S0-BZI-578

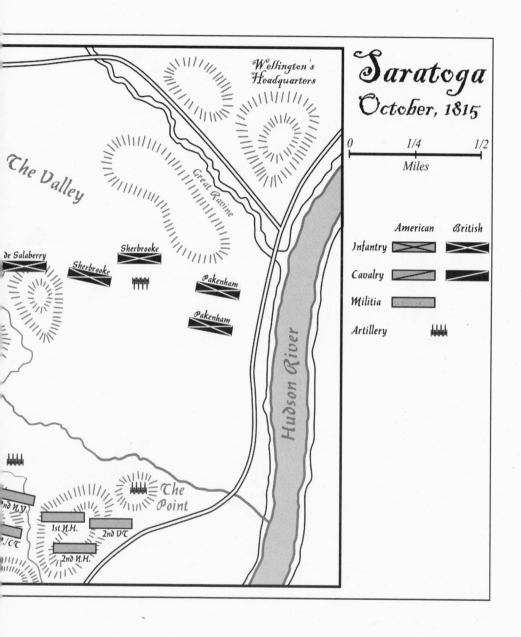

Saratoga
October, 1815

0   1/4   1/2
Miles

Wellington's Headquarters

The Valley

Great Ravine

Hudson River

de Salaberry

Sherbrooke

Sherbrooke

Pakenham

Pakenham

The Point

2nd N.Y.

1st N.H.

2nd VT

2nd N.H.

/CT

	American	British
Infantry		
Cavalry		
Militia		
Artillery		

Redcoats' Revenge

RELATED TITLES

Britannia's Fist: From Civil War to World War—An Alternate History
by Peter G. Tsouras

Napoleon's Troublesome Americans: Franco-American Relations, 1804–1815
by Peter P. Hill

Redcoats' Revenge

An Alternate History of the War of 1812

COL. DAVID FITZ-ENZ, U.S. ARMY (RET.)

POTOMAC BOOKS, INC.

WASHINGTON, D.C.

Copyright © 2008 by Potomac Books, Inc.

Published in the United States by Potomac Books, Inc. All rights reserved. No part of this book may be reproduced in any manner whatsoever without written permission from the publisher, except in the case of brief quotations embodied in critical articles and reviews.

Library of Congress Cataloging-in-Publication Data
Fitz-Enz, David G., 1940–
  Redcoats' revenge : an alternate history of the War of 1812 / David Fitz-Enz. — 1st ed.
    p. cm.
  Includes bibliographical references.
  ISBN 978-1-57488-987-1 (hardcover : alk. paper)
  1. United States—History—War of 1812. 2. United States—History—War of 1812—
Campaigns. 3. United States—History—War of 1812—Naval operations. 4. Imaginary histories.
I. Title.
  E354.F57 2008
  973.5'2—dc22

                                                        2008028755

Maps by Jay Karamales, after Lewis G. DeRussy.
Originals by Andrew J. Brozyna.

Printed in the United States of America on acid-free paper that meets the American National Standards Institute Z39-48 Standard.

Potomac Books, Inc.
22841 Quicksilver Drive
Dulles, Virginia 20166

First Edition

10 9 8 7 6 5 4 3 2 1

CONTENTS

ACKNOWLEDGMENTS

Canadian Chris Evans, a former Random House editor now with Stackpole Books, read *The Final Invasion* and asked, "What if the British had won the battle at Plattsburgh?" That did it; he was one of dozens of readers who had asked the question, and I could see that I was obliged to answer them. In London, I asked the "what if" question to a mutual friend, Lionel Leventhal, publisher of Greenhill Books. He reminded me, "The invasion of the United States by the British on September 11, 1814, was a horrific event but is lost these 187 years. In its time, however, the undertaking on the part of Great Britain was significant and is still shrouded in mystery. The Plattsburgh battle is sandwiched between two great events—the abdication of Napoleon ending the long war and the battle of Waterloo. You must awaken readers of history with a striking tale."

The largest challenge in writing this alternative history was transporting the British army to North America. I was surprised to find that the transportation of men, guns, cannons, ammunition, and provisions paled in significance to the movement of horses by ship across the Atlantic. In England, I combed through the archives of the college of Veterinary Medicine at Greenwich, the old Admiralty library collection at Whitehall, and the stacks at Chatham Royal Dockyard. I found a great number of gruesome stories and a rare drawing of a horse transporter. Veterinarian John Cogar of Lake Placid, New York, sent me to Cornell research librarian Susanne Whitaker of the Flower-Sprecher Veterinary Library. Within the month I received a ream of photocopied excerpts that filled in the gaps as to the care of the animals' conditions at sea. Veterinarian Darcy Wiltse, an expert in the treatment of horses, told me about her personal experiences that mirrored material dating from the eighteenth century.

I bounced the evolving plot off Steve Saffel of Random House, who gave me great encouragement. He cautioned, "Keep up the action," and sent me copies of Harry Turtledove's great series. "Read and learn," Steve advised.

Commander Liam Murphy, USNR, an Irish scholar, sent me the writings of Derek Warfield, acquainting me with the gravity of the struggle in Ireland and the men, seething with revenge and hatred for all things British, who were exiled to America. Mr. Celedonia "Cal" Jones of the Bureau of Manhattan History went to great lengths to answer my questions, narrowing down the exact location of something that may or may not have happened.

A friend and colleague, Colonel James Macdonough, furnished the saga of my main character, the Duke of Wellington, by sharing his fascinating research on the life of Sir William Delancey. Macdonough's novel, *Limits of Glory*, was an inspiration. Andy Broznya, who illustrated *Old Ironsides* for me, provided my narrative with excellent maps, which proved to be a most vital contribution.

I am grateful to my editors at Potomac Books, especially Julie Kimmel, Kathryn Owens, and Vicki Chamlee. The seamless presentation is the memorable contribution of John Church, production manager.

I can't conclude this recognition until I thank professional librarian Betsey Whitefield of the Saranac Lake Free Library and her interlibrary lending program, which located for me the most obscure titles, time and again.

Carol, my wife and researcher, read every word of the book out loud, which puts her among the angels. Other noted historians contributed ideas but declined to be identified for fear of going over to the dark side of alternative history. To quote only one, "Just don't mention my name." One who will share the blame is my editor, Michael Dorr, who prodded with a sharp stick to make it all come together. He alone would see it through to the end.

Research, even in a novel, is key. This work opened up innumerable possibilities.

AUTHOR'S NOTE

History is a powerful influence that entertains while providing a never-ending source of argument. As a nonfiction author, I was too steeped in realism to become involved with fantasy. In the later part of the 1990s, I researched at great length and then wrote the saga of the battle of Plattsburgh/Lake Champlain, which occurred on September 11, 1814. My book, *The Final Invasion: Plattsburgh, the War of 1812's Most Decisive Battle*, highlighted a long-forgotten but most important engagement of the War of 1812. The book won the Distinguished Writing Prize from the Army Historical Foundation and the Military Order of Saint Louis from the Knights Templar for contributions to military literature. The day of the book launch, the 187th anniversary of the battle, terrorists attacked New York City's World Trade Center—ten blocks from my publisher.

The subsequent notoriety of the date propelled book sales and led to television appearances on C-Span Book TV and FOX News Network. At Chicago Public Radio, I was asked, "If this or that changed, would the Christmas treaty talks at Ghent in 1814 possibly have reached a different solution?"

Alternative history is an intriguing possibility, I thought. My editor at Random House asked for a plausible story line that was believable yet altered. He referred me to one of his writers famous for the genre. The formula seemed complicated and fraught with pitfalls. I had to, on the one hand, keep history somewhat intact, yet on the other hand, find a natural break with history without an outcome that bordered on the ridiculous. While in England on a research trip for my book *Old Ironsides: Eagle of the Sea*, I was sent by Lionel Leventhal, publisher of Greenhill Books (distinguished for its alternative histories), to renowned author Dr. Paddy Griffin, a highly successful writer and scholar. In England, Canada, and the United States research turned the key. Griffin, formerly with the Royal Military Academy, Sandhurst, told me, "Writing alternative history is dangerous, as your imagination whirls off, you could lose the thread along with the reader." Paddy provided the solution to the puzzle. He advised that an altered history is most difficult to concoct because it is both fiction and nonfiction within the same cover. "Alternative history is like a railroad track. While one rail remains true to historic facts, the parallel rail waits patiently for an opportunity to break free of the gauge restrictions and touch the other rail ever so briefly before returning to the mandated distance, thereby changing the path of the journey. All you have to do is find a credible, seemingly minor natural change to the story that would give history a nudge and then sit back to see what you can make happen." As I began, I soon found how flexible history could become and still remain within the realm of plausibility.

In 1814 the Duke of Wellington, victor of the war in Spain, where he defeated Napoleon's army, turned down command of the British invasion forces that crossed the Canadian border and attacked northern New York on September 11. In *Redcoats' Revenge* Wellington accepts command, fights the subsequent battles, and traumatically amends the history of the United States. The true history of the turbulent time centered around the French Revolution, Reign of Terror, and Napoleon, which drove the new United States into choosing sides at a time it would have much preferred to remain neutral. Two years of niggling war against the British brought a financial crisis, which could have sent democracy back to colonial times. The first republic established of, by, and for the people was tested by the most powerful nation in the world, which bore a hateful grudge. What if the Duke of Wellington had served in North America?

I'll tell you.

CHAPTER I

An Eventful, Fateful Year

"In a rebellion as in a novel, the most difficult part to invent is the end."
—ALEXIS DE TOCQUEVILLE

Since 1775 and the start of the American Revolution, the Western world had been in turmoil. The war concluded with the Treaty of Paris in 1783 and provided both a respite from fighting and a hotbed for hotheads in France who took the government into their own hands in 1789. The French republic began a reign of terror that shocked the crowned heads of Europe and destabilized the continent. At first the new United States enjoyed unprecedented wealth, trading with the warring parties. Then Great Britain turned on her former colony, demanding exclusive trading rights while kidnapping thousands of American seamen and enslaving them below the decks of Royal Navy warships, where they remained for the duration of the wars with Napoleon Bonaparte.

Ambition Thwarted, America Imperiled

On June 18, 1812, Congress declared war on Great Britain. Conflict had been smoldering since before the turn of the century, when Great Britain, in order to man the fleet in an ever-escalating war with France, seized American sailors and restricted the sea trade of the neutral United States. In 1807 the situation came to a head when the Royal Navy frigate *Leopard* fired on an American warship leaving Norfolk, killing four and impressing a handful into foreign naval servitude. President Thomas Jefferson spent most of his time in office applying restrictive measures, but to no avail. His successor, James Madison, took matters more seriously and asked Congress to act.

Within a week of the war's start, American naval lieutenant Sidney Smith, commander of the war brig *Growler*, patrolled the northern-most waters of Lake Champlain where it flowed into Canada. His mission was to interdict American smugglers before they could deliver loads of contraband to the British forces. Soon, he was in hot pursuit of the illusive *Black Snake*, a notorious offender of the embargo, sliding north toward the Canadian border and safety. "I've got him in the bag this time!" Smith shouted, urging his crew to greater effort at the lines and sails. Smith could taste the impending victory and all it promised—redeemed honor, public acclaim, perhaps even reinstatement to his prior position as master commandant of Lake Champlain. With his sister ship, the brig *Eagle*, he was certain to corner and seize the enemy—during his very first action as commander of the *Growler* no less!

Smith was neither brawny nor handsome. His round shoulders cried out for the large gold epaulets of a navy captain to improve their appearance. The days he had spent contending with high winds at sea had beaten his complexion dark red and coated it with a spiderweb of purple veins. Thin-faced and hawk-nosed, Smith was acutely aware of his unmilitary figure, yet he believed that, despite his weedy appearance, he could carry off the sudden fame he would soon encounter.

A strong following wind encouraged his chase of the *Black Snake*. If he had been a pious man, he might have seen the manifestation of Providence in this mundane display of Nature, but he wasn't deeply religious. After all, he had spent the better part of his life at sea, and such experiences rendered in a man faith in the Almighty—or faith in himself. Smith was pleased to think he was in the latter category, though soon events would throw that confidence into doubt.

The *Growler* was a trim lake-built, eleven-gun, two-masted, square-rigged ship, large by lake standards and feared by smugglers who fled whenever she appeared out of the mist. Her nine-pound cannonballs had played about their heads and shattered their hopes of British gold coin on a number of occasions. Together with the *Eagle*, a nearly duplicate vessel, the Americans had sailed north seventy miles on a strong southern wind to sweep up contraband and sink long rafts stacked high with timber. Those supplies had been intended for use by the Canadian Provincial Marine, the naval authority of Canada, an auxiliary of the Royal Navy, at Ile-aux-Noix, an island in the center of the Richelieu River, ten miles inside Canada. The dockyard built naval craft and warships for service on Lake Champlain. Where the Richelieu emptied into the St. Lawrence north of St. Jean, the river turned rapid, preventing boat traffic, a condition the strong wind had mitigated.

Sailing Master Jarvis Loomis, commander of the *Eagle*, followed closely just off *Growler*'s stern. He waved his hat vigorously to gain Smith's attention. Loomis was aware of the prohibition against entering Canadian waters and thought his leader foolhardy. Both vessels were square-rigged and could not beat south without room to tack. The wind was blowing them north into perilous waters, and an attempt to turn around would place them full in the face of the twenty-knot breeze that had so effortlessly brought them there. The river grew shallow; the bottom could catch the keel in a slow turn and maroon them. The north-flowing river's mouth was a mere hundred yards wide. It was clear that it would not get wider the further it led into Canada.

At twenty-six, Loomis was the same age as his leader, though he had followed a different career path through the ranks, one arduous step at a time, to attain his naval warrant. His ability to read, write, and navigate caused him to stand out from fellow seamen. Also slightly built but half a foot taller than his diminutive boss, he wore his blue frock coat with distinction.

Loomis's frantic gesturing did not register with Smith. All the lieutenant could see was the *Black Snake*. All he could think of was the cargo's value, not in its monetary terms, though they were worthy of consideration, but rather what that cargo once captured would mean in his current predicament. A month earlier, the secretary of the navy, the seldom-sober Paul Hamilton, during one of his drier moments, had lost confidence in Smith's stewardship of the hundred-mile-long lake touching neighboring Canada. With the American declaration of war on England, he sent forward Commodore Thomas Macdonough, a senior naval officer, to take over as master commandant of Lake Champlain, thereby relegating Smith to the intolerable position of second in command. Whispers circulated in Washington and closer to home that Smith was thought to be "too timid in the face of war."

Lieutenant Smith felt the criticism acutely. Hadn't he been present at the Royal Navy attack of HMS *Leopard* on his ship, the USS *Chesapeake,* in 1807 when he was a mere midshipman? That violation of sovereignty helped spark war five years later. Smith boasted often enough about his service as first lieutenant aboard the USS *Wasp* in 1810 by declaring, "I served with distinction against bloodthirsty Caribbean pirates." But no matter how dishonorable and unjustified the allegations against him might be, he knew that it took longer to pull in such nets than it took to cast them out. Only in battle could he rout those aspersions decisively.

Determined not to take the censure lying down, he assured his new wife Evie, before kissing her farewell on the quayside at Vergennes, Vermont, "My detractors will eat their scurrilous words when I return." His father-in-law, the prominent Judge Frederick Everett, tried to view the situation in its best possible light, but he too had heard the gossip and saw daily how it distressed his son-in-law. "My boy," the judge said, "Lieutenant Macdonough is senior. The rules call for him to take command. I'm sure the secretary values your service or he wouldn't have left you here at this critical time when an attack is only a matter of when."

Smith thanked his father-in-law for his words of support but added, "Though I may tolerate it momentarily, I'm unwilling to accept this insulting relief of command. I will prove myself in combat—the only arena that counts!"

By now, the *Growler* and *Eagle* were entering that arena. In an effort to staunch the free flow of smuggling into Canada, Macdonough had ordered Smith to establish a blockade at the American port of Rouses Point. There he could make scarce the food for which the ravenous British army hungered and hinder the smooth trade in timber so desperately needed by the Royal Navy's boatyard. The contraband was vital to Upper Canada's defense because the population consumed all it produced, leaving nothing for the army and de-priving the Canadian Provincial Marine of materials to maintain their warships.

Likewise, the American military was aware of Lake Champlain's importance. It had served as the "old road to war" since the French and English first colonized North America. The narrow lake, dead straight north to south for a hundred miles, had been the highway for military expeditions since Samuel de Champlain discovered it in 1609. Officers like Braddock, Montcalm, Rogers, Carleton, Burgoyne, and Benedict Arnold found its use irresistible in designing their campaigns. With no roads through the wilderness, the water-way became the only axis of advance for trade, troops, and supplies. To control the water was to command the land on either side.

Smith's orders had clearly cautioned him "not to cross" the unmarked watery bor-der just a mile above Rouses Point. But the wind was behind his little flotilla, and the *Black Snake*, a good-sized craft, appeared to be loaded to the gunnels with casts of salt beef, surely intended to feed the enemy quartered in Montreal. If he could take her, the prize would be escorted triumphantly into Plattsburgh, New York, where the customs station warehouse would eagerly welcome the catch. It would be sold at auction and the money sent to the federal government to finance the war. Prize money wasn't paid for capturing inland waterway cargo or for seizing the vessels carrying such cargo, but such bold action and beneficial results were bound to find favor with the secretary of the navy. It would present the drunken Hamilton with incontrovertible proof of Smith's worthi-ness for command. His valor would excite second thoughts about his intrinsic value in those calling for his relief.

Of course, it would be the talk of the lake. "Did you hear? Lieutenant Smith snatched that infamous *Snake* from under the very noses of the British in Canadian waters? Didn't even fire a shot!"

Such an incursion would be the first of the war. When promenading with his wife on the streets of Burlington, people would point him out as the "Hero of the Lake." When asked, he would gladly offer, "While I was facing the enemy, Macdonough was busy build-ing boats. I prefer to capture mine."

The mate tugged Smith's sleeve, breaking his superior's reverie. He wasn't accus-tomed to touching his commanding officer, but the situation was becoming critical and his warning shouts had gone unheeded. "We're entering the river, sir! We'll be leavin' America soon."

Aware he was being pursued, the skipper of the *Black Snake* had jettisoned hogs-heads of contraband off both sides to lighten his ship, which improved his situation. The floating half barrels bumped and thudded against the wooden hulls of the American ships. The closure rate was not sufficient to allow the *Growler* or *Eagle,* both cruising at top speed side by side, to catch the slithering *Black Snake* as it sought to evade capture. The Americans' pursuit carried them through the estuary and into shallow water, confining the ships within a narrowing river lined with yellow and deep red oaks and forcing them into a single file. They were well within Canadian waters that threatened to swallow them whole. Smith had exceeded his orders but not yet his ambition.

As he closed in on the smuggler, now just a hundred yards ahead, his mate asked, "Shall we fire the chaser, sir?"

In those last moments before the battle, as the fading sun set the waters aglow, Smith's mind wandered one final time. He imagined the expected headlines that would appear in the Burlington newspapers the next day, July 7, 1812: "Lake Hero Beyond the Border." His eyes grew distant. "Taking the fight to enemy waters Lieutenant Sidney Smith boldly showed how this ignoble war ought to be won. . . ."

"Sir?"

"No," Smith said. "I want that slimy *Snake* intact." He was willing to refrain from firing his bow chaser (the cannon mounted in the *Growler*'s nose) if it could be avoided. He didn't want to damage unnecessarily the prize that would soon be his. He planned to board her, take command himself, and sail her back into American waters before the Canadian Provincial Marine patrol could be alerted, let alone intervene.

Loomis brought the *Eagle* in close behind *Growler*, nearly touching her as they continued up river at four knots, main sails set. Shouting through his big brass speaking trumpet, he hailed Lieutenant Smith. Finally catching his commander's attention, he warned the lieutenant that two gunboats to their rear were being loaded with riflemen on the western bank. In the lengthening shadows Smith hadn't seen them moored. Loomis feared the Canadian lookouts had raised the alarm when the Americans had entered the estuary.

Forced to fire or abandon his attack, Smith heeded his subordinate's warning, but not before making one last attempt to capture the *Snake*. Still hoping the chase would end in triumph, he swung *Growler* to starboard, firing a rippled five-gun broadside at the smuggler fifty yards to her front. As Loomis had feared, with the sudden violent turn, the brown worn flaxen sails lost the wind, stopping *Growler* in her tracks.

"Fire!" shouted the young American lieutenant.

The gunner's aim was in line but low at that distance. The black iron balls skipped across the water and smashed into the *Snake*'s stern on the first bounce. They struck like growls of thunder against the hollow hull and sent showers of splinters slicing like jagged knives through several of the smugglers' bodies. The six surviving crewmen jumped overboard and swam for the bank only twenty yards away.

In moments the guns were reloaded, but as far as Sidney Smith could see, there was no need for another round. He turned his face toward the *Eagle*, intending to wave her forward to take the prize in tow. It was then that he realized his trophy had become a trap from which he would be lucky to escape alive.

Two sixty-foot rowed Canadian gunboats had cut off his getaway route. An attack by the Canadian Marine had diverted Master Loomis's attention. The abandoned *Black Snake* drifted deeper into enemy water. Smith shouted to the *Eagle*, "We're in a pickle, Loomis!" But beyond that observation, he gave no orders to improve their situation.

Loomis seized the initiative, since it seemed if he didn't, no one else would. He brought his brig across the stream and held her steady. His five starboard guns were double-shotted with cannonballs. This was a risky procedure. The increased pressure had been known to burst gun tubs wide open. Not waiting any longer for orders, Loomis rippled off all five guns. Each in turn barked belching flame. A cloud of billowing white smoke concealed the *Eagle*.

Each American combatant was crewed with eighty men, but these lake seamen had never been in such peril. Smith had neglected to train them for anything other than harassing smugglers. The shots were not well timed with the ship's slight roll and only one cannonball grazed a gunboat, nearly capsizing it, but only nearly. The appalling noise and flame shocked and alarmed men on both sides of the battle. Soon, two more enemy gunboats, from the dockyard farther north, circled around the foundering *Black Snake* and joined the fray.

"I fear we're finished," Loomis said in a low tone beyond the hearing range of his helmsman, who spun the wheel in an attempt to turn the ship before it struck the bank. The crew scurried instinctively across the slippery deck to man the port guns and looked to Loomis to improve their aim, but the twenty-four-pound single gun in the prows of both oncoming gunboats interrupted the action on board the American brig.

"Down!" Master Loomis shouted as the bright muzzle flashes burst forth. There was scant delay between the shots' firing and their arrival, since the engagement had now closed to less than a hundred yards. The first shot, passing over the beam at a dozen feet, nicked the mainmast. The large cannonball's sizzle as it flew overhead startled the crew, who cowered momentarily on the deck. The second ball struck aft, shattering the port side just below the rail and clearing the gun crew off the deck, tossing them, screaming, along with a portion of the aft gun carriage into the churning sunset-burning water beyond. Their shattered bodies sank between *Eagle* and *Growler*, which were side by side, ten yards apart. Hot wooden fragments of the *Eagle* peppered the deck of her sister ship.

Stunned by his predicament, Smith watched his would-be prize float quietly away from his reach. The *Black Snake* was replaced by enemy gunboats, firing as they came. At that moment, a small sliver of wood shaved off the side rail by a musket shot and pierced Smith's coat. They were getting too close. He left the wheel and stationed himself between the number two and three guns. In a moment the enemy gunboats would shoot their twenty-four-pounders right at him. American frigates, like the *Chesapeake*, were similarly armed, and Smith knew the damage such a point-blank salvo could create.

He suddenly wondered if he had misplaced his faith on an object that had been found wanting. He prayed to God that the Canadians would hold their fire long enough for the *Growler* to engage with a broadside from her five nine-pounders.

Smith had only one chance and knew it. If they were to survive, he could not miss. The lieutenant was well aware that the enemy's single bow guns would be difficult to reload. They too would have only one shot. A well-aimed Canadian heavy cannonball would strip away *Growler*'s mast and rigging and leave her shattered and helpless. Expecting that the enemy was interested in capture rather than destruction, Smith fought from the starboard side, wedged across the narrow river. The odds in his favor could not have been bleaker, and he began thinking, *They're just gunboats.* A shot or two and they would turn and run. The *Growler*'s crew needed little direction as they waited nervously for the lieutenant to give the order to fire. It would come any second; they dare not take their eyes off the enemy or fire without his command.

Smith searched deep inside himself for some measure of courage. Recalling his boastful past, he considered the impending reality. He was being tested and had to demonstrate his vaunting exaggerations now by confronting the enemy. Still, he held his fire—was it from courage waiting for the best possible shot or simply, damningly, from fear? The naval lieutenant felt his sense of duty flowing away. The agitated river slapped against the wooden walls of the little brig, causing it to rock back and forth in a queasy rhythm, as he watched the enemy gunboats close the gap. The Canadian infantry were massing along the bank. The gunboats moved steadily, fearlessly, toward the Americans. Smith was losing focus and hoping that only his focus was being lost. His eyes darted from one approaching gunboat to the other, fixating on the muzzles of the menacing black iron cannons, which could take not only his life, not only his ship, but also his already tarnished honor. Moments ago, everything had been so clear. The *Snake*'s crew had abandoned ship and the prize was his. His reputation was going to be restored.

It shouldn't be like this, he thought.

The clamor at his back from the *Eagle* caught his attention. He snapped his head around and tried to embolden himself. After all, he *was* in charge; decisions had to be made. He was no longer a midshipman. The crew looked to him to save their lives. For the first time in his naval career Smith knew the visceral meaning of command. Before that moment he had taken position and responsibility in stride. He had excelled at the "talk of war." Shipmates had allowed that during certain armchair discourses he "transcended in heightened circumstances." Why was present-tense command so crucially different? He had been in combat early in his career and had fired many a cannon in anger from his two-gun sections. He had witnessed death and destruction and had taken it in stride. Everyone agreed that he had behaved well in battle. But today Smith had overreached and knew it. He had put his faith in himself but was turning out to be a shoddy idol indeed.

The big gun on the first approaching gunboat discharged its firepower in his face while he dithered. The missile sheered off the *Growler*'s mainmast, splitting it just below the yard. Billowing clouds of canvas descended on the crew, as did showers of wood splinters, heavy blocks, and coils of constricted rope. What had once been parts of the ship had become deadly weapons that wounded several of her fighting crew. The rattling shock of the strike against his ship brought from his lips the unexpected cry, "Fire!"

The gunners, stunned as well and hovering at the breach end, dipped their smoldering matches to the guns. Sparks flew from protruding goose quills, filled with gunpowder, at the touchholes. Flames plunged down into the main charge, and the guns fired in unison. A crescendo of sound and a belch of fire hurled five nine-pound cannonballs north into Canada.

The brig was not built to withstand the recoil of all five guns being fired at once. They should have been fired in rotation, but the crew could wait no longer. Two of the nine-pounder cannons broke free, ripping up the ringbolts, deck, and rail. The weight of the guns, mounted on wheeled carriages, sprung back and careened across the slippery deck into the silent guns on the opposite side. They carried their crews with them, entangling their limbs in the trailing ropes and trundling over prostrate bodies, crushing them.

To Smith's surprise, the American cannonballs did their job. One struck the muzzle of the British cannon and drove it out of position and down on the boat's weak-ribbed hull. Its slats were not stressed to take the weight. The two-thousand-pound bouncing barrel did not pause in its unexpected retreat but crashed straight through the deck. Its awkward departure created a giant hole, which quickly swamped the boat in cool river water. The fifty men aboard, along with their flintlock muskets, settled into the swirling channel. At least those few were no longer a danger.

The two American men-of-war huddled together. Master Loomis took the time to rope the two vessels side to side for mutual support in the face of the onslaught both knew was coming. It was just a matter of time before they began receiving small arms fire from the French-Canadian *chasseur* company gathering on the western bank. The chasseurs had come down the road from the boatyard in skirmish order, taking up firing positions behind the autumn oaks at the north-flowing Richelieu's very edge. Dressed in buckskins, which had faded from tan to white, and wearing pointed bearskin hats, the Canadians looked comical to American eyes. Loomis thought they resembled a convention of shaggy bishops, but he knew their rifles offered no blessings.

He soon learned how dangerous the gathering infantrymen were when a bullet plunged into his right hip, spinning him around, and depositing him like a discarded rag onto the cluttered deck. He pulled himself up, leaned against the back plate of one of his nine-pounders, and *willed* himself to resist the growing weakness in his legs and buzzing in his head.

Lying flat on the deck, the American crewmen returned fire with their single-shot muskets. To reload them, they were forced to stand and so sought whatever cover they could find on the jumbled deck. Enemy bullets bounced about the rails, bulkhead, and masts like hail. The chasseurs, armed with new rifles, poured an accurate and lacerating fire into the two stranded American vessels and prevented the reloading of the cannons that were still serviceable.

On the *Growler* the situation was no better, even though only one gunboat, fifty yards north, opposed it. Smith's crew continued to fire, but casualties were mounting minute by minute from the rifle fire emanating from the ever-increasing infantry on the banks. A full company of nearly a hundred riflemen strafed the *Growler*'s deck with lead bullets that ricocheted off the iron gun barrels, injuring even those not directly in their line of sight. Smith's crew looked to the lieutenant for relief, but he had collapsed onto his knees, his blue uniform jacket torn open to the waist and blood seeping across the front of his white shirt from just above his belt line. A jagged splinter, larger and far more deadly than the earlier musket shot, had punctured his midsection. The captain was still at his post, though he was now supporting himself with his sword, useful only as a cane.

Even as blood spilled from him, Smith's brain cleared. His professional advancement seemed of little consequence at the moment. Not even the gossip swirling through the capital mattered to him. He understood only two things: his opportunity had arrived and the courage he thought he had lost blazed in him. He couldn't see Loomis, but noise behind the lieutenant assured him that his comrade was fighting on. Because the two vessels were tied together, there could be no escaping back into the open water of Lake Champlain. The dual fates of the *Growler* and the *Eagle* were as one.

Raising his head, he saw that he was right. The gunboat crew could not reload the bow gun in the face of the cannonballs that the *Growler* was sending north from her three remaining guns.

The Canadian vessel turned about. The enemy's side was wide open, ripe for sinking with a well-aimed shot.

"Now, boys!" Smith shouted over the battle's discord. "Fire!"

Two of the three American guns leaped forward, sending death north as one cannonball left a bloody path through a cluster of oarsmen.

The gunboat continued turning until the stern was aimed straight at the *Growler*. Lieutenant Smith realized suddenly that the enemy ship held a stinger in her tail. She wasn't retreating at all. She carried not only cannons but also a carronade—the "smasher." Its short, fat, black barrel was unmistakable. It fired a heavier ball than the twenty-four-pound cannon but at a lower velocity. If one of those monsters struck the stricken *Growler* anywhere along her exposed side, the carnage would be catastrophic. Even one shot would be lethal.

Thinking of the crew and wishing to forgo a suicidal slaughter, Smith raised his sword reluctantly and pointed to the remains of the mizzenmast, which held the battered fifteen stars and stripes comprising the flag of the fledgling United States. Smith, the slighted officer, had intended to vindicate his valor and retrieve his prior command of Lake Champlain with this plucky action. Instead he surrendered the first lake action of the naval war to the enemy.

"Strike the colors, boys, and save your lives," he said, the blood loss exhausting his resolve and causing him to stagger.

The commander of the Canadian gunboat saw the lowering of the *Growler*'s tattered ensign before the carronade's fuse was lit. He called a cease-fire.

The battle was over. The Americans were prisoners.

Loomis had fallen unconscious on the *Eagle*'s shattered deck. His men crawled to his aid and dragged him behind a gun. Their resistance, though it spoke of the regard in which they held him, was pointless, and they soon realized it. Debilitated, wounded, or merely drained, the few crew still capable of moving didn't bother to raise their hands in the air but instead turned to assist their fellow shipmates calling for assistance. Dead crewmen, crushed and crumpled, lay on the blood-soaked deck, while others floated, forgotten, in the water next to the battered hull. The *Eagle*'s colors had been shot away before they could be lowered.

The Canadians jumped on board the *Eagle* and began clearing away the debris, some of it entwined with the corpses of the American crew. The Canadian commander, a Royal Navy lieutenant from the surviving gunboat, found Lieutenant Smith clutching his stomach and cramped over. Smith said in a choked voice, "Sir." This was followed by a long pause. When next he could speak, he said, "I'd offer my sword, but as you can see, I'm afraid I need it for support."

Each side attended to the casualties regardless of nationality. As two Canadian boats emptied out their wounded onto the river's bank, the chasseurs took their place. They swung out to the river to gain the captured American vessels and to aid in the evacuation of the wounded and the removal of the dead. Of the 178 American sailors in the battle, twenty-two had been killed outright and fifty-one were seriously wounded. Only a fortunate few had survived without an injury of some kind. Carried carefully to the riverbank, both Smith and Loomis were treated by the Canadian army surgeon attached to the unit. The doctor, twice the lieutenant's age, his beard already gray, informed Smith that he had tangled with more than three hundred defenders of Canadian soil that day and that he had never had a chance of victory once he had entered the river.

His one chance for fame had soured swiftly, but he suspected the stench would linger. Under such dire misfortune, Smith's thoughts returned to the trophy that had become a trap.

"Tell me, what of the *Black Snake*? What was her cargo?" he asked.

The surgeon cast a wry glance at the American officer. After a pause he replied, "The British army's most grateful to the Canadian Marine for saving their bacon."

The frivolous comment belied the importance of smuggling along the Canadian border from Maine to Lake Ontario. The climate above the 45th parallel, halfway to the Arctic Circle, limited the growing season in Upper Canada to one crop and that was often in peril. The Gulf Stream warmed the Maritime Provinces and fish were plentiful, but the provinces of Quebec and Ontario counted on cross-border trade to maintain a decent standard of living. The added burden of the British army's presence drove resources to the limit. The vital trade in food and commodities turned to smuggling once President Jefferson mandated restriction. Lieutenant Smith had been fighting for a cargo load of provisions.

Marquess of Wellington at Number One, Piccadilly

The eventful autumn of 1812 was turning out to be particularly fortuitous for Arthur Wellesley. He had recently been named the Marquess of Wellington for his military service in Portugal and Spain against the forces of Napoleonic France. Though a field general of high standing, he did not want to lose his political standing in the capital, and on this particular afternoon he expected to establish a presence in London. He had recently returned to England for the first time from a campaign he had been fighting since 1808. Those who knew him were shocked at how gaunt he had become and insisted that he rest. He intended to do so at the very spot at which he was sitting—his friend's London home, Number One, Piccadilly.

Even now, Lord Bathurst urged Wellesley to linger in England and enjoy her splendors, to recuperate and replenish his vigor. As if he were an invalid!

The marquess replied affably, "My 'rest' will have to wait a bit longer. I must still report to Parliament on the war's conduct."

"I can well imagine," the lord said, "that your perspective on our current tête-à-tête with France is eagerly awaited."

"Let them wait." Wellesley's words were as brusque as his temperament, but he tempered his tone somewhat by adding, "At least for the duration of this fine day."

Napoleon had turned away from Spain, denuding the Iberian Peninsula of some of his best formations and leaving its defense in the hands of the suave Marshal Nicolas Soult, whose ambitions had grown prodigiously since his early dream of becoming a village baker. Did the change of command portend a more promising outcome for Great Britain?

On this particularly nice autumn day, Wellesley vowed there would be no talk of war. He intended to finalize the purchase of Number One, Piccadilly, the home of his good friend Lord Bathurst, the colonial secretary. Wellesley's fortunes had risen markedly since his days as the younger son of a noble Irish house led by his elder brother, Richard, the governor-general of India. A member of the Irish parliament, Wellington was a politician as well as a soldier and enjoyed a wide array of important connections in that world of patronage. Notwithstanding his birthright, he had earned everything that had come his way, and as all powerful men in high places, he had detractors eager to see him fail and fall.

In the unusually bright light of that afternoon, Hyde Park looked pastoral through the window of Bathurst's study. The leaves of chestnut trees carpeted the ground and the rose gardens dominating the edges of Rotten Row were still resplendent with huge blooms of red, pink, and white. Number One, Piccadilly had been cobbled together forty years earlier from four five-story, mahogany-colored-brick row houses. The secretary's father, a horseman unconcerned with architecture or for that matter creature comfort, converted the buildings to a single residence to take advantage of the proximity to the park's bridle path. One of Bathurst's servants poured the two old friends dry sherry as they sat on the first-floor porch facing the park. The sun moved steadily behind the house, steeping the area where they sat in shade as cool and refreshing as their drinks. The back garden, which abutted the three-mile-long park, made the secretary feel as if he lived in the country. Wellington was attracted to the location rather than to the old house itself. He relished the countryside more than the city and found the park's great expanse a restful sanctuary in the center of London's chaos.

Both men anticipated the end of the wars with the Ogre, as Napoleon was known by his enemies, and believed it would happen within the year. They were meeting to make plans for a future dominated not by war but by peace. Their talk didn't encompass emperors and kings, campaigns and casualties, strategies and risks. Wellington simply wanted to buy the house as a base for his political career. His friend was moving to a country estate in Richmond, just up the river, and, when necessary, planned to take rooms in London. Bathurst wished to unburden himself of a house that "needed a great deal of work," as he had assured Wellington with a candor that the marquess admired and appreciated. "Arthur, if I were you," Bathurst said, "I'd tear the whole place down and start over from the ground up. That prize money you received from Portugal would allow you to build a palace here. That is, of course, to say nothing of your award from the British government for your astonishing victories. What better ground in London than Number One to house the hero of the Peninsular War!"

"Nice of you to think of me when you needed to sell," Wellington said, finishing his sherry. The servant, standing like a sentry just inside the door of the study, stepped forward to fill his glass once more. "I believe Kitty would be happy to escape the doldrums of the country for the society here in the heart of Westminster. Perhaps it'll even help bring her out of herself."

Bathurst thought it odd for his usually private friend to speak of his wife so openly. As a rule, her name never passed Wellesley's lips. The absence and distance between the marquess and Kitty necessitated by the seemingly unending war and myriad political duties were apparently to Wellesley's liking. Just the mention of her name brought on an embarrassing silence. Bathurst thought it best not to delve further into the subject of Kitty. He didn't want to say the wrong thing at this final stage of negotiations.

"Well, well," the secretary said, breaking the uncomfortable silence, "it's settled then? You'll take the house off my hands? Do with it what you will. I've no further interest in it."

The two gentlemen shook hands to seal the bargain. Relieved to be rid of the old mansion, Bathurst confided to his friend, "Frankly, knocking four decrepit buildings together didn't make for one decent one. The drains are a disgrace. The servants have gone mad running up one set of stairs and down another from the kitchen. You know, Arthur," he said with a laugh, "I haven't had a hot meal in the place in years. I wish your appetite better luck!"

The Judge Receives the Bad News

From a safe distance the American customs cutter *Valerie* had watched the *Growler* and *Eagle* disappear into the open mouth of the Richelieu River. The crew heard the cannon reports and feared the worst.

When darkness settled over the lake, the cutter abandoned its watch and turned south to report the incident. The southern breeze, which had propelled Lieutenant Smith to his defeat and capture, didn't diminish until long after the sun set and the full moon etched its bright silver streak on the water. The *Valerie* made its way swiftly toward Cumberland Bay, thanks to the vessel's staysail rigging, which permitted her to tack in a short zigzag pattern. A square-rigger would've taken twice the time to cover the twenty-mile distance between the river's open mouth and the bay. Captained by customs officer Howard Hollis and crewed by ten lake seamen, the thirty-foot *Valerie* was armed with a nine-pound cannon in the bow and a thirty-two-pound carronade mounted on a slide amidships so that it could engage the enemy on either side. Equipped for interdiction and inspection of cargo, the cutter was intended to seize craft and arrest smugglers.

It was late when the *Valerie* turned northwest into the quiet bay and docked in Plattsburgh. The town, smaller than neighboring Burlington across the lake, numbered only a thousand residents with six churches, three hotels, grist and lumber mills, two newspapers, and four bars. Plattsburgh served as a military base both for regular army and militia; the troop concentration often doubled the population. The customs headquarters was adjacent to the commercial docks.

Officer Hollis, the cutter's skipper, dismissed the crew as soon as the *Valerie* was secure and walked briskly to the home of Judge Peter Sailly. Still dressed in his official dark blue frock coat, with its single row of big brass buttons running down the center, Hollis took long strides up the steep sandy bank. With his spindly legs confined in tight dark trousers and swinging his thin arms to sustain the pace he had set for himself, he resembled Ichabod Crane. The gate banged behind him before he reached the sheltered front door of the most impressive house in town.

The judge lived in a whitewashed brick two-story surrounded by a low white picket fence two blocks from the docks. During the day he could be found at the U.S. Customs warehouse on the waterfront. Since the hour was late, Sailly opened the door himself, hiding behind his back in his left hand a small single-shot flintlock pistol. At the sight of his agent, he slid the gun unseen into his frock coattail pocket.

"Hollis, what on earth brings you out so late? Come in. Leave your cloak on the peg," he said, pointing the way to the sitting room to the left of the main hall, where a wide staircase led to the second floor.

Sailly was not what he appeared to be. He was born Pierre Marie in France, the son of a prominent mill owner. After attending the Royal Military Academy, he had served in the King's Guards, and as a result, the revolutionaries had branded him a Royalist. During the Terror of 1791, Sailly was nearly arrested because he refused to accept the new order. He changed his name, took what remained of his father's fortune, and escaped to America. Once there, he looked for a place to invest his father's money. He intended to bring his wife and two daughters to the New World to protect them from the ever-shifting danger of revolutionary France. In the interim his father died and his extended family was thrown into the prison at Marseilles. Working for Ezra Platt, a wealthy merchant in Poughkeepsie, Sailly viewed the shore of Cumberland Bay as holding great promise for immense wealth. He advised Platt to buy thousands of acres around the shoreline. By 1806, at age fifty, Sailly had promoted the town and established himself as its first district congressman. While serving in Washington, he engaged the assistance of the French ambassador, who intervened on Sailly's behalf. His wife and two daughters were released and soon joined him.

Back home in the summer of 1812, he was elected judge and highway commissioner. Maintaining the military turnpike that stretched across the northern tier of New York became his responsibility. Most significant was his federal appointment as chief of customs. Sailly's broad experience had taught him tolerance as well as the importance of the rule of law. He never again wanted to witness the chaos and carnage that had accompanied his homeland's transformation from monarchy to republic.

A nationalist in a time of states' rights, Judge Sailly was not in tune with the local merchants and farmers, who were distrustful of the federal government. Ever since President Jefferson had applied the various phases of the 1807 embargo against trading with British Canada, the Customs Service in the North Country of New York State had been waging a campaign to foil smugglers. The market for farm produce, timber, and potash lay at Montreal and the little communities along the Canadian side of the St. Lawrence (Upper Canada being sparsely populated). The harsh climate curtailed crop growing to a truncated season. As a result, much of the region's staple food came from Canada's southern neighbor. The only other market for Lake Champlain farmers was New York City, six hundred miles to the south, which required an arduous trip down Lake Champlain and at least two portages to reach the headwaters of the Hudson River. President Jefferson's ban didn't make the journey any easier or more profitable. The terrain of Vermont and northern New York was a virtual wilderness, more or less beyond the federal government's reach. The citizens preferred to smuggle their goods twenty miles north across the international frontier rather than transport them six hundred miles south—an economic fact of life that Jefferson failed to appreciate.

When the judge confiscated contraband, he deposited it in the federal warehouse on the waterfront for sale at auction. It was not uncommon for him to recapture the same item some time later and sell it yet again. Sailly was the person to whom Lieutenant Smith had intended to present the seized *Black Snake* and her cargo of food. The townsfolk, many of whom were involved in smuggling, harbored an acute and abiding grudge against the Customs Service for its interference. In their view, the dispute with Great Britain wasn't their fight. Neither did they share the federal government's passion for conquering Canada.

Warming himself by the evening fire with a tankard of hot rum punch courtesy of Madame Sailly, Agent Hollis recounted the tale of Lieutenant Smith's rash movement into Canadian waters, described the sounds of unseen battle that had rolled toward the *Valerie*, and ended his report by declaring, "Sir, they're surely lost!"

Judge Sailly, alarmed at the news and surprised that Commodore Macdonough would risk half of his armed sailing ships in a pointless raid, said, "Mr. Hollis, at first light you must take me down to Vergennes. We must coordinate our activity with Macdonough and discuss his change of strategy. First, though, when you return to the dock tonight, please notify the other crews to be on station first thing in the morning. We'll need them for our eyes and ears till our navy can once again assert its presence on the lake."

As soon as Hollis left, the judge prepared for bed. Before he turned in, his wife asked him about the reasons for the officer's unexpected, late-night visit. "Madame," he cautioned, "things are going to get very much worse long before they get better. I'm afraid our haven of peace will be short-lived. Have we brought the curse of war from France to this little enclave of serenity?"

Macdonough's Dilemma

At dawn, Sailly boarded the *Valerie*. Spray broke over the prow as the customs craft bumped and pitched its way south toward the American navy boatyard. It wasn't until the afternoon that the *Valerie* entered Otter Creek, a two-mile narrow channel to Vergennes and the boatyard at the foot of a dam.

Commodore Macdonough had sent out a watch for the missing flotilla, but it only warned of the cutter's approach. Happy to see his friend, the naval lieutenant, hatless on the quay, peered beyond the approaching cutter for the *Growler*.

Despite his age the spry judge jumped the last foot before the *Valerie* was even secured. Breathless as he approached Macdonough, he blurted out, "Lost! They're both lost!"

The commodore, thinking Sailly must be referring to his customs patrols, asked, "Who's lost?"

The old man had been tussling with the news of the incident, thinking of its varied ramifications and considering how Washington would receive such dire information. As a result, he had presumed too much and started the story at its end rather than its start. A little surprised that he was the first to bear the news to the commodore, he replied, "Why the *Growler* and . . . and *Eagle,* to be sure!"

Shocked and baffled, Macdonough thought the old gent had gone mad. "What do you mean lost?"

Sailly attempted to explain himself, "Sunk, burned . . . captured by the British . . . in the Richelieu. What were they doing there, I ask you, Commodore? Were they under orders? Why wasn't I told of this change of plan?"

Macdonough had been concerned that he hadn't heard from Smith, who had been ordered to send daily reports of his activity via customs boats, but with the southerly wind he assumed the weather had caused a delay. Bringing the judge to his office, Macdonough tried to calm him. He called for his second in command, Lieutenant Stephen Cassin, to join the discussion. Sailly blurted out the story, and Agent Hollis filled in the details in a most professional manner. The news was a staggering blow to the commodore: half of his principal forces had been most likely captured; nearly two hundred American sailors were dead, wounded, or taken prisoner; the first lake battle of the war had ended in utter defeat; and the defense of Lake Champlain had been seriously, perhaps irrevocably, compromised. While Cassin penned a report based on the conversation for recently appointed secretary of the navy William Jones, Macdonough ordered the *President*, a sloop of war, to prepare to journey north to plug the hole left by the previous day's losses. If the commodore failed to deny passage of smuggled goods north and passage of British troops south, industrial New England could be cut away from the agrarian southern states, thus breaking down the very fiber that held the nation together.

Within the month, Commodore Macdonough received a message addressing the state of the survivors that had been conveyed by a British patrol boat to one of Sailly's custom cutters. Master Jarvis Loomis's report included a description of the action, a record of the names of the dead and wounded, and a passage describing the wounds he and Lieutenant Smith (now resting comfortably in a Montreal hospital) had suffered. The text ended with his prognosis: "Though Captain Smith's injuries are extensive, he is expected to live but be very much diminished." Loomis included the details of his own parole and said he was "doing well living in the home of a British civil servant." In those days of gentlemanly warfare, parole meant that the officer accepted his captivity and promised not to escape. He was then free to roam within the confines of the community. As was the custom, the American Consul in Quebec City covered Master Loomis's expenses.

Meanwhile, the secretary of the navy had been informed of the failed action. Macdonough noted in his report that it was highly probable that the *Growler* and *Eagle* would be seen once again—under Royal Navy colors. The acquisitions increased the Canadian Provincial Marine's strength by 30 percent while Macdonough's effectiveness was halved. Loomis's final paragraph ended with the following prediction: "Sir, expect a significant enemy marine campaign to seize control of Lake Champlain by April 1813. The British army is compelled to continue foraging the edges of the lake for food since most of the Canadian-grown provisions are consumed by the public. It is considered too expensive to bring ship timber for boat building from Canadian forests when the nearby American supply presented by American smugglers is not only superior in quality but cheap. I believe the enemy intention is to swallow up the Lake Champlain Valley and convert it to a permanent enclave of English Canada."

The American Army Campaign of 1812

While Macdonough suffered the loss of two ships and sought the aid of Secretary Jones to confront the lake problem, the commanding general of the regular army, Henry Dearborn, had not been idle. Along with the other hawks and Secretary of War William Eustis, he had intrigued for the onset of war. Not concerned with the impressment of American sailors or Royal Navy blockades, his attitude could be summed up in the words of former president Jefferson: "The taking of Canada this year is a mere matter of marching." Jefferson had convinced President Madison that the French Canadians—by far the largest contingent of the population—were mortified by the British victory of 1759 that took control of their land. Jefferson argued that the majority of Canadians in Quebec would rise up against the oppressive English government if only the American army invaded, even in negligible numbers. "It will be the spark they need to establish a new rule for our northern neighbor, one that is more in concert with American society," Jefferson, former ambassador to revolutionary France, assured Congress.

Dearborn, a sixty-one-year-old Revolutionary War veteran, served as secretary of war under Jefferson. At his Albany headquarters, he devised a land campaign that was approved a month before the war was declared: invade Canada at three points—Detroit, Queenston, and Kingston—to separate the majority of the British army from Montreal. Press the main attack on the capital city from Plattsburgh, New York, transporting troops and supplies on Lake Champlain. To describe his military campaign as ambitious was pure understatement. He intended to deploy no fewer than ten thousand men along a front that stretched over a seven-hundred-mile length of wilderness, from the western edge of Lake Erie at Detroit to the mouth of Lake Champlain just south of Montreal. The quartet of attacks would occur one after the other. Included in the ten thousand troops were militiamen culled from Ohio and New York State.

Men with scant military experience from the War for Independence still resided in the country. Those who had been active in the Revolutionary War were now nearing sixty. Only the most senior officers—those who had recently been appointed generals—had ever seen a battlefield. The officer corps was appointed according to political affiliation and not merit. While Congress had initiated a program to recruit a regular force, it was barely in its infancy by June 1812. The spirit of the Massachusetts minutemen was long gone. Times were prosperous, and farmers were reluctant to leave their land. More to the point, there was no clear threat to the nation's safety as there had been during its earliest days. While the British impressment of American merchant seamen was a significant concern, it didn't threaten house and home.

The first attack was led by Governor William Hull, an officer in the War of Independence. He crossed the river from Detroit to attack Windsor Canada. Within a week the effort fizzled out, and Hull was court-martialed for cowardice. By early fall militia general Stephen Van Rensselaer, a Dutch patrician, attacked Queenston in an attempt to isolate western Canada from Montreal. The poorly planned crossing of the swift Niagara River left a thousand men stranded; they were later captured by the British.

From the *Albany Morning Times*, November 4, 1812:

On the third day of testimony over the battle loss at Queenston, New York Militia major general Stephen Van Rensselear testified in open court that he was ordered into battle without the support of the rifle regiment, which remained at Buffalo despite orders to the contrary.

When questioned by the board of officers as to the state of his command prior to the assault across the Niagara, he insisted that not enough time or material had been allocated to properly train and employ the militia. He noted that the regular army officers present were at first reluctant to serve within his command and that he had made the headquarters aware of the shortcoming. However, he admitted receiving some relief prior to executing the order. His orders read simply: "Conduct an assault on the Canadian city of Queenston in the most vigorous manner and secure it from use by British forces."

The board cited Van Rensselear's inability to cross the river with the entire complement, leaving nearly half on the New York shore. The defendant again cited the lack of watercraft to carry both men and artillery. The board ignored the logistical aspects of the battle and concentrated on his inability to inspire his troops to assist their fellow soldiers fighting and dying in the streets of Queenston.

The court will conclude testimony tomorrow with an expected verdict sure to relieve the New York general of both command and culpability. While there are undertones of political infighting—Van Rensselaer is a Federalist—it did not emerge in open court.

By November 1, Major General Dearborn had taken the two defeats philosophically and canceled the attack on Kingston from Sackets Harbor. But the main attack on Montreal, he assured his staff, "would succeed where the others had failed."

By October, he had assembled the regular army regiments at Plattsburgh and rounded up New York State militia from the northern counties. The largest force of the war— more than six thousand men—was composed mostly of infantry accompanied by a few field guns and a handful of light dragoons because both horses and artillery pieces were in short supply. Nonetheless, Dearborn launched a major attack across the border on November 20. His timing was prophetic. At precisely the same moment, in Russia, Napoleon was caught in the unrelenting grip of an early winter that proved to be fatal to his ambition and hitherto invincible army. The loss and decline of France would allow for a significant addition to the military might directed against America and ultimately cripple her ambition to take Canada.

It was no better for Dearborn. The leaden skies threatened and the wind howled— not the best time of year for an assault on Montreal, lying twenty miles straight north across a flat, wind-swept forest, where fallen trees lay across the unimproved tracks. Fearing an attack from the lake on his right flank, he called on Commodore Macdonough for naval protection.

Crippled by the loss of the *Growler* and *Eagle,* the naval master commandant of Lake Champlain nonetheless brought everything at his disposal to Rouses Point. Hugging the western shore, he put his meager forces between the American army and whatever response the Canadian Provincial Marine intended to launch. That late in the year the winds on the lake were fierce, and the safe maneuvering of sailing vessels was nearly impossible. Macdonough had to rely on the resilience of the frozen men at the gunboats' oars to fend off the enemy while his two remaining square-rigged brigs lay well off the rocky shore. To the credit of the Canadian Marines, they ignored the American land invasion and naval sortie and chose instead to remain secure and warm within the confines of the Richelieu River. Macdonough, not privileged to such decisions, remained on the lake as promised. Treacherous winds pummeled the little flotilla and threatened to blow them on the rocks.

Meanwhile, at the border, the New York militiamen balked, informing the commanding general, "Sir, we didn't join the militia to fight in foreign wars." With a third of his army remaining staunchly on the American side of the border, the morale of Dearborn's regulars began to wane. Six miles inside Canada, Major Charles-Michel de Irumberry de Salaberry, charged with defending the border in that area, cobbled together a force of fewer than a thousand trained redcoats, Indians, and French-Canadian *voltigeurs* (light infantry from French-speaking Quebec). Advance elements of American dragoons received sporadic fire along the road leading to the Royal Navy boatyard on the Richelieu River. At Lacolle Mill, the Canadian major set a defensive line and waited for the American infantry. But they never came.

Dearborn had lost heart when confronted by the malevolent weather and the meager prospects for victory. He realized that it was far too late in the season to initiate such an ambitious campaign. Under his orders, the entire American force withdrew in less than forty-eight hours, and the American navy sailed south for winter quarters at Vergennes. Dearborn proffered his resignation as the commanding general of the U.S. Army, but President Madison did not accept the offer. The disastrous battles fought by the amateur army, whose blood seeped into the ground on forgotten skirmish lines, should have moved the politicians in Washington to settle the war at the peace talks sponsored by the czar at Saint Petersburg. But blind to ambition, another campaign was scheduled for the spring of 1813.

The French Army Flounders

That same winter large portions of Napoleon's Grande Armée of 500,000 men perished during their retreat from Moscow. The emperor had drawn many of those formations from the French army that had faced Wellington in Spain. With the reduction of enemy forces on the Iberian Peninsula, England's Lord Bathurst, immensely relieved, began to turn his attention away from Europe and toward America. Jefferson and Madison had counted on the continued success of France to drain the British, but they neglected to consider the consequences for America if Bonaparte's fortunes declined.

Preparing for the Worst

"May on Lake Champlain can be mighty turbulent," Commodore Macdonough cautioned Judge Sailly. "Have your inspectors keep an eye on the Richelieu River and beware of an increase in contraband, which has been stored up all winter, and is most likely destined for St. Jean Beauharnais."

The judge had postponed his visit until spring, when the lake was relatively free of ice. He had hoped to see a new fleet ready to take control and relieve his cutters of the responsibility. But the winter of 1813 had taken a fatal toll on both the army, which had succumbed to a winter fever and an ill-planned raid on York, Canada, and the navy, which had been overwhelmed with preparations for the spring campaign.

"Commodore, those slimy smugglers can't wait to get their hands on British gold and gaily cavort about as if they own the waves. My spies in Canada tell me that the Provincial Marine boat-builders haven't been idle."

Those were not the words that Macdonough wished to hear. Noah Brown, who ran a boatyard on the bank of New York's East River, had two hundred shipwrights hard at work, but materials were in short supply for the American navy's ambitious building program. A considerable amount was expected from the ship chandlers in the faraway city, more than three hundred miles due south. Since the previous sailing season Macdonough's workforce had been seasoning timber, resting masts in ponds, collecting hardware, and cutting out blocks. The young commodore was convinced that his sole hope was to initiate a boat-building program that would not only replace the loss of *Growler* and *Eagle* but also increase his combat power. According to Sailly's spies, Royal Navy captain Daniel Pring was building a new flagship. The commodore's plan called for the shipwrights to construct two sloops of war with upward of twenty guns, vessels powerful enough to recapture control of Lake Champlain in the upcoming sailing season of 1813. The narrow shallow channel of Otter Creek, which led to the open water of the lake, would not allow any larger craft to traverse.

Perhaps by summer, with the constant interest, intervention, and assistance of the secretary of the navy, the *Ticonderoga* could be completed. She had been laid down as a steam-powered commercial sloop but was being converted to sail that summer because the commodore didn't believe that the steam plant was reliable during combat. Additionally, its workings were exposed to enemy action and easily damaged. To compensate, Macdonough expected to complete a larger sloop as well before the summer was over.

In the meantime, ten rowed gunboats were readied as an interim fix and sent to Burlington and Plattsburgh. The crafts sported a twenty-four-pounder in the bow and an eighteen-pound columbiad—a cross between a cannon and a carronade—fixed on a rotating circle amidships. The judge and commodore both hoped the boat crews would prevent the smugglers from going north.

The two men agreed that every bit of timber confiscated would be sent to Vergennes, their only construction facility. Just as serious as the lack of supplies and completed ships was the lack of lake seamen. Their concern over the recurring summertime outbreak of fever made seamen conspicuously absent. A shortage of qualified sailors on the lake was the rule even in good times. Most served in the regular navy or on privateers, where prize money was offered. Lingering pneumonia from the previous winter had further reduced the Americans' prospects of obtaining able sailors. It had also taken a heavy toll in the boatyard work crews, which slowed productivity drastically.

Britain's Summer Offensive of 1813

In late June 1813, Lieutenant General Sir George Prevost, governor-general of Upper and Lower Canada, visited Royal Navy captain Pring, who had been seconded as commander of the Lake Champlain Provincial Marine. Pring's immediate superior, Commodore Sir James Yeo, chose not to attend the meeting. He excused himself by claiming to be engaged in operations on the Great Lakes and left the lesser matters to his subordinates.

Pring was well aware that Prevost and Yeo didn't get along. The clash was a constant source of contention. Caught in the middle between supporting army operations and pandering to his naval boss in Kingston, who constantly second-guessed his decisions, the beleaguered Pring was at his wit's end. While Yeo was under the operational control of Prevost, he reported to the Admiralty in London through the Royal Navy Station in Halifax. By keeping the string on Yeo, the Royal Navy only hindered cooperation and made the simplest operation cumbersome. "Rather sticky," Pring was fond of saying in polite company, when only expletives could truly express his frustration.

There was really no need, though, for Yeo to oversee the visit. Pring was an experienced naval officer. As a young man, he had been a midshipman on warships out of Jamaica Station. One of Lord Nelson's young officers, he had witnessed the great victory at Copenhagen in 1801. In 1807—the start of Great Britain's most recent troubles with the United States—he had been given command of a schooner, the *Paz*, which ranged along the Atlantic coastline. Yeo, knowing he would be absent in Kingston and supervising the Great Lakes effort, had selected the aggressive Pring over more senior officers for the billet of lake commodore.

Prevost, an experienced commander and politician, was aware of the precarious position that Pring occupied. Personally, he liked the naval officer and believed that, in the absence of Yeo, he was more than adequate for the task. His young daughter, Anne, often praised Pring at the dinner table, where Prevost encouraged her to take an interest in the affairs of his high office.

A judge in Montreal had described Prevost "as a good, sincere man wrapped in a small sprightly body." His thick, curly head of chestnut hair topped an easy smile. His whole demeanor revealed a confident air of command. His father, Major General Augustin Prevost, had begun his military career as a Swiss mercenary in the Royal Court of Orange, where the Duke of Cambridge recruited him to raise a light infantry battalion to defend the American colonies against the Indians and French. There, in Hackensack, New Jersey, in 1767, George was born. After the defeat of the British at Yorktown, the teenager returned with his family to England, where his father retired, and was schooled in London at Lochee's Royal Military Academy and later in Colmar, Alsace. As a result of his training in Alsace, Sir George spoke French with no English accent.

As a member of his father's old regiment, he received severe wounds during the Battle of Cape St. Vincent. Later, he was cited for conspicuous action at St. Lucia and was appointed brigadier and governor of Dominica. At the approbation of the crown he was made a baronet in 1805. A favorite of the Prince Regent, he was appointed lieutenant governor of Nova Scotia in 1808.

As war loomed, the British feared that the French Canadians would rebel. The governor of Canada, Sir James Craig, was an oppressive Anglophile who was driving his French-speaking citizens into the arms of the Americans. Prevost offered a solution to this problem. (His French manners and understanding of the people would be crucial in maintaining their loyalty when the war began.) On his first day in office, he doubled the salary of the Canadian archbishop and appointed French Canadians to half of the government posts. These actions made him extremely unpopular with those who had been displaced, and they never ceased to criticize him both in Canadian and London newspapers.

On quayside, the crew of ninety-nine stood at attention as Governor Prevost inspected them prior to his boarding. Most were French Canadians, so Prevost worked his charm as both a politician and combat leader. Captain Pring directed his visitors onto the long planked dock, where his twenty-gun flagship, the *Canada*, bumped gently against the mooring. HMS *Canada* was a two-masted brig eighty-five feet long. The crew was all smiles as the red-coated general with gold-lace chevrons on both sleeves inspected the new vessel. As the son of an army family and the king's soldier, he had lived much of his life on sailing ships and was nearly as expert as the crew in nautical matters.

Canada lacked an executive cabin, so the coming campaign was discussed on the open stern. Pring, the commander of the expedition, left the land assault portion of the operation to Lieutenant Colonel John Murray of the King's 8th Regiment of Foot and commander of the land forces in the area south of Montreal, who was also present, and started with the naval action. The commodore began by reviewing the mission.

"Sir, we intend to accomplish two objectives. First we must ensure safety of movement for the smugglers who supply both boat-building timber and provisions for our army. Our capture of two American brigs last summer was a major blow to the enemy and made this operation possible." He gestured to his left at two vessels moored in the channel. The formerly American crafts had been renamed the *Chub* and *Finch*. The new names were painted on their bows in bold white letters. "We've converted them to His Majesty's service."

With that statement a signal was given and the two latest additions to the Canadian Marine fleet fired an ear-shattering gun salute to honor Lieutenant General Prevost. Sir George acknowledged the salute with a tip of his plumed hat. *It's a very neat trick*, Prevost thought, *and shows some flair on the part of my host. But then, Pring's known for his showmanship.*

Captain Pring pointed to the cannonballs stacked on the deck. "Both vessels are combat loaded, and the crews have mastered the eleven nine-pounders."

Sir George was pleased and asked, "What's your second objective, Commodore?"

Colonel Murray took over the briefing. "Sir, we intend to punish the citizens and the military for General Dearborn's invasion of the king's land. Though we drove them off with little fanfare, we want the Americans to realize that such behavior is neither acceptable nor encouraged. Therefore, I intend to take, by your leave, sir, six hundred soldiers, whom the commodore will transport and support, and with this force raid the communities along the lake. We'll also break open the stores of the customs house and seize war matériel."

Sir George broke in: "Naturally, you'll exclude our smuggler friends in your punitive action. We can't risk losing their support. Their contributions have fed my army."

With a nod Murray replied, "Of course, sir."

The commodore added, "If the American fleet, which I understand is quite weak, engages us, the resulting battle will turn the lake into an English sea that we'll use at our leisure." Pring believed his parry had preempted another interruption by the governor general but was mistaken.

Prevost, intrigued, asked, "How do you propose to lure the American navy into battle, Commodore?"

"We'll create such havoc within the neighboring communities that the local people will demand action from their navy. Once Macdonough is exposed, my flotilla will destroy him as we've destroyed his ocean-going comrades. You know, sir, as a result of the Royal Navy blockades, not one American frigate is active at sea."

Prevost responded with a touch of irritation, "Ah yes. Sir James Yeo keeps me well informed by regularly forwarding *all* of the Admiralty dispatches. The successes of the Royal Navy are always included prominently in his communiqués."

Pring could see he had touched a nerve.

June 1813

Early on the morning of June 22, Customs Agent Hollis was taking on supplies at the dock at Rouses Point. It was a bright day, the winds light and fitful. Shoving off, Hollis didn't expect to engage many of the traitorous cretins, since the *Valerie* was nearly becalmed. The cutter was able in the light breeze to sail well out into the channel, where Hollis intended to sit and welcome the warm day. There, at the narrowing of the lake, he would wait at anchor and enjoy a leisurely breakfast.

Scanning the water to the north before tucking into the warm bread procured just before sailing, Hollis caught a glimpse of a tall mast rigged in square sails.

"To your stations, men!" he cried. The judge had warned him of a pending Royal Navy incursion. "It can only be the *Canada* with those square sails," he shouted to the crew, who had also been at ease and attending to their victuals.

Canada's movement was ponderous; what wind there was did not favor her.

Within the span of a very long hour Hollis confirmed his suspicions to the steersman. "Yes, there are three of them, maybe more," he said. "It might just be a sea trial, my lad, shaking off the winter with a bit of a cruise." He recognized the brigs *Growler* and *Eagle*, led by a large sloop of war. "I was warned we'd see them again but re-flagged."

Soon he realized that the enemy fleet was intent on more than merely an outing. Pring seemed determined to challenge the American supremacy of the lake. "They're coming on. Look sharp, boys . . . look sharp now. We don't want to be caught within their range." The *Valerie* was brought around and sent south. Hollis's heart pounded at the impressive sight.

Commodore Pring didn't care if his fleet was seen. Emboldened by the size and power of his ships, he was sure that this day would be his. The *Icicle* and twenty transports that had been converted from gunboats to carry troops followed the billowing sails of the *Canada*, *Chub*, and *Finch*. The boats retained one cannon—placed in the prow—while a lateen sail had been rigged in the center to aid in keeping pace with the men-of-war.

In the opposing wind the gunboats moved quicker than the square-riggers and suddenly popped up into Hollis's glass. "My God," he gasped. "It's an invasion fleet! They mean business this time, my lads." Panic dropped into his stomach like an iron cannonball, but he managed, for the moment, to master his fear. Such a sizable fleet hadn't been seen on the lake since 1777, when *Gentleman* Johnny Burgoyne had taken an army south to

Saratoga and raided Bennington. A year earlier, in 1776, Guy Carleton, Baron Dorchester, had clashed with Benedict Arnold at Valcour Bay just a mile or two below what was now Plattsburgh, en route to Ticonderoga. Well aware of the history of this watery road to war, Hollis wasted no time and trimmed his sails for a run south. On his way, opposed every torturous mile by a southerly breeze, he met two other customs cutters, one with a prize in tow. The first he sent to warn Judge Sailly, and he ordered the second to cut the prize free and convey the news of an imminent attack to Burlington. Under present conditions, he couldn't stop to brief his chief but pressed on to Vergennes to warn Commodore Macdonough.

The Royal Navy commodore, familiar with the prevailing winds, expected them to shift soon. He needed them to sweep across his beam. Such a wind would be ideal for his square-riggers on the lake. But this day would not favor him, nor would the following. It was thirty-five miles to Burlington, which lay on a bay below Grand Isle.

"I expect the wind to favor us as soon as we get a little farther south," he assured Lieutenant Colonel Murray. "This southerly gale is becoming a blasted nuisance. We've made no more than ten miles headway. Even my gunboats are ahead of *Canada*." Pring complained, shaking his fist at the sky and spitting out the words as if he were chewing nails, "That bloody wind's killing my timetable."

The wind refused to cooperate, slowing progress south to a labored crawl. Colonel Murray's men were forced to bivouac onshore night after night. It offered only minor relief from the endless tacking and rolling of their flat-bottomed gunboats. The six hundred redcoats looting nearby farms for pigs and chickens sent waves of panic rolling south. American colonel Alexander Macomb didn't have soldiers to spare outside Burlington and was unable to engage the redcoats camped on the shoreline. His inaction did little to reassure the populace.

After a week Pring finally rounded the point into the open bay at Burlington—to the great relief of the Canadian soldiers, who were exhausted from the rowing. Royal Navy cannons began the bombardment while the troops landed just south of the city.

———

Hollis's brief account of the invasion fleet hit Commodore Macdonough like a hammer. He had expected to see his former brigs under English sail that spring but not in the company of a landing force. The lethal enemy fleet meant that he couldn't take to the lake with the fragments of the flotilla he had managed to cobble together during the winter. His gunboats were deployed at Plattsburgh and Burlington. There, at Vergennes was the *President*, sixteen guns, and the unready sloop of war *Ticonderoga*. The crew wouldn't be trained until August.

Within two days of Hollis's report, Judge Sailly arrived by cutter. He was full of news. "Thomas, I just witnessed an attack on Burlington. I laid off out past Valcour Island and could see the whole thing. It's Pring again, but this time he has a battalion of infantry loaded into nearly two dozen gunboats. Your boats are beached and abandoned. Colonel

Macomb's regulars and Major General Sam Strong's Vermont militia have come up and are fighting them off. When I left, only a few redcoats had managed to land. Macomb's field artillery has established a strong battery on the heights above the beach, and there is a hell of a battle going on."

In this situation, Macdonough could do little. The loss of *Growler* and *Eagle* was now a double-fisted blow to his mandate to defend the lake. Not only were the crews lost, but the vessels had also been converted and were now attacking the land where they had been built. All he could do was report the aggression to Secretary of the Navy Jones and plead for more assistance in obtaining a refurbished fleet.

———

The staunch defense of Burlington compelled Murray's force to turn away, and the southerly winds continued to flummox the expedition's plan. Pring was forced to turn northwest across the lake to Plattsburgh.

Since Brigadier General Zebulon Pike had evacuated the post early that spring for the ill-fated expedition against York, Macomb lacked sufficient troops to occupy Plattsburgh. As a result, the little town of a thousand citizens was at the redcoats' mercy. The people had heard the cannonade thirty miles east across the water and knew that they were next. The militia, under Major General Benjamin Mooers, consisted of several thousand soldiers spread out over four counties. Worse, the men were untrained and barely equipped. Mostly farmers, they were reluctant to leave their holdings during their busiest time of year to confront veteran redcoats and Canadian regiments and defend a town that was not theirs.

The people of Plattsburgh agreed that it would be folly to turn their streets into a battlefield for fighting that would surely result in burning and looting what little wealth they had accumulated. They opted instead for what their neighbors in Ogdensburg, on the St. Lawrence, had done and opened the town to the British by sending the militia away into the interior. Colonel Murray sent his boats ashore while Commodore Pring provided overwatch with his naval guns. Not a shot was fired as the redcoats fanned out among the houses. However, the kind treatment the townspeople had expected was not forthcoming. The prime purpose of the raid was to manifest the power of the crown. One citizen described the action of the invaders in a letter to her brother.

Reverend Abraham Shields   June 22, 1813
Riverside Methodist Church
Albany, New York

My Dear Brother,

Today has been an apocalypse. The wretched redcoats have pillaged our town. They came in like Lucifer running as rivers of red through the streets of our helpless town. At the shore they ransacked the customs house and seized anything they wanted in the name of contraband. They plundered Morrison's general store, burnt the gristmill, and tore up the planks in my barn loft looking for my good silver. They said Harold was a militiaman since he was not present and claimed that we'd hidden powder according to some informant. It is true that Harold and the others of General Mooers's boys left town along with the sheriff, so as not to cause gratuitous destruction and loss of life. Since they weren't strong enough to fight off the British in the streets, it was best to leave town. So here we sat at the mercy of the redcoats like ducks on a pond. They didn't kill no one, but they did take the customs boats and some fishing craft, leaving us marooned on the New York shore.

We got a few traitors in our midst, I fear. Lang Hubberd, you know, has been smuggling for them and took them straight to General Pike's cantonment. The camp been deserted ever since spring, so they burned the huts to the ground. All the useful things our soldiers had left behind had already been picked over by the townsfolk.

I'm told that at the military hospital on Crab Island they turned out the sick soldiers and took the medical supplies. We could see the smoke rising from the fires they set before leaving. They left the churches alone, didn't even go inside. Some folks figured on that and hid their valuables in the church cellars.

They put up proclamations everywhere saying that if we didn't resist we'd be safe. Leonard Mills talked to an officer who said they would be back if the American army set up here and attacked the border again. The captain was friendly, thanking those who brought food across the border and promising to pay in gold coin anyone in the future who was so inclined.

They set a lot of fires before returning to their ships. I tell you, my brother, it is a cataclysm. I never believed that we'd ever be invaded and done too like this day.

No one was killed, thank the Lord, but plenty of us were scared.

Ask your parishioners to pray for us all.

Your loving sister,
Adele

Pring brought the fleet home in triumph to St. Jean. Murray paraded his soldiers down the main streets to cheers and martial music of the regimental band. The commodore began a program to refurbish the weather-beaten masts, sails, and rigging. The entire operation had taken far longer than expected owing to the dastardly southern wind, but the purpose of the raids had been realized, as he noted proudly in his report:

July 1, 1813
His Excellency
Governor-General Sir George Prevost
Governor of the Canadas, Montreal

Sir,
I have this day completed my mission to raid and disrupt the communities of Vermont

and New York that adjoin the shore of Lake Champlain. Eight communities and settlements were attacked by naval cannon and troops put ashore, resulting in the destruction and seizure of contraband of war. The town of Burlington, Vermont, was invested and set ablaze and its gunboats and commercial vessels either taken or destroyed. At Plattsburgh, New York, which was undefended, the customs warehouse, commercial establishments, and military facilities were secured and contraband removed. Care was taken to ensure the continued supply of goods and services from agents supportive of our cause.

I wish to single out Lieutenant Colonel John Murray, of his Majesty's 8th Regiment of Foot, for his strength of command and conduct of the maneuver and commend the men of my command for their professional conduct of duty.

Your Obedient Servant,
Daniel Pring
Captain, Royal Navy
Commodore, Lake Champlain

Pring could assert that the lake was his, and as hot summer winds continued to dominate from the south, no response could be heard to dispute his claim.

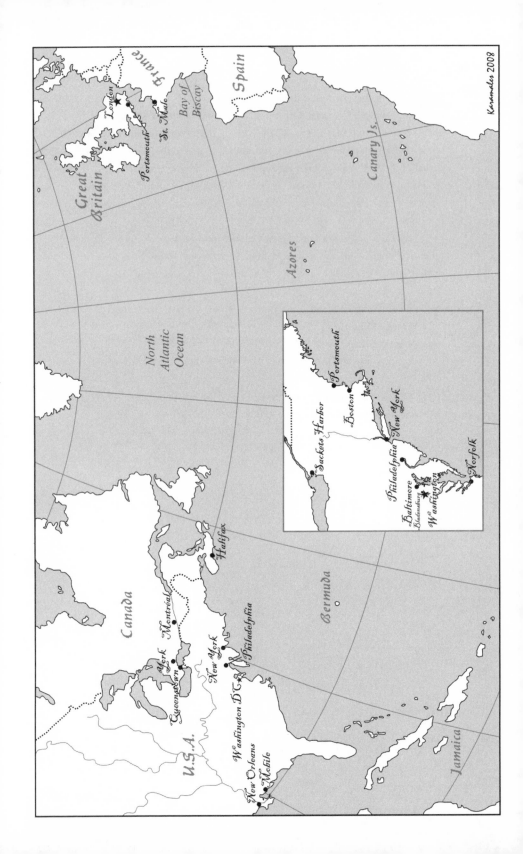

Kensander 2008

CHAPTER 2

The Early Lives of Future Adversaries

"In the first stages of his career I was his equal, in the last nobody was. Where did he get his magic?"

—JUDGE JONAH BARRINGTON ON WELLINGTON, LONDON, 1815

"I saw shoot in those eyes."

—BEAN ON ANDREW JACKSON

Decades before they faced each other in battle and as far back as their early childhood (one privileged, the other impoverished), when neither knew of the other's existence and destiny could still be derided as chance, the formative experiences of Arthur Wellesley and Andrew Jackson created future leaders who would strive to wrest glory from the other.

Born Worlds Apart

Andrew Jackson was born at Waxhaw on the border between North and South Carolina in March 1767. His Ulster-born father had died shortly before his birth from overwork at the frontier homestead, leaving Andrew's mother, Elizabeth, with three sons under the age of five. Andrew was poorly educated and writing never came easily to him; one biographer described him as "having a wall of ignorance about him, high and impenetrable." Jackson's mother and brothers were simple farming folk caught in a harsh, violent environment replete with marauding bands of Indians. Their survival depended on her relatives and the care of the surrounding community.

Jackson described his mother, known as Betty, somewhat sentimentally, as "gentle as a dove and as brave as a lioness." Her belief in self-reliance caused her to teach Jackson to settle his disputes on the field of honor, not in the courtroom. "Always protect your manhood," she instructed him. Betty was at odds with neighboring Indians and taught her son to be both an Indian fighter and an Indian hater. In her reductive but prevalent view, the land belonged to the "Christian white man" and had been bestowed by God. She expected the neighboring Indians to respect her divine, incontrovertible claim.

It is likely that Indians savagely killed Andrew's older brother, and his loss was deeply and unforgettably mourned. Betty Jackson couldn't forgive the Indians' disfigurement of the body. After his brother's death, Andrew learned to shoot a bow and read bird and animal calls the Indians used as they encroached on settlers' farms. He once saved a neighbor's family with a prompt warning.

———————

An aristocrat, Arthur Wellesley, born in 1769 (about three months before Napoleon) to an Anglo-Irish family, was the third surviving of four sons and one daughter. He was educated from youth at home by tutors and later at the Diocesan school in Trim, where he left an undistinguished record. Special note in the records is made of his slight stature and his eyes, which were a remarkable light blue. A silhouette portrait at the time shows a beaklike nose and sedate mouth. His eldest brother, Richard, inherited the family title of Lord Mornington and became Marquess Wellesley in 1799. Richard would distinguish himself in a number of high posts of great responsibility. Arthur was not favored at home because he was slow in learning and had a carefree attitude. He was sent to prep school at Brown's in London to buck him up. At Eton he was a scrapper, but his mediocre classroom performance continued and his despairing parents looked to put him in a regiment in hopes that he could find a place for himself. The four boys, though not close in age, were very close friends. Richard always championed Arthur, and his younger brothers idealized him. When Arthur reached age eighteen, he received a commission in the 73rd (Highland) Regiment of Foot. Over the next five years, the young officer progressed through the ranks. He was listed as serving in five regiments in five years, but although his name appeared on the rolls, he was physically absent. His influential family purchased his promotions to provide Arthur with both a social position and appropriate military rank.

The army officer corps was composed primarily of sons from landed and notable British Isle families. Holders of the king's commissions often sold them to settle debts or to enter into commercial enterprises. The commissions went to the highest bidders without consideration either of military education or field experience. It was the way young gentlemen of the day "got on." In the late eighteenth century, France and Spain threatened Great Britain's colonial empire. As units deployed, the officer corps was required to show up and actually lead men in battle. Little military training, outside of the personal use of a sword and pistol, was available. Army officers learned on the job—to the detriment of the soldiers and the empire. As a result, many young officers' careers were cut short [in] "some corner of a foreign field that is for ever England . . ." (as Rupert Brooke so aptly expressed it).

Nevertheless, despite cries from commanders for experienced replacements, the purchase system continued to provide large numbers of officers to the British army well into the early nineteenth century.

For heroic sergeants, daring battlefield exploits often led to promotions to lieutenant and captain. Those brave and proven leaders were highly effec-tive but rarely did they rise any higher because the officer corps did not regard them as gentlemen. Thanks to his birth, no such restrictions inhibited Wellesley's career potential.

During the Revolution

During the early stages of the Revolutionary War in the Carolinas, Andrew Jackson learned to fear the ruthless treatment handed out by the infamous sadistic lieutenant colonel of dragoons Banister Tarleton, whose marauding had nearly captured Thomas Jefferson at Monticello, Virginia.

At age thirteen Jackson joined the fight against the British army. Tarleton led the attack of the Royal Dragoons that slaughtered several hundred militiamen near Jackson's new home on the eastern edge of the Tennessee Territory. For a month afterward, Jackson and his mother nursed in their home those fortunate enough to be wounded rather than killed. The experience kindled in Jackson a hatred of the British army. Families fled to the mountains while redcoats, together with their Creek Indian allies, burned settlers' homes and stole their cattle. Jackson and his mother were forced to live like animals in the wilderness.

The young lad viewed the Indians as ignorant pawns susceptible to any invader. The British army supplied the Indians with muskets and promised to provide protection from the ever-encroaching frontier families. The British officers hinted at a sovereign homeland for the Indians when the war was over. Together, the redcoats and "redskins" disrupted and destroyed the valley he called home. These traumatic experiences impacted the young Jackson for the rest of his long, influential, and controversial life. In later years Jackson often stated in public forums and told the press, "They must go." Once patriots had compelled the British army to return home, there was no doubt that Jackson believed all Indians also ought to be eliminated from the land—either by involuntary relocation or the simpler solution of government-sanctioned extermination. It became an obsession that he nurtured all his life.

Jackson's hatred for the British and their Indian allies intensified during the war. As a teenager, he was stubborn, impetuous, quick to anger, and extremely contentious when he believed he was right. And according to Betty, her boy was nearly always right. However, he was unwaveringly loyal to his friends and soldiers. It was said that he was a "fighting cock all his life. He was very kind to the hens who clucked around him, but a savage killer toward any other cock who dared cross him." He had a tendency toward violence that fit his time and place. There was little sophistication on the frontier. Life was not only hard; it was often fatal.

Jackson became a messenger in the militia in 1780, attended drills, and learned firsthand the political and communal importance of the volunteer militia. Captured a year later, he was taken to a prisoner of war camp in Charleston, South Carolina. There, the young man was forced to serve a British army officer. A true son of liberty, Jackson refused to shine the officer's boots. Outraged by such impertinence, the officer slashed the unarmed youth across the forehead with his sword and, as the boy attempted to fend off the blade, sliced his left hand. During a lull in the fighting, his mother arranged to have him and others from their village included in a prisoner exchange. But the scar remained prominently on his face, and the memory forever in his mind.

Betty Jackson returned to the prison camp in Charleston toward the end of the Revolutionary War to tend the cases of smallpox. She walked the 160 miles to the prison ship, where she cared for her kin and soon thereafter contracted cholera and died. With the war over and orphaned at fourteen, Jackson went home to Waxhaw to finish his schooling and turned briefly to teaching. The loss of his mother and her ambition for him led him to sell the farm that had killed his father. Jackson had no love of sod busting and decided to go to the city to be a lawyer. He studied law for two years in Salisbury, North Carolina, and a companion there described him as "the most roaring, rollicking, game-cocking, horse-racing, card-playing, mischievous fellow that ever lived in the town." However, he possessed a charisma that drew people to him. A tall, thin piece of wire, he was a brawny brawler of a man who gave no quarter. Jackson had a strong jaw that jutted far forward and made his eyes look sunken under his wild eyebrows. His long straight nose had a sharp end. His striking appearance and outrageous manor drew homespun frontier clients to him. By September 1787, at age twenty, Jackson qualified to practice law in North Carolina. He moved to the western district of the territory that later became Tennessee. There, Jackson garnered the prominence and notoriety that stayed with him for his entire life.

The Colonel in Charge

Arthur Wellesley first saw action as a lieutenant colonel in 1794 against the French in the Low Countries of northern Europe. The newly minted revolutionary army of France, which took the field to defend its borders from covetous kings, gave a surprising account of itself. The new French formations not only drove off the attacks on their frontier but also gained territory from established armies mired in the purchase system. Wellesley learned two things from his initial combat experience: logistics must be systematized, and most important, he was meant to be a soldier. During the calamitous campaign Wellesley became aware of his natural talent for organization and leadership.

His administrative efficiency and battlefield efficacy came to the attention of the Duke of York, the king's son and commander of the British army. Wellesley had exposed the chaotic supply train apparatus. Officer baggage wagons clogged the roads and civilian teamsters deserted their wagons at the sound of the first shot. While some drivers were sound, if a bit jumpy, the officers, be they appointed or purchased, were incompetent and didn't care for anyone but themselves. His battlefield reports led the army to form regular units to transport munitions and supplies. In the first of his countless commands and expeditions Wellesley had displayed true compassion and concern for his men's welfare. He recognized the value of each soldier and demanded that none be squandered needlessly. Officers were relieved of their posts if the troops were found wanting, organized road marches were systemized, and leaders were held accountable for their actions regardless of their pedigree.

It must also be said of Wellesley that he was a snob, and he likely wouldn't have objected to such an appraisal. He associated only with persons of his own class and lived his life by the rules of high society. His staff and serving officers were always from families of distinction. He wasn't a man of the people by any means and would freely say of his soldiers, whom he deeply cared for throughout his life, "They are drunkards, brigands, wife beaters, and criminals." However, he wasn't afraid of them and spoke to them most directly, not as equals but as loyal citizens of the nations he was bound to protect. Soldiers were generic bodies to him, yet they relied on him and sought his protection. His only concern was that they meet his and his country's expectations, yet he became deeply depressed when he found them wounded or dead on the battlefield. He suffered from intense feelings of remorse for having contributed to their agony. He grieved for days over officers and commanders whom he had sponsored and who had died as a result of his patronage. Like many aristocratic young men too far down the family tree, he had few funds but was too highborn to get a job. Instead, Wellesley sought an event to make his fortune—and it was waiting for him on the other side of the globe.

In 1797 Prime Minister William Pitt appointed Arthur's brother Richard governor-general of India. Patronage was a way of life in most Western countries, so it was no surprise that Colonel Wellesley arrived in India on his brother's heels and was appointed commander of an infantry formation. As a colonel commanding a combined army of native and regular troops, he led from the front against the army of Tipu Sultan, who opposed foreign rule in India. Wellesley's victory overshadowed the criticism the Raj leveled against the new governor-general's blatant nepotism. In addition and perhaps more important, he received four thousand pounds sterling of the 1.5 million granted by the prize board for overthrowing Tipu, the ruler of the Mysore. His superior, a general who had criticized Wellesley's appointment, received 150,000 pounds, and the men five pounds each. Upon payment the general withdrew his objection.

Finally able to pay his debts, Wellesley remained in India and continued to excel in the military arts. When not fighting, he made a personal study of topography and always considered how he would fight from various positions. It became a hobby of sorts and inspired one of his favorite adages: "The land is an ally to multiply the force and diminish the enemy's capability."

He learned firsthand the realities of massed troops moving over hostile terrain far from their base. In 1803, while crossing the Kaitna River, he was nearly killed when an enemy artillery barrage decimated his column. A cannonball decapitated his orderly, who had been riding just behind Wellesley at mid-channel. The headless trunk remained in the saddle as the man's neck spouted blood. The sight spooked the staff, but not Wellesley, who, undaunted, rode on into a battle in which he was outnumbered six to one. A complex man, he appalled war but accepted his role with confidence. If war was necessary, no one could wage it better. He was best for England and Englishmen. The French, who wished to drive the English out of India, had trained the opposing force of Indian troops in the most modern field maneuver tactics. Moving as solid blocks—the better to control the formations—the Indian formations presented a formidable but densely packed target. Wellesley opposed the onslaught with a daring tactic: a thin overextended line of steady soldiers. With unrestricted fields of fire every British musket shot was felt. The advancing enemy was unable to return fire as the single shots fired by their leading rank could not be reloaded on the move. Wellington's well-trained infantry overwhelmed the French mass tactics, and he won the Battle of Assaye, which made his name. Throughout the countless battles that followed, the lesson of Assaye never left him.

Jackson in Tennessee

Five years before the Land Grab Act, North Carolina, caretaker of the western territory, allowed settlers to stake out Indian land in what would become Tennessee. The Indian tribes refused to allow trespassers, let alone settlers, and in a never-ending cycle of violence, the Cherokees tried to drive the settlers out while the militia punished the Indians. The Indians' ally, Spain, ruling over Florida and Louisiana, provided weapons and gunpowder. It was a cheap policy for the Spanish, who encouraged the tribes to stop the progress of the white settlers while husbanding their troops in the port cities along the Gulf. The Chickamaugans under Chief Dragging Canoe led the Indians' fight.

In October 1788 the McNairy party, comprised of about sixty settler families, took to the new road into Tennessee. Jackson and his fellow lawyers, about to set up practice in Nashville, joined the pioneering travelers to take advantage of the security of a large group on the 183-mile trek through hostile Indian territory. Beyond the gap in the Cumberland Mountains the Indians were thick on the ground and eager to kill settlers.

Moving slowly by day and night, only stopping for an hour or two to rest, and not daring to risk a static campsite, the McNairy party pressed on for more than thirty hours until it reached a defensible spot—natural high ground, cleared for nearly a half mile in all directions. As evening closed in on the slumbering camp, Jackson propped himself up against a tree and smoked a pipe, listening in the dark. Soon he heard the hoot of owls. Waking the camp leader, he explained what he had heard and that it was too early in the night for owls to begin hunting. Quickly, the settlers loaded up and moved out under moonlight, leaving their campfires burning. Later, a white trapping party took advantage of the old campsite and settled in for what remained of the night. Before dawn, the Indians slaughtered them.

The story of Jackson's cunning grew in Nashville, and he soon gained a reputation as an Indian fighter—a highly respected position in the community. Whenever a posse was called out to defend a farm or family, he would interrupt his law practice and take up arms.

Jackson took a prominent role under provisional governor William Blount in the Tennessee Territory. Tired of fighting Indians and prosecuting settlers for squatting on

Indian land, he threatened the federal government: "If you don't settle this matter, we'll look elsewhere for protection." President George Washington understood that Jackson meant to turn to Spain or even England.

Jackson led the bid for Tennessee's statehood, which succeeded in June 1796. At age twenty-nine, he became the first and at that time only member of the House of Representatives from Tennessee. The Honorable Andrew Jackson quickly gained a name in Congress for tenacity on behalf of his constituents. He fought hard for government assistance for families who had lost their homes and compensation for militia who risked their lives serving in the Indian-raiding parties.

He spoke on this matter on the floor of Congress: "The United States government has an obligation to protect its settlements if this nation is ever to grow. The absence of federal troops in the field doesn't absolve us of that commitment." In 1793 he sponsored through Congress a claim for compensation to recognize the militia's service. Four years later, the bill was still being debated. Some believed it was unjust to take Indian land in support of the settlers' unlawful claims. Even President Washington was not comfortable with this unbridled expansion. And so, in the fall of 1796, Jackson once again took the floor and, in his typical direct style, declared, "Gentleman, there were over 1,200 separate attacks upon our citizen-farmers that took place, which were totally unprovoked. Small clusters of painted heathen savages, like snakes in the grass, scouted the most vulnerable Christian pioneers as they toiled peacefully on chartered land. Then they stormed in whooping and hollering to kill, scalp, burn, and kidnap in the wilderness. The militia, the only forces capable of defending our communities and farms, took the fight to the Indians in their lair. The governor called them out and their superior officers, elected by the body of troops, directed them in their good work. Are you telling me that they should question such authority and confirm the rightness of their action? Should a militiaman be expected to get clarification from Washington before honoring the order to mobilize? Such a contrary doctrine would strike at the very root of subordination. Before you obey the command of your superior officer, does the fighting man have the right to inquire into the legality of the service upon which he is about to be employed, and, not until he is satisfied, may he refuse to take the field? Admit to this and you destroy the very basis on which military authority rests. You must agree with me that when a force is called to service, the men expect that they will be paid for their service and not negotiated out of it by uninterested parties at the federal level years later. If you do not uphold this claim, you can expect the word of your action to travel like wild fire across the frontier from north to south. Then where will your plans for progress be with no authority able to muster a single rifle to right wrongs? Ah, then where shall ye be, I ask you, gentlemen?"

The compensation was paid.

Monitoring the newspaper accounts, Jackson took credit for the long overdue and feared lost payments. In 1797 the Tennessee legislature elected him to the U.S. Senate. A year later, he walked off the job. He lacked the patience for the pulling and hauling required of any compromise. An appointment to the state supreme court lured Jackson back to Tennessee. The role of judge fit him more comfortably than the role of legislator. Serving for six years with great success, Jackson's honest black-or-white Christian justice was understood and respected in this frontier land of hard work and plain deals. The judge felt it was his sacred honor to interpret and uphold the law. He was fond of saying, without irony, "The land would never be civilized and safe for women and children if the rule of law was subverted." However, old prejudices remained deeply rooted within Judge Jackson. He showed no interest in defending Indian rights and supported every incursion into tribal land as a God-given right of white men. He was, in short, a man of his times.

Wellesley Returns

In March 1805, like so many strangers on the subcontinent of India, General Wellesley succumbed to fever and reluctantly left for home. In April he lingered at St. Helena, a British protectorate isolated in the South Atlantic that boasted a tropical climate and "good air." In addition to the fever, Wellesley complained of lumbago—a persistent annoying pain that plagued the small of his back—and rheumatism, which pervaded muscles and joints throughout his body and which the doctors of the day attributed to the long hours he spent horseback riding. (In the field in India, Wellesley, an excellent rider, had rarely trusted reports and preferred to witness the entire battlefield firsthand on horseback.)

Convalescing at the house on the island known as the Friars, he recovered his health before proceeding to England. Before Wellesley departed from India, his brother promoted him to major general of Sepoys, a theater rank that dissolved in the time it took to cross the warm waters of the Indian Ocean. Once he arrived home, at Horse Guards, the London headquarters of the army's commander in chief, the Duke of York refused to confirm Wellesley's elevation to permanent major general. However, Richard used his political influence with the king. In view of the victory at Assaye, George III granted the Order of the Bath, thus elevating the colonel to Sir Arthur Wellesley KB, Knight of the Bath, opening to Wellesley the doors of London society and the press.

A returning adventurer claimed headlines across England, and Wellesley was no exception. Outspoken as a rule and certainly unconventional in his views of the army's structure, he used his newfound fame to spread his electrifying ideas. Concerning the purchase system that regularly produced inept generals, he commented, "I've often said that if there were eight to ten thousand troops stuck in Hyde Park, only the best generals could get them out again." Such popularity didn't make him popular at Horse Guards, but it did cause a sensation in Parliament, which considered him as more of a politician than as a professional soldier. They liked his critical gaze born of field experience in a far-off war, even when it fell on the immovable Duke of York. Tweaking the nose of the king's son was great fun for members of Parliament, who couldn't directly attack the sovereign.

Wellesley spoke plainly. He used no lofty or convoluted language. He once said to a reporter, "I think that a soldier cannot know too much. From that I mean that he should be cross-trained on guns as well as rifles." Another time he espoused that "a commander's strength is in his attention to detail. The load of an oxen, how much a wagon can carry, the amount a man has in his pack, the availability of medical facilities, the quality of the victuals, the utility of the uniforms, the importance of daily cleaned equipment are of equal consequence with the valor of the attack. Officers must be professionally sound and aggressive if they are to be depended upon." Prime Minister Pitt, on his deathbed, commented to Lord Mornington, "Quite unlike other military men, he—Sir Arthur—never made a difficulty, or hid his ignorance in vague generalities. If I put a question to him, he answered it directly; if I wanted an explanation, he gave it clearly."

Press interviewers asked about the schools he had sponsored throughout India to train officers and British civil servants. Wellesley had learned on the job, but he didn't think that the army had the time to do that in the teeth of Napoleon's giant strides. What military training he had received took place at the Cavalry Academy in France. He now urged his own country to establish courses that concentrated on practical battlefield skills rather than on the personal art of the sword and pistol. Still, he was only a young colonel and his power base—his brother Richard—was a long way off in India.

Judge Jackson Gives No Quarter

Jackson came to notoriety in the frontier press for his "offer of terms" to Waightstill Avery, a fellow member of the bar. Following his mother's advice, he chose to resolve his personal affairs as a man and *not* as a lawyer. Dueling, though illegal, was regarded as a fair means of conflict resolution and therefore not punishable. However, only gentlemen were allowed such a privilege. Jackson challenged Avery to settle an insult concerning Jackson's skill as a lawyer. Each man fired his pistol, but neither injured the other.

In the spring of 1798, in a drunken rage, a culprit named Bean cut off his child's ear and, for the offense, appeared before Judge Jackson. Snarling at the judge, the defendant defied the court and stomped out, cursing the audience in the chamber. The judge sent the sheriff and posse after him, but they were cowed when Bean threatened to kill anyone who barred his way. Jackson, outraged at the behavior, told the sheriff to deputize him. The judge then left the courthouse to confront Bean in the street as the miscreant threatened the gathering crowd with a pistol. With a brace of loaded and cocked flintlock pistols, Jackson stormed through the throng of onlookers. At the top of his lungs the tall resolute judge, justice incarnate, bellowed, "Now surrender, you infernal villain, this very instant! Or I'll blow you through!"

Bean dropped the gun and later declared that when he gazed at Jackson's expression, "I saw shoot in those eyes."

At age thirty-five, Jackson was popular as a judge. The job wasn't an easy way to win friends but offered opportunities to display his great skills as a leader. Judge Jackson gave his name once again in the militia election for commanding general and won the position. As commander of Tennessee's militia and as a judge, Jackson now defined the law regarding land claims and enforced it on the Indians.

Parliament Beckons

Stepping out of uniform, Wellesley resumed his political career and sought an office in London rather than in Dublin. The Whig-Tory coalition, under the leadership of Lord Robert Stewart's supporting party, found a safe seat for the popular hero in Rye, Kent. It was a small provincial town, the Cinque Ports facing the English Channel.

At Westminster Palace his brothers happily formed an unashamed cheering section for their sibling soldier. While it was true that King George was the fountainhead, Arthur learned quickly that Parliament was the spring that supplied the water pressure.

"But first, Gerald, I must marry," he told his younger brother, the Reverend Gerald Wellesley. Sir Arthur's lineage compelled him to adhere to the strict rules of polite London and Dublin society. Wellesley recognized his obligation as a gentleman in his late thirties and thus took a wife. He had occasionally corresponded with his bride, Kitty, during his time in India, but it had been nearly ten years since he had seen her. Her thirty-four years had not been kind to her. She had always prided herself, as ladies did, on being rather frail, of a delicate constitution. She cooed about her "condition," and her doctor urged her not to become too excited. That, coupled with an early deterioration of face and figure, was not a good fit for the dynamic Irishman who proposed by letter in 1806.

The happy giggling girl of Wellesley's memory dissolved when he met Kitty on their wedding day. When he saw her for the first time coming down the aisle, he confided to Gerald, who was to officiate at the nuptials, "She's grown ugly, by Jove." Filled with regret that he hadn't followed his military penchant for reconnaissance before the engagement, he continued, "I've made a terrible mistake. Convention demands of me that I go through with the commitment."

The Irish honeymoon ended within the week. He asked Gerald to accompany the bride to their home in the city because Arthur's military leave was over. He later told Mrs. Harriet Arbuthnot, a lady friend in London, "I married her because they asked me to do it. I didn't know myself. I thought I should never care for anybody again and that I should be with my army, and in short, I was a fool."

The lovely Harriet took him in hand. "Arthur, never mind, my dear. We good ladies of London will see you through. You know that you can depend on us for everything." The married ladies of London society were gifted companions, caring for influential married men whose "wives did not understand them." Such intimacy, by mail and in person, with sympathetic ladies continued regularly for Wellesley's entire life. Sir Arthur's use of "military necessity" as a respectable reason for his frequent absences from Kitty became a defining feature of the couple's long, unhappy marriage.

Move the Indians

In Europe, matters of state between conquerors and kings continued to develop. Napoleon never forgot the loss of French land to Spain earlier in history, and in 1800, as he grew in influence, he insisted in the Treaty of San Ildefonso that Spain return Louisiana to

France. Spain agreed to relinquish to France the port of New Orleans in return for half of the Caribbean island of Santo Domingo. This kind of arbitrary caprice was why men and women had come to the New World. They could see that once the land, along with the government, belonged solely to the people, then their way of life and those of their descendants would be free from the interference and whims of crowned heads. Initially, Napoleon allied his country with the royal house of Spain against Great Britain. He then separated the Spanish king and his son from their crown and bestowed it on his brother Joseph Bonaparte, former king of Naples. This done, Napoleon prepared to sell the Spanish claim on the Louisiana Territory in North America to the United States. In 1803, President Jefferson, who had been ambassador to France prior to his presidency, purchased the vast tract of land west of the Mississippi for $15 million—nearly doubling the size of the country. The surprise expansion threw open the door to the West, revealing a breathtaking vista vulnerable to conquest, settlement, political development, and economic speculation and exploitation. Nothing for the young nation would be the same again.

By 1809 Jackson had grown in power and stature on the frontier and in Washington. He proposed to the new governor that an "exchange of territory" was the only solution to the unending Indian raiding parties that kept Tennessee from participating in the mainstream of progress. Jackson wanted to populate the southern portion of the Louisiana Territory with displaced Indian communities and force their welfare onto the federal government's shoulders.

"As simple as two and two makes four," the new governor said, agreeing that it was the perfect solution.

Jackson pointed out, "On that vacant land there is game for hunting, and a culture of other Indian tribes close to that of our own. You know that the idea originated with Jefferson and therefore has support of the federal government. It fits in with his agrarian plan for the United States by extracting the Indians and depriving the Spanish of their use of Indian surrogate soldiers. The Spanish, who cannot afford regular troops to protect Spanish Florida, and the territories of Georgia, Alabama, and Mississippi, have always stirred up the Indians at every opportunity. The removal of the Indians is the key to the president's plan for expansion. You know, Jefferson is opposed to manufacturing and foul factories. Jefferson sees the New World as the breadbasket, the supplier of fibers and food for Europe."

Jackson went on at length to remind the governor that the eastern tribes of Delaware and Yamasee Indians had been wiped out over land disputes that allowed farmers to prosper. "It is the kind thing to do. The removal of the Cherokee nation would save them from the inevitable white man's takeover of the state of Tennessee."

The governor agreed to their eviction.

When dealing with the Indian chiefs, General Jackson took the tone of an angry uncle scolding naughty children. He showed militia captain Sam Houston a letter that he planned to send to a half-white chief who had raided settlements, massacring settlers and enslaving many of the women and children. The letter read,

The Creeks have killed our women and children. We have sent to demand the murderers. If they are not given up, the whole Creek nation shall be covered with blood, fire shall consume their towns and villages, and their lands shall be divided among the whites. I am your friend, and the friend of your nation, but if you persist in allowing Creeks to have access through your nation, my friendship and the friendship of the United States will stop. Remember how the entire Creek nation came to destroy your towns and how a few hundred Chickasaws aided by a few whites chased them back to their nation, killing the best of their warriors, and covering the rest with shame. Remember, brother, we will do the same if the Creeks dare to touch you for your friendship to us. So be warned. Mark what I say. If you suffer any more scalps or stolen horses to be carried through your nation by the Creeks, your father, the President, will know that you have violated your treaty with us and have taken our enemy by the hand. Give me the names of the murderers, the identity of their towns, and the place where they have carried the women prisoners. You say you are the friend of whites. Now prove it to me.

Taking the letter back, he said, "Sam, I don't trust those red devils. It's best to set one tribe against the other. Never forget that fear is better than love when talkin' to Indians. You gotta put the fear of everlasting damnation in them. Make no mistake. It's the only way to deal with the savages."

The raids continued unabated. When Jackson learned that Martha Crawley had been abducted during a raid against her village, he mounted an expedition to pursue the abductors. In addition, he sent Captain Houston to arrest and prosecute the white settlers who had violated the treaty agreements and squatted on Indian land, though he did not burn them out, kill them, or send their women and children into captivity, as he did with the Indians; he sold their stock at auction. When Houston asked, "Andy, why do you inhibit whites from squatting on Indian property?" the judge replied, "I believed such white behavior only destabilized the law-abiding settlers and puts 'em in jeopardy from retaliat'n savages."

When Jackson's expedition crossed into Indian land, the militia found the renegade camp still occupied, killed eight of the offending Creeks, and restored Martha to her community. She was unable to walk because of wounds inflicted during her ordeal, and it was apparent that her mind had become deranged.

War in Portugal

In 1808 Wellesley's life changed radically. Lord Cornwallis, who had lost the Battle of Yorktown during the American Revolutionary War, died. Sir Arthur replaced him as the regimental colonel of the 33rd Regiment of Foot, a post of honor coveted by distinguished military officers. Not a field command but a leadership post for life, the position brought prestige and responsibility. The Honorable Sir Arthur Wellesley resigned his two political posts, a seat in the House of Commons and his responsibilities as chief secretary of Ireland in Dublin. The honor, colonel in chief of his old regiment, bestowed on him by

Horse Guards, touched him deeply. However, he would not be able to rest on his laurels for long.

After installing his brother Joseph as king of Spain, Napoleon bolstered Joseph's throne with 200,000 crack French troops and set into motion his plan to annex Portugal. Great Britain, long an ally of the Iberian country, stepped in to assist Portugal. Napoleon's army hunted down the British army and smashed it against the coastal town of Corunna, on the northern tip of Spain. In January 1809, Sir John Moore, commander of British forces on the peninsula, who evacuated the majority of the army as far as the port, was killed in a last-ditch rearguard action.

Determined to defy Napoleon's glaring aggression and efforts to upset Europe's delicate balance of power, England established another army with the mission of expelling the French from Portugal and of assisting the loyal Spanish to do the same. Great Britain set a naval blockade around the French coast. By 1813, Austria, Prussia, and Russia decisively engaged the Ogre on the continent. Even with multiple adversaries and fronts, Napoleon dominated all battlefields.

Wellesley's appointment as commander of the new expedition was a direct result of patronage. Once in Portugal the new army of 26,000 would be combined with a force of 6,000 Portuguese, who had been well trained by British major general William Beresford. Wellesley earnestly believed, as a result of past horrendous voyages, that the god of the sea, Poseidon, held a grudge against him for some unknown transgression. His trip to Lisbon only confirmed this feeling. Confronted in the channel by high winds and mountainous waves, the passage worsened in the Bay of Biscay. Nearly floundering, the general refused to put on his boots, because "I can swim better with them off."

His belated arrival as a result of the tempest prompted Napoleon to provide the new British commander with a nickname. Napoleon, who had no respect for the British army, intended to run the "drowned leopard" off the peninsula along with the second wave of British troops, but having other fish to fry in Austria, he left Wellesley for his marshals to defang. When Wellesley heard of the "honor" bestowed on him by such an important personage, he was flattered and referred at times to himself as the Leopard.

Always the aggressor, the new British commander planned first to attack the French, who had settled in the middle of the country on the banks of the Douro River, and then second to liberate the town of Oporto. French marshal Nicolas Soult squatted on the banks of the Douro River with an army of 23,000 veteran soldiers; Wellesley had roughly the same number of troops. Soult fortified his flanks and prepared to receive a frontal assault. However, the enterprising Wellesley feinted at the center, while sending his main force upriver, where the soldiers found boats and rafts. Wellesley surprised the marshal and routed the French.

Suffering few casualties, Wellesley remained while Soult fled to Spain. The aggressive British leader turned south immediately, picked up strength from incoming formations, and struck out across the border for Madrid. Adding Spanish elements along the way, he discovered that coalition warfare was more challenging than meeting the enemy on his own. Spanish generals were always reluctant and rarely made the blocks on time or in advertised strengths.

While waiting for the Spanish forces to arrive at Talavera, Wellesley scouted the horizon from the top of a tall stone tower while his escort, a troop of British light dragoons, enjoyed a siesta below. Suddenly, a formation of French voltigeurs appeared at the base of the tower and began to slaughter the dismounted hapless dragoons. Wellesley and Major William Delancey, his assistant quartermaster general, clattered down the tower's wooden steps and onto their horses. The enemy fired at the fleeing figures and wounded their horses, forcing them to go on foot. According to Delancey, "The general cursed the British dragoons mile after mile."

"The bloody cavalry can't be trusted with serious campaigning. They belong in a steeplechase on Wimbledon common, somewhere safe where they can't hurt themselves. They take nothing seriously and are only happy galloping about breaking things. God, I wish I were rid of them. They can't be trusted." His old friend from India commiserated and promised to have a word with Colonel Frederick Ponsonby, the only cavalryman commander the general trusted to listen to his complaint.

———

England wanted desperately to avenge the losses suffered at Corunna in 1809 during the evacuation of the corps under Sir John. Wellesley was determined to give that vengeance to them. At the defense line constructed at Torres Vedras, north of Lisbon, he made his mark. He picked his ground carefully and packed its center with redcoats behind a hill known as Cerro de Medellin. On either side he employed the Spanish allies. Using reverse slope defense, in which the majority of his men were hidden and protected behind the crest of the hill, he settled to wait for the attack. The French assumed his center was weak. The British ranks were safe from direct artillery fire, thereby nullifying the French supporting attack. Shooting at the top of a hill is nearly impossible. The cannonballs fell short or careened well over the top, falling deep behind the defenders.

Frustrated, the experienced Marshal Claude Victor realized after probing the ground that it would be no easy task to rout the British this time. He decided to attempt a risky night attack. Night attacks, as a rule, were conducted only against fixed fortifications because the attacking formations had a tendency to get lost in the dark and lose focus. However, despite the evident risks, Victor realized the surprise gained that evening could well be the deciding factor that would carry the French to victory.

The sudden shock of the night attack won the crest from the British and threatened the entire line. As expected, great confusion tore through the thin line of pickets. The regiments, their arms stacked, were tucked up in bedrolls clustered around great glowing fires. The initial units were overwhelmed; the French bayoneted the men in their blankets. Soon, others, clad in shirts and underwear, rose up, but the French chased them farther down the reverse side of Cerro de Medellin. Other regiments, given only moments to organize, closed the gap quickly in hand-to-hand fighting. Flashing thirteen-inch bayonets rent from arms stacks reflected amber light from the abandoned fires.

The attack began to lose its way and break up into snarled tangles of confused and disoriented soldiers from both sides. Grooms hastily brought saddled horses to Wellesley and General Rowland Hill. Standing in the stirrups of his chestnut stallion Copenhagen, Wellesley led the 29th Worcestershire Regiment toward the crest of Medellin, where men were still fighting in clusters. The hatless British, in white shirts and trousers, were a stark contrast to the French in their full campaign dress and plumed shakos; at one point, Wellesley's plain dark blue frock coat confused the French into thinking he was a civilian. Gradually the British gained back the lost ground and the enemy abandoned the attack, fleeing over the crest of the Medellin, where it was black as pitch.

The expelled French, stumbling and cursing their way back home, scurried down the front side of the steep hill, thereby allowing General Hill to restore the line. On frothing mounts in the gloom the two leaders met. They were exhausted yet relieved that little harm had been done. Each side gained respect for the other that frightful night, and Wellesley never again suffered a surprise night attack.

———

At noon the enemy assault, led by a full-face attack of 4,500 densely packed French line infantry, rushed that same scarred hill in a determined column. Wellesley demonstrated amply that he didn't fear the French as other European generals did.

Delancey commented, "General, you don't look worried."

"I'd never offer battle that I haven't already won. Remember Assaye and Tipu. You were there. Am I mistaken or have we seen this specter, half a world away, before?"

"Sir Arthur, handle them with care. All they have to lose at your hands is their reputation."

Wellesley addressed Hill. "General, three straight lines abreast, if you please. Steady your troops and set an example for the Spaniards. This day the French will fall like nine pins. Those formations resemble large coffins, wouldn't you agree?"

Hill concurred. "Sir Arthur, we're ready for them in fine order. If the fatigue from the climb doesn't spend them, our fine lead balls will." Hill sent the bulk of his troops forward over the crest of the Medellin like long, thin, red-piped ribbons along the leading edge of the steep bluff. Waiting for the enemy, they stopped and sighted down their muskets' long, brown metal barrels. There on the forward slope the infantry took aim at the French grenadiers in dark blue coats marked out in red. The plumes of their shakos bobbed in unison with their labored strides over the rocky ground.

Astride Copenhagen as the horse shifted nervously at the sound of the low-throbbing French drums, Wellesley remarked, "Supremely confident I'd say! They come on as if we aren't here. No need to rush, Hill, the combination of the steep slope and rolling musket fire will turn them away."

In thickly packed blocks the French soldiers began stumbling over each other, yet they came on as they had on a hundred battlefields over the past fifteen years. Their hearts pounded in unison with their musicians' strike. Trailing a few paces behind, the drummers halted out of range but continued their thundering throb. Crushed together, the infantry at last reached the range of the British muskets. The soldiers listened to their sergeants' deep voices intone, "Steady there, lads. Wait for it."

While the French formations had shock power, little musket fire was possible. Only the soldiers in the first two ranks of the advancing columns were able to shoot. The urgent pace prevented them from reloading their single-shot fusil flintlocks.

Suddenly, every British musket belched fire. The first file of the French formation and part of the second disintegrated. Those who followed tripped over the bodies of their screaming comrades. The redcoats' regimental sergeants kept control as officers commanded the second rank to discharge their weapons. Line after line of Frenchmen were threshed as soldiers fell under foot and a dozen formations slowed, wavered, and stopped well short of their objective. The attack had been broken. The momentum, so crucial to Marshal Victor's plans, waned in the face of his steadfast foes. His columns faltered and finally turned and ran.

"Sir Arthur, we've done it, by God!" General Hill exclaimed as he trotted by, waving his black hat with its gold acorns dripping from each end. Sir Arthur acknowledged his boast by lifting his *chapeau de bras* in return and tipping it forward to hide his smile. His mounted staff clustered around the man of the hour. The victory at Talavera, a place until that day unknown to the people of the British Isles, caused church bells to ring in every English village.

"Delancey," Wellesley mused, "dozens of seamstresses must now learn how to spell Talavera, for it's a battle honor that will emblazon these colors here today for generations to come. Metal workers will carve it into badges and glaziers will remember it in stained glass. But all that won't matter unless we notify the Continent, as we did here, that Napoleon's armies are far from invincible."

Another Laurel for Wellesley

To: General Sir Arthur Wellesley, Marquess of Wellington, Generalissimo of Spain, Duque da Victoria of Portugal

Greetings.
It is my honor to inform you that his gracious Majesty, George III, King of England, Scotland, and Ireland and the dominions beyond has at the passing of Lord Buckingham appointed you to the Most Noble Order of the Garter as knight-errant this first day of March 1813.

Harold Egerton
Earl of Sutherland
Knight at Arms to His Majesty King George III

Wellington received the news of his elevation while on campaign in Spain. He slipped the missive, without fanfare, into a drawer in his brass-bound mahogany campaign desk, which had accompanied him since the beginning of his military career and which held all his private papers. He was well aware, as was every British subject, that since the establishment in 1350 by Edward III, the Garter had become the premier royal order of chivalry. Many sought the honor, but only a select few were chosen.

"Delancey, on which shoulder is the blue sash worn—left or right?" Although seated, he held it up on one and then the other. "Ah well," he confided before putting the wide ribbon to one side, "I'm sure the king will provide instructions at the ceremony." The general was known for his dry sense of humor. He accepted honors as a matter of course. "Really, the accumulation of baubles doesn't compare to the challenge on the field," he said. Despite his claims to the contrary, in his hierarchical world, the general was determined to acquire ample power and position.

Although forty-four, Wellington appeared much younger. His decidedly slim five-foot-nine-inch figure and dark reddish-brown unruly hair gave him an aristocratic air. Even though he put the announcement quietly away, the award reminded him of his unremarkable youth, which had shown so little promise.

Jackson's Federal Service

With another war with Great Britain started in June 1812, President Madison appointed Jackson as a temporary major general in the regular army and sent him to New Orleans to reinforce the garrison. Suspicious as to the motives of the president and his political cronies, Jackson didn't leave Nashville until January 1813. On his way to New Orleans he recruited a small army of two thousand men; it was winter and there was nothing for the farmers to do until spring, at which time they expected to be discharged from service.

Five hundred miles from home, traversing the wilderness in the grip of a harsh winter, Jackson received a change of orders from Secretary of War John Armstrong. The general was told to stop, discharge his force, abandon the expedition, and return to Nashville immediately. Major General James Wilkinson, a favorite in Washington and a rascal of the first order, commanded the American forces at New Orleans. The original plan combined Jackson with Wilkinson in an invasion of Spanish Florida. However, the militarily possible operation became politically unsound when the czar of Russia offered to host and mediate treaty talks between Britain and the United States, and Madison scrapped it.

Jackson received the order as an act of treachery intended to relieve him of his rightful command. He believed that Armstrong fully expected the men to continue on without him. Maintaining the formation (for it was folly for a disorganized band to backtrack in Indian country), Jackson turned for home. The men agreed with Jackson's assessment of vengeful Indians waiting to pick them off a handful at a time and followed their leader, who, because Armstrong refused to pay the militia for its efforts, reimbursed them with his own funds. The trip to Tennessee was arduous. More than 150 men became so ill that they had to be carried on horses. Jackson walked every step of the way and urged his troops onward with a cheerful yet strong display of will and affection. His men called him "as tough as old hickory." The nickname stuck.

————

While the United States and Great Britain continued to fight the war into the summer of 1813, the British sent Tecumseh, war chief of the Shawnee, from his home on the Upper Wabash River to meet the tribes of the southeastern United States. Backed by England, which promised to supply arms from its facilities in Spanish Florida, Tecumseh intended to unite the tribes into one fighting nation and promised, "We'll drive the accursed waves of white men back into the sea."

Major and minor chiefs arrived, surrounded by their most trusted braves, decked out in multicolored feathers and paint. The meeting took place on open land north of Mobile, Alabama, under the admiring eye of their Spanish hosts. The Spaniards supplied crates of new rifles and paid in gold coin to have game brought. For several days hundreds of Indians feasted, danced, and waited for the great visitor from the North to appear from the lodge that they had built for him and his medicine men. Each night, when it became clear that "big medicine" was not yet made, the dancing continued while tensions rose. Campfires blazed anew and the chanting grew deeper, more ominous. Tecumseh was setting the stage, like the magician he was, before he laid before them his vision of the future. It was no secret to the Creeks that the white men were growing more powerful with each season. They also believed that their medicine was strong and could be brought down on the white man's head, wiping him from their fathers' land. The old chiefs from the Creek, Cherokee, and Chickasaw tribes were working with Jackson to compromise over the white man's expansion into Indian territory, and the chiefs were uncomfortable with this firebrand from the North.

Tecumseh was secluded in the lodge for nearly four days. Finally, he appeared as the sun was about to set and strolled into the center of the square. Face painted red and black and towering at six feet, he carried a war club stained with the white man's blood. Over the previous days, storytellers spread tales of the Shawnee victories against American soldiers and enraptured the audience with visions of war whoops and swinging tomahawks. The long, highly decorated, and feathered smoking pipe of the Shawnee was passed, but only after Tecumseh took the first draw. While the sweet smoke was still about their heads, he began to speak slowly and seriously as if he were digging his words from the depths of his soul. His eyes burned with supernatural luster. Every limb and muscle quivered with emotion.

"Listen, oh Muskogees, brethren of my mother. Brush from your eyelids the sleep of slavery and strike for vengeance and your land. Join your brothers from the North, who have won great victories. While the white men press us everywhere, we will defy them. Let the white men perish. They have seized your land, made you into women, and stood triumphant on the graves of your fathers. Send them back across the water in a trail of blood with tales of war beyond all war. Burn their dwellings, destroy their stock, slay their wives and children that their very breed will perish."

His words set fire to the huge throng of painted warriors. They became one, whooping their approval and pounding their leather moccasins hard against the ground so that the thumping would awaken the Great Spirit that gave them the land.

Tecumseh finished his speech with the rousing rallying cry, "War now, war always, war on the living, war on the dead! The Great Spirit told me that it is his will."

His brother, the medicine man, adorned with the horns of a buffalo and the yellow paint of the anointed one, danced behind him.

The great speech may have produced hysteria in the tribes but not in their leader. The senior chief of the Creek, Big Warrior, now stood and said, "I will not bring my people against the white man for too many will die."

Tecumseh told them that he had made big medicine and stomped his foot hard on the ground before the assembled tribes. But all the chiefs agreed with Big Warrior.

With fire in his eyes and vengeance in his head, the Shawnee chief cried out for all to hear, "I will go to Detroit and you'll feel my mighty battle here in this square."

Shortly after Tecumseh led his party north to fight without the Creeks, an earthquake shook Tookabatche village, razing houses and slaying a number of inhabitants. Now the young Creeks believed that the Great Spirit had spoken to them; they broke away from their old chiefs, who they said were filled with white blood. The fiery braves, along with their prophets and medicine men, left the circle and formed the "Red Sticks." These renegade warriors from Tennessee joined Tecumseh's fight to the death against all white settlers. Broken into bands several hundred strong, they moved north looking for trouble.

The Creek War began in August 1813. The Red Sticks' first action was to butcher women and children at little-known Fort Mims, forty miles north of Mobile. Their leader was the half-white William Weatherford, known as Chief Red Eagle. In all they massacred 500 settlers. The Indians swung settler children by their legs and battered their fragile heads against trees. They scalped pregnant women and, while they were still alive, sliced them open to disgorge their infants onto the ground.

General Jackson called 5,000 territorial militia from Tennessee, Georgia, and Mississippi. Georgia and Mississippi didn't hold Jackson in the same esteem and refused to join his command. Jackson, undeterred, issued a clarion call in Tennessee's newspapers: "Your frontier is threatened with invasion by a savage foe! Already do they advance toward your frontier, with their scalping knives unsheathed to butcher your wives, your children, and your helpless babes. Time is not to be lost! We must hasten to the frontier or we will find it drenched in the blood of our fellow citizens."

President Madison directed that "all militias must defeat the Red Stick tearaways" and provided federal funds to organize a force of 1,200 infantry and 800 cavalry. Volunteers, on reading the horrors of the massacre, joined the expedition. Within days of the presidential order Davy Crockett left his family in the Kentucky Territory and joined a contingent of mounted infantry. They struck south to Alabama Territory and moved through the wilderness at the phenomenal pace of thirty-four miles a day. The force intended to destroy the renegade Indian parties that had terrorized not only white communities but also the peaceful Indian villages that didn't support Chief Red Eagle. Jackson's Tennessee militia traveled along the western spine of Lookout Mountain, where two supply forts, Forts Deposit and Strother, had been established. No sooner was Fort Strother cut from the wilderness than a friendly Creek alerted the fort's commander to the hostile village of Tallushatchee, thirteen miles away. The cavalry and mounted infantry, under Brigadier General John Coffee, rode out immediately and surprised the Creeks, who were slaughtering people where they stood. Crockett said of the attack, "We shot them down like dogs." Trapped inside cabins, the Indians weren't able to fight in the open. The entire town was set on fire and razed to the ground as an example to Red Eagle's followers. Jackson's swift action, attacking from the march, was a stunning victory and sent the Red Sticks reeling.

Examining the battlefield, Jackson came across a dead Indian mother holding a live baby in her arms. He was told that friendly Indians had discovered that the entire family, save the baby, had perished. They recommended that since no family member had survived who could care for the child, the infant be killed. But the general, remembering his own experience as an orphan, took the child to his tent and fed it brown sugar dissolved in water. Then he asked an officer who was returning to Tennessee with the wounded to take the child to Jackson's wife at their home, the Hermitage. He sent along a letter to Rachel asking her to "raise the child as our own in the house, even though he is a savage."

Rachel Donelson Jackson had been the center of controversy from the time the two fell in love in October 1788. Years before, when a budding lawyer, Jackson had arrived in Nashville and had taken up residence in the Donaldsons' rooming house. John Donaldson had been killed recently by Indians. His daughter Rachel, a lighthearted, happy-go-lucky young woman, was married to the absent Lewis Robards, a frontiersman working in the Kentucky Territory. On Robards's return he accused Rachel of committing adultery with the family's boarder, Jackson. Much was made of the romance, and Robards divorced Rachel. She married Jackson in 1794.

———

In November 1813 Chief Red Eagle prepared to wreak vengeance on the Indian town of Talladega, where Creeks friendly to Jackson dwelled. The general had pledged in letters to Big Warrior and other chiefs that they could depend on his support and asked them to hold on until he arrived.

While waiting to receive badly needed supplies to feed his small army at Fort Strother, Jackson received a message that Talladega would soon be under siege from a major Red Sticks war party. The village couldn't hope to withstand an attack from more than a thousand warriors. The army left that night, stumbling thirty-four miles through the wilderness to Talladega. Jackson intended to attack Red Eagle's men from behind. The Indians, believing that the militia wasn't a factor they had to consider, focused on the beleaguered village. By moving swiftly, Jackson was sure that he had gained the element of surprise. The Red Sticks were unaware of his presence in the neighborhood. The tactic allowed him to concentrate his entire strength on one point.

Jackson attacked right from the march with no respite for his troops. The militia moved in a fighting square formation with mounted troops on the sides and the reserve behind. According to a messenger who claimed that Red Eagle was within a quarter mile of Talladega, there would be no time to lose. Not pausing to organize further or rest and feed his soldiers, Jackson ordered a dawn attack. He felt the surprise assault would catch the enemy with their backs to him. He expected to inflict major casualties, while minimizing his own. He thrust the lead elements of the infantry forward to engage the Indians. It was a feint. As soon as contact was made, the Red Sticks turned and attacked in a disorganized frenzy. The general withdrew the force quickly into the safe position in front of his reserve. He then sent the mounted formations on either flank forward like the horns of the bull, thereby keeping the reserve as yet in place. He planned to draw the Indians into the killing ground formed at the middle of his U-shaped defensive position.

The battle went according to plan. All one thousand whooping savages turned and charged the withdrawing militiamen. Unfortunately, the center gave way with the ferocity and shock of the redskins' response. For a few agonizing minutes, the survival of Jackson's entire command was in question. It had been an enormous risk, but one that paid off. Jackson, highly visible on a white horse, placed himself at the head of the reserve. He brought his troops forward at a trot to seal the gap like a stopper in a bottle. He stabilized the center and stopped the fleeing infantry just in time to see the mounted horns of the bull close in behind the trapped enemy.

"It was like shootin' fish in a barrel," said the eloquent Crockett. The Indians swirled in ever-smaller numbers until they managed to break through a weak spot in the left flank, where an infantry unit had failed to close. The panicked braves rushed through, leaving nearly half of their force dead on the killing ground.

Wellesley Continues Campaigning

Wellesley's victory at Talavera was good for a headline, but taking Madrid and expelling the French from Spain were other matters altogether. Far from his Lisbon support base, Wellesley didn't have the troops or the supply train to campaign any longer. It would take four more years—from the defensive lines of Torres Vedras through the siege of Badajoz and beyond—before decisive victory was achieved. The government chided Wellesley for spending too much money, skimped wherever possible, and questioned every request. Time and again only Wellesley's victories would silence his detractors on the opposition side of the Commons chamber.

With each campaign new honors arrived. Talavera brought Wellesley a peerage in his own right. The College of Arms, responding to the king's request, searched for a suitable name. His brother William stood in for him and suggested Viscount Wellington of Talavera. In a letter to Arthur he justified the selection: "After ransacking the Peerage and examining the map, I at last determined upon Viscount Wellington of Talavera and of Wellington, and Baron Douro of Welleslie in the county of Somerset—Wellington is a town not far from Welleslie. . . . I trust that you will not think that there is anything unpleasant or trifling in the name of Wellington."

Wellesley approved. "Viscount Wellington of Talavera is exactly right. You could not take for me Lord Wellesley's title. . . . You were quite right in not taking Vimeira and in that situation I think you have chosen most fortunately."

While Wellington accepted elevation to the captain-generalcy of Spain, he turned down the pay on the grounds that he wouldn't burden the Spanish people, who were "on short rations."

After the hard-fought Siege of Ciudad Rodrigo in January 1812, he became the Earl of Wellington. At Vitoria, his men captured a marshal's baton, which had belonged to one of Napoleon's favorite commanders, Jean-Baptiste Jourdan. Wellington presented it to the Prince Regent, who had assumed power in England when his father had been declared insane. (The condition was a temporary one but also recurred intermittently.) The prince, who had always been a supporter, was so struck with the gift that he granted Wellington a personal reward: "You have sent me among your trophies of unrivaled fame the staff of a marshal of France, and I send you in return that of England." Field Marshal Wellington soon justified the honor.

After the stunning destruction of the French Imperial Corps at Salamanca, Spain, he was ennobled as the Marquess of Wellington. A considerable amount of money and land accompanied each title, thereby making Wellington a very rich man. Back home in England, Kitty reveled in his prosperity and filled her letters with accounts of the antics of the affluent social set who came to call.

The British army's steady march east since 1811 became stalled just short of the French frontier outside the formidable gates of San Sebastian. England could no longer afford to replenish Wellington's provisions and combat losses. Additionally, England's six-hundred-ship navy, sailing around the world, was a colossal financial burden. Great Britain's gold and goods had to sustain her allies—Russia, Prussia, and Austria—as well.

At this critical juncture, the coffers of the Old Lady of Threadneedle Street, as the Bank of England was affectionately known, were empty. British agents arranged a loan from James Rothschild's bank in Paris. (The banker had garnered guarantees from Napoleon's political opponents.) Customs agents failed to notice coins packed in the wardrobes of the Parisian women sent to visit French soldiers garrisoned in the city's fortress. With such traitorous monetary encouragement to weaken the defenders' resolve, San Sebastian fell, and Wellesley's victorious campaign continued unabated. By March 1814, the British army had crossed the Bidassoa River and invested Toulouse. Within a month, the allies entered Paris, Napoleon Bonaparte abdicated, and Sir Arthur was rewarded with the title His Grace, Duke of Wellington.

Charges of Treachery

Soon after the fighting at Talladega ended, Jackson enjoyed a triumphant entry into the village. There, to feed his gallant militiamen, he purchased food with his own personal funds. He was proud that his Tennessee woodsmen and farmers, though not professionals, were more than a match for the renegade Red Sticks.

In the two battles, Jackson had suffered 20 killed and 121 wounded. The renegades had nearly 700 dead or captured; there was no count of Red Eagle's wounded. Jackson sensed that, if nothing else, then Red Eagle would have difficulty recruiting more braves to his cause. The fire that Tecumseh had lit would become an ember after news of the staggering defeat spread among the tribes. Word of the battle reached the Hillabees and Fish Pond tribes, who quickly surrendered. Indians believed that war should be entertaining and profitable and allow for individual coups of glory. If its nature, when fought against white men, failed to meet their expectations, they wanted no part of it. Additionally, Jackson knew they would not approach a line of battle when artillery was present. Therefore, he always dotted his formations with small, highly mobile horse-drawn guns. Jackson let it be known to the tribes that "long shall they remember Fort Mims with bitterness and tears."

To protect those tribes that had opposed Red Eagle, Jackson announced that the fight would not stop until he laid waste to the Red Sticks and all those who had supported the savages—including the Spanish. It was generally accepted that the Battle of Talladega had finished the Red Sticks, but such an interpretation was more optimistic than realistic. Owing to the lack of coordination and the difficulty in communicating across the harsh landscape, Jackson's counterpart in eastern Tennessee, General John Cocke, attacked several Hillabee villages, killing and seizing hundreds of captives. Although the Indians settled with Jackson, the news of the battle in the east outraged the tribe. They cried treachery and remained on the warpath to avenge the deaths of their people.

The Last Major Battle of the Creek War

The peace talks with the British, which had begun a year earlier in Russia, ended without result. In Washington the news spurred Secretary of War Armstrong into action. As the army expanded in early spring of 1814, most of the regular units were given to Major General Wilkinson, who had launched yet another attack across the northern frontier from Plattsburgh, this time aimed at Montreal. Like all the previous expeditions, the goal was to attack Canada and bring the country over to the U.S. side—willingly or not. Armstrong was well aware of the Royal Navy's blockade of the American coastline, spanning Maine to New Orleans and preventing the American navy access to the sea. The secretary feared a British invasion from the Gulf of Mexico. To form a credible defense in that area, he turned his attention to the Tennessee frontier and the soft underbelly along the Gulf Coast. The 39th Regular Infantry Regiment was sent to augment Jackson's Tennessee militia. The general was overjoyed when they arrived at the precise moment that his new recruits were exhibiting an impressive display of incompetence. With nearly five thousand well-provisioned troops at his disposal, Jackson struck out for the Horseshoe Bend Indian cantonment.

There, a thousand braves from the scattered Creek nation were meeting with their prophets to bolster their courage. They believed, mistakenly, that Jackson had been routed in a recent encounter and were eager to wipe out the American's army provisioning at Fort Strother. However, Jackson was confident—some might've said too confident—and determined to make use of his expanded command. He boasted, "I'll send the last vestige of Tecumseh's renegade Creeks to their happy hunting ground!"

Leaving a small decoy formation behind at Fort Strother to guard the provisions, Jackson marched straight south with a force of 3,500 infantry, 700 cavalry and mounted infantry, and 500 Cherokees and 100 friendly Creeks.

When he arrived two days later, Jackson was astonished at the preparations the Red Sticks had made. More than 1,000 Indians, along with 300 women and children, had settled on a piece of land neatly surrounded by a colossal loop of the river. Across the open end they had constructed a breastwork of logs over six feet high, cut through with loops for rifles. The sawtooth barricade provided crisscross fire protection. The Indians had learned from their enemy the tricks of building a safe defensive position. It was true that a good fort could provide as much as a four-to-one advantage in the defender's favor. But the more Jackson considered the matter, the more he realized that the Indians had constructed their own cage. Sending the cavalry and friendly Indians around to the opposite side, Jackson easily surrounded the fortification. He massed artillery opposite the log wall and beyond the range of Indian rifles. His allied Cherokees set fire to the log houses inside the cantonment with flaming arrows.

While the gunners bombarded the breastwork, Jackson yelled, "Charge!" Supported by cannon fire, he led the 39th Infantry attack, which carried the outer defenses. He was in his glory, as happy as a man who loved a fight could be. He knew that the Creeks would crumble and that their war whoops would not be heard again in Tennessee—or anywhere else—after that day. At the wall the infantry used its wooden remnants as firing positions, turning the table on the scattered panicked Indians. Crockett was in the thick of the mayhem. He swung a hatchet with one hand and worked a skinning knife in the other. The Americans and their Indian allies routed the Red Sticks. In a swirling dust cloud of feathered bonnets, war paint, and musket fire, the clearly outnumbered Indians inside the cantonment searched desperately for an escape route, but there was none.

The years of defiance and resistance to protect their land and families were coming to a calamitous end. They found themselves fighting according to the white man's rules within the cantonment's lethal confines. Deprived of open ground, the bewildered braves couldn't melt away into the dark dense forest to regroup and recharge. They had run out of options and could only fight or surrender. They chose to fight.

The battle proceeded at close range in hand-to-hand combat. The pent-up emotions and promised vengeance held so personally by the white men had ferocious effects on their behavior. For years they and their families had lived in fear of night-raiding parties that burned them out, killing their women and children or carrying them off to a fate no one dared imagine. Finally, the carnage exhausted itself, but not before a mass of twisted half-naked bodies were heaped in the center of the smoldering ruin that had once been the Red Sticks' stronghold. There, the Indians had given up the ghost to the Great Spirit.

Of the thousand Creek warriors presumed in the camp, twenty survived the attack to escape into the woods and to carry the tale to the tribe's surviving elements. Jackson had lost only seventy-two from his various elements; double that number had been wounded. Many of the wounded wouldn't survive long, however, without medical treatment.

Jackson was not a one-man band and never pretended to be. He freely praised his subordinate leaders and the soldiers, whom he loved. "There never was more heroism or Roman courage displayed," he told the newspapers. He singled out Major Lemuel Montgomery of the 39th Regular Infantry for special mention. He didn't forget the invaluable assistance of the friendly Creek Indians and their half-white leader, Major William McIntosh. Of one man, his wife Rachel's nephew, Private Jack Caffery, he wrote, "Jack realized all my expectations. He fought bravely—and killed an Indian. There was no weeping over the pile of savages. Nor was there remorse when their stronghold was burned and the women and children taken into custody."

During the entire campaign 3,000 of the 180,000 Creek Indians were killed on the battlefields. Within the white settlements, nearly a thousand militiamen and family members perished during the Creek War. Those days were most costly for the new republic in its early expansion west. To Jackson, who had lost close kin to savage raiders, there was solace that the red scare was at last at an end. He was proud of his service and contributions to the outcome. In Washington, Jackson, though not liked, was admired for his ruthless campaign.

Hurtling toward Immortality

Wellington and Jackson each had unique experiences that impacted their development as men and commanders. With skills aplenty and the possibility of defeat and triumph seeded within the nature of their characters, both were now poised to take their part in what would become a legendary campaign culminating in a decisive engagement between their nations that would forever alter the men's reputations.

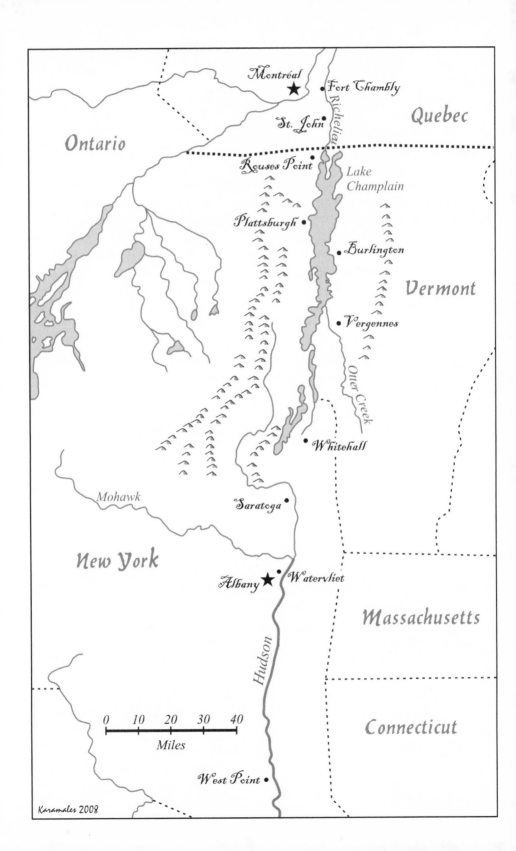

Montréal ★ • Fort Chambly

St. John •

Rouses Point •

Lake Champlain

Plattsburgh •

• Burlington

Vermont

• Vergennes

Otter Creek

• Whitehall

Mohawk

Saratoga •

New York

Albany ★ • Watervliet

Massachusetts

Hudson

0 10 20 30 40
Miles

Connecticut

West Point •

Karamales 2008

Quebec

Ontario

Richelieu

CHAPTER 3

The War Intensifies, the Stakes Rise

"Do what you can, with what you've got, where you are."
—THEODORE ROOSEVELT

I n the fall of 1813, while Wellington was whipping the French in Spain and Jackson was destroying the Red Sticks in the South, American smugglers in Vermont and northern New York were aiding the British army in its efforts to resist the American army, which was intent on taking Canada.

Pring's Boast

On Lake Champlain, Royal Navy commodore Daniel Pring, flush with success from the attacks on Burlington and Plattsburgh, saw an opportunity that he couldn't ignore. Pring had already recognized the possibility of sealing up the American navy like a ship in a bottle, but now Vermont smugglers, paid in British gold coins, disclosed to Pring why the American navy hadn't defended Burlington and why he had ranged the lake so freely, burning and bombarding the communities that pleaded desperately for Commodore Macdonough's assistance. The American navy not only was dealt a heavy blow by the loss of *Growler* and *Eagle* but also had just a single American sailing ship, the *President*, fit for duty. Two others were under construction at Vergennes, but they wouldn't be ready that sailing season.

Winter came early on the Canadian border, which rested on the 45th parallel, half-way to the North Pole. Howling winds would soon wrap around land and lake followed closely by never-ending snow. The loss of a number of American gunboats on the beach at Burlington had further crippled the fleet. Only a handful remained to chase the smugglers. Pring's sole mission was to protect the smuggling trade and their uninterrupted passage on Lake Chaplain at all costs. Provisions supplied by the smugglers sustained Prevost's Canadian army; likewise, the Canadian Marine boat-building yard depended on American timber. Still, Pring hoped for a challenge more ripe for martial glory than this naval babysitting.

The smugglers had been busy all summer bringing cut lumber north to the Canadian boatyard at the Ile-aux-Noix. There, Master Builder William Simons turned the rough planks into a new sloop of war. The HMS *Linnet*, Pring's new flagship, carried sixteen cannons and six carronades. Confined between the wooden stocks of the yard, the shipwrights covered her exposed ribs and stuck her with a mainmast 150 feet high. Her topping out could be seen over the flat farm fields and on the streets of St. John, several miles north.

Pring looked forward to the ship's completion—and to breaking her in doing battle with the noisome Americans. Quoted widely in Montreal's newspapers, he announced, "Let me provide fair warning to my opponent, Commodore Macdonough. *Linnet* is more than a rival for the *President*. She's the new guardian of Lake Champlain. I challenge the American commodore to come out and meet her. I can stand off a mile and turn that 'Head of State' to driftwood. There'll be no need to heat up the guns on *Chub* or *Finch*. I'll bring them along to pick up the survivors."

Smugglers saw to it that copies of Pring's provocation were distributed all around the rim of Lake Champlain. Lieutenant Colonel Murray and his red-coated infantry wouldn't be included in this foray. In their place, 150 Royal Marines embarked on board rowed galleys to form the land contingent, while provisions were carried on the HMS *Canada*.

The British commodore had also neglected to inform his superior, Commodore Yeo, of the battle plan. He reported it as only a punitive expedition intended to guarantee the flow of naval matériel north to the Canadian boatyard for the remainder of the sailing season. Pring didn't want to reveal his scheme until the American fleet was in the bag—or the bottle. False promises didn't create a career. Great deeds did.

Sailly Sounds the Alarm

The American customs patrol recorded every detail of Pring's flotilla as it swept out of the Richelieu into Lake Champlain. Bulletins of sightings from land and lake piled up on Judge Sailly's desk. The most alarming report came with Agent Hollis's arrival: "Sir, a dozen barges, loaded with rocks, are in tow."

The old man voiced his suspicions. "Hollis, Macdonough's boatyard is located at the far end of the three-mile-long Otter Creek. Where it pools before the Vergennes, Vermont, dam, the channel becomes very restricted long before it opens into Lake Champlain." He paused to think and then continued, "If I were Pring, I'd clog the mouth of the inlet. The troops must be a landing party to protect the barges. That's it, Hollis! Their gunboats will position the rock-filled barges and sink 'em. That'll strand our navy vessels in the creek. Pring can afford to leave *Chub* or *Finch* on station, offshore, to prevent the rocks from being cleared."

"What irony," Mister Hollis remarked. "To be held captive by our own captured vessels! That'd put a stopper in the bottle."

Together Sailly and Hollis left Plattsburgh on board the *Valerie*, Hollis's customs cutter. On the same day Pring's fleet plunged south into American waters. Spread out before the south wind, the ships composed an impressive flotilla. The *Valerie*, held back by a stiff southerly breeze, was forced to tack.

"Mister Hollis, this chop isn't to my liking," the judge said. "It only slows our progress, which I fear will cost us a great deal. Sail as close to the wind as you dare, though we can't risk springing the mast. I'm very much afraid we'll be too late to warn Macdonough."

Wet with spray, Hollis held his course. "Sir, what's hard against us is doubly hard against that square-rigged *Linnet*."

Rain beat down on Judge Sailly's oilskin cap as the wisdom of Hollis's observation sank in. More relaxed now, the old man braced himself with both hands and descended below, out of the storm's worsening conditions.

The voyage, which should have taken five hours, took twice that long because of the gale. Watching the sails stretch and shiver below the rolling dark gray clouds, Hollis knew it was a blessing in disguise. The churning lake, 400 feet deep, was known for taking sailors for wild rides. The storm would likely scatter the enemy fleet, thereby allowing the messengers enough time to alert the navy. Hollis tried every trick known to an experienced lake sailor to defeat the southern tempest. The cutter was rigged with staysails that ran parallel to the deck and allowed her to maintain a line that a square-rigger could never match. By late in the day, the judge rose from the forward bunk below deck, surprised to find that Morpheus had overcome him. Feeling strong with purpose after his rest, he climbed the ladder, which resisted each of his unsteady steps. The wet treads and plunging hull recommended caution. A severe downpour splattered him as he emerged on deck. A smile came to his cold trembling lips; bad weather was good news.

"Mister Hollis, how's the glass?" he asked. "Falling like a rock, I hope!"

The singing of the wind in the lines made it difficult to hear. Hollis cupped his ear and the old man staggered closer, repeating his question with increased volume.

The skipper nodded, "Just above 28, sir." He pointed to the pennant tearing itself apart at the top of the mast in the harsh southerly gale. The weary master of the *Valerie* shouted, "It's good for us, sir, because it's bad for our enemies farther north."

It had been a long day, but at last they reached the point on the lake opposite the narrow entrance to Otter Creek. Hollis relieved his steersman and took the cutter inshore. Turned abeam, *Valerie* took the wind and shot across the water as if, for the first time all day, she were relieved to be with the wind. Relishing the crosswind, Hollis turned her due east. The turn caused *Valerie* to heel over radically. Sailly lost his footing and grabbed for a lifeline that had been stretched the length of the narrow deck, but was tossed into the skipper. The two men clung together for a moment, frozen at the wheel.

"There, sir, hav'ya got your feet now?"

A little out of breath, the judge clung on. "I thank you, sir. Is that the Otter's mouth?"

The sight disturbed Sailly: there was no preparation for defense. *What can Macdonough be thinking? Is he so preoccupied with boat building that he's left this vital gate ajar?*

But as soon as they reached the opening, a gunboat on the south side issued a challenge. The vessel's captain and crew had been watching from the shelter of the tree-covered bank as the cutter approached. The guards hadn't expected to see anyone in such a storm.

They managed the three miles of easterly travel upstream along the length of Otter Creek at a steady pace. The rain had driven everyone under cover at the yard. Sailly found Macdonough pouring over plans for a new ship. It was nearly quitting time; night fell earlier that far north. The young commodore listened intently to the master of customs' excited synthesis of information gleaned from spy reports.

"Thomas, the British have a new ship, *Linnet*. Very well armed. There's evidence that an entire company of naval infantry has embarked as well. The *Finch* and *Chub* are at her side, and at least a dozen merchant barges loaded with rocks and cut-stone blocks have joined her. I think they're coming to draw you out to fight. Or, mind you, if you don't come out, they'll sink the barges at the mouth of the creek and block the channel."

Macdonough began to pace the broad rough boards of his sparsely furnished office, which looked out on the unfinished shell of the *Ticonderoga*. While her hull and single deck were in place and watertight, the carronades and cannons hadn't been taken aboard. He saw the workers wresting four eighteen-pound and eight twelve-pound cannons next to the first five thirty-two-pound carronades reserved for the *Saratoga*. Useless in their present state, the weapons were merely black iron tubes nestled helplessly on dunnage. The *Ticonderoga* might indeed save the Americans one day, but not this time. Macdonough's prized ship was reduced to the unenviable role of bystander.

The threat described by Judge Sailly weighed heavily on Macdonough, who didn't want to add yet another tale of loss and humiliation to the short history of the U.S. Navy. He was well aware of the turning tide in the naval war against the invincible Royal Navy. The first eight months of the war had been replete with glorious single-ship victories over British frigates. The country grew delirious with joy—imagine, a little upstart breakaway country like the United States tweaking the nose of the most powerful navy in the world! But now, in the summer of 1813, the euphoria had proven unsustainable in the face of six hundred men-of-war increasingly employed against America's twenty-one warships.

Macdonough was determined to keep Lake Champlain from falling permanently into the enemy's grip and to open once again that terrible road to Albany and, ultimately, New York City. Though not the capital of the new republic New York was the financial center of the hopeful land. Without Macdonough's steadfast defense of the lake, an invasion could again overshadow the country's great gains earned since the early days of the Revolutionary War.

The American commodore called for his staff, which included civilian Noah Brown, owner of Brown Brothers, Brooklyn's leading shipwright firm and prime contractor for the navy. (At this early stage of U.S. naval development all warships were constructed under contract one vessel at a time.) Calming the judge down, Macdonough offered him the comfort of his own soft leather chair. He introduced each member of his staff as they entered the room strewn with rolls of nautical plans. By the time they had all assembled, a scheme was forming in Macdonough's mind. He couldn't take his tiny flotilla out on the open lake to fight. That would be suicidal folly. There must be an alternative. Unlike Sidney Smith, he refused to commit a reckless act to prove his courage. He needed to stall for time, so the twenty-nine-year-old commander asked the judge to repeat his bad news to the gathered staff.

Once they were apprised of the facts and apprehended the peril of the situation, he knew they would look to him for a solution. His mind raced to latch onto a strategy they could believe in and support wholeheartedly. He wanted to fire them up to meet the enemy. Strongly convinced that they would defeat the invaders, Macdonough had little to muster against the attacking British force, but regardless of resources, the American fleet had to be saved. And such salvation was on his shoulders.

When Sailly had relayed the bad news and the ensuing discussion drifted to the situation's gravity, Macdonough called on Mister Brown to provide an update on the progress in the yard.

"Well, sir, the *President* is fine. All eleven guns are right and ready. *Ticonderoga* has her masts and yards and is being rigged. It's taken much more time to convert her from steam to sail than I'd expected. I agree, though, don't take it as criticism, Thomas—*sir*," he said, checking his familiar tone since the commodore's subordinates were present, before continuing. "The steam plant was much too fragile to stand up to Royal Navy guns. Then, where would we be, I ask you, gentlemen?" His attentive audience nodded as he had expected. "Her sails left Albany a week ago and should be here any day now."

Macdonough broke in abruptly, "They must be delayed at Fort Ticonderoga, Mister Brown. Send a messenger boat tonight with instructions for their temporary storage. We can't chance that Pring's fleet will intercept them."

Brown nodded. "Right you are, sir. Consider it done. Now we've a good start on the piece parts for *Saratoga*. We could be laying the keel within a fortnight. The hardware, for the most part, is in for the carronades and cannons. Two of the twenty-four-pounders are mounted on carriages and nearly a dozen of the thirty-two-pound carronades are on slides. There are five still loose on dunnage. You can see them out the window there along the quayside. I don't have any restraining tackle as yet, but I've the ropes. Within the month we'll have 'em, along with the metal fittings, out of the blacksmiths. The masts are cut and on their way. Of course, we'll cure them in the pond till spring."

The commodore, who knew all this beforehand, let him summarize the yard's progress more for the staff and the judge than himself, though it did give him the needed time to formulate his plan. "Thank you, Mister Brown. Keep up the work, steady as she goes. There's no reason for your crew to delay. We'll need those ships for the next phase of this little war of ours." It was not a casual remark as his subsequent comments confirmed. "This is not Armageddon, gentlemen. There'll be plenty more war to come and I plan to win it. Those *Saratoga* cannons and carronades will be crucial to our defense."

Macdonough looked around the room but found only vacant hopelessness welling in his comrades' eyes. He called for suggestions, but a resigned silence greeted his request.

At last, Lieutenant Stephen Cassin, second in command, spoke up. "Sir, *President* is fit to fight, sir . . . but we can't change out her light guns for those heavies. The recoil from the twenty-fours and thirty-twos would rip up her planks and destroy her rail."

A smile curled Macdonough's lip. "Correct, Mister Cassin," he said, accepting his lieutenant's estimate. "But we don't have to fight on the lake. We'll choose our ground, by God, and build an earth fort at the mouth of Otter Creek. The long twenty-fours, with their range of more than a mile, will keep the principle ships out on the lake. The carronades will prevent the gunboats from entering the mouth of the creek and might even sink a barge or two—where the British don't want them sunk."

His delivery was light and confident. The men felt the fight rise within them. Macdonough was not one for hanging crepe. He paused and peered at the ceiling before speaking again. "Yet, we'll need some infantry to protect the guns from a landing force of Royal Marines. I'll appeal to Colonel Macomb for a few troops from the Burlington garrison."

Macdonough had borrowed soldiers before to crew the *President* after losing *Growler* and *Eagle*. The assemblage doubted his ability to succeed in a second appeal for troops. Macomb might be reasonably reluctant to assist. After all, the navy had been unable to prevent Murray's raid on Burlington earlier that season, and the army might resist defending the navy yard at the expense of Burlington's safety.

Not waiting for comment, criticism, or approval, the commodore began issuing orders. "Mister Brown, prepare the guns for movement to the mouth of Otter Creek." Turning to Cassin, he said, "Lieutenant, move the guns, cannonballs, and powder to the creek's mouth. Cut down the trees, and put the logs in the water to prevent passage upstream. Revet the guns on either side of the creek behind a dirt redoubt and garnish it with storm polls. Top it with an American flag and we'll call it Fort Cassin!"

Macdonough knew how to motivate. Having done so, he left his staff to their work. He called for his horse and directed his servant to pack the saddlebags for an overnight stay in Burlington.

An Appeal for Troops

The forty-mile, buttocks-numbing journey gave Macdonough time to develop a persuasive argument. The next day he entered the city's limits via the lake road and saw ample evidence of the British bombardment.

A nervous sentry challenged him. A dozen drenched men in the bushes stepped out beside and behind his horse, causing the creature to shy. The foul weather hadn't confined itself solely to the lake. The small gold eagle in the center of the black rosette, held in place by two gold bands on his high flat black hat, was identical to those worn by their own officers. The eagle identified him as a friend. He was allowed to pass into the city center, as the unrelenting rain drove the guard back under cover.

Macomb's headquarters, a brick building behind the heights in the village's center overlooking the lake, was lit by torches that sputtered in that wet moonless night. The smoky cook fires reflected the grave faces of soldiers coming and going with no apparent purpose. A guard, looking as tattered as a militiaman's coat, stopped him and asked his business. Before he could answer the soldier's challenge, a regular army officer stepped out and ushered the commodore inside.

Escorting the commodore, the officer took pleasure in chiding him. "Macdonough, I'd hoped to see you through my glass coming up behind Pring's fleet during the recent attack on the city."

The lieutenant had expected the jibe. After all, his mission was to protect the towns surrounding the shores of Lake Champlain.

"Don't worry, Macdonough," the officer continued. "Your gunboats are safely on the beach. In pieces, of course, shot through with British cannonballs."

The tone was getting ugly; the officer's remarks implied cowardice and such a charge, however subtly intimated, was probably meant to be unmistakably understood. If the conversation went any further in its course, a call out of honor and a duel might result.

The commodore stiffened but was saved from further embarrassment when the large hands of the brawny Colonel Alexander Macomb spun him around. "Macdonough! Am I glad to see you! Come with me," he said, tugging the naval officer out of harm's way. The two men, only three years apart in age, were good friends. "How are my soldiers-turned-sailors doing for you?"

Macomb was a New York City native, the son of a revolutionary staff officer and the largest holder of land in western New York State. As a boy, he had listened to his father and General Washington discuss the campaigns of the Revolutionary War. The president had lived in the Macomb home during the new nation's first congressional sessions when the capital was situated in New York. Commissioned into the regular army at age twenty through patronage, Macomb grew into a fine professional soldier. He admitted freely to learning more from blundering superiors than inspirational ones. When Major General Dearborn had divided the army the previous winter, he had appointed Macomb commander of the Vermont wing of the northeastern army.

An orderly entered the small chamber. "Hot tea for you and your guest, General?"

Macomb's promotion to brigadier general was expected momentarily, so much so that his staff, jumping the gun, addressed him by his new rank.

"In view of the weather, Corporal, hot tea with *rum* would be better."

Macomb was anxious to regale the naval officer with his successful defense of the city. Macdonough listened to the details of the attack on Burlington and asked questions about the Royal Navy fleet's composition. Macomb, proud of the defense, praised his artillery gunners for the victory.

"The concentration of cannon fire alone was key to our survival, my friend. The few redcoats who landed were dealt with in short order. Some became separated, detached by choice so to speak, and are still hiding nearby, hoping for amnesty, no doubt. The federal government's offered any deserter two hundred dollars and forty acres. What they don't tell the fellows is that the land's in the Illinois Territory!" He laughed heartily at the thought of ex-British soldiers fighting Indians in that wilderness. "Believe me, they'd be much better off marrying some good Vermont girls and settling here in God's country." His red face lit up at his own joke. He banged the tabletop, causing the cups of strong tea to shiver in their saucers.

Steering his host back to the battle, Macdonough interjected, "Sir, your comment about massing artillery is what my visit is about. Your words are right out of Jomini's *Field Tactics of Napoleon*." The commodore was familiar with the employment of guns in Europe. Napoleon, an artillery officer at heart, was a hero to the American military. Macomb's mentor, exiled French general Moreau, frequently visited Burlington, and Macdonough, along with his officers, had been invited to a session with the venerable instructor.

"Sir, I didn't forget Moreau. In fact, I'd like to apply his strategy to save Otter Creek from an assault I fear is imminent." He gave Macomb a brief review of the spy reports and added, "I believe the stone blocks in those barges are to be sunk at the entrance to the navy's outlet to the lake. My fleet's behind schedule and can't be deployed. I must admit that Smith's loss of *Growler* and *Eagle* has left me tied to the dock. I can't meet Commodore Pring on open water. Instead, I propose throwing up an earth fortification bristling with naval guns and anything you can spare. A virulent lake fever has weakened my complement. I've only enough men to service the batteries. I look to you, sir, for the temporary infusion of infantry to protect the guns and ward off any landing parties of Royal Marines that I'm sure will come."

While Macomb was rightfully concerned that Pring could take another swipe at Burlington, he felt compelled to support the navy. He realized the vital significance of Macdonough's command to his own continued well-being. Macomb agreed that Pring intended to bypass Burlington and invest Otter Creek, which made him uneasy.

"Pring's no fool. He's intent on shutting down your warships as the British have done on the high seas. Since those barges are loaded with rocks and not Murray's infantry, I'm convinced Burlington has little to fear. But you—you're surely in for a hot time." In addition to a thousand regulars, Macomb could depend on three times that number in Vermont militia.

"Well, Thomas," he said, pausing for dramatic effect and watching Macdonough, whose eyes glinted with anticipation, "you'll need the army's help, to be sure. Stay the night, while my men make ready. I'll send you three companies of experienced troops. That'll be just the ticket."

Macomb called first for his chief of staff and then for a decanter of brandy. The two comrades sat up discussing military affairs until the crystal carafe was clear once more.

Macdonough returned home the following morning accompanied by Lieutenant Colonel Roger Henson as well as several artillery and infantry officers. Macomb had attached them to his naval headquarters to assist in Fort Cassin's design. Confidence deepened in Macdonough when he noticed the cloud of dust rising up behind him. Following in wagons were three hundred infantry, expected to close in at Vergennes before midnight. Macomb was as good as his Napoleonic cognac.

The next day the weather held damp and dreary. The wind was steady from the south, much to the irritation of the Royal Navy fleet tacking its way past Burlington.

Perched on the edge of the artillery heights, Macomb watched them through his glass. They managed to tack just outside the range of his anxious gunners. The general turned to his chief of staff. "The secretary of war will soon be able to boast that the army saved the navy on Lake Champlain."

Pring Thwarted

After two weeks in American waters the weather was still set firmly against Captain Pring. It was a repeat performance of the Murray raids. In the age of inboard mechanical propulsion, it is difficult for modern men to accept a time when the direction and velocity of the wind were the determining factors in all naval engagements. A square-rigged vessel couldn't plunge straight ahead into a gust coming over the bow. Tedious zigzagging took its toll on men, morale, and, especially, the mission's momentum. In the second week, the circumstances forced Pring to retreat for supplies. On the lake, naval vessels carried few provisions to allow more room for shot and powder. The need for replenishment, combined with the time lost to bivouac the marines each night onshore, destroyed Pring's timetable. During the third week, the maelstrom from the south made necessary his anchorage in Valcour Bay, directly across the thirty-mile-wide lake from Burlington. Now, as Pring bobbed around his anchor chain, he had time to fret over the wisdom of his ambitious plan.

In late October when the wind finally shifted to the northwest and allowed a very frustrated British commodore to swoop down the last few miles, all hope of surprising the enemy had evaporated. Peering through the spyglass, Pring could see that in the interim Macdonough had used his time well. While the British fleet coiled out of range, their commander pondered the changes wrought at the creek's mouth. The Americans had cut back and cleared the forest on both sides as well as on the point that hooked around to guard the entrance. Logs, like cattails, stuck up a foot above the water's surface in the shallows. The Americans had sharpened the tops to cut open the bottom of his gunboats. On the beach long dark mounds of dirt, ten feet high, were pierced by slits, which mounted the muzzles of several sizes of cannons. The gunners weren't wearing the red-piped uniforms or red plumes of field artillery. *They must be navy*, he thought.

Pring suspected that such a prepared defense would contain regular infantry, but he couldn't detect any such troops. Perhaps they were hidden just inside the woods on the flanks to prevent his marines from securing a foothold? One thing was clear: Macdonough wasn't coming out to fight on the lake. Pring feared the expedition's plan wouldn't unfold as he had intended and began to alter his objectives. The loss of surprise hung over the Royal Navy commodore like a pall. He had freedom of action, since he had been wise enough not to disclose his strategic intentions to Commodore Yeo. It was time to test his resolve against the enemy's.

The Battle for Otter Creek

The winds lightened, the sky cleared, and the cursed weather lifted at last. The water was the truest of blues highlighted by the sunlight that skimmed and skipped across the rippling surface in all directions. The maples surrounding the graceful lake burned red and orange like muzzle blasts from muskets and rifles. The air was pure, without a hint of man's stale presence. This placid environment was about to shatter like a pane of stained glass, its fragments flying into a cloudless sky.

Pring, a decisive man, wasted no time once the entire flotilla was in place. The mix of craft, both sail and oar, that had spread out during the southern trek closed together under his calculating gaze. On the previous day, leaving the gunboat crews to toil without relief on the final leg south, he had rested his marines on board the *Canada*. It was clear that cannon fire from his three principal ships would have to reduce the beach. Pring relished the bombardment that would be laid down by the *Chub* and the *Finch*, formerly the pride of Macdonough's command and now a scourge.

Calling his leaders together on the *Linnet*, at anchor in the lake's center, he stood at the rail and directed their attention with the point of his drawn sword.

"There it is, gentlemen. The enemy's prepared a reception, but it won't prove effective, will it? I'll lead with *Linnet*, followed by *Chub* and *Finch* in line, to within 800 yards off the point." He indicated it by swinging the straight silver blade with a sweep of his arm. "There, outside the effective range of most of the enemy guns, we'll anchor. All guns must conduct counterbattery fire at the American artillery to take it out of action and prevent the Americans from engaging the Royal Marines when they land."

Pring turned to Maj. Harold Lime, commander of the Royal Marines, who stood out in his red coat with its dark blue cuffs piped in gold bullion. Across his chest were thick horizontal gold bands an inch apart. Joining the commodore at the rail, he listened intently.

"You'll land on the point, take the enemy from the left flank, and roll him up against the northern shore. Any opposing infantry will likely attack from the left out of the woods. *Linnet's* close enough to reach the trees and provide covering fire."

The commander of the marines replied, "Aye, aye, sir."

"A few enemy cannonballs will reach the fleet, no doubt, but it's the short-range carronades that are meant for our boats and barges. Boat commanders, you won't be attacked until you're inside 500 yards of the beach. The gunboats will tow the barges to the mouth of the river and sink them as far up the channel as possible."

No longer did Pring expect to dominate Otter Creek in the face of the Americans' improvised, implacable defense. While the attack would be far less vigorous or decisive than planned, it could still serve Pring's purpose. A ship could be left on station to preclude tampering with the British sunken barricade. Macdonough would be trapped. Such a naval blockade would bring the commodore's career the climatic, laudatory notice he desired.

———

Fort Cassin was as secure as it could be. Macdonough's second in command had prepared emplacements for fourteen guns divided onto either side of the creek's entrance. Four surviving gunboats, bow forward and anchored inside the mouth of Otter Creek, supported the defense. Confident in his preparations, Macdonough had only one concern: his dread of casualties. He couldn't afford to lose trained sailors.

A veteran of combat, Macdonough had earned a most impressive reputation as a fighter. As a midshipman, he'd served with Lieutenant Stephen Decatur during the clandestine torching of the USS *Philadelphia* at Tripoli in 1804 during the Barbary Pirate War. The unfortunate vessel had run aground in the harbor and was captured along with her crew, who languished in the dungeon of the pirate castle. Midshipman Macdonough's highly dangerous mission was to set fire to the *Philadelphia*'s forward magazine. Boarding the American frigate at night from a captured pirate sloop, he fought his way with sword and pistol down the ladder to the bottom deck. Leading a small party of incendiaries, they left flaming torches on barrels of powder. He and his men made a swim for it when the rescue boat meant to pick them up was sunk.

In another later incident, at Gibraltar, with his captain ashore, Commodore Macdonough faced down a Royal Navy captain who had attempted to remove a crewman from an American merchant ship. That incident appeared on the front page of every newspaper in the country. When captured by the British the following year, the talented and versatile officer escaped by stealing a British officer's uniform and seizing a boat.

This would be Macdonough's first land battle.

He believed, though in truth he was by no means certain, that the Americans' forward position on the very edge of the water would prevent the British from proceeding upstream enough to block the passage to the lake.

Macdonough watched as the large ships maneuvered into line by turning first to the north. Then, like birds of prey, the naval column swung around to seize the wind and cross in front of Fort Cassin. Of the twenty-two guns on Pring's ships, only those on the port side could be employed. It was nearly a match of cannons, as the army advisers provided by General Macomb had predicted. Macdonough held his fire and accepted the first salvo. Like a good sailor and leader, he was not being passive, but rather learning as much as possible about his enemy's capabilities before exposing his own. As in all artillery duels, the first shots were highly inaccurate. Trees behind the fortifications lost their limbs, while other cannonballs skipped across the water as if they were pebbles tossed by a boy. They splashed several times before plowing into the soft dirt of the Americans' fortified position. The blasts' accompanying noise proved more effective in its demoralizing purpose than the shot. Many American gunners were novices, unaccustomed to the shock of naval cannon, which were larger and therefore more fearsome than land guns. The commodore could see his men recoil and look to the woods for an escape route. With his naval sword drawn, Macdonough took giant strides until he reached his guns.

"Prepare to fire." He then shouted, "Fire!"

At that he swung his sword toward the ground in a great arc. The flashing blade signaled to Cassin on the creek's south side to employ his guns into action.

Four moored gunboats held the creek's broad mouth that separated the two gun batteries. They were both under the command of Midshipman Simon Pauling. As planned, he held his fire, awaiting the assault of the British gunboats, which were expected to tow the stone-filled barges into the channel. Locked together now, each opponent could only play out his own fortune.

Pring anchored his ships to steady their fire. He let his ships' guns rip while the marines rowed forward. They were expected to land at the point, so Pring suspended the *Linnet*'s covering fire, thereby allowing the smaller craft to row down the center. At such close range no elevation was cranked in; the naval cannon's trajectory was as straight as a rifle shot. With little arc to the zinging cannonballs, Pring's fleet endangered all those headed for shore.

The lull allowed Macdonough's gunners a free shot or two. As the British boats came into range, American shot bounced, skipped through the ranks, and swept away the odd craft and splintering oars. One gunboat, her bow smashed, filled with water and wallowed in cold lake water until she sank, pulling a barge of rocks down after her. The sailors clung to chunks of wreckage and swam back toward the fleet.

———

Macdonough debated with Lieutenant Colonel Henson about allowing the Royal Marines to land before engaging them. "Colonel, it could be mightily unwise to rely solely on the expected success of your counterattack. I prefer to sink the boats soon as possible. Discourage the passengers, wet their powder."

"Commodore, with respect, you mustn't divert your guns from the main attack."

Macdonough replied, "I pleaded with General Macomb for your assistance, so I must bow to your advice. Fight them where you will. If you need me, look to the guns."

So it was that 150 dry, red-coated naval infantry landed and organized within two hundred yards of Macdonough's right front. But the American army did not let him down. Out of the woods, to his right rear, came 300 members of the 6th U.S. Infantry Regiment clothed in dark blue trimmed in white buff with white cross belts. A startled Royal Marine major recalled his skirmishers to steady a line three deep and to receive the attack. No strangers, these bluecoats were the same fighters who had met the British army two months earlier on Burlington's shores. As the marines formed into a tight group, Henson opened with a hidden battery of field guns. Witnessing the Americans' counterattack, Pring swung his fire a few degrees to the left, redirecting the support for the barges to his beleaguered marines.

Macdonough concentrated his ten cannons at the moored fleet. The oncoming rock-filled barges, bobbing along behind the struggling British gunboats, distracted him. There was the real threat. If sunk in the narrow channel his fleet could be written off, but the big ships were key to the enemy attack and had to be engaged first. The marines' attack only added to the confusion. Shell and shot, bright flashes and muzzle blasts, smoke and flames were all concentrated at the small clearing on the end of the lake. A hundred yards in any direction, beyond the range of the Americans' guns, all was detached and serene. Except for the cannons' muffled boom, which at a distance could be mistaken for thunder, the fear, fright, and forlorn hopes of a thousand men at war was unknown to the rest of humanity.

————

While the American infantry impressed the Royal Marines, the redcoats didn't give an inch. There they stood, separated by a hundred yards of flat ground, firing away with little to show except the holes in the static ranks, which grew wider with each smoke-filled volley. Cannonballs, lobbed in from ships, competed with the American field artillery's sweeping fire. Macdonough thought he saw the American 6th begin to waver, and for a moment, he considered moving two eighteen-pound naval cannons out of the battery to assist the regiment. But then the field artillery battery at the woods' edge to his right rear picked up the tempo.

Commodore Pring, at the rail of his flagship, saw only wisps of the enemy through the billows of white smoke spewing forth from his own cannons. Once the battle was fused, he could do little while isolated on his ship. Choosing to risk it all in one main attack, he held back no reserve. Pring abandoned the marines and focused on the barges' deployment. If he could manage to sink the barges and block the creek, then he could claim victory. By confining the American navy to Otter Creek, he would secure the smugglers' continuing course on Britain's behalf. He directed signal flags to be hoisted to the top of the mizzenmast to tell the attacking forces to shift the action to the center. The success of the British attack was in the hands of the men pulling the barges. As they rowed, they discharged the single cannon in each boat's bow as they closed in on the creek's mouth.

Macdonough shifted his smashers, the carronades. They quickly found the range and let loose a sizzling salvo of giant proportions. The blasts rolled across the water, deafening all those in their line of assault. The thirty-two-pound solid shot splintered gunboats, sunk barges, and dismembered crews. Wave after wave of projectiles criss-crossed the front of Fort Cassin, churned up cold green water, and laid a smoky mist just above the lapping waves. Boats, barges, cannons, and men—they vanished below the bubbling surface.

Pring's hopes evaporated in the erupting plumes of frothing water, fragments of shattered wood, and the cries of the wounded. Following within minutes, another salvo of murderous black iron balls chased half-loaded marine galleys back toward the anchored British ships. The British withdrawal had begun.

Macdonough wished to pursue the fleeing Canadian Marines fleet, but he hadn't the means. Repelling the attack had been miracle enough and would have to suffice.

The Enemy Within

A shocking event occurred before the citizens of Plattsburgh snuggled down inside their homes to await winter's appearance once more in the North Country. Hollis was towing in a skiff that belonged to a local merchant, a prominent citizen known for his loyalty now sat in irons on the open deck. Opposed to the smugglers' treachery, Ezra Knoles had spoken out against their traitorous deeds. In a way, he had prospered from the capture of their goods: he purchased at bargain prices a considerable amount of their contraband from the customs warehouse and then offered it for sale in his own store.

The crowd on the dock clamored for an explanation for Knoles's arrest. A silent Hollis paraded his prisoner up the cobbled road to the judge's office at the warehouse's far end. The crowd, loudly demanding answers, followed. Ezra was a popular man because he extended credit at his store when no other merchant would. When they noticed that no goods had been confiscated, some questioned Hollis's crew, but the crew was as reticent as their skipper.

The judge was startled when Hollis led the prisoner straight into his office without knocking, leaving the outer office staff to deal with the rising commotion that followed the two men.

"Agent Hollis, what are you thinking—"

But the irate officer cut the judge off. "Sir, Ezra's a spy for the redcoats!"

The agent dropped a dark leather portfolio, bound in straps and buckles, on his superior's desk. Sailly pulled the portfolio toward himself and began to undo the brass buckles.

"This better be *full* proof, Mister Hollis. Ezra's a good friend and model citizen."

The judge was hedging his bets, trying to stay neutral as he fumbled with the shiny buckles. The damp hide and swollen leather ties made it difficult to open.

"Sir, I looked inside the case when we stopped Ezra on the far side of Isle Lamont. We had to chase him down. Just before we caught him, my boys saw him throw this here valise over the side. One of the boys had to dive for it." Hollis pointed a long, thin finger at the papers as the judge was retrieving them from the case. "There! Those are military plans and maps of Burlington and Plattsburgh, along with a lot of numbers. Hollis was afraid now that perhaps the evidence, which had seemed so convincing at first, might have another explanation. He directed the judge's gaze to drawings of the hospital, then under construction at Crab Island, and the new earthworks around the point of Cumberland Head a mile to the north. Another page showed the gun emplacements at the heights in Burlington. Notes on the margin indicated their size, while crude marks revealed their location. There was no mistake. Even the powder magazine was shown.

The judge looked up at his restrained friend with disbelief, which soon turned to outrage. He thrust an accusing finger straight at Knoles's hanging head. "Why, Ezra? Good God! Why?"

Hollis added, "He was heading for a rendezvous with some lobster backs who'd promised to make him rich, I'll bet you," he said, tugging on the traitor's chained hands.

Sailly's immediate concern turned to the commotion in his outer office, which was crammed with townsmen. While the judge's anger rose from his collar, turning his face bright red, the discord cut his rebuke short.

"Get him out of here *now*," he demanded. "When they find out what we've got here, they'll lynch him." Without asking the accused any more questions, Sailly said, "Hollis, go through the warehouse and take him over to General Macomb's military tribunal. I'll occupy the folks in the outer office to give you time."

Justice Mercy

The Burlington guardhouse was a small sturdy log blockhouse with two crude cells and a dirt floor. There were no windows, only a single barred door. A posted sentry kept visitors and spectators at bay.

Knoles's involuntary neighbors included Sam Stratton and Ray-boy Long. Stratton, who had a record as a barrack thief, had been guarding his unit's broken-down supply wagon. Private Long had been left with him, so one could sleep while the other watched. Stratton convinced Long to join him in a swindle that he assured the young soldier had worked before and would work again. They would desert the Vermont militia, go to Albany, and there enlist in the regular army. Once they received their bonuses, they'd leave again and travel to New Hampshire, where Stratton's relatives lived, and enlist again, changing their names each time. As a rule, since volunteers were in short supply and the need for infantry universal, no questions were asked. With his head filled with the promise of wealth, the simple Ray-boy followed the older and "wiser" sergeant willingly. The scheme led not to prosperity, but to captivity.

The tribunal lost no time prosecuting Knoles and the other two miscreants. Within two days all three men were tried before a panel of officers and found guilty. The sentences were read out on the parade ground behind Burlington Heights. There, the regiments had arranged themselves into a three-sided formation. The ranks stood at attention, well aware of the event they'd been summoned to witness. Desertion and spying were the highest of crimes, which demanded the ultimate penalty. These crimes hadn't occurred under the stress of battle; scant pity for the condemned dwelt in the ranks. Every soldier understood the fright of battle and wondered how he'd fare. They could comprehend how a man might lose courage at the last moment and run. They accepted the military law that condemned desertion and hoped that they would never be led to the posts. However, all three men had been motivated not by fear but by greed—and such a motivation was unforgivable.

Three stout, rude, eight-inch-thick wooden posts waited, their stark shadows resting on the warehouse's brick wall in the early morning sun. The prisoners, dressed in light shirts and dark pants and confined between soldiers armed with fixed bayonets, were marched into the square to the sound of muffled drums draped in black crepe. A black-robed chaplain from St. Giles read aloud as he led the small group of soldiers and three prisoners. He read from the liturgy of the dead. The prisoners, protesting one moment, pleading for mercy the next, were dragged to the posts.

Ezra Knoles suddenly fell silent at the sight of his disgraced family whom he hadn't seen since his arrest on the lake. Isolated as a dangerous spy, he hadn't had an opportunity to explain away his actions and frame them in the best possible light. How could his devoted wife stand behind the counter of their store and face the customers? He knew that they'd have to live with this burden long after he had paid for his foolishness. Ezra wanted to express his sorrow and love for his wife and children then, but such an emotional display would be too unseemly before so many witnesses.

He remained quiet, tied to the post, as his sentence was read. The men strained at their cords and begged in loud voices for mercy. When the sentences had been fully read, the firing party was marched across the field, halted, and given a left face. Their heels clicked in unison as they turned to face the trio of condemned men. Drums, which had beat a slow march earlier, now picked up the pace and rolled the last sounds the prisoners would ever hear.

The regiment's sergeant major tied a black blindfold over the eyes of each man. The two soldiers lifted their heads to see out through the bottom—without success.

The officer in charge of the firing squad drew his sword and raised it above his head in anticipation of the downward stroke. He called out, "Make ready firelocks."

The men snapped to attention.

"Load firelocks."

The soldiers drew paper cartridges from their leather boxes that hung at their side on a broad cross strap. The thirteen members of the squad tore the musket balls from the paper cartridges, holding them in their mouth. A light charge was tipped into the open firing pans of the cradled muskets. Almost at once, with an unmistakable thud, they dropped the butts of their guns to the ground.

The prisoners, despite their blindfolds, recognized that sound.

Knoles jumped, startled.

The soldiers emptied powder with a careful pour down the upright barrels, followed by the paper packages, which were soon rammed down tightly by long thin straight rods drawn from under the barrels. The soldiers spat the musket balls down their barrels and gave them a final tap with the rods, before they were returned to their brackets.

"Ready—" Then a pause. "Aim—"

The field commander, Henson, called out, "Cease fire," with a rather casual voice considering the occasion. The assembled troops audibly sucked in their collective breath. The adjutant, who'd read the sentences, proclaimed, "In view of Private Long's youth and service to date, the convening authority, Alexander Macomb, has commuted his sentence to one year's confinement. Remove the prisoner to the guardhouse, sergeant major."

The senior commissioned officer cut the bonds and removed the blindfold. "Now, lad, straight as a soldier, march off the field." But try as he might to walk, two sentries, one on either side, had to help Private Long.

The ominous sequence began again, without consideration for the two rigid prisoners. Stratton continued to sob uncontrollably.

"Ready, Aim, *Fire!*"

The crash of arms followed. The sudden relaxed slump of limp bodies pulled unsuccessfully at the two posts. The adjutant drew his pistol and marched to the condemned; the chaplain, praying in whispers, accompanied him and made the sign of the cross over each man. Both men were shot through. A finishing shot behind the ear wasn't necessary.

Plattsburgh Revolts

In Plattsburgh discontent over the handling of contraband was rampant. Living on the frontier was hard and goals were often short-term and shortsighted. The war was *very* unpopular.

People held no grudge against Canada or the Canadians who provided a market for their hard-earned labor. The federal government was a long way off and held little importance to life daily in the harsh land. While the war in Europe was of interest and U.S. involvement was intriguing, the embargo meant to punish the British turned the citizens in the Champlain Valley bitter at Madison's meddling in their business. One's living was scraped from the land by muscle with no help from the government, which at the time provided no safety nets for its struggling citizens. Hardships were endured in the hope for a better future, but the detested war made tempers flare out of control.

The customs warehouse, a federal presence, was like a thorn in the town's side. All revenue was sent south into the government's coffers in Washington. Yet, little came back in the form of sorely needed protection. Where had the federal government been the previous summer when Murray raided local businesses and burned the town? While Knoles's crime was reprehensible, so was the neglect the citizens had suffered after the army had left them defenseless. It gnawed at the business community that it hadn't yet been compensated for the credit extended to house and feed the troops during the winter of 1812–13. Their vouchers were returned accompanied by promissory notes. Word filtered back that Washington bureaucrats felt the community should be glad to maintain the troops, who, after all, were there for its protection.

Judge Sailly, working at the warehouse in the late afternoon, became aware of a crowd gathering outside the Exchange Coffee House, fifty yards up the cobbled street at the corner of Margaret and Cornelia. The commotion was unusually vehement, so he sent his clerk out to see what was happening.

On his return the excited clerk, who had lost his hat coming down the hill, burst into the judge's inner office. "Your Honor, they're a-comin' for us! I heard 'em plain as day! Hartley, Rose, and Jennings from the sawmill, and all the others from the exchange, are comin' to demand that we open the warehouse and share out the goods. They say it's rightfully theirs and they mean to have it. All the other goods hauled in by the cutters, too! They're lookin' mighty mean and some brought guns. Wilber Myatt is wavin' a pistol and I think it's loaded! There's fifty if there be two dozen, sir."

Sailly sent the clerk out the back to Major General Benjamin Mooers's house to summon the militia while the judge fortified the warehouse with the help of the agents at hand. Soon, the clerk was back, banging at the judge's side window and wanting to be let safely back inside.

"The general's missing," he said. "He hurried out about an hour ago taking his valise with him—heading south, I think, toward the Salmon River. You know, sir, he ain't the kinda man who likes trouble."

It's true, Sailly thought. That past summer when the British appeared, Mooers had also been conspicuously absent. Appointed by the governor, Mooers had scant military experience and was unlikely to become acquainted with the profession of arms other than on the village common on a bright Sunday afternoon after church.

Under Sailly's direction, some agents covered the windows with blankets and blocked the doors with wooden crates while others scurried about looking for powder and ball, which they deposited on the stone floor in piles next to firing positions. The red brick building, a story and a half in height, was long and thin, with large, swinging plank doors, now closed, at either end. They had been preparing for an auction, so the facility was crammed with slabs of bacon in cheesecloth bags, barrels of salt meat, sacks of grain, and milled flour. Crates of iron bars, ready for the smith, were next to boxes of nails and ingots of lead. Taken from smugglers, the contraband had originated on the properties of New York and Vermont citizens, some of whom were marching down Margaret Street toward the Customs House.

The judge's first view of the mob shocked him. It was far larger than he had been told an hour earlier. The discontent had apparently spread rapidly. Sailly recognized every man, and as they closed in, he began to take note of friends and foe. The sheriff was notably absent, most likely out of town with the "courageous" General Mooers.

Harold Rose was a tall angular man with huge hands. He raised one now, stopping the crowd just short of the front door of the Customs House, and called out, "Your Honor! Give up the goods and share them in good faith. We both know how handy, how necessary, they'll be this winter. It's our right to reap the fruits of our land! We aren't a part of this here war, and you know it."

A prominent farmer who owned several homesteads, Rose was suspected of not letting the law and blockade interfere with his trade and profits.

Sailly told the gruff-speaking spokesman, "Tone your voice down, Rose. These are federal goods. Go home before you step in too deeply."

Rose stepped forward defiantly and continued to jaw. The crowd pressed against the big warehouse doors, causing them to creak against the heavy crosspiece on the inside that kept the protesters out—for now.

The customs agents, far from popular, feared that momentarily a torrent of angry men would break in and overwhelm them. They pulled free pairs of pistols, snagged onto their belts by metal clips, and cocked the hammers back to the firing position. The judge directed them to form a line behind the barrels and boxes in the warehouse's dim light.

Sailly yelled through the door, "Rose! Listen to me! We don't want any blood shed, but we're armed and sworn to defend government property. Calm down, folks, and think. This is a federal offense you're embarking on here. You *know* what that means. Go home to your fami—"

The rotten crossbar snapped from the crush of the mob. The doors sprang open. Townspeople, to their surprise, fell in onto the stone floor in front of the customs agents. Spooked by the sudden violent incursion, the agents fired half a dozen pistols. The noise was amplified under the confines of the slate roof. The echo bewildered everyone—inside the Customs House and out.

There was no need for a second volley. The townspeople pulled back.

One man lay dead on his back, a thin rivulet of blood leaking from a small charred hole in his forehead and widening into a dark puddle on the warehouse's dusty floor.

The United States Prepares for the Next Round of the War

Commodore Macdonough was unaware of the trouble in Plattsburgh. Relieved that his forces had driven off the Royal Navy, he renewed his efforts to convince Secretary of the Navy William Jones of his dire need for assistance. Unable to leave the lake, he had to rely on correspondence, which he hoped would be circulated through the offices of Congress. However, official Washington was glued to newspaper accounts of the disturbing events unfolding in Europe. In the winter of 1812, Napoleon had retreated from Russia before Christmas. The campaign season of 1813 now found the once-aggressive Napoleon defending France's borders. The diminishing threat on the continent meant only one thing for President Madison and his adviser Mr. Jefferson: Great Britain's armed forces in the Mediterranean and English Channel could now be used in an English effort to penalize America for attempting to wage war on Canada.

America's support of the Ogre gave Britain's secretary of war carte blanche for punitive retaliation. Considerably more warships would soon become available to intensify the blockade of America's commercial ports as well as to deploy further troops. Recalling the Burgoyne war plan of 1777, the British again regarded Lake Champlain with keen interest. It appeared on the map of North America as a dagger pointed due south at New York City, a water route that, if taken by force, could split the new nation.

In Washington, Secretary Jones could also read a map. In November 1813, more naval assets were sent up the Hudson, over the portage at Lake George, and arriving at the Vergennes boatyard before the lake was closed off by ice. The closure was a blessing as well as it had also confined the Royal Navy within its own borders nearly a hundred miles north. During the spring of 1814, Noah Brown and his brother called for more men from Brooklyn to complete the *Ticonderoga* and the flagship *Saratoga*. The Browns and Macdonough expected that the new boats would be a match for the Royal Navy's *Linnet*, which had ruled the lake during the previous sailing season.

Captain Pring's Proposal

Commodore Yeo summoned Captain Pring to his headquarters in Kingston, Canada, near the mouth of Lake Ontario. He intended to quiz Pring about the recent operation on Lake Champlain. But Pring had good reason to accept the summons, also. Once in Kingston, the captain asked to tour a new Royal Navy frigate, which was dry-docked to protect it from the crush of the winter icepack clogging the St. Lawrence. He knew how fond Yeo was of frigates, the navy's light cavalry.

Commodore Sir James Lucas Yeo, RN, RCB, a distinguished sailor, enjoyed an enormous reputation for heroism under fire. However, this didn't make him a pleasant fellow, and despite his many worthy qualities, his equals said he took himself too seriously while those of lesser reputations described him as insufferable and unwelcome as a tempest. Sir James didn't care what others said. In fact, it complemented his position as commander of the Provincial Marine in Upper and Lower Canada. As a member in good standing of the senior service—the Royal Navy—he regarded Sir George Prevost, a lieutenant general and governor-general of all the Canadas, as just another army officer. After all, hadn't Wellington himself admitted, "The struggle over the North American border called for the use of naval power and not army boots"?

The Canadian Marine commodore despised the army and expressed his disdain often enough. He was far too fiery when dealing with Prevost, who actually was just as battle hardened as he. In truth, he envied Prevost's fame, royal connections, and diplomatic presence.

Unfortunately for Canada, these two honored men, so respected within their own services, were unable to put aside the self-sustaining animosity between armed services, which manifested itself in public as well as in private. When Yeo commanded the nautical arm of Prevost's force, the two invariably squabbled continually over every combat operation. Prevost recognized that controlling the water was more important than nearly any other consideration, since the lines of battle, supply, and communication were drawn on the water. The St. Lawrence River defined much of the border between Canada and the United States. Lake Champlain, a deep trench that divided the Adirondacks from the Green and White mountains, ran a hundred miles south toward Albany. A portage or two farther south found the headwaters of the Hudson River. The river plunged ever downward before pooling at last against the docks in New York City's harbor. Prevost used the navy to transport men and supplies but recognized that it took men on the ground to hold and defend the land. He often pointed out to Yeo, much to the latter's consternation, the limitations of naval gunfire. Yeo, at high dudgeon, would reply, "Without ships and cannon fire the army would never get to the fight or, if it did, it couldn't sustain an attack without the support of the navy." Like the study of history, the argument was unending.

The day of his meeting with Yeo, Pring intended to walk a high wire between the two superior officers and propose the construction of a thirty-six-gun frigate at Ile-aux-Noix. The commodore was essential to the plan because he controlled the money for naval construction.

"Sir," Pring began, "my spies tell me that Macdonough's building two twenty-gun brigs and a twenty-six-gun sloop of war this winter. They'll likely be ready for next year's sailing season. When they take to the lake, we'll be flummoxed for sure. However, if I were to counter the Americans' new addition to the lake with a frigate, more formidable than all his vessels combined, we would continue to rule Champlain."

Yeo, a former frigate commander, was intrigued. A frigate on the small lake would be invulnerable and satisfy Prevost's worry of losing the vital support of smugglers. Yeo's quick tongue, as usual, got the better of him. "Have you seen Sir George lately, Captain? Did he suggest I build a frigate for him on Champlain? I understand that you're *quite* close to the family."

Pring ignored the commodore's insinuation that his loyalty might be questionable. He said, "Sir, I haven't spoken to Sir George about the building of a frigate, since that is very much within your purview. Wouldn't you agree, sir?"

As Pring pressed on, Yeo cooled to the possibility of his subordinate's disloyalty and warmed to his idea of a frigate. It was the obvious solution, one for which the commodore intended to take credit.

"I agree, Captain, and will send representation to the Naval Board for funds and hardware to construct a frigate for the inland lake."

To Pring's pleasant surprise, before the close of 1813, he received plans for the frigate. He was notified that the necessary hardware, anchors, and cordage would arrive in the spring with the breakup of the ice on the St. Lawrence.

But while Pring had promoted the initiative to make 1814 the year that the Royal Navy would float the largest ship ever seen on Lake Champlain, he had failed to endear himself to Yeo. Reports of the captain's regular presence at dinners at Ramezay House with the governor's family in Montreal, his burgeoning friendship with Anne Prevost, and his frequent briefings to the governor made their way back to Yeo, irking the jealous commodore, who was known for his less-than-forgiving disposition. Much to Pring's astonishment, on the same ship as the shipwrights, hardware, sail, and rope for the new frigate, Captain Peter Fisher—Pring's replacement—arrived. A known bootlicker, Fisher had been Yeo's lieutenant in the Mediterranean. Sir James didn't deign to provide an explanation to Pring, who relinquished command to the senior officer as a matter of rote. Still, the demotion hit Pring hard, and as a professional, he had no recourse but to assume the unenviable role of second in command.

Fisher seemed less concerned with the military situation than with pumping Pring about the politics and intrigues within the Canadian command. There was currently no serving admiral in Upper Canada. Fisher gossiped that his former superior would soon be elevated and that Fisher had been, more or less, promised to succeed him at Kingston. By implication, Fisher strongly suggested that Pring should kowtow if he knew what was good for him.

"Well now, Pring, tell me all about Sir George. I hear he has a pretty daughter who likes men in uniform. Do 'we' go there often? Socially, that is?"

Unlike Yeo, the captain was adept at holding his tongue when necessary. His discretion and deftness had seen him through thus far, and he believed they would see him a bit further still.

April 1814

While the church bells in Paris were silent, they rang to the cracking point across the rest of Europe. In England there was a particular sweetness to their resonance. The coalition of Russia, Prussia, Austria, Sweden, Spain, Portugal, the Netherlands, and Great Britain had—at last—defeated Napoleon Bonaparte. Before the fatal Russian Campaign in 1812, no one had believed the Ogre could be deposed. But Napoleon had overextended his army, exhausted his resources, and underestimated the climate. The French Campaign that began that summer died a horrible death before Christmas in early snows and bitter cold that swept with a vengeance across Russia. Beginning in the spring of 1813, the French emperor had fought some of his most impressive battles, but after each one, a weakened French army withdrew ever closer to Paris. The final blow came at the very gates of the capital, when the French marshals could no longer sustain the French army and begged their emperor to abdicate.

Within the month the Duke of Wellington relinquished his military post and arrived in Paris as the new ambassador from the Court of St. James to the restored house of Bourbon at the court of Louis XVIII.

In Washington the news came as a bitter blow to the administration of James Madison, who had risked his gambit based on the assumption of Napoleon's continued victories. Not only did the United States lose French sponsorship, which Jefferson had strove so hard to preserve, but with Napoleon's defeat England's mighty military machine was now left idle.

That spring the American navy was put out of action. British warships previously dedicated to the Mediterranean were shifted to the Royal Navy fleets out of Halifax, Bermuda, and Jamaica. An intense blockade put a lid on American merchant shipping. The citizens of New England were hollering for relief, as trade profits plummeted and crops from the southern ports rotted in waterfront warehouses. Americans had thrived on the prosperity created by years of European warfare. As a neutral nation in the continental war, Americans had traded with anyone willing to pay their price. The merchants were unwilling to surrender their lucrative status for Mr. Madison's war based, in their view, on a grudge held by Jefferson and the Republican Party.

Yet, Madison persisted with the American War. He refused the efforts of the czar, who had sponsored the peace talks held in Saint Petersburg between Great Britain and America that, however noble or vainglorious, had collapsed.

Lord Bathurst, the colonial secretary and secretary of war during the American War, considered the conflict a needless and expensive proposition that cried out to be concluded quickly. As spring moved toward summer, he searched for a solution that would profit Great Britain, which had spent lavishly on its wars with France since 1794. Members of Parliament pointed out that the former colony was on its knees, ripe for conquest by the most powerful army and navy extant that happy English spring. Newspapers agreed, offering advice on extending the war to conquer the "colonies" and take back what was rightly theirs. They could easily sandwich the United States between English Canada and the English Caribbean now that the French possessions were defenseless.

Members of Parliament called for an invasion that would restore a portion of the land that had been stolen by the disloyal radicals a generation earlier. This time there would be no France to intervene and rescue the rebels. England had seen to that by defeating Napoleon. Members discussed openly the allure of snatching the land south of the Canadian border. They proposed that, since there was a French ancestry problem with

Quebec, any new acquisition of territory should remain separate from that province—and that a new country, loyal to the king, should be established.

Wellington's Conference in Paris

Just before arriving in Paris on May 1814, Arthur Wellesley was elevated to duke for his contributions to the nation and the king. The Prince Regent, Prince of Wales—his supporter and the man who would become George IV—accompanied the new Duke of Wellington to the salons of Paris and participated in the discussions of how best to secure England's advantage in an evolving Europe. The gatherings, both official and social, were replete with the most glittering uniforms. The sovereigns, Czar Alexander I of Russia and Frederick William III of Prussia, were full of themselves over the destruction of the "usurper." They chose not to utter the name Napoleon ever again. Russia's foreign minister and his Prussian, Austrian, and French counterparts kept to the grind of government business while generals toasted themselves at champagne parties thrown by the restored aristocrats of France—the few who had survived the French Revolution.

At one such joyous dinner, given by the czar at Fontainebleau Palace, the duke found himself under fire once again. This time it was his allies who assailed him. All conversations among the allies were conducted in French, which the duke, having been educated in France, spoke fluently. (In Russia the court language was French, a legacy of Peter the Great and his daughter Catherine, who believed that Western culture began and ended with France.)

King Frederick William III began the discussions by extolling the virtues of his general staff and the part played in the victory by Field Marshals Gebhard Leberecht von Blücher and Karl Philipp Fürst zu Schwarzenberg on the field of battle. He explained how the Prussian military staff system was geared to produce expert officers bound to conquer the Ogre in due time and how none could compare with the Prussians.

Before Wellington could respond, the czar stepped in. "You see, Your Grace, it takes more than talent to be a field commander. The Russian general staff has produced a number of fighting officers like General Kutuzov, who not only could fight, but also outthink the Usurper. I know that had you only had the chance to fight the French emperor in person, you may have been lucky as well."

Wellington was well aware that his reputation outside of Great Britain was tainted by the fact that he had never met Napoleon in battle. The French emperor had defeated Sir John Moore the year before the duke arrived in Portugal. From that point on, Napoleon left the Iberian Peninsula in the hands of a series of French marshals—all of whom Wellington had vanquished.

Speaking up for himself and the British army, the duke said, "Sir, it's true I haven't seen the Ogre on a white horse, but I've defeated his plan, his troops, his generals, and his system over a period of six years."

Frederick William, who, unlike Alexander, had not been present on the field for much of the fighting, backed his companion. "But, Your Grace, you must know that

Bonaparte's very presence on the field gave him an advantage of 40,000 troops—or as much as your entire field army."

The emperors gave each other congratulatory looks for the cleverness of their arguments.

Wellington, wanting to retire from the conversation as a suave diplomat rather than a bellicose general, said, "Ah, yes, it's true. I never had the pleasure of stomping my boot on the little rascal's neck."

This was a clever reference to the famous low-topped riding boot named for the duke. Every person in Europe knew of Wellington's exploits, but many had never heard of Alexander or Frederick William. A skilled politician with considerable experience, Wellington began to surmise that this war, which had lasted twenty years, was not nearly over. The defeat of Napoleon and, more important, his continental economic system had created a vacuum. The independent states—and there were many between eastern France and the Prussian border—that the French emperor had gobbled up were now free of entanglements. Weak electors from feuding families ruled Baden, Hessen-Darmstadt, Westphalia, Kleve-Berg, Saxony, Brunswick, Nassau, and Oldenburg, which were temptingly ripe for the taking. They might be looking for a good paternal friendly empire to ensure their safety in an uncertain world. From listening to and watching the collaboration between the diplomats and generals of Prussia and Russia, the duke got the distinctly unpleasant impression that there was a new coalition in the making, a garden party to which Great Britain was not invited.

A Sudden Trip to London

When the celebrations began to cool and the dignitaries grew restive, the distinguished visitors slipped out of Paris. The Holy Roman Emperor in Vienna called for a congress. Francis I, grandfather of Napoleon II, the usurper's only son, was at home there with the boy's mother at Schönbrunn Palace.

Rather than establish himself in Paris, Wellington left the city and rode to the channel coast on Copenhagen, his Arabian charger. Always a horseman, he preferred the saddle to a coach. Copenhagen's story went back to the days of Wellington's first campaign in Denmark, when Lord Grosvenor promised him the foal. Perhaps his closest friend, Copenhagen had been with the general on all his campaigns in Spain and France.

In London, Wellington went directly to his old friend Earl Bathurst. The long-suffering minister had been waging war for most of his adult life. Yet, he had never left the safety of Westminster Palace. Since Napoleon's exile to the Island of Elba, Bathurst had turned to the nagging American War. That spring he was perusing the plans for reigniting the American peace talks that had broken down earlier in Russia. A meeting was planned at Viscount Palmerston's home, just across Piccadilly from Green Park.

The duke felt that his concerns were far too volatile to be discussed in Bathurst's Whitehall chamber. Wellington walked the quarter mile from his London residence, Apsley House, at Number One, Piccadilly. The day was unusually bright and clear, and the stroll gave him a chance to do some last-minute thinking before he put his foot in it. Unsure of himself in the new role of ambassador, he needed a sounding board. The duke trusted the minister yet was concerned that his first wager as a diplomat might prove far too fool-hardy. He depended on his old friend to provide an honest, straightforward assessment.

The two-story house was a gray stone Palladian with a picked-out relief on the gable above the front door. Large by London standards, it was set just off the busiest street in town beside a sandy courtyard large enough to accommodate several horse-drawn carriages. The two stone arched gates were on the left and right with a small pedestrian opening on one side. A footman, expecting the duke, had propped open the black iron grill.

The two gentlemen sat on small French chairs at a green-felt-covered table in the card room. The room was small, perhaps fifteen feet by twelve, with a painted ceiling marked out in a relief of fancy filigree. Its charm, however, was found in the quiet ano-nymity it provided.

Wellington, with hands folded on the table and leaning forward, said in a low voice that was almost a whisper, "Lord Henry, while in France it occurred to me that England's about to be excluded from the Continent once again."

Bathurst winced. What he thought was finished may not have yet resolved itself.

The duke ignored his friend's reaction and continued. "I believe our good friends and allies, the Prussians and Russians, are about to formalize a pact intended to dominate the central states and divide the spoils of the war between them. They feel it's their right, since they suffered such great losses over the past twenty years at the hands of Napoleon. Russia naturally is expecting to assume the Duchy of Warsaw while the Prussians are eyeing a new western border abutting the Rhine. If they're allowed to annex those lands, Austria will have no choice but to join. Of course, England cannot permit such a center of gravity that could exclude our interests and trade."

Wellington leaned back to let Bathurst ruminate.

After a brief pause, the duke went on. "We must approach the Austrians and the French with a proposed alliance to block such a move and weaken the czar. Of course, the Low Countries will join whoever dominates as will Denmark. Perhaps Sweden would be more inclined to go with the Prussians. We'd lose access to the timber for ships from the Nordic forests, hemp from Riga, and tar from Sweden."

Bathurst was not surprised by Wellington's estimation, but he was unprepared to respond before he reviewed all possibilities. The scenario, as sketched out by the duke, was intriguing to the old statesman.

"Well, Your Grace, you've been learning all those years in Spain and not just how to fight. What you say *is* possible. I've been working on an alliance with France myself."

Wellington switched to his military hat and soldiered on. "Sir, if this comes to pass, England will need an army prepared to fight again next summer. Today, our army's sitting in southern France, Spain, Portugal, and Ireland—trained and ready to fight. However, if left without an obvious threat, it'll dissolve before our very eyes. No peacetime nation will stand the cost of a large army unless there's a commensurate danger." He raised his right hand as if taking an oath and said, "I predict that most of our best units will be demobilized and the rest dispersed to India and the Caribbean, where they'll decay. They'll be good for nothing except guarding shipments of tea and sugar. When called to action the army will be swept away on the Continent as it once was before 1808."

Bathurst knew that Wellesley was correct. He leaned back to ponder the possibilities. "Your Grace, you've articulated an important consideration. Of course, the navy isn't the question. It'll be kept busy on the seven seas potting at pirates, escorting convoys, exploring new worlds, and carrying diplomats into far-flung ports. Yes, the army's the problem that must be solved. Wellington, you don't have the whole picture, though. While you know India and Europe, you're not acquainted with North America—as I am. We've been engaged, against our will, with the United States, who's been suffering under Jefferson's rule since the last decade. President Madison believes he can annex Canada, if only he can get the French Canadians to rebel. However, his New Englanders are fed up with the arbitrary embargoes that are strangling them. You've been the beneficiary of their generosity."

Wellington smiled. "Lisbon Harbor's been filled for six years with their cargo ships. I couldn't have campaigned without American goods."

Bathurst added, "They've defied their federal government to line their pockets with our gold coin. We've witnessed disloyalty that has disturbed Jefferson and his Republicans. The former governor of Canada, Sir James Craig, sent spy reports in the spring of 1812 that reported a split of fifty-fifty between those who'd favor a return to the monarchy. Americans are all about money. And they call us a nation of shopkeepers!"

The joke caused a hearty laugh from both men, who needed such a break. There was a knock at the door. The butler entered with a tea tray and placed it on the side table. He served them without interrupting the conversation. The two men continued as if he were not there.

"Now, Arthur, my old friend, what if I were to ask you to prepare a campaign to end this pesky little war in our favor? After all, they started it!"

Wellington was unaware of any past events in the conflict, focused as he had been on the Iberian Peninsula. However, he commented that the tactics employed in America were inappropriate.

Bathurst said, "I myself had the Orders of Council repealed within months of Madison's objections, but it didn't matter. Jefferson had talked his war hawks into it and Madison wouldn't oppose his mentor. I'll give you a job that'll keep your army keen and return them in time to meet any threat that may come our way in Europe. What do you say to that, my good fellow?"

Bathurst was more than pleased by Wellington's initiative, and the duke embraced the challenging task eagerly.

"Write a plan for the successful conclusion of the war with America. If it preserves your army until it's sorely needed in Europe once again, all the better."

Within the month the work was ready, and a copy was sent to Prevost in Montreal.

SECRET
The Military Reinforcements allotted for North America
and the operations contemplated for the employment of them.

Sir,

I have already communicated to you in my dispatch of the 14th of April the intention of His Majesty's government to avail itself of the favorable state of affairs in Europe, in order to reinforce the Army under your Command. I have now to acquaint you with the arrangements that have been made in consequence and to point out to you the views with which His Majesty's Government have made its considerable augmentation of the Army in Canada.

The 2nd Battalion of the Royal Scots of the strength stated in the margin —768— sailed from Spithead on the 9th ulto. direct for Quebec and was joined at Cork by the 97th Regiment destined to relieve the Nova Scotia Fencibles at Newfoundland; which latter will immediately proceed to Quebec.

The 6th & 82nd Regiments of the strength as per margin—980 8 / 2. 8 37—sailed from Bordeaux on the 15th ulto. direct for Quebec. Orders have also been given for embarking at the same port twelve of the most effective Regiments of the Army under the Duke of Wellington together with the three companies of Artillery on the same service. This Force, which when joined by the detachments about to proceed from this country will not fall far short of ten thousand Infantry, will proceed in three divisions to Quebec. The first of these divisions will embark immediately, the second a week after the first and the third as soon as the means of transport are collected. The last division, however, will arrive in Quebec long before the close of the year.

Six other Regiments have also been detached from the Gironde and the Mediterranean, four of which are destined to be employed in a direct operation against the Enemy's Coast, and the other two are intended as a reinforcement to Nova Scotia and New Brunswick, available (if circumstances appear to you to render it necessary) for the defense of Canada or for the offensive operations on the frontier to which your attention will be particularly directed. It is also in contemplation at a later period of the year to make a more serious attack on some part of the Coast of the United States, and with this view a considerable force will be collected at Cork without delay. These operations will not fail to effect a powerful diversion in your favor.

The result of this arrangement as far as you are immediately concerned will be to place at your disposal the Royals, the Nova Scotia Fencibles, the 6th and the 82nd Regiments, amounting to 3,127 men; and to afford you in the course of the year a further reinforcement of ten thousand British troops—10,000—

When this force shall have been placed under your command His Majesty's Government conceives that the Canadas will not only be protected for the time against any attack that the Enemy may have the means of making, but it will enable you to commence offensive operations on the Enemy's Frontier before the close of this campaign. At the same time it is by no means the intention of His Majesty's Government to encourage such forward movements into the Interior of the American territory as might commit the safety of the force placed under your Command. The object to your operations will be, first, to give immediate protection. Second, to obtain if possible ultimate security to His Majestiy's possessions in America. The entire destruction of Sackets Harbor and the Naval Establishment on

Lake Erie and Lake Champlain come under the first description. The maintenance of Fort Niagara and so much of the adjacent Territory as may be deemed necessary and the occupation of Detroit and the Michigan Country came under the second. Your successes shall enable us to terminate the war by the retention of the Fort of Niagara, and the restoration of Detroit and the whole of the Michigan Country to the Indians. The British frontier will be materially improved. Should there be any advance position on that part of our frontier that extends toward Lake Champlain, the occupation of which would materially tend to the security of the province, you will if you deem it expedient expel the Enemy from it and occupy it by detachments of the Troops under your Command, always however, taking care not to expose His Majesty's Forces to being cut off by too extended a line of advance.

If you should not consider it necessary to call to your assistance the two Regiments which are to proceed in the first instance to Halifax, Sir J. Sherbrooke will receive instruction to occupy as much of the District of Maine as will secure an uninterrupted intercourse between Halifax and Quebec.

In contemplation of the increased force that by this arrangement you will be under the necessity of maintaining in the Province, directions have been given for shipping immediately for Quebec provisions for 10,000 men for 6 months.

The Frigate which conveys this letter has also on board one hundred thousand pounds in specie for the use of the Army under your Command. An equal sum will also be embarked on board the Ship of War which may be appointed to convoy to Quebec the fleet which is expected to sail from this country on the 10th or at latest on the 15th instant.*

> *I have the honor to be,*
> *Sir,*
> *Your most obedient*
> *Humble Servant,*
> (signed)
> *BATHURST*

---

* The secret order was found among the private family papers of Sir Christopher Prevost, 6th Baronet, at his home in Portugal. The order remained secret into the next century. The famous American naval writer Adm. Alfred T. Mahan knew of the order and the gist of the content but had not seen it, when he wrote about the battle in 1905. It was discovered at the English Public Records Office in 1922 but lost again soon after. A portion of the order exists in the Canadian Archives. Sir Christopher Prevost, 6th Baronet, unearthed this order of his ancestor, Sir George. It does not appear in the record of the court-martial held by the Royal Navy in 1815.

CHAPTER 4

The British Are Coming!—Again

"We should have to fight hereafter not for free Trade and sailors' rights, not
for Conquest of the Canadas, but for our national existence."

—Joseph Nickolson

America's Strangled Coastline

New York Times, June 1, 1814

They, that is Mister Madison and his prophet Mister Jefferson, should have known
better. They are such brilliant men, creative inspired scholars, and inheritors of their
own vision. How they have risked it all! And for what? Expansion to the frozen north
of Canada, when they could freely absorb a whole trackless continent to the west,
green and lush. So driven by cavalier and blinkered attitudes, they have brought our
new nation-state—not yet dry behind the ears—face to face with the destroyer of the
French and her revolution. As bright as our own, yet far more troubled, the French
Revolution has had its flame extinguished by England and her cronies. Now the master
of the Western world, Britain will likely bring her military machine, honed in Europe,
back to her former colonies and attempt to reconstruct the past. Are we to host raging
redcoats in our streets once more? No voice in America dares boast, "Fear not." Any
man can plainly see, after England's great victory over Napoleon, Britannia can do as
she pleases. Obviously, the Atlantic Ocean's wide expanse is no protection from the
greatest sea power in the wide world. The trade winds that sustain our maritime also
provide a highway that will sweep Royal Navy fleets onward to the North American
shore like dust from a broom. Mister President, what can you offer us now—other
than pain and panic? The British are coming, the British are coming once again.

————

The spring winds racing across the Atlantic brought only bruised clouds laden with foreboding to the United States. Mr. Madison's war had begun with the hope of great gains but, with Napoleon defeated, had turned tail on the Republicans. They had counted on Napoleon's invincibility, as it had been forged in the decade prior to 1812. The Republicans had believed him when he boasted that his reign was just the beginning of liberty, equality, and fraternity throughout the world.

But now it seemed it could not be worse for the fledgling republic. Every American port was blockaded, the American navy was impotent, the army was riddled with incompetents, and New England's Federalists were crying for Republican blood. Frustrated citizens watched British men-of-war, under billowing sails, choke the maritime trade that sustained them. In the South scant cargo eluded the patrols and slipped safely out to sea. Once left open in violation of the U.S. embargo to support the redcoats, then at war in the Iberian Peninsula, the southern ports had been closed down and were now withering. Charleston's food and fiber were no longer given free passage and high-seas protection to feed and clothe Wellington's army. Europe's vital markets, open once again for business, were out of reach. Yankee merchant ships, shut in like ill children, waited helplessly for relief. Norfolk, Virginia, usually the replenishment station for the Royal Navy, lost the lucrative arrangement to Bermuda, Jamaica, and Halifax.

In the early months, the American navy had manifested an impressive display of fortitude and daring in the Atlantic theater. Its aggressive attacks on Great Britain's merchant lifeblood had begun brilliantly. London newspapers demanded that its formidable navy to stop "these humiliations." Inevitably, with the destruction of the French and Spanish navies, the Royal Navy was now free of foreign entanglements. The English had overwhelmed all other contenders. Only one maritime service stood on the seven seas, and its ships hoisted and flew the Union Jack.

From the first hour of the first day of the War of 1812 the battles along the northern frontier went badly. The Niagara Campaign had devolved into a stalemate. Major General Jacob "Embargo" Brown and Brigadier General Winfield Scott, with four thousand regulars and militia, vied with the redcoats but attained nothing more than needless casualties. In addition, the watery border between Lakes Ontario and Erie was under continuous contention, but nothing had been resolved. American Oliver Hazard Perry's victory on Erie over a smaller fleet remained the only bright spot in 1813.

While the year 1812 had seemed like an ideal time to start a war with Great Britain, events had thwarted all optimism. True, the crown had little time or resources to allocate to the "American Sideshow." After its withdrawal from colonial America thirty years earlier, England had normalized relations. The intransigence of American members participating in the Saint Petersburg talks, though, angered the British government, which realized that America's obstinacy toward settling the conflict arose from its hope of annexing Canada. The Napoleonic Wars had hardened the attitudes of Parliament. When the British had come out from under Napoleon's shadow, the men at Westminster were eager to punish America for courting Napoleon and threatening loyal Canada.

Down to Business with Castlereagh

Meanwhile the newspapers reported gossip: Wellington had attended a soiree with Lady Anne Bernard and the Prince Regent, as well as a number of notable men unaccompanied by their wives. The duke was not in London by accident or to visit Kitty at Apsley House.

In fact, warnings from English master spy Francis McGee had prompted Wellington's withdrawal from the French capital. Increasingly vocal Bonapartists threatened not only Louis XVIII but also the English ambassador, commander of the British army residing in Belgium. The French army's loyalty to the king was dubious. Louis had wasted no time in slashing veterans' pensions, fragmenting formations, and reducing army pay. Surprisingly, the restored Royalists saw Wellington as an intriguer, a villain even. His best intentions were suspect. Even though Wellington followed His Majesty's instructions to the letter in dealing with the monarchy's restoration, the duke was a lightning rod for anti-British feeling.

Wellington was in London for the business of empire. No longer a mere field general, he was being promoted by his friend Robert Stewart, Viscount Castlereagh, the foreign minister in Lord Liverpool's government.

Castlereagh, the son of the Anglo-Irish Marquess of Londonderry, was born in Dublin the same year as Arthur Wellesley. Of the same stock, they had been friends and neighbors from youth. Castlereagh had risen in the political realm while Wellesley ascended in the military one. In an effort to maintain political visibility in London, Wellesley corresponded frequently with Castlereagh while on campaign, and during Wellesley's brief stint of 1806 in Parliament, Castlereagh looked to his friend for military advice. Wellesley was straightforward in his assessments; this candor helped build a strong bond between the two Irishmen. Castlereagh had served frequently in previous governments and in 1807 held the post of secretary of state for war and the colonies at the time of the HMS *Leopard*'s attack on the USS *Chesapeake*. Castlereagh saw to it that some time later that the commander of the *Leopard* was admonished for the attack as well as the subsequent impressments of four American crewmen, but only after the newspapers referred to the act as *unfair*.

After Sir John Moore's disastrous evacuation of Spain, Castlereagh planned a reentry to the Iberian Peninsula and appointed Wellesley as its initial commander, a move that had been badly received. After the assassination of Prime Minister Spencer Perceval in 1812, Cartlereagh, with no one to rein him in, dominated Parliament. He became most unpopular in the political and public spheres, but his ability always saw him through. He bore his unpopularity like the mantle of distinction worn by many misunderstood historical figures posthumously vindicated. Sure of himself in all things, he believed that he was ahead of his time. He regarded the members of Parliament as oafs and freeloaders unwilling to work, sustained by the accidental privilege of their birth. The party provided most seats in Parliament through safe constituencies. It wasn't necessary that a member live in his district or, in fact, even visit there. Universal suffrage wasn't in place at the turn of the nineteenth century in Great Britain. In the majority of representative seats in the House of Commons, party machines controlled votes. The House of Lords, which could obstruct, for a time, legislation proffered by the Lower House, was composed of hereditary peers and those proposed by the party in power at the time. Castlereagh menaced anyone who opposed his initiatives with a premature political demise.

Outwardly, he was slim, tall, wiry, and good-looking with sandy red hair. Those who met him socially found him pleasant, cultured, and amenable. His dark eyes and fine features captivated the ladies, who found him clever and amusing. Known to be unremittingly fearless on amorous afternoons when pursuing a hostess in her chamber, he could also be impulsive and generous with allies and equally sudden and ruthless toward his antagonists in the House Chamber. His manner was businesslike, often abrupt, but when in the duke's company, these characteristics became less strident. He regarded the successes in the land war with France as a direct result of his own good judgment, since he had championed Wellesley throughout the war and against numerous detractors in the House of Commons. Castlereagh prided himself in sponsoring the creative funding for the war and in charting the international strategy that cost Napoleon his throne.

The time had come to conclude this nasty business with the United States. Castlereagh's successor at the war and colonial office, Lord Bathurst, had approached Wellington for a solution. This determined triumvirate needed to convince the Prince Regent that the military strategy and expedition, as outlined by Wellington, would win back many of the former colonies. It would also punish America's arrogant upstart government for attacking His Majesty's provinces and provide a good lesson globally.

Lord Liverpool, the prime minister, agreed with this assessment and suggested that the trio "educate" His Highness as soon as possible. In the meantime, Bathurst got the ball rolling with the help of General Sir David Dundas, former head of Horse Guards. Wellington was kept out of the discussions with the general, who had left his post the previous year but had maintained the staff's loyalty. Wellington's latest elevation above more senior officers to duke had pushed more than a few noses out of joint. Many of Wellington's critics, ensconced in the musty halls at Whitehall and Liverpool, could be convinced by Dundas, who had overcome the opposition. The general's promised peerage would be proposed on the occasion of the next honors list, soon to be submitted by the prime minister to the Prince Regent. Dundas, known as "Old Pivot," was a passionate admirer of the Prussian system of military training, which dwelt on strict formation drill. He had succeeded the Duke of York, George III's son, after the scandal of January 1809 broke. The Duke of York's former mistress, Mrs. Mary Anne Clarke, had exposed her illicit relationship and how, through the bedroom exploits with the head of the army, she had sold commissions and appointments. She even admitted pinning notes to the Duke of York's bed curtains to remind him of his promises.

The Prince Regent wasn't expected to be an obstacle, but it was considered bad form for him to be the last person in London to learn about the proposed campaign. Lord

Liverpool primed the pump by requesting an audience with the Prince Regent that, unfortunately, he couldn't attend due to a sudden crisis in Vienna, where the conquerors of Napoleon were carving out a place for themselves without the benefit of British assistance. He would leave the explanation and exhortation in his colleagues' capable hands.

Wellington preferred to travel the congested streets of London on Copenhagen; the horse had become more famous than the duke. The sight of the chestnut stallion with the white blaze on his nose and chest drew such crowds that the animal impeded the traffic flow; mothers sent children to pet the sleek horse, who seemed to relish the attention. Bowing and shaking his noble head, he stood still despite the duke's urging.

Castlereagh solved the problem by sending his carriage, which slipped into the courtyard of Apsley House early that spring morning, to retrieve Wellington. A smart pair of small, matched black horses, marked with white fetlocks, pulled the black-enameled brougham. Seated on the box was a liveried driver and footman dressed in forest green piped in yellow worsted with low top hats, held on with the thinnest of leather bands under the chin that turned their faces red. The carriage clattered down Piccadilly with the duke concealed inside.

The duke was apt to be understated in the field as well as in public. For the royal visit he dressed simply sans sword. Wellington had received a number of gold and jewel-encrusted medals but didn't care for ostentation in any form, calling it "frippery and fuss." The year before, while in Spain, he had written his brother requesting "a standard officer's brass hilt straight sword in a leather scabbard, since mine has gone missing on this last move." If he wore a sword, it would be as simple as his dress. He was most upset when the court painter Thomas Lawrence displayed at the Royal Academy the duke's portrait, showing him holding a massive gold sword of state, which His Grace found "most inappropriate." Such aggrandizements did nothing for him; they only provided ample kindling for his critics. He was sure that morning that the Prince Regent would be wearing a field marshal's red military coat, complete with orders and stars. It would be unwise, under the circumstances, to compete with the monarch by wearing the same decorations, which the duke had won in battle. While it is true that Wellington was a snob, the incomparable warrior knew his place when walking with kings.

The coach turned down Duke Street just before Fortnum & Mason's emporium and left again at Jermyn Street. Castlereagh's house, at Number Four St. James Square, was only a couple short blocks from St. James's Palace, where the prince resided. The coach slowed; the cobblestone street was covered in straw to muffle the clop of the horses' hooves. *A severe illness must inhabit number two no doubt*, he thought. Leaning slightly forward and tipping his hat, Wellington peered out the window for the first time since leaving his home.

Castlereagh's home, like those on either side, was constructed from flat-fronted white limestone. Before the carriage came to a complete halt, the footman jumped down at the northwest corner of the quiet square. Only sixty feet wide, marked out by large windows, the dwelling seemed modest. The lowest floor, below street level, was crammed with laundry facilities, cupboards, storage lockers, kitchens, a scullery, and a wine cellar. The ground-floor foyer led to a large reception hall with a molded ornate plaster relief ceiling supported by white fluted Doric columns gilded at their tops. A liveried servant took Wellington's hat and passed him on to the butler, who led him up the white marble staircase, which was wide enough for five men to march up arm in arm. Covered with a royal blue carpet, the staircase spiraled back on itself before reaching the formal first floor, where the family lived.

At the top of the stairs the escort directed, "His lordship is waiting in the library, Your Grace."

Wellington could see that the house was much larger than it had appeared from the outside. It continued at least forty yards before connecting to the carriage barn in the rear. While his residence, Apsley House, was most impressive as a stand-alone sandstone dwelling, it was similar in overall size to that of the minister's. Ushered into a splendid room, the walls and ceiling of which were paneled with the lightest of sandalwood squares, he was glad to see that both Bathurst and Castlereagh were contemplating a ten-foot-high wall map of North America.

"Ah, Wellington, right on time! We were getting the measure of our expedition," said Castlereagh, glancing over his shoulder.

Bathurst held a long stick and ran it up the U.S. coast, resting the pointer on Halifax.

Wellington always found his superior, the third Earl Bathurst, to be rather curious looking. He liked the earl, who was a very fine friend and supporter, as well as a man of action who never disappointed. But Bathurst didn't look like a warrior: not too tall and rather lardy about the middle, he looked every bit of fifty-two and then some. Even less inspiring, Bathurst maintained a permanent worried look on his pasty face. His grayish washed-out hair was receding, revealing a forehead that was rather more pointed than domed. His sideburns were grizzled and not long enough to hide the weird combination of dropping jowls and a strong chin, which made his teeth appear to be pushed in and flattened across the front. Few laugh lines surrounded his broad mouth and none at all lingered at the corners of his green eyes. His shoulders were considerably smaller than the cut of his red-brown flocked coat, which hung on him as on a hook. There was a pronounced stoop to his stance, as if he were descending stairs. Serious, polite, and politically powerful, he spoke in a measured voice. The earl dived right into the heart of the matter, using the direct approach with which he intended to engage the prince later that morning. He aimed at leaving the Regent no choice, but the duke found the technique abrupt and brusque.

"Arthur, dealing with our prince is a simple matter," Bathurst assured him. "We won't offer alternatives. To do so could be dangerously counterproductive. He might pick the wrong one!" Bathurst paused, allowing his comrades to absorb the argument. "I'll express the goal of the endeavor at the start. You know, 'This will guarantee a successful conclusion of the war with the United States decidedly in our favor.' Of course, I'll remind him of how the treacherous French snatched the colonies from his father's benevolent hands by funding the rebellion. Then I'll recall the humiliating surrender at Yorktown. His Highness will certainly recognize the aptness of our campaign. He'll also find the reacquisition of what his father lost to be irresistible."

Wellington was silent but nodded his agreement.

Castlereagh stepped in. "I'll cover the political scene in Canada. He's a keen supporter of Prevost. He elevated him to a baronetcy after a most successful campaign on Dominica and St. Lucia, and then he promoted him to lieutenant general after his encounters with the French in the Caribbean. Prevost was born in New Jersey so I think he'd be happy to return to his boyhood home at the campaign's conclusion."

The two ministers shared a chuckle. Castlereagh cleared his throat before continuing. "After we speak, Arthur, you'll run through your military plan—leaving out much of the detail. If he wants to know more, he'll ask. Be particularly clear when you report the added advantage of diverting attention *away* from the northern invasion of New York."

Wellington felt comfortable with his role in the audience. He was well acquainted with the Prince of Wales both professionally and socially. If all other discourse failed to persuade, then Wellington would rely on his more personal connections with the prince.

Plucking the Eagle

The three were rather cramped together in the carriage for the short ride to the Mall entrance to St. James's Palace. There was an absence of majesty in its architecture. The old reddish-brown palace, which had seen better days in its three-hundred-year history, was a labyrinth of crammed corridors and tiny chambers. It was filled to capacity with courtiers and servants, who clattered about on the plank floors. One servant escorted the visitors quickly up rickety steps to an antechamber, where he indicated that they should seat themselves on frayed damask-covered chairs.

Once seated, Castlereagh remarked, "It appears we've been brought in through the servants' entrance—most fitting for the king's ministers, don't you know."

Bathurst agreed and added, "It'll be a treat once the conversion of Buck House at the end of the Mall has been completed." Turning to Wellington, he said, "That'll be convenient for you. It's just around the corner from your place. I never should've sold it to you. It'll become prime real estate, adjoining as it does the back wall of Buckingham Palace."

Wellington replied, "You're feeling frisky. I do believe you're up for this meeting."

A venerable courtier, wearing a black frock coat with satin collar and shiny knee stockings, a mixture of the old and new, appeared. He managed a slight bow and with his right hand swept them up and through the double fourteen-foot doors into the map room at the near end of the library. There, an eager Prince Regent met them in the dress uniform of a general. His red coatee lapel was turned back and buttoned, revealing the dark blue of a royal regiment. The thin white duck leather breeches were skintight. (When seen from the rear, they failed to flatter.) He led them to a large map of North America, the same one his father had used before the creation of the United States.

"Gentlemen, I'm looking forward to our discussion," the prince said. "Lord Liverpool has briefed me, and I'm anxious to get this maneuver under way. It's long been a dream of His Majesty, my father, who we all pray will return to good health, touched by God's grace, to recover our possession."

The prince centered himself at the map with the party to his left—it was protocol to stand to the left of the monarch. The foreign minister spoke first, as planned, and launched into the political tale, reaching back in history to his father's early reign for a running start. But the prince, impatient with the diatribe, waved it off.

"Now, Lord Robert, we know all that. What's your part in this, Lord Henry?"

Bathurst, a most astute reader of royal moods, deferred immediately to the duke with the words, "I believe Your Highness is well acquainted with my message of colonial misbehavior. Let's hear from the warrior next. I'll reply to any government questions you may have in the fullness of time."

Without warning, Bathurst had thrust Wellington prematurely into the action. But the duke welcomed it, since he didn't want to listen to the morning's discussion one more time.

Wellington began, "This isn't a simple campaign. While the enemy forces are not formidable, the terrain and logistics are. The Atlantic Ocean devours time and ships. The campaigning season is reduced to half that of Europe. The road system in the North won't support our army. This reality forces us to rely on water transport." He pointed the six-foot-long wooden stick at full arm extension to St. Lawrence Bay and traced it down to the opening of Lake Ontario. "The Canadian border lies on the 45th parallel, halfway to the North Pole. What's needed in Canada isn't an army, but a navy to seize and hold the waterways during the summer and autumn. Once winter sets in at the end of October, all fighting stops. It won't be till next May that we can fight a decisive engagement."

This wasn't at all what the Prince Regent had been expecting. He referenced the French Campaign of 1812 in Russia. He neglected, by design, to utter the name Napoleon.

Wellington commented, "Precisely, sir. Of course, you're agreeing that a winter campaign is much too dangerous and would lead to total defeat." He used the term "sir" rather than more regal prefixes because the prince was dressed in a military outfit. Wellington paid homage by addressing him as the senior serving officer.

The prince cut in again: "Field Marshal, I wish I'd followed my brother and become a serving soldier. I do believe I've a talent for military matters and the field . . . and . . . well . . . you know."

"I would've been proud to serve under you at Ciudad Rodrigo, sir." He was careful to say "under" rather than "beside." The prince's eyes glazed over as they drifted to the fresco painted on the ornate ceiling depicting Ares in the midst of battle.

Encouraged, the prince continued. "What would you have done at the gates of Moscow, Field Marshal?" The conversation's tone was becoming clubby.

"I would've been more patient about rushing to occupy Moscow. And then what? The French should've wintered at Borodino, established a supply train, and waited out the winter rather than pressing on into Moscow and oblivion."

The prince replied, "We've all learned a lesson, right so, right so. Pray continue, Field Marshal, with our conquest of North America."

Wellington was gaining strength. His companions stepped back from the line of fire and left the military men to play at soldiers.

"Sir George Prevost sent an assessment of the enemy that he's been successfully fighting for the past two years. He reports that the enemy land force is composed of regular and militia infantry with little artillery and some cavalry. The officer corps is appointed according to political favor from civilian ranks. Only the most senior officers have seen service and that was more than thirty years before during the rebellion, sir. They're too old, ignorant, and syphilitic to be of use. Many have been replaced with young men whose experience has been only in minor skirmishes. Some may be capable. The regulars are paid a bounty of money and the promise of land for an enlistment of two years. Training is done at the convenience of the commander, and it is, therefore, inadequate. Caught in a conventional battle, it's doubtful they could establish a line that'd withstand our veteran regiments. Their artillery batteries are often short of pieces, horses, and effective leadership. Since the terrain's covered with few roads that can support heavy movement, the country doesn't lend itself to mounted formations. The American navy on Lake Ontario is confined to Sackets Harbor in the west and rarely ventures out owing to its cautious commander. On Lake Champlain we have superiority and are likely to maintain it for the foreseeable future."

The prince asked, "Once you've assembled the army and arranged the navy to transport troops and supplies, how will we proceed?" The prince had leaped over the mundane, meticulous preparations for battle and, like most newspaper readers, wanted to get on with the bloodletting.

Wellington wasn't seeking guidance, so he outlined the field campaign in the broadest terms. The Prince Regent was only an armchair general despite the honors hanging heavily on his uniform. "Sir, I'm going to seek the wisdom of another ill-fated military expedition for inspiration. This time it's English and not French. Major General Johnny Burgoyne in '77 attempted to capture New York but failed because his force was too small and General Henry Clinton failed to support him. This time a diversionary force will harass the eastern seaboard, drawing the American army away to protect the seaports. With their strength and interest elsewhere"—Wellington placed his pointer twenty miles below Montreal—"I'll attack with the main force from Canada. Lake Champlain is a deepwater route due south, where it links up with the Hudson River and plunges like a dagger into the heart of the United States. The Royal Navy will secure the lake and capture American craft to move my regulars, the best regiments from the Peninsular War, down that old road to war until I can force the American army to engage me. There," he said, stabbing the map hard with the pointer's tip at Albany, "I'll end this foolish, fraudulent experiment in democracy."

While the prince pondered the dynamic proposal, Bathurst interjected his voice into the accruing silence. "While Wellington's preparing his expedition, we—that is, Lord Robert and I—will endeavor to resuscitate the peace negotiations and participate from a *far* more powerful position. Sir, we have their measure and I—that is, we—believe that with the British army squeezing their jugular, we'll end this outrageous war in our favor."

Castlereagh added, "The prime minister believes it's probable that Your Highness can expect to recover a good portion of the industrial center of New England."

The three men thought it unnecessary to elaborate further. Too much detail at this stage could become arduous and distracting for the prince. As Lord Liverpool had hoped, the Regent's was desire to retaliate against the United States for its attack on York, Canada, and to right the wrongs perpetrated on the United States' peaceful neighbor.

"Gentlemen," the Prince Regent declared, "I insist that the United States be punished for its capture of our merchant ships and for the sinking of Royal Navy vessels in international waters. You have my support to crush the Americans with all speed and severity. Pluck the eagle and reveal its true nature—the dodo."

The prince's remark elicited a round of laughter, and the royal audience, which had accomplished its task, descended into the day's gossip and a discussion over the shape of the new cavalry hats.

Madison's Nightmare

Taking the temperature of the allies one more time, the prime minister returned from talks in Paris and Vienna. Within the week Lord Liverpool convened a meeting of the upcoming campaign's principals. The setting was Bathurst's chambers at Horse Guards.

The duke took advantage of the clear, bright morning air and walked the quarter mile across Green Park and down the Mall to the base of St. James's Park. Few were out promenading on a weekday with the exception of ladies' maids on errands and nannies pushing prams. That Monday morning, the adjacent Constitution Hill Road catered to delivery wagons with groceries for the cooks, dust men picking up horse manure, and water buffalo (wagons that sprayed water) wetting the streets to keep the dust down.

As a result of numerous depictions of his distinctive profile in newspapers and curios, Wellington was recognized now and again along his walk. Exaggerated caricatures emphasizing his nose weren't that far from the truth. Passersby giggled, hands covering their blushing faces. When he overheard a young lady say to her companion, "He's more handsome in person, don't you believe," it brightened his mood. His pace was slower than usual. He took a moment to watch children feeding ducks in Green Park. Without a job for the first time in his adult life, Wellington was enjoying the respite from military responsibility.

At the rear entrance to the gray stone edifice of Horse Guards, next to the more imposing Admiralty building, he slipped in, unnoticed by the reporters who hung around Whitehall scavenging for crumbs. Seated in the outer chamber, Wellington waited quietly for word that the prime minister, foreign secretary, and secretary of war were ready to begin the conference. He watched the sun climb the wall. Fetched at last by a clerk, he was ushered into the War Department's map room, which had been reserved for the occasion. Lord Liverpool looked worried, more so than when Wellington had first told him of the possible coalition arising in the vacuum left by the French collapse in central Europe. Slightly taller than Wellington at just six feet, he was also a year older and forty pounds heavier. Their resemblance ended at what the press referred to as their "aristocratic noses." Deformed with a large bump in the middle, Liverpool's nose was similar to Wellington's but wasn't nearly as prominent.

The son of the 1st Earl of Liverpool, Robert entered politics at age twenty after schooling at Charterhouse and Christ Church, Oxford. Serving in Tory governments, he was elevated to the House of Lords in 1801 as Lord Hawkesbury. When a deranged bankrupted businessman assassinated Prime Minister Spencer Perceval in 1812, Liverpool, the secretary of war and the colonies, was asked to form a government. He served as its secretary of war and the colonies prior to becoming prime minister. A blue-eyed son of his Viking ancestors, he would have been at home with a broadsword in his hand as much as with a parliamentary order paper. As fiery as his red hair, Liverpool was the best choice for a wartime leader. Single-minded to a fault, he directed all his energy and the nation's wealth toward victory and declared, "Compromise and negotiations with the Ogre aren't a possibility." With Napoleon vanquished, the English bulldog would become a nightmare for stooped, balding Madison.

Lord Liverpool felt deeply that the United States had taken unfair advantage of England's plight by attempting to annex Canada. The upstart parody of a nation still looked to England for its culture and went to great lengths to ape it. To Liverpool and many others, the United States was like an unreasonable, ungrateful child who had offhandedly rejected England's overtures, extended in 1812 and again in 1813. Now America would pay for its arrogance and ignorance and pay *dearly*.

Wellington didn't posses the venom toward the United States cultivated by his countrymen. In fact, he had given little thought to the American War during his bellicose years of thwarting France's Iberian ambitions. Now he was spending one of those glorious days that the Almighty seldom bestowed on London. And here he was cloistered with three ministers, all of whom had experienced conducting warfare from the boardroom at Whitehall and equally possessed not only egos as sensitive as bruised berries but also a tendency toward the verbose rather than the concise.

The prime minister's first words didn't surprise the duke. Lord Liverpool enjoyed getting his teeth into a new adversary. "Gentlemen, the Holy Alliance—the czar calls it the Sacred League—is nothing more than Christian nations from the East being brought together to plunder and dominate western Europe. Composed of Russia, Prussia, and Austria, it intends to sweep up all loose confederations like Bavaria, Württemberg, Baden, and the Palatine, with Nassau and Neuchâtel eager to join. We along with the French and the Dutch haven't been considered worthy of their notice." Giving credit where it was due, he nodded in Wellington's direction. "Our field marshal first alerted me to the possibility of this grave development coming to pass as it, alas, has."

Castlereagh spoke up, "Must it mean war once again? Our allies, whose bills we've paid for many years, will repay us with cannonballs minted at Woolwich Arsenal?"

Bathurst interjected, "Our people are demanding that we demobilize the expensive army and navy now that there's no clear enemy. War has exhausted the public, as I suppose it must if we're not to annihilate ourselves in quick order."

When Liverpool spoke, his tone was low and serious. "It's not only a matter of money. The politicians don't trust a standing army, regular or militia, in times of peace. They know firsthand the awful pitfalls."

Bathurst longed for a sip of port or at the very least a good pot of tea. "Yes, your point's well taken, Prime Minister, but that's ancient history. There's no Cromwellian threat of civil war today. Last time we acted in accordance with the public's sentiment, but at what cost? Paying off allies? Buying mercenaries?"

Castlereagh supported his colleagues, "Wellington's proposal to busy the army in North America far out of the range of both public and party critics isn't for public consumption. If questioned, we'll explain our maintaining the armed forces as an expansion of the war in America fueled by a sense of just retribution. With the American War won and our army intact, we can effect a strong new alliance with France, Spain, Portugal, and the Netherlands in time to subdue the ambitions of our eastern neighbors."

All agreed heartily, though Bathurst's thoughts did drift back to that imagined sip of port. He said, "Deploying an army takes time. I set the machine into motion last night. The army, most of which is still in France, is preparing to embark for North America. Many of the soldiers will never touch English soil and disrupt the public's placid pulse. Out of sight, out of mind, eh? I ordered a cutter to be dispatched with a copy of the plan for Prevost. I'm sure he'll receive the plan, built on offensive operations along his southern border, gratefully. And of course, the Admiralty has notified Halifax Station. Our hounds are straining for the hunt, and I'm certain there's a Yankee fox trembling under a bush."

Lord Liverpool turned to the duke. "There's only one thing left to do before we adjourn. Marquess Wellesley and indeed your younger brother William have put you forward, Arthur, to command the expedition, and I concur. The government and crown support me, Your Grace, in that decision. I suspect this doesn't come as a shock. I've a copy of Lord Bathurst's letter to you offering you the command. I understand that you declined by restating your belief that what's needed along the Canadian border isn't a general and soldiers to secure the province but a naval presence. But we're concerned with far more than just protecting Canada's existing border. We can justify the retention of a high number of troops only if the English public can interpret our invasion as retribution and an attempt to restore what was ours. The English newspapers drip with venom toward America. We can capitalize on that mood by sending our greatest national hero on this great national endeavor. I trust no one other than you with this responsibility."

Wellington was aware that the command wasn't being offered; indeed, he had been involuntarily appointed. This was a challenge of his character. It was the same as years earlier, when he had withdrawn from military service to serve in Parliament. Then he had turned his back on the military life for good. But his appointment as colonel of 33rd Regiment, his regiment, which he hadn't sought, was placed on his shoulders when Lord Cornwallis died. He was given no choice then as now but to set aside his own expectations and accept. There in the map room he thought he could smell gunpowder once again.

"In India," the duke mused, "they have a phrase *nimmukwallah*, which roughly translates as 'I have eaten of the king's salt.' Once one tastes of that salt, it becomes one's duty to serve with unhesitating zeal and cheerfulness, when and wherever the king or his government may think proper to employ him."

Wellington could see now that the morning meeting had little to do with any other business. He was the center of attention, and it wasn't just three against one. They wielded the approbation of his brothers. He was sure that it had been offered at the Prince Regent's insistence. He had deluded himself into believing that his declining Bathurst would suffice to put the matter to rest and that his service to king and country would be only as a military adviser. The duke believed in himself, but like all men he also doubted himself on occasion. Perhaps agreeing would be the first instance of his overreaching; perhaps all would come crashing down. Although sometimes self-doubting, he was rarely, if ever, daunted.

"Gentlemen," said the duke, "I accept the honor and will strive to bring further glory to His Majesty."

With that, he left.

Tea for Two

The plan for "operations in North America" was a closely guarded secret; only three written copies existed. They were distributed to the Admiralty headquarters, the governor general of Canada, and Admiral Alexander Cochrane, commander of the Atlantic maritime force tasked with executing the campaign's diversionary portion.

Yet, members of Parliament had been consulted, and soon the whispers reached the ears of Sir Josiah Wedgwood, a backbencher from East Anglia. Although opposed to the French Revolution, the English potter was a vocal supporter of the American revolt over taxation without representation. His pottery firm had long idealized the American struggle for international recognition through images on his famous earthenware. He had continued to champion the American cause and had been pivotal in the restoration of normal relations formalized in the 1794 Jay Treaty. His affection for the eaglet overwhelmed his nationalism, which had been unassailable during the wars with Napoleon. Now in his old age, he couldn't surrender his sympathies. He saw no compelling need to punish America for her resistance since 1812 and believed England should pursue a harmonious end, not more bloodshed.

Wedgwood's good friend Albert Gallatin, formerly the American treasury secretary, was one of the peace commissioners present at the new treaty talks, which had begun again in Ghent. Gallatin was passing through London on his way to Belgium. The two men arranged to meet at Twining's Teashop across from the law courts. As members of the Sovereign Military Order of the Temple of Jerusalem, they planned to meet after ceremonies at the Temple Church off Fleet Street. Because they were Knights Templar, they didn't generate any suspicion for being seen together a block from the seven-centuries-old church. Additionally, the special bond established within the international order, which dated back to the Christian Crusades, was dedicated to keeping the road open to Jerusalem. In Wedgwood's mind, America was the New Jerusalem, a place of peace where

Christians had gone when oppressed by the Old World. There, they could worship freely. For that reason he didn't want to see American democracy come tumbling down.

Twining's, in business since 1706, provided the finest teas from India, Ceylon, and China. They favored Wedgwood crockery and had commissioned from Josiah's firm special pieces. The establishment was long and narrow, lined on both sides with stacked shelves of large ornate tin and pottery caddies that reached to the richly decorated plaster ceiling. Within the first forty feet of the shop the owner dispensed loose tea expertly over narrow counters on either side and provided valued customers with personalized blends. Lady customers were squashed together by sippers who sneaked past to the building's rear, where tiny tables were clustered together. There, Wedgwood and Gallatin secreted themselves.

Gallatin wasn't a man anyone would notice. In his late forties, he was small and slim with a very high forehead and a dark, unmanaged fringe of hair that wrapped around the back of his head from ear to ear. He gave the appearance of being a bookish man; his bright blue eyes were viewed through the ever-present, thin, silver-framed spectacles that perched on the tip of his pointed nose. Always in poor health, he seemingly suffered from every malady known to man.

Wedgwood turned the initial pleasantries to much sterner stuff, once the petite pinafored waitress had strained a portion of tea into their blue-and-white cups.

"I must tell you, Albert, there's much more to this treaty talk than the previous negotiations in Saint Petersburg. While the impressment of sailors has stopped with Napoleon's demise, the military blockade is still very much part of the future. England, now liberated by its victory from its entanglement in Europe, intends to end the dispute with the United States."

Wedgwood gave his friend a chance to consider the news and form a reply. He sipped his hot black China tea; he never permitted milk to cloud his cup. Gallatin didn't expect further military developments and believed that the English involvement in the talks was motivated by a shared sentiment to conclude the war as quickly as possible. President Madison's instructions were clear: "Insist on an end to the naval blockade as soon as possible and return affairs to the status quo prior to the declaration of war in 1812."

He assured Wedgwood, "My friend, we've no ax to grind and hope to avoid any further naval engagement since Great Britain has lifted the naval blockade she had imposed." Gallatin believed that Wedgwood had been sent from the government to exploit their friendship and smooth the talks before they began in earnest. He was pleased by what he believed was an informal gesture there in the teashop and waited for substantive overtures from his brother knight.

After admiring the quality of his cup, Wedgwood began again. "You see, my friend, there's a military plan, which I've not seen, that details a large-scale military invasion of your country. You must appreciate my position and the attendant risk in telling you this, which I do in the greatest confidence. This conversation never occurred. Inform your government to prepare as soon as possible."

Gallatin, stunned, let his tea grow cold. As a former secretary of the treasury, he viewed the threatened invasion as a deathblow to his country. While others would certainly turn to military matters at this crucial moment, he knew there was a much more critical component with which to contend. Wars consumed money, and U.S. belligerence had already tallied up a substantial sum. This time there was no France to help fund the endeavor. The country was in no condition to establish and maintain a large field army and navy.

The navy, most costly yet slowest to bring to a boil, was overseen by William Jones, who had just proposed that half a million dollars be spent on Robert Fulton's steam launches for the defense of New York City's inner harbor. These boats would've been of little use against the might of the Royal Navy. But although a feeble program, it was beyond the budget. Jones, who had taken Gallatin's place as temporary secretary of the treasury, was dragooned into wearing these two hats until the senator from Tennessee, George Campbell, could be sworn in. Campbell knew nothing about banking and finance but was a good Republican.

"Sir Josiah, my very dear friend," Gallatin sputtered, grateful for the information, "allow me to clarify for you the financial crisis facing us at home."

His voice betrayed the gravity of what he had just heard. He extended his right hand across the tiny table's surface, placed it on top of Wedgwood's, and left it there for the duration. Gallatin was aware of the risk involved for a member of Parliament to divulge such a secret to the enemy. It was nothing less than treason, a death sentence, and enmity for his family; it was an action that would be woven into the very fabric of British history. But Gallatin couldn't conceal the overwhelming concern that filled his reeling mind. As treasury secretary, he had scraped together and scavenged for the pittance that had financed the past two years of small-scale war in North America. But financing a defensive response to such a large invasion was another matter altogether.

"The varied embargoes that have come and gone have ravaged our treasury. Believe me when I say that they've devastated our economy when ironically, they were intended to decimate yours." Concerned about revealing a state secret to an Englishman, Gallatin continued in hushed tones. "Last year, the federal government collected taxes and other sources of revenue in excess of $16 million. Due to the necessity of supporting this war, we've expended $30 million more than we've collected in the vaults. As my last official duty as treasury secretary, I proposed a tax increase in all sectors. But, of course, Congress wouldn't hear of it and decided to float more loans that will only further weaken our position in the market. I speculated that we couldn't service our current debt, even if more paper was issued. But the foes of taxation dismissed my suggestion—and me. The last I heard, Congress voted to print $10 million more in treasury notes and to seek loans in the amount of $25 million. A similar scheme in 1811 failed owing to a lack of confidence in the government. This summer $4 million in notes sold for $2.5 million, or just over half their value. The administration's seeking loans from the banks in New York but hasn't been successful. I fear that when your news becomes public, they'll go bust. To date, the federal government has kept its head just above water by increasing the import tax from $2 to $6. But such tweaking is not enough. Not this time."

Wedgwood interrupted by raising his hand to signal for another pot, thereby giving his distraught friend a break. It was going to be a long discussion.

"Albert, I thought you intended to follow Alexander Hamilton's guidance and establish a national bank, one free of state connections. What came of that?"

Waving his hand at the Englishman, Gallatin expressed his regret. "I attempted to do so three years ago, but my initiative failed. We labored throughout the spring to generate interest in a $30 million loan, but the banks preferred to keep their money in New England establishments and cut us loose."

There was more to this meeting than Wedgwood's alarming message that the British were coming in force. He had already investigated America's grim financial picture with assistance from friends in London's banking community. As a board member of Scoff's Investment Bank, an old and highly respected firm, he knew that his bank and many like it were heavily invested in the growing prospects of the United States and had been even *before* the American Revolution. In fact, English money had financed the formation of many of North America's colonies from the time of the pilgrims. The banks had been steadfast through the colonial period and had influenced the crown to send troops to defend the colonies during the French and Indian War, which had resulted in England's capture of Canada from the French. The fiduciary interest in New England's industry and the southern plantations never wavered—neither before nor during nor after the rebellion. London's banking institutions, established as early as the crusading Knights Templar, the first international bankers, had been adept at adjusting to the changing political climate for centuries. Both men were cognizant of the wisdom of backing both sides during times of crisis. With that in mind, Wedgwood's cohorts had urged him to inform his banking friend, Gallatin, of Wellington's audacious secret plan and to propose an equally audacious and secret loan that would enable the United States to resist the looming invasion.

Gallatin ended his dismal financial review of the treasury. He felt somewhat better. He hadn't summed up his nation's dire plight, even to himself, until now. It sounded even more hopeless when spoken rather than merely read off from balance sheets full of red ink.

"Albert, there are those here in London acutely aware of the crisis caused by your struggling economy, and these persons don't intend to abandon their American friends so easily."

On hearing the message that his country was the sole target of the greatest military machine in the world, Gallatin had assumed that Wedgwood was relaying the information to convince him to settle quickly at Ghent before the invasion could be executed. He was grossly mistaken and overjoyed to be so wrong as he listened to Wedgwood.

"I'm afraid," his English friend said, "that we can't do anything to alter the government's intention to end the war in England's favor. We aren't military men, but there's more to national power than soldiers and sailors. They're but one means a county has to influence events. While we can do little to deny funds for the government to conduct its military adventure, we can and indeed will provide encouragement to resist the

Duke of Wellington and the best army in the world. Your assistance will be both needed and welcomed."

Gallatin, a sophisticated and astute man, understood exactly what the potter and his friends were proposing. They were going to bail out America just as the French had during the American Revolution. He was also aware of the need for the strictest secrecy. If the crown were to discover Wedgwood's plan to assist the United States, the outcome would be disastrous for all concerned.

"We must be exceedingly careful, Sir Josiah. I'm sure your exchequer's well aware of the extent of offshore investments. A direct overture to the U.S. Treasury will certainly garner scrutiny and be foiled before it begins. While your friends have inroads into our system, so does the Bank of England. Little occurs that they're not party to via the Anglophiles who still lurk in the American financial system."

Wedgwood was well aware of the dangers posed by circumventing the Old Lady of Threadneedle Street. "Albert, we have a very good and influential friend at the heart of the Bank of Philadelphia. And he has promised us his utmost service."

Enter the Irishman

Mathew Carey was the only American who fit Wedgwood's image of an American. Carey was one of the most prominent Americans of the post-Revolution period. Born in Dublin in 1760, he was apprenticed to an owner of a printing company and bookselling establishment. There, he learned the power of ideas and the influence books could wield. At that time, the visiting American ambassador to France, Benjamin Franklin, spoke in Dublin. Young Carey listened to him with enraptured interest. Afterward, he abandoned his job and returned with the venerable diplomat to France. Carey was employed as a pressman at Passey. There, he befriended the Marquis de Lafayette, the lionized hero of the American Revolution.

By age twenty-two, Carey had become a fierce Irish nationalist and a supporter of everything American. He was back at home when the independent Dublin parliament established the Bank of Ireland in 1782. Reinventing himself as a writer, Carey founded *The Volunteer*, an Irish nationalistic newspaper that soon became the leading chronicle of the day. He also became a student of economics and quoted liberal thinkers. Irishmen were beginning to fault London's intervention in Ireland's financial interests. Carey's newspaper quoted in glowing terms the ideas of Dr. Lucas, Henry Gratin, and Joseph Flood, all of whom were on the British blacklist. The writings of Molyneaux and Jonathan Swift influenced him as well. He resurrected Swift's treatise "A Modest Proposal for the Universal Use of Irish Manufactures." Carey, whose philosophy derived from these great thinkers, wrote eloquently, "The American system is designed to reward the individual for his labor within a community that has supportive educational and industrial institutions. . . . Growing populations were necessary of a growing economy, contrary to the English philosophy of thinning the population for increased profits."

He deplored the clearing of land in Scotland a hundred years earlier and found it to be shortsighted and antisocial. Carey argued that the system of monarchy and privilege was fundamentally irreconcilable with republican principles. He was detained in 1784 and sent to Newgate Prison in Dublin. The Lord Mayor secreted him from custody and sent him and his family to America. Other firebrands of the Irish Rebellion who followed the same path, like Thomas Russell, were publicly hanged for sedition.

In Philadelphia, the Marquis de Lafayette backed his friend's printing and publishing business. Carey became prominent and urged Benjamin Franklin to establish the Government Printing Office. His radicalism was evident when he assisted Theobald Wolfe Tone's planning session, which was held in Philadelphia, for the French invasion of Ireland in 1796. Thousands of Irish nationalists were expected to join the 5,000 French regulars deployed at Bantry Bay, but the opportunity was lost when a storm scattered and sank the fleet.

Most important for Wedgwood, Carey had been made a director of the Bank of Philadelphia in 1802, and thereafter, he became a member in good standing of the American banking community. A staunch supporter of both Jefferson and Madison, Carey went on to write *The Olive Branch* in 1814. It listed the causes of the conflict to come between the American system of political economy, which placed value on labor, and the British system, which placed capital over labor and reduced workers to the level of destitute wage slaves. The book called for a militant bipartisan approach supporting the current war with Great Britain and recommended enlisting the efforts of moderates of both parties. Carey plotted to undermine the Anglophile secessionists among New England's ultra-Federalists while he rallied support for the financial and military measures needed to win the war.

Naturally, Gallatin, Carey's good friend and supporter, thought of him after the meeting with Wedgwood because they shared many of the same ideas. He delayed his passage across the channel and extended his visit to London by claiming illness from the climate and the crowded metropolis's unhealthy air. Space was provided in one of the secluded chambers of Scoff's Bank, which Gallatin entered via a passage from a neighboring building on the other side of the block. A men's tailor shop provided a necessary cover in case he was being watched. The rear of the establishment also connected to the chambers of Madame Beck, who was known to entertain gentlemen in the afternoon. As a result, the tailor's business appeared rather brisk, if only somewhat innocuous.

Mister Kind, a senior officer at Scoff's, sponsored the bank visit. In a dark-paneled office the two men exchanged information that established the methods by which funds would be moved and arms purchased. Some of the military equipment was beyond the capability of the American arsenals. Kind would consolidate the investment from other London banks and outside sources that would remain confidential. Gallatin was expected to provide the funds required, a timeline of payment, and a list of collateral.

To conceal the transactions, Scoff's would establish letters of credit at the Bank of Ireland in Dublin. Secretly, the Dublin parliament of 1784 had backed Hamilton's attempt to establish his Bank of New York at the same time it established the Bank of Ireland. The Irish parliament didn't trust the London government's resolve and, at Carey's urging, protected its assets with the American alliance. A few years later, London absorbed the Dublin parliament. Since the Irish bank was a solvent institution, it was able to function despite the break up. Internally, a transaction in the Bank of Ireland was an automatic transfer to Hamilton's bank. Since there was no national bank of the United States and since banking was not regulated or overseen, Hamilton's bank could move money transparently within the country or overseas through any other bank.

When Gallatin finished the week's worth of negotiations and had signed the letters and agreements, subject to Mathew Carey's approbations in Philadelphia, his doctor proclaimed him cured of the ague. It was a marvel of medical care.

Before leaving in late July for Ghent, he met once more with Wedgwood at Twining's Teashop. "Sir Josiah, it has been a most heartening visit and one that I can safely say could determine the outcome of our second War of Independence. It would not have been possible without your courageous involvement."

With that the two men finished their tea and parted—never to meet again.

Prevost's Spirits Soar

Prevost was the son of a British soldier who had fought in the Battle of Quebec in 1760. Seven years later, the young Lieutenant Augustin Prevost, a Swiss mercenary in the Court of Orange, defended the American colonists against the Indians. His son George was born in Hackensack, New Jersey, during that period.

A true North American by default, Sir George sat comfortably in his elegant quarters in Montreal late one evening in the spring of 1814. He was enjoying the fireside with his wife, Lady Catherine, and his eighteen-year-old daughter Anne. It was after dinner and the three sat alone on one of the shortest days of year. Dark by midafternoon, it was decidedly cold forty miles north of the contiguous border with the United States.

Lady Catherine was a comely, diminutive woman in her early forties. Her doe-like brown eyes, her most stunning feature, were large with sleepy lids and thick, long, curled lashes, which vamped at anyone caught in her soft gaze. Her complexion had a healthy pink glow. Her nose turned up slightly at the end, which lent an impish air to her appearance. In short, she was a natural charmer.

The displaced daughter of the landed and titled La Grand family of St. George, Brittany, Catherine had slipped out of the country to Switzerland at the start of the French Revolution. Many of her relations hadn't been so lucky and were among the missing during the Reign of Terror. She had seen hard times. Tucked away in Canada, she wrote a steady stream of letters to people and places, hoping to allay her growing fear that few of her kin had survived the revolutionaries' zeal.

She sat quietly now on the settee next to her husband and waited patiently to hear the news the governor had bottled up while their dinner guests were still in the mansion.

At last, Sir George began to speak. "My father, God rest his soul, is here with me tonight, my darlings." He looked across the parlor at the portraits of his parents, close together in art and memory as they had been in life. They were not a pretty pair. The paintings had been completed late in life. Wisps of white hair protruded from his mother's beribboned lace cap, which framed a long, drawn face. The lack of a smile betrayed the harsh life of a soldier's wife. Prevost's nearly bald father, in a bright red uniform coat, was upright and steadfast. His steely gaze bespoke a man who performed his duty. A hint of a smile belied the overall stern expression and suggested that he had been a happy man who must've told a good joke now and then and who was fond of nights spent at a campfire sharing a bottle of liberated rum.

Sir George pointed to his father's image on the golden damask-covered wall. "He was here once in Montreal, Anne. He marched by on his way to Quebec and the Plains of Abraham." Sir George's eye was drawn to the left side of the old man's forehead, where a depression had been painted in proudly. "He had to be trepanned as a result of a Frenchman's spent bullet. My father wore the dent with distinction all the days of his life. It was seen by the troops when he raised his hat in victory over the Americans at Savannah in 1778. And now, by God, I'll raise my hat to him in victory over the Americans in 1814."

Lady Catherine continued to prick her needle into the hoop-held cloth in her lap and left Anne to respond. "Oh Father, these last two years of dreadful Yankee attacks have burdened our spirits. What's happened to put you in such a fine mood?"

It was true; his spirits were more buoyant than they had been on previous evenings by the fire. The past two years of constant border crossings by Canada's southern neighbor, whom Prevost believed had no valid ax to grind, had worn him down and taken its toll on his family, however supportive and resilient they were.

While Napoleon was on the loose, Horse Guards had precious little to spare in troops, ships, supplies, and funds for Canada's defense. He credited the success of his defensive series of military maneuvers to the troops and officers of his British regiments, who numbered fewer than four thousand. They were combined with a couple thousand fencible regiments of English-speaking Canadians and native Indians.

It wasn't just the Americans who nagged him. The Royal Navy's waterborne forces in Canada were known as the "Canadian Marine." The Admiralty denied Prevost overall command of this force and allowed him only operational control. A similar but not as stringent arrangement existed with the Royal Artillery, which remained under orders of the Ordnance Department at Woolwich. The Canadian Marine provided transport and resupply, controlled the waterways, and orchestrated the naval gunfire. The Canadian Marines fought alongside the army when it was suitable or, as Prevost remarked to Anne, "suitable to Sir James Yeo." A hundred miles west along the St. Lawrence River at Kingston, Yeo had established his headquarters, thereby denying Prevost the ease of daily contact. Quite apart from Montreal's demands and influence, Yeo busied himself with the defense of the Great Lakes to ensure that the fur trade enjoyed a secure path to Quebec City—a need that he viewed as equally important as the myriad others Prevost often cited. The result of this feud cost lives.

Still, Yeo was not Prevost's primary concern. Feeding the land and naval forces was a constant headache. While the Maritime Provinces of Nova Scotia, New Brunswick, Labrador, and the archipelago that comprised the sea approaches to Canada were prosperous and could sustain Lower Canada, they were frozen and out of reach of Quebec City, Montreal, and the army that had to eat—even in the winter. The snow and ice came early. By late October, winter had established a grip that would not be broken until late April. Prevost increasingly relied on smugglers from Vermont and New York to sustain his forces. The growing season above 45 degrees northern latitude was short. Farms could barely feed the 4.25 million citizens under his protection. Yet, the American farmers were more than willing to send food and timber north on Lake Champlain. Jefferson's and Madison's punitive embargoes had little effect on dissuading farmers and merchants from making frequent use of the attractive markets in nearby Canada. Prevost had the good sense not to ask for credit and always paid in gold coin.

Smugglers had cut a road through a northern county of Vermont forest, which they referred to as "Embargo Road." They drove herds of live animals across the border without the knowledge of the not-so-watchful customs officials. The lake was the most successful avenue, however. Along with the grain and meats, the traffic in potash and cut lumber was so great that even the customs cutters couldn't stem the flow. Even iron ore made the cross-border trip. It wasn't just a one-way ferriage. Americans sought furniture, tableware, machinery, sugar, rum, chocolate, and medicine from the Caribbean. The Canadian Marine boat-building program acquired masts and spars as well as planking for their warships, which would be used to attack American settlements. Without the nightly arrival of low-slung craft at the St. Jean's dock, Prevost's army wouldn't have survived during the past two years of the American War. Sir George frequently thanked the Americans in the Montreal newspapers for their generosity, which drove official Washington crazy.

However, smuggling was a tenuous link on which to hang the long-term well-being of the British army. Prevost feared that American naval forces would put a stopper in this bottle and that his Yankee provisions would come to a sudden halt. The worry etched on his face that clouded his kindly countenance concerned his daughter. She was relieved to see him jovial once again.

"So why the good cheer, father?" she asked again, being less patient than her mother.

"My dears, I must tell you a secret, one that you'll not have to keep for long. Today I received an order from Secretary of War Bathurst that I've been hoping for since the Ogre was caged on Elba. My plan has always been to stop the invasions by punishing the Yankee army to the point of exhaustion, but resources had not been sufficient. This new plan offers far more than I could've hoped for. I've been concerned over a change in the American army brought about after the court-martial of their General Wilkinson. I've been told that the politically appointed officer corps was at its end. There's a new class of young bucks who will assume command across the board. I've been particularly impressed with the exploits of Major General Andrew Jackson. But it doesn't matter any longer what they do. For the Americans it is all over."

His eyes sparkled as he leaned forward and whispered huskily, "In short, my dears, Wellington is coming."

CHAPTER 5

Both Sides Prepare to Escalate the War

"For Prosperity doth best discover Vice; But Adversity doth best discover Virtue."

—Francis Bacon

A Patriotic Fourth

Gallatin had thought long about who ought to receive his vital message once the American fast cutter *Rover* reached the United States. He couldn't afford to leave it to chance and potentially risk that the message would go unheeded. If he sent it to Secretary of War Armstrong, he would roundly disregard it for he had his own agenda. If it went to Gallatin's replacement at the treasury, George Campbell, it could create more confusion than clarity. Gallatin was unsure of Campbell's position, if indeed he had one. Perhaps he could trust Thomas Jefferson, whom he knew well, but the former president was likely to fly into a diatribe about the "bloody British." Besides, Jefferson, a blabbermouth of the first order, would spread the news all around town or, for that matter, all around the country. Secretary of the Navy Jones was a good man, but did he have sufficient presence inside Congress to influence action? In the end Gallatin settled on the president. Although an intellectual, Madison had the practical experience of the past two years and knew the hard facts of war.

On the dockside, Gallatin met the *Rover*'s captain and passed on his instructions. He held the officer firmly by his right hand while he transferred the light brown vellum muniment into the captain's possession. On the red wax flap was the impression made by the signet ring the American envoy wore to the Ghent peace talks. The seal assured the recipient that Albert Gallatin had inscribed the contents within and therefore they should be taken at face value.

As soon as Gallatin released his grip, satisfied that he had conveyed the critical nature of the communiqué, he started to worry about the voyage ahead. Ships floundered and, in doing so, changed history. Should he send a second copy via another craft, perhaps a slow merchantman, just to be doubly safe? The message was vital to his country's well-being, but he dare not risk the existence of a second message. Now that word of the invasion had been sent, Gallatin felt marooned in England. Alone with his doubts, Gallatin packed up and left for Ghent.

Leaving Plymouth, England, and flying Portuguese colors to deceive the Royal Navy, it took the *Rover* twenty-one days to reach Philadelphia. It wasn't considered bad form to fly illegitimate flags, but rather the practice was accepted as part of the high-seas game. Often, warships disguised themselves to entrap an enemy or indeed to acquire safe passage.

An early tropical storm that blew the *Rover* hard across the Atlantic along the outer edge of the Caribbean aided her quick passage. The trade winds swept her north along the Carolina coast, around Delaware, and into the safety of the Delaware River estuary. The *Rover* docked at the port of Philadelphia rather than adding more time to the voyage by rounding Hampton Roads and sailing up the Chesapeake Bay to Baltimore or up the Potomac to Arlington, Virginia. The bay's winds could be tricky, and the vessel might lose time tacking in narrow waters.

The *Rover*'s captain passed Gallatin's catastrophic communiqué to Thomas Hope, the energetic young cavalry officer at the courier station next to the dock. The silver chevrons on the base of Hope's sleeves marked him as a lieutenant of the 2nd Light Dragoons. The captain emphasized the urgency for a swift journey and the importance of the mission. "Give it directly to the president and no one else."

The courier changed mounts four times before clattering across a long wooden bridge at Blandensburg Crossing that provided access to Washington. The rider was forced to take the congested route, which was clogged with revelers on that holiday evening, slowing his urgent progress to a crawl. The courier office would surely be closed by the time he arrived.

The capital after dusk on July 4 was caught up amid celebrations and fireworks. Hope was familiar with the city, in which all the festive streets led to Capitol Hill. Colorful paper lanterns were strung throughout the city in celebration of the nation's birthday. As evening gathered, the tall windows of three-story red-brick homes reflected the flickering colors from the illuminated lanterns.

Hope headed for the War Department, which had recently moved into the new stone Palladian-style government building on the southeast corner of the federal block of government buildings, which were dominated by the Executive Mansion. The city plan had called for one major government department housed on each corner of the presidential mansion grounds. Earlier, the war offices had been spread among six adjoining row houses on Fifth Street. By July 1814, two of the four structures were finished. Work had been suspended as the war consumed more and more funds. The country's administration was maturing into an expanding central bureaucracy housed in the hither-too-obscure southern village. Hope had expected to find the duty officer at the War Department, but the door was locked. The duty officer had closed up early to join the festivities and was somewhere enjoying the merriment.

The courier turned toward the Executive Mansion, his next destination. Once there, he expected an escort to guide him through the crowd to the president. Flares and flashes of fireworks lighted the grounds. Mister Madison would be hard to locate in the crush of citizens. He doubted the family would be in seclusion on the one night a year when independence from Great Britain was recalled with high spirits and great joy. Now the nation was engaged in what the newspapers called "the Second War of Independence," which made this Fourth of July that much more poignant in the new capital.

That patriotic night the Executive Mansion sparkled like a glass showcase bursting with America's finest goods. First Lady Dolley Madison, famed as Washington's hostess, was presiding over a lavish gathering that filled the first-floor formal rooms of the presidential mansion. She wanted to show off the mansion's renovation, accomplished entirely with American furniture and trappings. The press was especially prominent among the guests in hopes that they would approve and join her in endorsing her "Buy American" campaign. The embargo had prevented the importation of preferred English furniture and French decorations. New England's craftsmen had lost their market and were turning inward, prompting Americans to purchase Yankee furniture, which, it must be admitted, was of equal quality to that originating in the Old World.

The diminutive Dolley, even shorter than her husband, the five-foot-five chief executive, swept around the room in a pale yellow empire-waist gown. She was attempting to divert the politicians from the grim state of affairs recounted by the newspaper stories that arrived on neutral ships all along the eastern seaboard. The latest news or rumors (and often it was impossible to discern the difference) about Great Britain's gathering strength found their way to the capital as if carried by lightning. It was no secret that many an English merchant, manufacturer, and merchandiser was eager to bring down the American government. The embargo was deadly unpopular in both the Old and New worlds.

It was getting late. Lieutenant Hope spurred his horse on.

Mister Madison's stately house was a blaze of candlelight and the lawn filled with inebriated guests who had been watching the pyrotechnics. The scent from drifting clouds of spent gunpowder, mixed with the smell of beer-soaked revelers, assaulted the courier's nose as he pushed his way toward the side door, hoping to find someone in an army uniform to assist him in his quest for the president. It was no use, however, and he entered the house through a forest of arms that patted him jubilantly on the back and congratulated him for his patriotic service. It was hot, even at that late hour, and Hope sweated under the short, tight, dark blue tunic crossed with rows of silver lace in the Hungarian style.

Once indoors, Hope tucked his black leather helmet with its silver faceplate in the crook of his left arm. The attached flowing white horsetail hung down the back of the helmet nearly to his knee and twisted in the rings of his sword belt. His wide-bladed, highly curved saber scabbard banged on the ground as it dragged behind, bumping along the floor. His thin, white duck, leather pantaloons were tucked into short, black riding boots trimmed in silver with sparkling bullion tassels attached to the front lip. His spurs occasionally scraped the floor or clicked against the bottom of his scabbard. He could've cradled the steel scabbard in the crook of his other arm, preventing it from tripping him, if he hadn't been burdened with the case containing the message. His right hand, encased in a white leather gauntlet, held the communiqué. He feared some drunk might wrench it free in the crush of the crowd.

Fortunately for the young officer, the president found him. A rather large gentleman—wishing to be remembered for his prodigious knowledge of feathers, "which came in numerous, textures, shapes, and sizes, and were of great commercial value and which should be supported by government interest"—had cornered the president, confining him against the fireplace in the blue salon. When he saw the dragoon wander by with a dispatch case in hand, Madison seized the opportunity to take his leave (much to his relief).

"Excuse me, Mister—," the president had forgotten the speaker's name in the evening's confusion. "I believe that messenger is looking for me." He stepped away brusquely and trailed Hope until he caught him at the door to the central hall.

Madison called out, "Sir," using a polite address, though knowing that as commander in chief, he clearly outranked the courier, who whirled immediately in the president's direction. The light from hundreds of candles shone on the bright plate on the front of Hope's helmet. The chief executive recognized the emblem—a running horse, with a rider leaning forward, at full gallop below a federal eagle—as the symbol of one of his elite corps.

"Is that for me?" he asked, hoping that the courier's business would steal him away to a quiet corner and beyond the reach of the melee. The celebration was getting to be too much for the introverted president.

"Yes, it is, sir. I've come from Philadelphia, where the captain of the cutter *Rover*, recently arrived from England, passed it on to me for delivery for your eyes only." Hope was running on, breathless in the presence of his leader, the head of state.

The president did not take it but beckoned for the cavalry officer to follow him up the staircase, which led from the central hall to the living quarters on the floor above. At the top of the marble stairs they passed a uniformed guard, who followed closely behind down the wide central hallway and into a private library. The room, though empty, was well lighted as a part of the festivities that night.

Lieutenant Hope stood at attention by the door as the president unfolded the contents of the letter on his large clean desk. The officer wondered if he would be dismissed or if there would be a reply. Madison, lost in the words, forgot he was not alone.

"Damn and blast, will they never stop interfering? Don't they have anything else to do but turn on us? Why can't they just accept the status quo? It's that blasted king—"

He looked up and saw the young officer's face. Madison paused before rereading the letter. In the brief lull the chief executive thought, *What of this generation of young Americans? Will they be up to the Armageddon that will surely come?*

The president waved his hand at the dragoon, who stood rigid. "Nothing more. Dismissed."

The officer was trained to inquire about a reply but stopped himself, thinking it would be best not to speak to his irate commander in chief. Hope saluted, pivoted about, and left the room, but not before carefully closing the tall solid door silently behind him.

Madison wasn't known for friendly repartee. He had a keen intellect and had finished the four-year course at New Jersey University in just two years. His small physique, frail health, and introverted personality didn't lend itself to manly banter and horseplay during youth. Now sixty-three and still only a hundred pounds, this son of a wealthy Virginia planter was, according to Washington Irving, "a small scrawny wizened man, who appeared old and worn." Nagging illnesses stalked him, yet it would be his two vice presidents, George Clinton and Elbridge Gerry, who would die in office.

It was his mind, not his body, that had been indispensable to the framers of the Constitution. He was a giant at the convention; its delegates welcomed his ideas and prose, which not only formed the fledgling nation's Constitution but also informed the Bill of Rights. Known also as "Jefferson's brain," he had convincingly argued for the Constitution's ratification. Madison shared Jefferson's hatred of anything English and pinned his hopes on Napoleon in the latter's struggle against the crowned heads of Europe.

A very serious gentleman of vision, he felt strongly about the federal government's role as distinguished from that of the states. No humanitarian, he wrote, "Charity is not part of the legislative duty of the government." He left that up to the states. Madison saw the presidential role as one of ensuring the protection of the country's sovereignty and its citizens' well-being. He said, "It's a universal truth that the loss of liberty at home is to be charged to the provisions against danger, real or pretended, from abroad." When he spoke of abroad, he meant Great Britain. So it shouldn't have been too surprising when, two years earlier, he had asked Congress to declare war on England in light of its aggression.

However, that Independence Day evening, he wished he had never ventured into war. The conflict had gone against Madison, even more so since Napoleon abdicated. Madison had no choice but to keep the dispatch secret. It was late, and he would sleep on it.

The Morning After

There was no point to rising early. Madison's ministers would be lying on steaming beds that humid Tuesday morning, the morning after a hard-drinking night in a stifling Washington summer. The Executive Mansion's high ceilings would protect him from the suffocating atmosphere that, by noon, was bound to creep in through the open windows and doors. The president would have time to assemble his thoughts before summoning his cabinet.

He called to his butler, a free black, for a cold repast to be served for lunch on the shady side of the veranda, where he hoped to welcome a quiet moment before the storm broke. Although the son of a Virginia slave owner, he wasn't opposed to blacks being free. Madison didn't see any dichotomy in his attitude. According to the wisdom of the age, the southern plantation was highly dependent on massive amounts of slave labor to be profitable. The abolition of slavery in the Western world—which, within a few decades, would roll like thunder across the national landscape—had yet to gain public support, even in England, that summer of 1814.

That morning, the president had copies of Gallatin's missive sent to each of his principal advisers. But before he joined the men in the first-floor cabinet room, tucked in the great house's southeastern corner, he informed Dolley of the looming threat. With husband and wife seated side by side on the silk-covered divan in their upstairs quarters, he spoke furtively, first recalling pleasant memories from their lives and then revealing how everything would soon change for the worst.

"My darling," he began, "I've a letter from Albert Gallatin from London. It's most distressing. Now I'm telling you this not as a prelude to asking you to alter your expensive ways, my dear, which you know I find charming—as does the entire city. But, as First Lady, you must be informed."

With that, he read aloud the message. He did so quickly, skimming over the verbiage and highlighting the salient points. Each word, each stray detail, filled her with the gravity of the days, weeks, and months ahead. She knew the problems of the past two years had been caused in large part by the shortages of men, morale, and munitions. She knew the nation was edging toward bankruptcy. She also had shared her husband's belief in the inevitable changes for good that Napoleon would bring to the world, overturning Great Britain's stale dominance and vindicating her husband's decision to go to war. But events had not gone as expected.

Dropping the letter and taking her hand, he said, "It means, my dear Dolley, that if we can't defend our cause in the field, then one day soon we could be prisoners of the redcoats."

In her mind she saw the newspaper drawing of Marie Antoinette riding in the cart toward her death, looking old and defeated. She shuddered.

"I'm afraid the old days are back, but this time we've no French ally to bail us out." There was no mistaking that the British blamed Madison and other American officials for their crucial role in pursuing a cowardly and opportunistic war. "If we lose this war and the British occupy the city, I'll surely be convicted of crimes against the mother country stretching back to the early days of the Revolution. The entire cabinet and I can expect to be confined in an English prison while our families will be left to the questionable mercy of the new government, which would most likely be run by returning American Loyalists. In short, my ignoring Washington's warning about foreign entanglement and venturing into this war may doom us after all."

Still shocked, Dolley responded in a soft awestruck tone: "My God, James, their fleet could sail right up to our back door." Panic began to creep into her voice. "What on earth can we do?"

"It's up to me and my advisers," he said, "to right this most grievous affair. I don't believe this situation to be irrevocable or the English government's mood to be as vindictive as Albert portrays. We'll need to provide instructions for our envoy at Ghent. The diplomatic front may yet save the day. All will be well; all will be well."

But Dolley was an intelligent woman, not at all the flibbertigibbet portrayed in the Federalist press, and she was able to assess the nation's dire predicament. Her exceptionally cheerful mood shifted to one of determination and service. Although not elected, she had duties to perform. Her example would be crucial to the public's perception and morale. Putting on her mistress-of-the-house face, she went about cautioning the household staff to ensure an ordered atmosphere and to exclude unnecessary guests from the premises. She retired to her upstairs sitting room and began preparing an evacuation plan for the household. For the time being, she wouldn't tell the staff or further question her already beleaguered husband. As First Lady (a title the newspapers had imposed on her), she felt responsible for the safety of the staff and the preservation of the young republic's demeanor.

As his wife went about her business, the president realized that he would be cloistered indoors all that scorching day and well into the sweltering evening. He went out to the veranda, where he paced, breathing in the thick heavy air that hung over the tidewater swamp. Madison sighed and begrudgingly returned to the steaming confines of the executive mansion. As a tobacco plantation owner, he might've been expected to smoke while he thought, but his delicate health restricted such habits and compelled those in close proximity to refrain as well. Most believed that smoking was natural to man and enabled them to "think in straight lines," which on this occasion would certainly be needed.

The butler prepared the chamber. Small dark-wood desks were brought in and placed in an oval in the center of the large room. Over the unlighted fireplace was the portrait of George Washington, a man every cabinet member had known personally; Madison himself had served under him during the Revolution. On this day, the president found it acutely difficult to stand in Washington's place. Alone, shaking his head, he began to mutter out loud, "What will history say of me, this dwarf disguised as a president?" He looked again at Washington's portrait and prayed, "Give me your guidance." This instance of reverent humility before America's preeminent Founding Father degenerated quickly into curses and censure for those who had led him so astray. "Those blasted war hawks stampeded me! My God, I never should've listened to them! Damn, how could God let this happen? America's faced with destruction! Under my watch, no less! This—this is—this is just a setback. Somewhere in this pernicious mess our salvation awaits discovery."

Madison, by no means a coward, though certainly panicked, pulled himself together with Jefferson's energetic arrival. The noisy cabinet followed soon after. They had been conferring together in a separate room in an effort to formulate a unified response. These men weren't of one mind in any matter—except where the English were involved. Only the political bond held them together.

"Mister President," Jefferson said, "if war's what they desire, we'll give it to them. By God we don't need the French this time! We'll greet them on the beach and toss them back into the sea from where they came."

Heads bobbed in agreement in those first moments of rash defiance. The president sat at his table hoping that, as the only man still standing, Jefferson would take his seat at the next desk. Before the room heated up any more, Madison wanted to get the issue outlined for discussion and an agenda agreed on. This was going to be a slog; there was no time to waste with speeches.

"Gentlemen, my esteemed colleagues, I thank you for coming so quickly. In the spirit of that promptness let me waste no further words. Now—to the issue at hand."

For the next month the secretaries were in denial. They dithered and diverted attention away from their departments, hoping that Gallatin was wrong and that it was all a ruse to get the American government to call off the war. Everyone, that is, except Secretary of State James Monroe.

The English Banker and the Irish Patriot

A special passenger had been on the *Rover*—Harold Scoff, the oldest son of Malacton Scoff, head of Scoff's Investment Bank, whose board was crammed with brothers, nephews, and cousins of the ancient banking family. They had married into the nobility at various times and boasted a marquis, a count, and two barons as members of the board. The bank itself dated from the Marshal family, knights of the Temple of Jerusalem.

Malacton Scoff wanted the true measure of this Irish banker he was entrusting with the money and his secret. Deeply embedded in London's pulse, he chose his son Harold to establish a liaison with Mathew Carey. This was one of the reasons the *Rover* had chosen to dock in Philadelphia rather than Baltimore: once on the high seas the captain had changed his ultimate destination to the port of Philadelphia to accommodate the banker, who was monetarily ungrateful.

Scoff, middle-aged and gaunt with a waxy complexion, also carried a letter from Gallatin. He wore a short beard to conceal a receding chin and a pale complexion pockmarked from a brush with smallpox that left him in delicate health. But his father insisted that he broaden his horizons and had assured him that his first sea voyage would "buck him up." Unsure of his sea legs, Scoff was reluctant to embark on the mission. All the shipwrecks for which the Lloyd's of London insurance exchange, where he represented the family interests, had to pay out didn't ensure confidence in transatlantic travel. Scoff was grateful that the sea voyage turned out to be relatively quick and uneventful. A born worrier, as soon as he disembarked, he began dreading the return voyage, especially since he would likely encounter the rough winter seas of the North Atlantic.

Normally, an officer of the bank's local branch would have met a man of Scoff's stature at the dock, but no one had been alerted to his arrival. Once on land, he thought it best to avoid a conspicuous public presence and traveled under the assumed name of Liam Corcoran. He didn't look Irish; his speech wasn't encumbered by an accent. Still, Scoff intended to pass himself off as an upper-class Irish landowner educated at Charterhouse. It wasn't uncommon for the landed Irish to set themselves apart from the "natives" through an education abroad. Besides, Corcoran was a prominent Irish surname. The Corcoran clan was known to produce numerous offspring, and he hoped to be easily lost in the crowd.

Scoff sent a note to Carey urgently requesting an appointment in a discreet location. The next day, a gentleman in a closed carriage called for him. They drove outside the broiling city to Valley Forge and the country house that General Benedict Arnold had used when he commanded the Philadelphia garrison in 1779. Set in the Pennsylvania Dutch farmland, the dwelling was the summertime residence of the Careys, who regularly fled the oppressive confines of the city in July and August. Mathew renamed the residence "Miranda" after his mother, whom he had been unable to visit since the British had expelled him from Ireland thirty years earlier. The British kept him from his homeland and his family, and it riled his Irish soul.

"It looks a great deal like Ireland around here, don't you think, Mister Corcoran? A bit like home to you, I expect."

Scoff, as Corcoran, agreed with his host's observation.

Once in the large dark-wood study, they prepared for refreshments brought in by servants. Scoff asked if they could be alone for discussions of a delicate matter. Carey was used to confidentiality concerning fiduciary matters and dismissed everybody else from the room. He poured some tea for himself and his guest.

"Sir, I beg your pardon, but I've presented false credentials. I'm not Mister Corcoran or even Irish. I'm Harold Scoff. You may have heard of my family's firm in London." Before Carey could acknowledge the revelation and accompanying apology, Scoff pressed on: "My father, with whom you've corresponded on many an occasion, has sent me with a very serious communiqué."

Bewildered, with a rising sense of betrayal settling in his gut, Carey accepted the creased papers. Rather than read the text, he looked first at the signature at the bottom of the last page. Carey was a close friend and admirer of Albert Gallatin and respected anything penned by the man. Yet, he wondered why Gallatin would have sent this envoy from an English bank when he was in Belgium remonstrating with the British over terms of a settlement.

Carey looked up at Scoff, whose eyes were fixed on the lengthy letter limp in the hands of his host. Sitting in the same room with an Englishman, particularly a prominent English banker, made the blood rise above Carey's collar and flush his fair Irish skin. He had absolutely no regard for anything British—except pounds, shillings, and pence. The use of the Corcoran name had indeed deceived him into believing that his visitor might be from the "United Irish," where Michael Corcoran of Sligo was well-known, and into opening his home to this interloper. Angry, he shuffled to his desk, sat down, and reassembled the pages. In an effort to be civil, he gestured to his guest to be seated in the leather chair near the window, where Scoff could catch the breeze. Now that Carey knew the man to be English, he refrained from offering further refreshment or comfort. It took some time for Carey to read and comprehend the shifting world the pages before him represented.

Carey soon realized that an accommodation had to be made to the Englishman and that he would have to make it if he hoped to save his adopted country. A prominent, monetarily endowed *English* banking conglomerate was offering the United States its only chance to save itself in this monumental crisis. Carey understood that the offer wasn't altruistic but merely an adjustment necessary to protect financial interests that transcended war and political wrinkles. The Parisian financial houses had helped defeat Napoleon by funding Wellington's battles in France that past spring, so there was, of course, a small yet decidedly satisfying irony in this matter. Carey pretended to reread the letter while actually contemplating the implications of the extraordinary offer.

Scoff studied the man at the desk who would soon be negotiating on behalf of American interests. Carey had an undeniably Irish look about him, in the London banker's view. He wasn't tall but rather sturdy and, despite his fifty-four years, powerful looking. The Irishman's shoulders were broad and beefy, unusual for a man who toiled in an office. He knew that Carey was not only a financier, but also a publisher who, in his youth, had worked the labor-intensive presses. Scoff had learned from a file (provided by his father) of published articles dating from the 1780s that Carey had a well-earned reputation as a political and financial rebel. Scoff thought he discerned a rebellious sparkle in those green eyes that popped up from time to time from the page and caught the light from the window.

"Well, Mister Scoff, the turn of events in Europe isn't the outcome we'd expected. We're in a trouble, I'm afraid. Mister Gallatin has spelled it out in the most compelling terms. As you clearly know, I'm no supporter of the British, a thorn in my side all of my working life. I truly thought I was rid of you all, but more of your 'lobster backs' are coming and *not* to dance with us."

Scoff, though this was business, winced at his host's anti-British tirade. *After all,* Scoff thought, *without the United Kingdom there would not be a United States.* But being here in a business capacity, he stilled his tongue.

Carey continued, "We'll resist, of course, but Gallatin's assessment of our ability to fight in the field is damnably correct. We must be honest with ourselves. We're severely deficient in the field and at sea and everywhere in between. And why? For a simple reason: we've run out of money and wars are fought with gold as much as they're fought with men. Your generous offer," Carey said and paused, suddenly and amazingly rendered speechless for a moment before uttering the words that threatened to choke him, "is our only hope."

Carey didn't need to discuss the particulars of America's plight with the English banker because the facts were obvious and compelling. The regular army numbered less than 20,000 of the 62,000 that Congress had authorized. The desertion rate in 1814 had increased dramatically to 13 percent. "Bounty-jumping"—that is, enlisting, taking the bonus, and then deserting to approach another recruiter to enlist once again under a different name—was rampant. Newspapers began running columns naming deserters to encourage the bounty hunters to earn the $50 reward for returning the culprit. Although desertion was a crime punishable by death, first offenders were sentenced to a term in the stockade. However, second offenses resulted in firing squads. By 1814 executions had risen to 146 from 3 in 1812. During the American Revolution, the militia contributed significantly to the field army, but by the time the minutemen's sons had replaced them in the current conflict, James Monroe conceded that it took three militia regiments to equal one regular. Perhaps the most compelling reason for desertion was the lack of compensation. It was common for a regular soldier to go more than six months to a year without pay when the treasury could not come up with the coin. An attempt to pay the militia with paper money led to more defection and the selling of the government claim to discounters. The apothecary general was unable to buy medical supplies and prisoners of war were ill fed because of the lack of ready cash.

Carey had experienced many tough moments in his turbulent life, but this one was nearly beyond his ability to manage. He had been spared from the hangman's rope in Dublin and had taken on the mission to build a brave new republic in North America. He could only hope God's hand rested on his shoulder for that great purpose. The United States was under assault once again from John Bull. The invasion had to be stopped and defeated, even if he had to go to the field himself. But an English banker, one of those money lenders from the very Temple of Jerusalem, where Christ threw them out on their ear, was in his parlor and tempting him with a treachery that he must not only accept but also become a member to in good standing.

Gathering his strength Carey shoved his meaty hands deep into slits of his front pockets. "I'm sure there'll be strings attached if we succeed in defending our land, that is, with your 'charitable' assistance," Carey said, lingering on the adjective "charitable," his voice tinged with irony. "What will the terms be—exactly?"

Scoff sensed the venom in his host's posture and the delivery of his carefully chosen words. He could see the former leader of the rebellious Irish hadn't lost his lethality with relocation to America. It lurked just barely beneath the surface. Carey didn't disguise the distrust in his voice, but Scoff's offer was the best and the only available accommodation. The world had turned upside down since the American Revolution, and now the British were trying to right it again. With Napoleon's defeat America stood alone. Certainly, the French, under the restored monarchy, were now in the enemy camp and Britain's European allies weren't willing to cross the Atlantic with help of any kind for the far-flung United States. This proposal wasn't a grant but a debt that, if the United States prevailed, it would have to repay. Yet, Gallatin had spelled out no terms; those were for Scoff to articulate.

Scoff's task was to clinch the deal on the best possible terms for his banking partners in crime. His instinct urged him to go for the jugular, but his reason told him to be careful of this already angry man and not to provoke him unduly.

"Sir, we're willing to buy, through the Irish National Bank connection with the Hamilton Bank, $10 million of the government securities you've been unable to sell." Scoff took a modicum of pleasure tossing the weakness of the country in the estimation of the international market in Carey's face. "Additionally, we'll provide your treasury with loan guarantees of $25 million, to be backed with land grant security for development of the Mississippi Valley and Louisiana Territory. We believe—that is, Mister Gallatin believes—that it's reasonable compensation when considering the risk we *Englishmen* are taking in opposing His Majesty's interests."

It's true, Carey thought. *The offer's a tremendous risk if the British government were to crack down on what's certainly a treasonable transaction.*

A practical man, Carey was aware that the crown was unlikely to intervene and might be willing to play it both ways, since a great deal of the banking community's wealth originated with the royal house coffers. No matter which way the conflict ended, the crown would surely profit. It was the way of the world.

Off to War—Again

From the *London Times*, August 1, 1814:
The time has come to give the treacherous Americans their due. In the past two years those "scoundrels of the marsh"—Washington, D.C.—have violated His Majesty's sovereign Canadian border with galling attacks and crimes. Like thieves in the night, they tried to knock down the back door while the wolf—*Napoleon*—was besieging the front gate. Sir George Prevost's gallant British, French, and native troops have thrown themselves up against the invaders like human barricades time and again. Now we will put a humiliating halt to Mister Madison's scurrilous ambitions. The taking of Canada this year or any other year is not a mere matter of marching, Mister Jefferson! The king has called upon our victorious army and navy to squash the interlopers like cuckoos in the nest. Royal regiments are preparing in London for their transit to the New World, which once more will become a jewel in our king's crown. British battalions in French ports are being loaded onto Royal Navy ships, destined for Canada and beyond, where they will end Yankee calumny on the deadly points of their shiny bayonets. Once there, they must make once again the lands of their peaceful brethren to the North safe for generations to come. Let us wish them God's speed and a safe swift voyage across the high seas. Our cavalry will sharpen their swords on the granite steps of America's new Capitol Building. Our eye is keen, our cause is just, and God is with us.

The bombastic palmistry of Fleet Street scribblers failed to impress the men who had to fight. The public didn't know the reality of war—only the romance of booming cannon salutes, glittering uniforms, massive parades, and martial music. The Duke of Wellington had stopped reading the London press years earlier, when they had printed every parliamentary popinjay's derisive diatribe concerning his conduct of the Peninsular War. Now he had been handed the familiar task of transporting an army of tens of thousands across the Atlantic. This time it wouldn't be to Iberia or India, but a perilous 3,500-mile sea voyage to a northern wilderness, where winter came early and often stayed late.

Wellington's mandate demanded a decisive victory before the snow flew. Furthermore, the army didn't exist as a cohesive force that summer but was spread out between the continent and the lands of the British Isles. Before he could grapple with the logistics of such a challenge, he needed a staff. The headquarters of the British army, known as Horse Guards, was back under the shaky command of the Duke of York and administered by a phalanx of army courtiers bereft of field service despite thirty years of conflict in India, America, and extended continental Europe.

This time, though, it would be different. The government, that is, the politicians in Parliament, had united behind the expedition—as had the crown. Beyond the army's sluggish red tape sat the triple-headed monolith known as the Board of Ordnance, the Naval Board, and the Royal Navy. These three venerable bodies were a world unto themselves. Yet, they too could be tamed with whip and chair and made to sit obediently if the prime minister could articulate the immediate threat as well as the expedition's benefits.

Finding the right men for the right jobs wasn't as hard as it had been in the past. Wellington's position, secure in British history, his reputation as a winner, and the state's strong sponsorship meant he would attract a multitude of office seekers. In the past Horse Guards had ignored his requests from the field. Weeks would pass as communiqués were exchanged to no avail. Now, face to face in London, the temper of the Iron Duke wasn't to be trifled with. He would require a military secretary (in continental terms, a chief of staff) to conduct the daily business of his field headquarters. While Napoleon had established a large well-oiled, functionally organized staff under the genius of Marshal Berthier, which was quickly copied by opponents, Wellington had resisted. The duke recognized the difference between his conduct of war and that of Napoleon. While the emperor had deployed armies as large as half a million, Wellington didn't have that luxury. Within the confines of the Iberian Peninsula he had never commanded more than 40,000 British troops. Even when the contingents of Portuguese and Spanish troops were added, the sum never came close to 100,000. When confronted by a large French corps in 1810, Wellington went on the defensive at Torres Vedras, Portugal, multiplying the effect of his forces through the wise use of terrain. With such a compact collection of infantry, cavalry, and artillery, he preferred to keep them under personal scrutiny and control.

In North America he planned to tailor his force to the terrain and the composition of the American army. The first step was to establish the military secretariat. Wellington was a creature of habit and not fond of change. Therefore, he turned naturally to Major General Lord Fitzroy James Somerset to head the staff and cobble together the same team that had served him so well in Iberia. The son of the Duke of Beaufort and nineteen years younger than Wellington, Somerset accompanied his superior to Portugal in 1808 and remained throughout the war, rising from major to major general over the course of the campaign. Rather tall and gaunt with a thin nose and hollow cheeks, he was the picture of an aristocrat. Owing to his impeccable breeding, he occupied an unassailable position in society, fearing no man, yet officers found him highly approachable and rather a figure of fun who took the edge off the sparse mess. Wellington said of him, "He could read men's souls just by looking into their eyes." Unlike his French counterparts, who were famous for large expensive throngs of needy staff officers, Somerset's talent for headquarters business reduced the numbers to a manageable few and kept the staff nimble.

"Ordinary officers need not apply" was the implied message on the board of the ground floor of Apsley House. Perhaps it ought to have read "common" rather than "ordinary." Wellington preferred the company of people with a background similar to his own. Despite this elitism the duke certainly appreciated commoners as leaders of his formations. It was just that, within the confines of his mess, a strong connection to a title was expected. However, such aristocratic lineage wasn't a license for poor performance. His staff members would have to be well connected but also highly competent—a difficult combination to find at the time, since there were few academies qualified to teach military science. Yet, Wellington's many years spent with military men in India and Spain produced a list of candidates that his military secretary knew well.

Next in importance was the position of quartermaster general, the key to a functioning army. The department coordinated logistical support with field operations. It translated the commander's orders into written instructions and delivered them promptly to all subordinate elements before, during, and after battles. Wellington's old friend George Murray was too ill to endure the transatlantic voyage and the wet woods of North America, so he had to find a new candidate.

A young man, just under six feet, dressed in a smart dark suit, was sitting in the ground-floor hall of Apsley House. He was decidedly handsome with thick, dark brown wavy hair that resisted control but spoke of virility. His blue eyes matched the color of his cravat, which was tied tightly around a strong neck that rose from the stiff white collar. Called forward, he passed the sentry at the foot of the winding, sand-colored marble staircase at the mansion's east end and climbed one flight.

"He isn't expecting you today," Somerset said on seeing the young officer. "I told him of your honeymoon plans for the Highlands. He'll be most gratified to see you. Come. I warned him before he sent the offer that it was impossible for you to accept the quartermaster billet because of your recent marriage. My concern made no impression, though. But then you know him much better than anyone!"

Somerset led his companion while jabbering at him over his shoulder. These three soldiers had fought side by side for eight years in Spain, but Colonel Sir William Howe Delancey, the former assistant quartermaster general, had stronger ties to the duke than Somerset had. He and Major General Arthur Wellesley had campaigned in India in the 1790s. Like so many aristocrats, Delancey was an offspring of Huguenots and Irish landlords. His ancestor, Etienne of Caen, was born in 1663 and came to England in 1685 to escape persecution. Later, his son received the family jewels and went to America, where he grew the investment into a fortune. He married into the influential Dutch patron family of Van Cortlandt. On the other side of the Atlantic, his ancestor was the Vicomte de Laval, Guy de Lancy. The De Lanceys formed a regiment in the British colonial army and fought at Ticonderoga, New York, in 1758. Both sides of the family supported King George during the American Revolution. His father, Oliver De Lancey, was the colonel of the DeLancey regiment when his son William was born in 1781 on Staten Island. After the Americans defeated the British, the Delanceys—changing the spelling of their name—escaped, like so many Loyalists, to England, where their young son was educated. Once in England, Oliver Delancey became a prominent owner of sheep farms and woolen mills in the Yorkshire Dales. William's aunt married General David "Old Pivot" Dundas KB, who offered the patronage needed for the sixteen-year-old boy to become a soldier like his father.

As a lieutenant of the 45th Infantry Regiment of Nottinghamshire, he served in India and came to Wellesley's notice. Wellesley mentioned the lieutenant in dispatches; such attentive praise was most unusual for a young officer to generate. Elevated to the general's personal staff as a liaison and later an aide-de-camp, Delancey remained healthy for the entire campaign and returned with Wellesley to England. When Wellington was campaigning in Spain, he seconded Delancey's promotion to assistant quartermaster general. In that capacity he performed with remarkable distinction, even though he was twelve years younger than Wellington. At the close of the Napoleonic Wars, the duke sponsored his elevation to the Order of the Bath.

That same summer his sister Susan married Sir Hudson Lowe, a fellow aide to the duke. At the wedding Delancey met his bride-to-be, Lady Magdalene, ten years his junior, the comely daughter of Sir James Hall of Dunglass, Scotland. Hudson Lowe had earlier described her to his family as an English Rose: "She's willowy in limb and most slight of body, but nearly as tall as her husband. Her hair has a remarkable red tint to the rich chestnut color. Large, very large green eyes, with flecks of amber, rest very gently upon you. She has a wide mouth with strong teeth that seem to flash a perpetual smile."

Her father had been rowed out to the skiff to interrupt the couple's brief time together sailing on the highland lake at Inverness. While Magdalene did not understand the haste of her husband's departure, she accepted the fact that her handsome accomplished husband served the great duke and had to go when summoned. She never expected that he wouldn't return for the rest of that year of 1814.

In the chamber at the top of the stairs the two men paused. Fitzroy handed Delancey a copy of a letter that the duke had sent to General Dundas at Horse Guards the previous week. It was the response to a list of officer appointments for the campaign. It read,

> To tell you the truth, I'm not very well pleased with the manner in which the Horse Guards have conducted themselves toward me. It will be admitted that the army's not a very good one, and, being composed as it is, I might have expected that the generals and staff formed by me in the last war would've been allowed to serve under me again, but instead of that, I'm overloaded with people I've never seen before, and it appears to be purposely intended to keep those out of my way whom I wish to welcome. However, I'll do the best I can with the flawed, paltry instruments that Horse Guards has so thoughtfully sent to assist me.

Delancey was amused by, as a postscript, one of his leader's never-ending chides directed at the army headquarters: "Are we once more to be burdened with witless direction from Horse Guards?"

Handing the note back to Somerset, he said, "Some things never change." He was referring to the endless battles fought not with the French but with much more intransigent foes—bureaucracy, nepotism, and mediocrity.

They were conversing in the house's grand front reception room, which was dominated by a massive white marble statue of Emperor Napoleon, its top nearly touching the arched ceiling. Meant as an allegory, the statue, totally nude excepting a laurel on Napoleon's brow, was holding the Roman staff of state.

Somerset, who had to eye it everyday, commented, "Hideous, isn't it? A gift from the czar, taken—or should I say stolen—from Les Invalides in Paris. It was originally meant to adorn the way to the emperor's tomb in the center of the church. This is the only room that'll accommodate the monstrosity. We had to haul it in through the window via an artillery siege derrick." He gestured toward one of the glass double-door French windows lining the house's entire first floor. "They had to remove the stone railing to squeeze it through."

Delancey was surprised that it not only dominated but also destroyed the salon's yellow decor. "My God, that's an exaggeration of the first order," he said, referring to the extremely generous detail (which wasn't concealed by a fig leaf). "What does the chief have to say about it?"

As the commander in chief of the expedition, Wellington commanded the entire North American theater of war; the position placed all but the Royal Navy under his command. But since the commander in chief reported directly to the king, naval collaboration was implicit (though many doubted that Wellington would achieve cooperation without a fight).

Inclining his head toward the closed door to Wellington's office, Fitzroy replied, "His Grace ignores the statue for the most part—except when a notable's caught staring at it. Then the duke regards it as a great joke. Yet, not wanting to offend the czar, he insisted we put it here. The duchess refrains from entering this room, which keeps her off this floor entirely—to His Grace's delight. What a display of strategy, eh?"

Well aware of the duke's lack of interest in his wife, Delancey smiled slightly before delicately inquiring, "So nothing's changed since he took up permanent residence with the duchess?"

"Well, there's no longer a need for her to send carping letters. At least for now. I've come to believe that he's accepted this assignment in North America to free him till the expected continental campaign next year. He spends as little time as possible here at *home*."

Delancey would have pursued the topic further, but an aide interrupted to summon the pair to follow. When the two senior officers reported to the duke, he was busy computing the strength of units proposed by Horse Guards and ticking off the names of their commanders to himself: "Barnes, Selkiek, Romney . . ."

Looking up, Wellington waved his left hand, indicating that they relax their military pose. "Sir William, I need your talent once again."

The duke lingered intentionally on "sir" in a subtle effort to remind Delancey of the knighthood that the duke had secured (though he hadn't been present at the dubbing by the Regent). It was hardly politic for Delancey to decline the duke's request that he accompany the expedition—especially after such a significant honor.

Delancey, bowing slightly to the figure in the plain coat seated behind the desk, replied, "Sir, Lady Delancey and I are most grateful for your gracious patronage." He paused, expecting the duke to inquire as to the health and perhaps happiness of his bride, but such queries weren't forthcoming. The field marshal wasn't known for exchanging pleasantries or engaging in small talk. In Spain, the evening meal had often been cut short if the table talk sank into gossip rather than business.

"Have you come to accept my summons to North America? This will be a quick show, home by All Saints', maybe—certainly no later than the Epiphany, before the North Atlantic kicks up. The main event will come in the spring—mark my words—when the unholy alliance makes mischief on the Rhine. This expedition's going to be merely a matinee performance."

The prospect of a six-month jaunt appealed to Delancey. How could he refuse a promotion to quartermaster general in light of his recent knighthood and a plea for assistance from the man who was a hero to him and the nation? At age thirty-three, Delancey viewed the offer of quartermaster general for what it was—a golden opportunity.

"Sir, I've come at your gracious request to honor your concrete expression of confidence in me with my gratitude and acceptance." He felt Wellington sigh in relief, which was an even greater compliment than the proffered position, for it meant he had been the field marshal's first choice.

———

Wellington believed that while soldiers fought the enemy, the staff provided the battle's direction. The duke brought his immense experience, talent, intellect, and, above all, judgment to the venture. An able cohesive staff wouldn't lose sight of his intentions during the execution of his instructions and orders. He gave considerable thought to the officers' selection and expected those chosen to accept graciously. He knew his stature and the power he possessed. To turn him down was most unwise; His Grace never forgot an insult, rejection, or betrayal.

But Horse Guards wasn't finished with Wellington. The following morning, the military secretary noted with exasperation that Major General Sir William Stewart, Wellington's adjutant general in Spain, was settling into the room next to Delancey's, in the space reserved for the new adjutant general. Since returning from Spain, Stewart had recovered from the ague that had plagued him during the final year of the Iberian Campaign. But Wellington, not a fan, had hoped that Stewart's ill health would continue to render him unfit for service.

"Morning, General Stewart. I'm surprised to see you. Have you an appointment with His Grace?"

General Stewart waved him off. "Here's a jolly note from Horse Guards. I thought I'd bring it over myself, save some time, and so forth."

Somerset accepted the paper Stewart thrust under his nose. He was well acquainted with this unannounced visitor, half-brother of Foreign Minister Castlereagh. The opposite of his half-brother, the general had been described by contemporaries as a "sad *brouillon* [bungler] and mischief maker, whose petty intrigues turned many officers against Wellington's conduct of the war." The duke had redressed Stewart in front of others for his varied transgressions but kept him on because he was exceedingly competent at his job and even ordinary competence was always difficult to come by.

"Sir, Horse Guards has intervened once again," Somerset said, attempting to soften the blow as he handed the letter of appointment to the duke, who was seated at a small corner table in the gallery. From his spot overlooking Rotten Row, Wellington amused himself by watching the pageantry and mischief as the military and civilians, male and female, exercised their horses in Hyde Park—a well-known meeting place for sparking sexual adventures. Wiping his hands on the large serviette tucked into his collar he took notice gingerly.

"Those bastards! *Ah*, well, we must get on with it, mustn't we?"

The military secretary thought the expletive must have been for his own benefit, but he was sharp and realized that the duke's theatrical outburst was far from spontaneous. Wellington had been forewarned of the assignment, probably by Castlereagh. Also the duke knew that General Stewart would be more of a problem for his staff than for himself. The adjutant general would be a spy for the duke's political opposition, reporting any perceived misstep taken by Wellington, but better a devil he knew than one he did not. The duke was secure with himself and with his position within the government arena.

"Let him do his harm," Wellington thought aloud. "I didn't seek this honor."

Aides-de-camp

The quartermaster department was authorized to appoint two personal servants (batman and groom), an officer aide, two field officer assistants, one company officer deputy assistant, five sergeants, and nine clerks. When they arrived, Delancey hurried to put in place the process that would ensure the timely appearance of equipment and provisions at Montreal. Somerset soon moved the quartermaster office out of the mansion and into the space provided at the Duke of York's headquarters, where the work of fielding the force was to take place.

Aides-de-camp filled many roles and varied in age, grade, and experience, but generally they worked as special assistants to the commander in chief. Some were young riders who could remain in the saddle day and night to relay a crucial message. Others, who were more senior, interacted with unit commanders to convey the duke's personal instructions. It was not uncommon for a senior aide to take command of a unit in an emergency. Some were observers—either reporting conditions or reconnoitering the enemy. Still others were old comrades expected to provide good company and perhaps advice.

The commander of the expedition was authorized nine aides-de-camp. All aides were under the military secretary's direct supervision. Somerset undertook the task of vetting each before offering the names to Wellington. The prospective list contained the usual suspects. They were called, one by one, from nearby gentlemen's clubs, officers' billets, and local residences. The younger, more vigorous officers waited at the snooker tables, long bars, and smoking lounges. It was an age of patronage. Civil and military positions were offered to friends, sons of friends, relatives, kin of creditors, schoolmates, and associates of pretty women (in the Duke of York's case). Patrons bent Somerset's ear at parties while endless notes and reminders of past favors were hand delivered. The proposed list was set as follows:

Major General Torrens, an old campaigner and Somerset's close friend

Major General Galbraith Lowry Cole, a onetime suitor for the duke's wife (Wellington often wished Cole's wooing had been more successful than his)

Major Sir Hudson Lowe, a loyal comrade from the Peninsular War

Lord March, the young son of the Duke of Richmond, Wellington's great personal friend

Captain Ulysses Burgh, later Lord Downes, a staff member

Major Lord Aylmer, former member of the quartermaster staff

Major Colquhoun "Colley" Grant, Wellington's most trusted spy and intelligence officer

Count Miguel Ricardo Alava (known for his flamboyant uniforms and plumes), former commander of the Spanish army, on board the Spanish fleet at Trafalgar, and shot in the rump at Orthez, which amused Wellington, his great friend and confidant

There would be others to come, including perhaps, on the king's insistence, a member of the royal family. For now, however, this list was enough to get things under way.

A Rather Unpleasant Fellow

Horse Guards selected the general officers, who were rarely to Wellington's liking. He preferred men with known track records who had served under him previously. Both Parliament and General Dundas had bills to pay and would ignore the list that Somerset submitted. It became an exercise in pulling and hauling. Horse Guards would insist and Wellington would threaten to resign. And so it went.

Reluctantly, Somerset granted a personal interview with newly promoted Major General Frederick Robinson, who came from a very distinguished family of American Loyalists. His father was Beverley Robinson, formerly a colonel on the British staff in New York City during the American Revolution. As spymaster to General Henry Clinton, he had masterminded Major General Benedict Arnold's defection and, in the process, sacrificed British major John André to the hangman. Robinson had served in the Loyal American Regiment, a British militia unit, in New York when he was only fifteen. He was captured in 1781 and spent six months in an American prisoner of war camp at Lancaster, Pennsylvania. Benedict Arnold had occupied the Robinsons' home, Van Cortlandt Manor, across from West Point when he defected to the British. Young Frederick, like Delancey, had been educated in England and Europe prior to becoming a soldier. Through patronage and wealth Robinson had purchased his way to the colonelcy of the 32nd Infantry Regiment. Although he was successful in command, only his family connections had assured Horse Guards naming him an independent commander of an expedition along the eastern coast of Spain. Wellington took exception to Robinson's appointment as a brigadier general. Normally, a positional rank was dropped once the job was concluded. However, Robinson ignored the convention and continued to wear the insignia of a brigadier, not an uncommon occurrence by any means but one that Wellington roundly disapproved. As the war continued, Robinson proved eminently capable of taking responsibility and achieved success on several occasions before the war ended. Parliament had championed Robinson's candidacy for promotion. By the end of the Iberian Campaign, the duke gave him his due and approved his elevation to permanent major general.

Frederick Robinson was a driven man. His imprisonment and treatment at the hands of the American rebels as well as the loss of his family home and extensive property in the New World had seared his soul. Disliked by his contemporaries, whom he was known to tread on at every opportunity, he had no real friends outside the Robinson clan. His younger brother, William Henry Robinson, was the equivalent of a brigadier general in the commissariat and en route to Canada at that moment. The two brothers were quite different. While William was a bookworm and bean counter like his father, Frederick was the proverbial man of action. Robinson never hesitated to use whatever leverage he could find to secure advancement. This wasn't lost on his fellow officers, who kept their distance and took every opportunity to denounce him in influential circles. Unmarried, Frederick devoted himself to his career. From a distance, he was handsome, above average height, and slim from years of missing meals on the road to war. The closer the encounter, the more apparent the sun damage to his face became. His countenance was red with deep lines that looked like sword cuts on his cheeks. At forty-nine, he easily passed for ten years older than his actual age. He was balding with a nasty fringe of gray hair sticking out like bristles on a brush from under his high flat hat. His uniform wasn't designed and sewn by the best of Saville Row tailors, for he was as parsimonious with his money as he was with his affection for his fellow man. Yet, on the battlefield this lion of a man was well worth his salt.

When he strolled into Somerset's office on the ground floor of the mansion, his heavy sword banged against the door jam, announcing his presence. The ceremonial weapon had recently been bestowed on him at a dinner given in his honor by the city of London. As a rule, such weapons were left for ceremonies or hung on a wall, but he wore it everywhere. The piece was in the style of the light cavalry with a very wide, severely curved blade, which was blued and gilded in a scene from a battle in Spain. The scabbard was of highly burnished copper, which caught the light as a rich red-gold hue. The quillon had the face of Hercules for courage, and a serpent denoting wisdom wrapped itself around the single-bar knuckle guard. The gold pommel depicted the head of the British lion.

Startled at the intrusion, the military secretary maintained his composure and remained seated. As a rule, Somerset would stand and cross the room to greet a fellow comrade in arms from the Spanish Campaign, but he refrained from custom with *this* fellow. Robinson liked it that way; he gave a salute instead of offering his hand.

"Ah, General, right on time I see. Come with me."

Robinson followed the secretary to the bottom of the staircase, which Delancey had used earlier. There they paused, and the military secretary directed him to a stiff high-backed wooden chair next to the red-coated sentry.

Somerset didn't offer pleasantries. "Just a moment. I'll see if His Grace is available."

He left the unpleasant man seated uncomfortably. It was best to remind the visiting general that he was at the military secretary's beck and call and, even more important, to stress this point early in the relationship. Wanting to conclude the interview quickly, Somerset returned within ten minutes. He already knew the outcome before Robinson reached the first floor. From midway up the stairs he called out to the major general, "His Grace will see you now, General. Come up."

Somerset entered the chamber with Robinson slightly behind him. The duke was seated at his ornately carved and gilded French desk, a prize taken from Malmaison, Napoleon's home with Josephine. Once Robinson was standing before the duke, the military secretary left the two soldiers alone to make peace—or war.

Looking up from a list of units that had already embarked from Ireland for Canada earlier that month, Wellington spoke first: "What is it . . . you . . . want, General?" The lack of warmth in his voice would have been evident to a deaf man.

Robinson favored the direct approach, a throwback to their professional relationship in Spain. "I'm here to solicit your acceptance of Horse Guards' appointment." Earlier in the week, his name had appeared on a list of proposed brigade commanders for the expedition.

Dryly, Wellington replied, "What makes you think I've any influence over appointments originating from those fine fellows at the Duke of York's? Like you, I'm just a servant of His Majesty."

Robinson ignored Wellington's remark. "I've come to make peace with you, sir. I don't desire to serve in a command capacity under a hostile field superior. I'd like you to recognize me as a fighter rather than a courtier."

The duke knew that the man standing before him shared a temperament similar to his own. Neither man was well liked; neither gave a damn. Wellington never considered popularity an asset. While he felt no affinity for his visitor, he didn't condemn him merely for his gruff manner or his overpowering desire for recognition. Initially in Spain, he kept

Robinson at arm's length, hoping he would betray his backers among Wellington's opposition in London and fall on his sword. He could then be sent packing. However, Robinson proved to be an effective commander who cared for his troops and made every effort to preserve his scant force from unnecessary and costly risk. Robinson was not compassionate, but he was practical. He had been successful no matter what the mission or condition of the enemy. He was not a griper and didn't tell tales in his correspondence home to Whitehall. In short, the duke had already approved the appointment. He was entertaining himself by making Robinson sweat inside his new major general's coat, hoping that the cheap red dye would run.

When the duke gave him the chance to speak, Robinson launched into the usual rant concerning his harrowing early life in America and ended the narrative by saying, "I assume you'll follow the old American road to war that ends on my father's land. I'll do all in my power to make that possible. I hope and pray that God will allow me to restore my family's land that was stolen away in my youth."

So there it was. He wanted to make certain that Van Cortlandt Manor, some fifty miles west of New York City on the Hudson River, wouldn't pass to anyone but the Robinsons. While Wellington had never met Frederick's father, the duke was aware of old Beverley Robinson's service to England and loyalty to the king and, therefore, approved of his motive. The duke held great estates himself, in Ireland and England, and while the Robinsons weren't of the nobility, they were certainly gentry.

"As do I, General," Wellington said, "as do I."

One Man's Traitor Is Another Man's Hero

Somerset's next appointment would take London and later America by storm. A young man, with good looks that favored his mother, passed through Apsley House's heavy double doors. Dressed in a smart dark civilian suit, cut to fashion, he wasn't yet thirty but walked with a limp that betrayed his profession. He should have carried a cane, but he didn't want to suggest that he wasn't up to the task. He gave his tall hat to the liveried servant and took a seat on the bench against the far wall. The bench was already occupied by two other older men, both in the dark blue uniform of a light dragoon regiment. They moved over quickly, recognizing both his countenance and infirmity. Robinson, on his way out, recognized him with a slight bow before leaving the building.

Coming down the stairs behind Robinson, Somerset didn't bother to bid good-bye to the major general when he recognized the new arrival. "General," he said, "His Grace has been anticipating your visit. Shall we go straight up?"

It didn't bother the two other bench sitters that they had just been passed over. From images printed in the newspapers they too recognized the son of the famous American traitor and English hero, Benedict Arnold.

Brigadier General Benedict Arnold Jr. was the first son of Major General Benedict Arnold, late of the Continental Army, who had defected in 1780 to the British. His mother,

Peggy Shippen, was a Loyalist and close friend of Theodosia Prevost Burr. Theodosia's house had been Peggy's refuge until she reunited with her husband in England after the signing of the Treaty of Paris. Arnold, perhaps the Continental army's greatest fighter, grew disaffected by the Continental Congress's carping. Not only had its members refused to pay him in seven years, but they also attempted to court-martial him for irregularities in the handling of funds during the Canadian Campaign in 1775.

Believing that the American rebels would ultimately lose the Revolutionary War, Arnold attempted to endear himself once again to his mother country by betraying the fortifications on the Hudson River at West Point. He sought command of the strategic force, which was crucial to the district's protection. In the process, he betrayed his great friend and supporter General Washington. By denuding the area of defenders, he planned to permit British general Clinton to seize the choke point on the river and cut industrial New England off from the agrarian southern states to win the war. However, the capture of his British contact, Major André, tipped off the Continentals, and Arnold fled to New York City. There, he accepted a commission as a brigadier general in the British army and raised an infantry brigade of Loyalist deserters, who, like himself, fought until war's end against his former comrades. Once back in England, General Arnold and Peggy became courtiers to the royal family and raised a family of three boys.

Somerset nudged the rather modest Arnold into the chamber. The son, named for his father, now stood before Wellington at the request of the Prince Regent. The field marshal had no misgivings about this appointment. The young general had proved himself worthy of the rank in the campaign of Walcheren Island in Holland in 1809, where, as a brigade major, he had led from the front and been wounded in the hip (as his father had been at Saratoga). Once recovered, nearly two years later, he had been a colonel commanding the 2nd Foot, the Queen's Own, at Vitoria in Spain. During the final years of the Napoleonic Wars, he was invalided out and recovered from fever at home with his mother, while his errant father, a broken man, wandered through Canada.

Wellington's mood reversed as the young man entered his office, and he exuded charm. He rose and came to greet Arnold. "How's your dear mother? I haven't seen her for months. We had a delightful time at Lady Anne Bernard's dinner party, but I was worried that your mother looked a little . . . fragile."

"I must admit my mother always looks somewhat vulnerable. It's a part of her great charm, don't you know."

A brief smile crossed both men's lips as the general and the duke recalled the lovely lady who had helped entice the mighty General Arnold in Philadelphia into switching allegiances. Wellington didn't speak of the father, though he thought of him as a reincarnation of General Monk of the English Civil War, who changed sides at a critical moment and, as a betrayer, succeeded in bringing the country back to royal rule.

"I'm particularly happy to welcome you to join me on this noble quest to restore to the king that which is rightfully his."

Arnold bowed deferentially and followed the motion with a crisp salute.

As Wellington received this formal courtesy, he couldn't help but think, *A newlywed, an American Loyalist, and a traitor's son—we're gathering an odd lot, but skilled at war, thank Heaven. Let's hope the Americans are gathering men less odd—and less skilled.*

This was war, after all, and Wellington intended to win it.

CHAPTER 6

Bureaucracy and the British War Machine

"It may be considered as one of those misfortunes incidental to warfare which human prudence can neither foresee nor prevent."
—GENERAL KARL VON CLAUSEWITZ

Delancey on the Move

While the appointments, patronage, and political pulling and hauling dominated the duke prior to his embarking for Canada, the real work of transporting an army across the wide Atlantic fell to Colonel Sir William Howe Delancey. In the first days of July, Delancey took over spaces in the Duke of York's headquarters and cobbled together a small staff of cronies from the previous campaign. Once the campaign began, they'd be the nucleus of a much larger effort; however, there were tasks that required the quartermaster general's personal attention.

No longer just a military aide-de-camp, special assistant, or old and valued friend of the high and mighty, Colonel Delancey had risen to a position of high individual responsibility. His glittering marriage, performed during the triumphant days following the French defeat, captured the public's interest as an embodiment of the happy ending they sought in the Napoleonic Wars. Nearly every household, high and low, suffered a loss on some distant land or sea. Drawings of Lady Magdalene and Sir William appeared in newspapers and were sold in tobacco shops along with the young beauties and notables of London society. His knighthood had also brought him into closer, more equitable contact with the nobility. If he desired, he could spend every evening at the supper table in a great London house. While his fame whirled about Delancey's head, the responsibilities of office weighed him down. He sought advice from the wise and experienced Somerset, who filled his days not with puffery but with appointments.

"Sir William, you're an unknown quantity. There are those who envy your success and strive to spread pernicious rumors concerning your character and connections. This is a dangerous city for the unwary. The only way to establish credibility is by visiting the halls of power regularly. You must confer with agencies and agents that know about the rigors of waging war. Request assistance from the influential. Introduce yourself as a deputy of His Grace. Be specific but not demanding. The work you accomplish before our expedition will later pay off exponentially in the wilderness."

The young quartermaster general had received his first lesson straight from the shoulder. Soon it would be solely up to him to make his reputation.

———

A major subset of the fighting Royal Navy was its Naval Board, which was responsible for moving men, animals, equipment, and supplies by sea. The board was a formidable organization that predated the British army's formation. Therefore, as the junior, the army approached, hat in hand, the mighty sea lords for their approbation. So it was on this day a cab was arranged to carry Delancey to the Naval Board.

Within London's confines, it was impractical to use a personal mount unless there was a stable nearby to maintain the animal. With the stabling came the need for a groom, who had to be not only paid but also housed and fed. While commercial livery stables abounded down every alley, they were an expense for which the newly promoted colonel wasn't prepared to pay. It could be just a matter of days before he departed for a port city and the great adventure beckoning beyond. Besides, Horse Guards subscribed to a cab service for officers on official business. The forerunner to the London taxi was a single-axle cabriolet carriage made of black-lacquered wood and able to accommodate just two passengers. Its crowning feature, particularly on this wet windy day, was the enclosed sides and top. The driver sat high on a seat, which was attached to the back wall and, unfortunately for him, open to the rain. A single horse of nondescript lineage dragged the vehicle through the maze of traffic at something less than the walking pace of a fit pedestrian; at midday the narrow streets were congested with all representations of wagons, carriages, and pushcarts, each demanding forward progress.

Delancey wouldn't be alone when he negotiated with the Naval Board commissioners. Accompanying him was his trusted aide, newly promoted Captain Basil Rymer, who owed his Royal Staff Corps appointment to Wellington. The corps, numbering fewer than a hundred, was very select. Bestowed directly by the king, the assignation was a significant event in a young officer's career. As a junior member of Wellington's mess in Spain, Rymer had not only amused but also impressed his leader with his professional approach to campaigning—a trait most others lacked.

Snared every few yards by an appointment seeker, Delancey negotiated the long complicated passage of the musty gloomy headquarters. The colonel longed for the coming campaign, which would free him from the confines of corridors and the crush of the crowds. Emerging from the rear of the ground floor, he found Rymer waiting with the cab at the edge of the sodden pavement.

"The cabby tells me the traffic's at its peak, sir," the aide reported.

Delancey cringed inwardly at the news, which he had expected but nonetheless dreaded. The dark blowing sky had produced its promise of rain, which sent the public rushing in a rude desperate search for any covered conveyance. The pavement was thick with opened black umbrellas that twisted in the wind. Hands held hats in place and soaked woolen capes covered pedestrians' slumped shoulders.

The colonel climbed into the cab under the protection of his aide's "brolly." The captain jumped in beside him and swung the black wooden knee protector in place, which warded off the damp and any debris kicked up by the draft horse. A comfortable, dry, black-padded button-leather seat welcomed the passengers. Rymer rapped on the lid above, a signal to the driver to open a small hinged hatch.

"Naval Board, quick as you can, driver."

The driver snorted derisively at the plea for haste.

The carriage crossed the Horse Guards' parade ground and swung out into the Mall's stagnant traffic. The black cab slowly and painfully negotiated its way toward Admiralty Arch. Numerous homes and structures had been razed on the other side of the arch, where work was progressing on the memorial to Lord Nelson. The Prince Regent proclaimed the space Trafalgar Square to honor the great naval victory in 1805. The demolition had changed the shape of one end of Whitehall. There, a statue of Nelson, atop a column, would look past the Admiralty and Horse Guards toward Westminster Palace. Along Whitehall's roadway the tops of street lamps would be adorned with model warships. It was a noble undertaking but "a damn nuisance" that wet morning, as Delancey muttered more than once during the seemingly endless ride. Single-file traffic from the confluence of seven major arteries nearly ground to a halt. Wagons filled with white marble blocks were jammed front to back in a line reaching down to the barges on the nearby Thames. Flimsy wooden derricks, which warped under the weight and strained the frayed hemp ropes, unloaded the slabs for the square. The wagons only added to the stalled fray.

Delancey outlined the tribulations to come as a diversion from the frustration of waiting. "Today we entreat the Naval Board for merchant ships to transport the soldiers, horses, cannons, powder, ball, food, and supplies. The venerable board's under the eye of the Admiralty, which, by the way, doesn't care for the Naval Board any more than the army does. They're a law unto themselves. A friend, a contractor to the army, said something last summer that illustrates my point: 'The Naval Board's hours of business are spent discussing difficulties of little consequence until the pressing occasion forced them to order things, not as they should, but as they could be done.' I'm telling you this, Basil, because I learned the hard way. In Spain I fought many difficult, embarrassed bouts that could've been avoided if I'd not been so ignorant. The local Naval Board agent was key to getting supplies landed, cataloged, and on their way to our elements and allies. That, however, doesn't mean that we should abandon our efforts today to impress upon the Naval Board's members our specific unique needs that only they can provide. But, I caution you," he said, looking his junior in the eye, "anything that can be done properly here will benefit us immensely once we're in Canada."

Captain Rymer, though new to his duties as a staff officer, understood the importance of the appointment that lay just ahead on Fleet Street. The meeting would be his baptism. Previously, he had been a minor aide, detached from his dragoon regiment, a mere messenger in Wellington's Corps of Guides prowling the Iberian Peninsula's dusty rutted roads. "Sir, some instruction may favor me, that is, if you might take the time to describe the workings of the Naval Board."

Delancey accepted the challenge as the cab lurched forward and just as abruptly halted, cut off by another squeezing in from the left side. The horse shied and stepped back, but the snap of the harried driver's long whip urged the reluctant animal forward. The two officers were tossed about the coach's tiny interior. Rain splashed in, soaking their knees through the light summer cloaks covering their white military trousers.

"Basil, it's a very complex matter. I doubt if anyone, even Naval Board members, could rise to that task, but I'll try for your sake." For a moment Delancey paused, striving to simplify his painful campaign experiences with bureaucracy into lessons learned. "The board falls under the purview of the Admiralty, which reports directly to the king and cabinet. However, one mustn't count Parliament out, since it also plays a major role. The House of Commons appropriates the money, through the Admiralty, to operate the board. There's an inherent conflict there, since the Naval Board tends to accuse the Royal Navy of skimming their funds prior to releasing them to the board. There are 145,000 men in the Royal Navy and at least 600 vessels. The board builds men-of-war and hires merchant ships to support the Royal Navy, His Majesty's army, and the Ordnance Board. Last year alone, more money was spent than allocated, leaving the Royal Navy and Naval Board in permanent debt. I know from naval officers that the shortfall was so severe that some sailors weren't paid that year, which—I am reliably told—led to mutiny." With a smile pursing his lips, he continued, "Thank God, that isn't our problem, Captain."

The cab was stuck at a combative junction crowded with coaches, wagons, and meandering pedestrians. Rymer accepted the delay with quiet grace, a trait most beneficial to a tyro quartermaster general.

"Admiral St. Vincent, the First Sea Lord, heads the Royal Navy, while his controller chairs the Naval Board, which is composed of invalidated Royal Navy sea captains *well* past their prime. Also sitting on the board are experienced shipwrights and naval clerks who, at one time or another, served at sea. However, it's rumored, mind you," he said, placing a finger beside his nose as a caution not to repeat the tale, "that the board isn't free from political interference."

Since returning from the war, the captain had learned that everything in London was for sale. But an officer with no family fortune girding him was generally priced out of nearly every market.

Delancey, interested in his own astute analysis and rather amazed at his accumulated knowledge, which he had never articulated before, continued: "The Naval Board's charged not with fighting or defending, but with providing. Within its ranks, spread out across the empire, its agents offer technical and financial support to British and allied forces. But here in London its real power lies in its authority to appoint all warrant officers—that is, ships' cooks, carpenters, masters, surgeons, and pursers. Such power exposes the board to cronyism, criticism, and corruption—or the appearance of corruption. The board also oversees all dockyard building programs and refurbishment of vessels—man-of-war *and* commercial—initially constructed with government money. In short, the Admiralty and board spend one-quarter of His Majesty's funds each year. And yet, it's still not enough."

Basil encouraged his superior to speak further on the subject by saying, "I'd no idea the board was anything more than a bunch of old men playing at ships, sir."

"Basil, I've just begun. There are subordinate boards as well! The Naval Board budgets for the Victualing Board, Transportation Board, and the Sick and Wounded Board. Power lies in the hands of those who control the purse strings, much more so than in the head wearing the crown. That is the Hydra-like organization that we're seeking to tame to our ends."

The driver finally turned off and crossed the pavement, pushing aside pedestrians with their heads down. Somerset House was an imposing four-story, white stone building less than a mile from Horse Guards on the Strand and abutting the Thames.

A Royal Marine, smart in his red coat crossed with white shoulder belts and his curious hat (the brim turned up on the left side and held in place with white cording), guarded the gate. The sentry, holding his bayonet-fixed musket firmly across his chest, stopped their entry through one of three tall arches dominating the facade.

"State your business, sir." He snapped his weapon to a salute when the captain announced, "Sir William Delancey to see the board president."

The cabby passed into a large open courtyard. The rain had flooded the central green lawn, but the carefully laid cobblestones shunted the water toward drains and the brown water of the broad river beyond. The only benefit of the day's deluge was the masking of the Thames's stench. The river was little more than an open sewer. Thick curtains treated with sulfur hung in all the windows in an attempt to filter the foul air, which many believed brought incurable fever and death. Considered a divine curse, the noxious smell permeated the lives of the great metropolis's citizens. The only alternative was life in the countryside or a voyage at sea.

Signs in the quadrangle's inner courtyard directed the two men to the far side by the river. Delancey paused. "Basil, don't let these old men intimidate you. They're here to serve the duke, and it's our job today to remind them of that fact."

Naval Board Encounter

It was customary to be announced when appearing before the Naval Board. Delancey located the clerk in a drab office crammed with paper on the ground floor. As a rule,

Delancey took a page from the duke and rarely wore his splendid uniform in London. Today, though, was an exception. He wore his red undress coat with thick silver epaulets and the star of the Order of the Bath. Captain Rymer, however, was dressed to the hilt in his new Royal Staff Officer's uniform, which Delancey's tailor on Saville Road had made for the captain. The cost was paid out of the allowance provided to the Quartermaster General Department. Rymer had shed his blue short coat with the yellow markings of his dragoon regiment and donned a shocking red tailcoat with a high, dark blue, stand-up collar and cuffs piped in silver lace. The collar forced his chin up uncomfortably and chafed his neck. Tight white leather pants were tucked into polished boots that came to his knees. His high flat hat with silver acorns protruding from within the folded ends was tucked under his left arm. Still a young man, despite his eight years of war service, he was a dashing figure. His dark brown hair was trimmed and curled like Delancey's—very much the fashion now that white powdered wigs had been abandoned. Not as tall as Delancey, Rymer was the perfect foil for the noted quartermaster general, whose arrival was awaited by the curmudgeons sitting on the board.

The two soldiers were expected, the clerk assured them, and the board was "in session and eager to serve the duke in his noble cause."

"A hopeful sign," Delancey remarked to his assistant, as they climbed the red-carpeted marble staircase. At the top they came upon a set of doublewide fourteen-foot polished doors, which swung open from the inside as they approached. The chamber was quite large and ornate. The walls were covered with panels depicting naval exploits on swelling seas and tossed ships with billowing white sails. Prominent on each exalted vessel was the exaggerated image of a streaming Union Jack. The domed and gaily painted ceiling amazed the officers. A giant image of Poseidon, trident in hand and seated on a rocky shore, ruling the seas on behalf of a comfortable Britannia, dominated the space above them.

They sat before the long dark table (constructed from salvaged chunks of once gallant ships). Their chairs, drawn up close, nearly touched the smooth surface, since the hearing of several members was seriously impaired. The room's expanse allowed voices, if they weren't vigorous, to trail off.

"Welcome, Sir William," said Charles Middleton, Lord Barham—the controller of the navy and president of the Naval Board. Middleton began the proceedings without any further compliments beyond saying, "Congratulations on your well-deserved honor. I only hope the small supporting role we played in your exploits as assistant quartermaster general during the duke's long campaign was of some modest assistance."

Obviously, he expected some expression of gratitude for the board's support during the Peninsular War. It didn't bother Delancey to indulge them by replying that the board's past cooperation had been vital. Of course, he neglected to remind Lord Barham how the board's obstinacy had often hindered plans and delayed the victory by months—if not years.

"Your Lordship, I accept your congratulation in the full knowledge that, without the approbation of this august body, I would surely have been overlooked during my years of service to His Majesty. May I simply thank the Board, and may I continue to expect its invaluable support?"

Barham, one of the most powerful men in government, sat quietly, his bony hands clasped before him on the polished table. Delancey had never met him until now but was aware of his reputation as a confident manipulator and tyrant of his fiefdom. A thin smile and slight nod from His Lordship's rather large head, which sat on his sloped shoulders like a ball on a stick, told Delancey that his words and attitude were acceptable.

"Let's proceed then. You'll be gratified to find that we haven't been idle waiting for this meeting. The navy passed along to us the duke's plan for the operations in North America in the earliest days of June, and with security foremost in mind, we've been moving most swiftly on his behalf. Contracts, with no destinations noted, mind you, were given to commercial carriers, which, in turn, have picked up troop formations in Brittany, Ireland's Bantry Bay, and in homeports along the channel. Their routes and destinations will be revealed once under way and not a moment before. Two elements still require our attention. The diversionary force of Major General John Ross and Vice Admiral Sir Alexander Cochrane, along with provisions, is currently at sea. The Royal Navy will interdict any American man-of-war or privateer still capable of eluding our blockades. Our squadrons under Admiral Sir George Cockburn will likely be at the entrance of the Chesapeake to escort raiding parties within the month.

"The Transport Board has contracted 150 merchant ships to carry your force and the necessary provisions. That is, generally speaking, two hundred men and equipment per vessel. The contracts are indefinite and each will probably make a minimum of two, if not three, passages. I'd expect, at a convoy speed of four knots, the process of transporting the bulk of your troops will consume four to five weeks—weather permitting, of course. It's hard to predict an exact schedule during hurricane season." His Lordship didn't take a breath as he laid out the complex execution as a mere trifle, something they did every day, which indeed they did.

"The main force's lead formations are approaching the St. Lawrence and perhaps," he added with a flip of his right hand, "have already landed. A courier vessel ought to reach Portsmouth soon and will provide the status by signal system to our station atop Somerset House. Commissary General William Robinson, Frederick's brother in Montreal, has the necessary specie to purchase those perishables that are inappropriate to ship on such a long voyage. We members of the Transport Board hope that what we've accomplished to date will meet with the duke's approbation."

Surprised and regretful of the diatribe he had unleashed on the impressionable Captain Rymer in the cab, Delancey could only utter, "Well . . . most accommodating, gentlemen. . . . Your work on our behalf is . . . most impressive, most encouraging. . . . Yes, indeed. Speaking for His Grace, as I do or as I can on this occasion . . . thank you for such an immense effort on our behalf." Getting a hold of himself after that totally unexpected broadside blast from the board, Delancey ventured to express concerns peculiar to North America.

"Critical to our plan's success, gentlemen," he said, pausing to turn his face to each member in turn, "is that provisions for the primary force be in place before winter descends and compels an end to the campaign. I'm confident we'll be well past the northern border of the United States before we must establish a winter camp. Therefore, the early and timely movement of supplies will influence significantly our ability to sustain operations into the following spring—if that's required. We must plan ahead, since the St. Lawrence freezes shut before December and only thaws in early April. Lake Champlain will offer our only means for conveying men and supplies. May I presume to remind you of the plight of General Burgoyne's expedition nearly thirty years ago? Traversing the same track, he squandered far too much on maintaining his means of survival to the detriment of his strategy and fighting capability." Delancey chose his concluding words carefully. "I am, Your Lordship, most concerned."

Delancey's warning didn't even stir Barham, who was clearly pleased that he had seized the meeting's momentum.

"Sir William, the Naval Board's acutely aware of His Majesty's previous attempt to dominate the Hudson Valley. We remain convinced if Burgoyne had been a campaigner equal to your eminent superior, then the board's support, properly allocated, would have contributed substantially to a noble victory instead of an ignoble defeat."

Delancey realized he had been put in his place and wished he hadn't referenced Burgoyne. To the board, Delancey was a nascent latecomer to the business at hand. While they recognized his previous experience as a minor player in the last war, they weren't going to pay any credence to his admonishing account of the Burgoyne debacle.

Having made his point, Barham moved toward concluding the encounter on an affable note. "Sir William, we must have a complete troop list for all the follow-up elements. Please include a separate gazette for His Grace's personal needs and preferences regarding transport and amenities. We can then calculate from the tables the total shipping amount and its ideal configuration. A liaison team, I expect, will be forthcoming from your headquarters, which we welcome on our premises now and throughout the campaign. I know from *experience*," Barham said, pausing slightly to let the jab sink in, "that the task will be arduous. After all, we're not discussing the moving and maintaining of a regiment, but some 30,000 troops bifurcated to pursue two distinct missions at two distinct geographic locations. Such an audacious endeavor will require continuous support over the next year."

Lord Barham let loose another smile thinner than a spider's leg. Clearly, the board held the upper hand. "Have you anything to ask us—your humble servants?"

"Lord Barham, distinguished members, my prior *experience*"—it was Delancey's turn to pause for emphasis—"in working with the Naval Board will help me form a liaison of formidable and enduring cooperation, which will in turn lead to victory and the restoration of His Majesty's dominions."

"Sir William, with our business concluded, shall we all adjourn to the library for some light refreshments?"

The board's members rose with much creaking and shuffling. At the far end of the opulent chamber two more doors swung open. Barham joined the two army officers at the end of the long conference table and escorted them into the Naval Board library. The other members followed, trundling along at their own labored pace. While they had been able to conceal their varying deteriorating states of health at the table, the pitiful parade toward the refreshments in the center of the library unmasked their staggering decrepitude.

Now unduly gracious, Lord Barham said in a tone as sweet as the tea a servant offered, "I envy you young people at the start of a glorious adventure, which will bring renown and fortune to those who will . . ." The word he'd been about to say—"survive"— snared in his throat.

Noting his host's discomfort, telling through Barham's fidgeting with his tea cup, Delancey stepped in. "All such expeditions, if they are to achieve greatness, must take great risks. Each is fraught with danger. And this one will be no different." As the colonel spoke, he realized it was the first time since he had been dragooned into the campaign that he had confronted the certainty that some would perish. A shiver, followed by a trickle of sweat, ran down his spine. He gazed at the giant map of the Northern Hemisphere and traced the long hazardous voyage across the Atlantic's blue expanse. Soon he would embark with only his kit and a miniature portrait of his new wife. Leaving the English Channel, past the mouth of the Mediterranean, his ship would strike out across the Atlantic and stop at the Canary Islands to catch the winds off Africa. On the map, in mid-ocean, a drawing of a whale blowing spray reminded him that summer was indeed hurricane season. If still in one piece, the ship would graze the northern Caribbean, then travel north between the Bermuda naval station and North America's eastern coast. The trade winds would carry the vessel quickly north a hundred miles until it anchored deep within the St. Lawrence.

Barham spoke: "Sir William, I wish I could go along. The journey alone would be worth the candle. To say nothing of putting Yankee Doodle firmly back where he belongs—under His Majesty's benevolent heel. It'll be worthy of a cracking good memoir and might even make you famous, I wager."

Delancey replied, "Yes, indeed, Your Lordship. Assuming, of course, that before departing I don't become a casualty to another's great ambition."

Barham allowed himself a chuckle at the officer's barbed wit. The board president could see in his guest the qualities that Wellington admired. "May we all be so lucky," he said.

Across the courtyard the two soldiers found their next appointment and were soon immersed in a luncheon provided by the Victualing Board. The board held a royal charter to provision the king's soldiers and sailors. Deptford, south of London, was the prime depot for voyages departing from ports along the Thames; smaller but similar facilities were located at Portsmouth and Plymouth. Its long-sitting president, Lord Ixworth, was a powerful peer, a direct descendant of Cardinal Wolsey of Tudor times. One of the wealthiest men in England, Ixworth prided himself on devotion to duty and regarded his department as a servant of the people. Those on the receiving end of the board's efforts remembered not the largesse of its intentions but the lack of results. Every soldier could recall the myriad times that food ran short or was so rotten not even pigs would deign to put their snouts to it.

The formal dining room provided a splendid setting. A trestle table seating twenty dominated the room, which contrasted sharply with the ornate library they had just left. This space was clean and bright and flanked along one side were ten-foot-high windows overlooking the Strand. Noise from the traffic hindered conversations, though. Delancey strained to hear his host, who sat at the customary far end of the dining table.

"Sir William," Lord Ixworth said, seeking the colonel's attention. "I hope to replicate a similar meal each day for His Grace during the long voyage. May I speak for the board?" He paused, looking both left and right along the rows of diners, who smiled back in agreement. "We consider ourselves fortunate to be asked to support His Grace on yet another courageous venture. I trust you find the meal wholesome? It's complete, but not lavish—salted meat and fish, vegetables, grain, and a savory. The wine, of course, is Portuguese. We haven't forgotten His Grace's aversion for all things French."

Ixworth waited for the low chuckles at the table to fade further into silence.

Delancey acknowledged the joke with a smile and nod and then, regarding the plate before him, replied, "My lord, if you achieve this repast each day for the month or more that we'll surely be at sea, I assure you that we members of the mess will also be *most* grateful."

At this moment the quartermaster general neglected to highlight the army's near starvation during the Peninsular Campaign or the rotted meat and weevil-infested biscuits. Delancey intended to mend fences, not tear more down, especially since the entire force would be at the board's mercy.

Ixworth seemed to note Delancey's emphasis on the word "most," and his smooth tone reflected the grit of his underlying irritation. "We're aware that, in the past, some improprieties have occurred, but I assure you and His Grace that we've reevaluated our agents and their suppliers. We now subject them to the highest standards and accept only the finest quality food for both men and animals. We're in the forefront of the science of food preservation. We were the first to pack meat into tin cans. Our coopers make the finest barrels in the land—*any* land. You can count on any package bearing the board's broad arrow of approval. That beer you're enjoying has been brewed in our own facilities and the biscuits baked in our own bakery. I know that newspapers seek scandals for their profit and at our expense."

His Lordship's voice rose well above the cacophony in the Strand, his jowls jiggling and turning bright red. With fist raised in defiance, he stood and proclaimed, "But I assure you, Sir William, there's no truth to their stories of corruption!" An overheated Ixworth removed a handkerchief from his lace-cuffed sleeve and mopped his brow.

"Your Lordship, I'll inform His Grace of this splendid fare and assure him that you will provide flawless support for the coming campaign." Delancey rose and Rymer followed suit. "We have much to do and the day's getting late. We'll be overdue for our next appointment if we don't bid you farewell now. Only a few days remain before we embark for Canada, and much must still be accomplished. Please, gentlemen, excuse us and accept our thanks."

When Delancey and his cohort left, Ixworth was still standing, still mopping his brow.

Munitions

Delancey left his aide behind to communicate the previous day's events to the staff while he made his last coordinating visit outside of London. Lord Barham provided his launch for the trip down the Thames. The forty-foot single-sailed craft contained a comfortable enclosed cabin that offered shelter from the weather and odor of the Thames.

While transportation and food were primary concerns, the next meeting was even more crucial to the quartermaster general. Great Britain's ability to defend herself, her interests, and her possessions was divided among the Admiralty, the army, and the Ordnance Board. The latter was an independent body that, in a curious arrangement, reported to the minister of war. Housed at Woolwich Arsenal, a massive facility forty miles south of London on the Thames, the Ordnance Board was responsible for the experimentation, manufacture, and supply of all firearms, cannons, ammunition, powder, and pyrotechnics. Moreover, the master general of ordnance—known as the "master gunner"—Lord Mulgrave directed the board, and his deputy commanded the Royal Artillery. Mulgrave was also responsible for training officers and gunners at the nearby Royal Military Academy high on the hill above the river. Royal Artillery officers weren't part of the commission purchase system so long ingrained in the army. Their cadets were required to pass examinations before being commissioned. As members of the scientific branch, they would be attached to the field army under Wellington's operational control. The master gunner's cannon parks and ordnance depots could be found from the Thames Valley to Calcutta. The garrison, field, and siege artillery all fell under the domain of the Ordnance Board. Once all men-of-war, regardless of size, were ready to go to sea, they stopped to pick up guns and powder at ordnance docks before sailing.

The Royal Military Academy also trained the small corps of military field engineers soon to be attached to Wellington's army. They were responsible for mapping, bridging, and field fortification. Not only did they build forts, they also destroyed enemy emplacements by employing siege guns, mines, and explosives. As technical advisers, they left the digging to the soldiers.

On Delancey's return to London that evening, he summoned his two dozen or so remaining staff for the last time. The rest had already departed from the Chatham Royal Dockyard on the Medway River, a tributary of the Thames. "My day at Woolwich was most encouraging. Besides acquiring a pledge of 'all the arsenal's assets' from Mulgrave, I witnessed Sir George Murray demonstrating the timeliness of his telegraph system." Delancey held up a message sent from Portsmouth that morning. "This note was carried on board a fast frigate bound from Montreal via Halifax to Portsmouth. A station at that port sent this message just over an hour ago, as soon as the fog lifted. It reads, 'June 13, 1814, Master General Mulgrave, Ordnance Board Headquarters, Woolwich. Fort Chambly Depot, Canada, established this date on the north end of the Richelieu River. Receiving troops and provisions in large amounts. Gunpowder stored under cover. Full report for you on board HMS *Laurel*. William Robinson, Commissary General.' Not too shabby, eh?"

Delancey's staff agreed. It was indeed impressive.

Last but Not Least, Horses

Of the four commodity categories—men, matériel, provisions, and horses—transporting horses safely was the most daunting. Delancey went to Apsley House the next morning after returning to London. There, he joined Somerset and His Grace for a late breakfast in the second-floor study overlooking Hyde Park. An unusually congenial Wellington filled the first few minutes with prattle about Lady Charlotte Lamb's dinner party, which he had attended the previous evening. After all the guests had left, he had stayed. His lingering was bound to add fuel to the gossip smoldering in London society.

Breakfast dishes were removed, and the three soldiers stood around the map of North America spread flat on a table in the center of the study. If Lord Bathurst had been invited, he wouldn't have believed the enormous change in his old house's study. The room was bright with the sunlight streaming through tall windows and the walls paneled in a rubbed pale-wood finish. The outside of the house was no longer dark, crumbling brick with rotten and peeling window shutters but rather a shining example of Palladian honey-colored stone. There was no remnant of the previous structure. All of London admired the changes the duke had wrought to this corner of Hyde Park, a prominent crossroads for promenaders.

The conversation at last turned to business. The duke, obsessed with detail, quizzed the young quartermaster, who had answers for all his superior's questions except one: the all-important transport of horses by sea. Delancey had left the arrangements for the type and quantity of horses to the end because the issue was the most contentious.

"Sir, your guidance concerning the deployment of mounted units, draft horses, and remounts is most necessary and would be most appreciated."

Delancey was aware of Wellington's dislike for cavalry. The reason for the duke's antagonism was the cavalier attitude of the leaders at all levels of the corps. Time and again, Wellington had witnessed the waste of good men and horses as their officers turned cavalry maneuvers into headlong foxhunts. Exasperated, he had relegated them to reconnaissance, communications, and picket duty.

"The matter of horses," the duke informed Delancey and Somerset, "has occupied my mind far more than any other subject. It's not just a question of horses but one of terrain, the first variable in the planning process. My first experience as a commander was in the Flanders Campaign of 1794. It taught me the importance of tailoring the force and supply train to the lay of the land. I've been studying the writings of past commanders who fought in northern New York and interviewing officers who fought the French from Fort Ticonderoga to Montreal in 1759. In fact, Prevost's father, Augustin, has been one of my recent venerable guests. His memory of Lake Champlain and Ticonderoga was *most* enlightening."

Wellington pointed to the maps overflowing his campaign desk, the surface of which, though inlaid with gold-trimmed leather, was rarely seen because of the sundry clutter. The table drawers, with recessed brass handles, were so stuffed with charts and maps that they no longer closed. Defying order, corners of faded paper stuck out from the front. Eight feet long, the campaign desk rested on two folding wooden horses; most practical, the table could be broken down quickly and slid into a wagon. The scuffed piece of furniture was totally out of place in the gilded palace.

Wellington's voice brought Delancey's attention back to the matter at hand. "That old boy served Johnny Burgoyne on his ramblings to Saratoga in 1777. Augustin brought with him an old naval gentleman who'd been with Governor Carleton the previous year when they took Ticonderoga from General Philip Schuyler before an early winter compelled a retreat. One thing's become clear to me: it's not cavalry country. There are few suitable roads that can bear the weight of our columns, which will be three times larger than Burgoyne's. Supplies will be moved primarily by water. Remember that the unavailability of provisions drove Burgoyne to partition his force. The excursion to Bennington, Vermont, for food and fodder resulted in disaster. Besides, a study of the map shows that there's little open country where massed cavalry can maneuver. If I take the cavalry in any number, most of their time would be spent finding fodder and running amuck. They would be high cost and little use."

Delancey took a breather from Wellington's lesson in tactics to assess the impact on the transportation plan now that it no longer required moving the weight of thousands of horses over thousands of ocean miles. The subsequent reduction in the number of horses to be conveyed would be welcomed at the Transport Board.

Referring to the map, Wellington continued his assessment. "One very important factor favors us. An estimate sent by Prevost assures me there's a willing community of New York and Vermont smugglers who will support the British army. As Prevost expresses it in a recent correspondence, 'The patriotic Spirit of '76 wasn't inherited by the present generation. The farmers will not take up arms against us. Better yet, they'll supply provisions in exchange for gold.' Come this autumn, gentlemen, our invasion will absorb those smugglers behind our lines. As newly acquired subjects of His Majesty, they can be expected to supply us, which should relieve you, Delancey, of much of your worries."

Happy to hear the duke thinking that far ahead, the quartermaster general said, "Good news indeed, sir, but that's for tomorrow. I'm truly concerned about getting us all there in a state to win the first battle. An exact number of horses needed to pull the artillery, draw the carts and wagons, and carry officers is the problem for today. Your

Grace, twenty thousand soldiers will be led by nearly eight hundred officers, all of whom expect to ride rather than walk."

Somerset cautioned Delancey, "I've been told that the northern states aren't known for horse breeding. The maritime islands of Lower Canada and New Brunswick, which raise heavy horses, can support draft remounts in some numbers. While they're not suitable for the saddle, they're adequate for drawing field and siege artillery."

Delancey noticed that Wellington's fingers were tracing a path southward that stopped short of Albany at the headwaters of the Hudson River. Did this indicate that the plan involved only limited objectives? Once south of Albany, New York, the countryside was cleared for farms with open pastures fit for grazing. Surely, that was cavalry country. Could it be that later, once seaports were pried open along the New England coast, the makeup of the army and its mission might alter? The business of this meeting didn't embrace such speculations, intriguing as they were. In any case, Delancey was relieved to hear that the mass transport of horses wasn't part of Wellington's vision.

"Sir, because of the sea voyage's duration, the Transport Board's records indicate there would be little success in importing horses from the British Isles or the Caribbean to Canada. The records of horse carriers on trips lasting more than five days are appalling. As a result, I'll not ship Copenhagen. Instead, I've arranged for Horse Guards to furnish you with several hearty mounts of good temperament."

Wellington smiled. "Good thinking, Sir William. I'll put him out to stud. Perhaps he'll prove to be as good a breeder as he has been a friend."

Delancey had his marching orders. Only one cavalry squadron, the 19th Light Dragoons numbering two hundred sabers, would be transported. Artillery would be limited to six companies of foot artillery, one of siege artillery, and one of Royal Marine heavy guns. The tally was three hundred dragoon mounts, four hundred artillery, and a hundred each for the two siege batteries. Each officer was allowed one personal mount, to be transported at his own expense if space allowed. Availability would be on a first-come basis. The Transport Board found that only twenty horse transporters were certified to cross the Atlantic. Even though they would make continuous transits, the slight number severely limited the movement of animals, since each vessel's capacity varied from one hundred to two hundred horses per ship. When the meeting concluded, Delancey understood that acquisitioning horses in North America would be his worst nightmare.

Just a Stable Boy?

Captain Basil Rymer wasn't one of the quartermaster staff officers invited to accompany Colonel Delancey on board the *Endymion,* named after the Greek god of fertility, to Canada. Instead, he was directed to take personal charge of the horse transport flotilla. The captain questioned the necessity of such an unsolicited assignment, but the colonel told him that it fit perfectly within a staff corps officer's duties. In the past he had been a cavalryman, a proud warrior, a line officer, a member of a fighting unit that made history. With his current orders came the realization that staff officers were anonymous clerks, even though they sat at the feet of the king.

Delancey was surprised by Rymer's chaffing at a duty that was of primary importance to the entire expedition's success. The captain squirmed in his chair and lost eye contact as his superior cautioned him on the peculiar problems he would encounter at sea. Rymer's attention was elsewhere. What had he done to his career by leaving the regulars? Could it be that the "sainted staff corps" was nothing but a bunch of shop assistants clad in uniforms that were more glitter than gold? Miserable, Rymer returned to listening to Delancey's instructions, which only reinforced the dispiriting image of an officer turned groom.

"Basil, you must be meticulous. Every accommodation must assiduously follow army regulations and Naval Board standards." It was obvious to Delancey that Rymer was less than eager to accept the assignment. "You do realize this is no channel crossing? I'm charging you, Captain, with a vital, demanding assignment!" Delancey, lacking the patience to indulge his underling's peevish feelings, was becoming angry. He reminded Rymer of his promotion to captain and all the patronage he had spent on the young man's behalf in the halls of power.

To calm himself, the colonel returned his focus to the topic of equine transportation. "Basil, horses are as crucial as men and ammunition. Remember, the time and trouble you take now will pay off once at sea." Delancey took one more stab at inspiring the young officer. "Be my eyes and make sure all that can be done to preserve the animals on the long passage is done. His Grace is most concerned, as am I, with the survival of the horses in your charge."

Captain Rymer, shamed, responded, "Yes, sir," but he did not look the colonel in the eye.

Rymer's sudden detachment from his colleagues dragged his spirit down. He thrived in the company of military men. With his kit lagging behind in an army wagon, he plodded on his horse along the Dover Road toward a dockyard south of London. He rode beside the bank of the calm, deep Medway River, a tidal branch of the Thames. In the fading light, ships, sails flapping, drifted like ghosts as they neared their moorings. His horse's hooves clopped on the bridge's wooden planks before Rochester's ancient gate. A ruined stone castle, broken from old age, watched mutely over narrows once guarded by Roman soldiers. Looking down at his mount's bobbing head, he realized that he had become the servant and his horse the master. It had been a long ride, but he had no desire to stop for the night at a tavern and drink with the locals. Candlelit shops, cheek by jowl, spilled light into the cobbled street and illuminated the wooden sign that read, "Chatham Royal Dockyard 2 m." He pressed on beyond the town, along the water, to the red brick arch that framed the entrance to the dockyard. The Royal Marine sentry provided a guide to the officers' mess. His comfortable quarters lay on a low ridge above the sprawling acres of warehouses, mold lofts, blacksmith sheds, dry docks, lumberyards, and a quarter-mile-long rope factory. Even though the sun had set, the yard never slept. The smiths were idle during the day; July's intense heat in the face of the hearth prevented them from forging. In the evening silhouetted gangs stoked fires and banged red-hot metal into anchors. Bright sparks, dispatched by horse-operated drop hammers, scorched the night sky. The din kept him awake. He watched the moonlight reflect off the bobbing masts that choked the river beyond.

The next morning, a Transport Board port agent met Rymer after breakfast in the mess and escorted him to the water's edge, where a skiff waited to take him—and his kit—on board one of the twenty horse transporters. One of the vessel's comprising the flotilla, anchored downriver where the Medway widened into a shallow lake before meandering into the lower Thames, would be his home for at least the next month. Purely utilitarian, the wide stubby ships wallowed at anchor, as barges disgorged cargo, slung in rope nets, up over the side and down into the hot dark recesses belowdecks. Their tubby lines made him want to weep. He had counted on "the ride of his life" across the ocean via a sleek frigate crewed by "tars"—Royal Navy sailors—expert at the lines and clambering aloft at the slightest change in wind direction. There would be rows of massive black-iron guns run out to shoot at a marauding French privateer to enliven the passage. Unfortunately, the little rowboat bumping against the discolored strakes of the *Washburn*, a commercial horse carrier, belied his hopes. Worn wooden steps were attached permanently to her side to accommodate the boarding of passengers. The reek of brackish water slapping the hull turned his stomach as he climbed reluctantly up the flat side onto the main deck. Two dark-skinned deckhands, already sweaty in the early morning sun, went to retrieve his boxes. Rymer cautioned them, "Be careful with my kit. There are items of value there." (He was most concerned for the black bottles of rum prescribed to ward off illness and comfort him during the interminable lonely voyage that lay ahead.)

The escorting agent, who climbed up behind him, said, "They don't speak English, Captain."

Being confined at sea with a crew of foreign cutthroats didn't brighten Rymer's mood. Shortly thereafter, he met the first mate, Mr. Lang. Clad in chopped-off pants, wooden shoes, and a loose cotton shirt, he hardly inspired confidence and was readily mistaken for a boatswain mate. He didn't speak like an officer either. "Cap'n Rudge ta shore at his digs. You'll share his cabin, which I'm surely bound to say"—he paused, searching his vast vocabulary for some fine-sounding words—"will accommodate your needs, sir."

Rymer, dressed in a glittering red tunic (an attempt to make a strong first impression), replied, "Mr. Lang, where are the other officers?"

"There ain't none, sir. This ain't no pleasure craft." The first mate chuckled at his inestimable wit. "Mr. Rainsby's the vet'nery. He bunks nearby with the fleet commissioner here." He pointed a dirty finger at the little man who had just emerged from the open hatch. "Beggin' your pardon, sir, my duties require my presence. I leaves you in his care."

"Arthur Cherry at your service."

The fleet commissioner extended his hand, after wiping it with the handkerchief drawn from the sleeve of his navy blue cloth coat. It was devoid of embellishments except a single row of large convex brass buttons engraved with "TB," for Transport Board, that descended from the high stand-up military collar to the plain wide black belt.

On the lower portion of his sleeve was a single circle of gold lace that the sea air had tarnished to a dark bronze.

"Captain Rymer, I'm charged with the health and welfare of the animals. You know what Shakespeare said, 'Put no trust in horses' health.'" He stopped a moment, gazed at the deck, then said, "Or was it 'Put not hope in horses' health?'" He shook his head to resolve his conflicted recollection. "Well, no matter. It's all the same, wouldn't you agree, Captain?"

Small boned, short, sprightly, Cherry wore a black felt flat hat, in the military style, decorated with a tarnished gold stripe on one side. He removed it, not as a gesture of respect but to wipe the flowing perspiration that dripped from his brow with the same handkerchief he had wiped his hand on moments ago. Bald, he was able to mop his entire head, including the thin fringe of dark hair that wrapped around behind his ears. He then applied the rag to his spectacles. Still, sweat dripped onto his black boots. Deep creases lined his cheeks and forehead, which made him appear old. Rymer found him most agreeable, though, because Cherry clearly regarded the captain as his superior.

"It must be stifling hot down there in the hold, Mr. Cherry. Have you loaded any animals?"

"Yes, indeed, sir. It's a bugger below, but we won't load stock till I've approved the ship and vetted the cargo. The evening before an ebbing tide, two days from now, will be all at once frantic with grooms and horses. You see, sir, if we loaded 'em now, then the animals would surely bake like bread down there," he said, pointing down the open hatch. "That would not do, sir. His Majesty's regulations demands loadin' takes place after sundown, in the cool of an evenin'."

Rymer was relieved to hear that some thought had been given to the welfare of the stock. Mr. Cherry had it all under control.

"Tell me, sir, have ya ever been on board a horse transporter in past campaigns?" Before the captain could answer, Cherry continued: "Beggin' your pardon, might I show ya the accommodation below? I think you'll find it most instructive, sir."

Rymer was about to be treated by the self-assured fleet commissioner to the intricacies of livestock transport. A school-trained specialist and self-taught philosopher, he laid down his views before beginning the walk around.

"The transport of horses is a vocation and Arthur Cherry"—he placed his hand on his breast—"is, if I may say so, a master of the trade." After a short pause to ensure that Rymer offered no objection, he continued, "Remove the cause, and effects will cease. Prevention is better than a cure." A second pause gave the captain a moment to absorb this wisdom. "Shippin' horses by sea is an exercise in preventable wastage," Cherry said.

It was a curious phrase, and Rymer asked, "Wastage? What wastage?"

"Sir, are you aware that horses ain't equipped to sail like you or me and find it most distressin'? They're highly social animals, they are, who herd. The confined environs of a ship, any ship, is most distressin'. Initially, the conquistadors kept their mounts belowdecks with calamitous results. Later, Spanish explorers left their horses suspended in hammocks on deck, exposed to the weather, on a four-thousand-mile voyage lasting two, perhaps three, months. The results was no better, sir: losses were over half. Little changed in these modern times. In 1756 the enclosed horse carrier *Medcafe* lost half her stock on a five-day voyage from Dover to Edinburgh. That, sir, was the standard. Half the horses transported was expected to perish! The army refused to sustain such losses and turned to buyin' horses after debarkin' on foreign soil. The cavalry, artillery, and—may I say—the officers, once they've landed abroad, have never accepted the idea of delayin' a campaign to break in horses. However, since the turn of the century, the Transport Board has instituted procedures that have cut down losses to two in ten."

He paused once more for effect and to draw attention to his next pronouncement. "May I say on my own behalf, sir, that on many an occasion when Arthur Cherry's been in charge, that number has come up substantially." Not sure exactly what substantially meant, he added, "If you know what I mean, sir?" The fleet commissioner placed his hands behind his back and appeared to stand a little taller than his normal five feet one.

Congratulations were in order. "Well done—most impressive, Mister Cherry. How, exactly have you—and the board, of course—achieved such splendid results?" If the long voyage was to be pleasant, Rymer knew he must humor the commissioner—that is, until the first horse died.

Accepting the compliment with a slight bow, Cherry launched once more into his favorite topic. "Well, sir, it's all in understanding the nature of the beast. At Land's End, the Office of the Remount General, which a veterinarian holds mind you, schooled Transport Board agents in the pathology of the horse." He began quoting from his studies. "Horses are surprisingly fragile. They can change their physical appearance in a few days, one way or t'other. Therefore, a trained seagoing farrier must be employed to treat valetudinarianism with dispatch."

Captain Rymer was as impressed as he was bewildered by the terminology. He followed the commissioner down the ladder, where the air thickened and the breeze was lost.

"When the Guards Regiment insisted their regular grooms and troopers accompany the stock on a voyage," Cherry continued, "the result was a hands-down disaster. The soldiers, not being accustomed to life at sea, became so sea-sickened they neglected the horses, which suffered from inattention and died. Since then all soldiers were put on troop transports, and the horse transporters were sent trained farriers."

"Now, Mr. Cherry, you do surprise me. I can't fathom such an alteration to cavalry regulations. But I must say I'm no stranger to mal de mer myself, and when caught in its clutches, I'm totally debilitated."

"Sir, the majority of indisposition in horses ain't from ship's motion, but the result of improper care and feedin'. If need be, a man can function on a pound of meat and a pound of bread per day. But an active horse must have *ten* pounds of grain and *ten* of forage each day. On board a ship the feed's cut by half, since the animal's static in the stall. The bulk of provisions limit the number of horses each carrier can accommodate on a long voyage. If we're going on a two-week jaunt to Spain, then the *Washburn* could add another fifty horses. Greedy eaters, a horse takes five minutes to consume a pound of grain and fifteen for a pound of hay. They bolt their food. You know army horses, sir. They never know when they'll eat again." Cherry could see Rymer's interest waning, so he finished quickly. "Between the lack of exercise and bulky diet, digestive problems is the order of the day, sir."

Captain Rymer, a former cavalryman, was familiar with the delicate digestive tract of horses. "What special remedies have you up your sleeve?"

"We pack a large quantity of linseed oil to flush 'em out and locust beans to buck 'em up. However, Captain, I'm sure you'll agree that those are poor substitutes for proper hygiene. If a horse stands in muck all day, you can't expect him to be free of disease. Horses shit at *least* six times a day, even on reduced fodder." Cherry smiled, knowing what was coming, then added, "Two hundred horses produce eighteen tons of manure a day that must be scraped up and thrown over the side. Each animal gulps down six gallons of clean water, which nearly causes a constant stream of horse piss flowing between the planks, down into the bilge."

Rymer calculated the resulting smell and nearly gagged at the thought. The sheer amount of provisions and barrels of drinking water, which Cherry's speech implied, concerned the captain. "Do we have space in the hold for such enormous quantities of consumables?"

The little man lowered his high-pitched voice and shifted his eyes. "Cherry's fleet will break all records for efficiency on this passage, Captain."

Rymer, despite his war experience, was awestruck by the complexity that Cherry laid before him. As they probed each corner and examined broad arrow–stamped containers, he began to understand the importance of care and cleaning. Delancey had been right to insist on his high-level oversight. The captain began to appreciate the significance of the assignment. Perhaps he had been hasty with his complaints. The successful accomplishment of his mission, with the help of the expert Mr. Cherry, could be an opportunity for advancement.

The somewhat worn, bedraggled exterior of the *Washburn* masked her efficient innermost workings. Once back on deck, it was obvious that she was prepared for inspection. She was a carrier of utilitarian design, her line unlike other transports. Like a frigate, she carried three masts, each with three yards and a sunken waist. That morning the multiple hatch covers were stowed aside on the spar deck to reveal a cavernous hold. With the exception of a four-foot-wide lip around the main deck, the hold was open to the keel. Between the raised quarterdeck and small forecastle, crewmen teetered on the edge of the gaping hold that plunged straight down four decks into total darkness.

Waiting in the water on the port side was a large flat litter boasting three tall derricks, each strung with block and tackle. The crew winched provisions off the litter high in the air and lowered them, out of sight, into *Washburn*'s innards.

As they walked together, Cherry picked at the standing and running rigging lines feeling for dry rot, a fungus that attacked fibers. "Look here, Captain." Cherry undid a line wrapped around a belaying pin. Stressing the cord, he bent it over and twisted it with his slim fingers. "There's serious wear. A Riga hemp rope will fray, strand by strand, givin' plenty of notice before it snaps. Ya gotta watch every line, ya know."

Mr. Lang, following behind, took note.

Cherry dismissed the offense with a wave of his hand. "Replace it, First Mate," he insisted.

After thoroughly inspecting the topside, the party once again descended the ladder to the crew quarters under the quarterdeck. Even the diminutive Mr. Cherry had to stoop, since the quarterdeck beams above reduced the overhead to just five feet. A sea of empty white canvas hammocks swayed at the anchored ship's slightest movement.

Lang explained that the *Washburn* required a crew of forty-five. "Of course, they're not all able seamen. Most are ordinary. I must admit havin' a handful of land's men, too, who signed on to avoid impressment into the Royal Navy."

Rymer's expression grew distressed at the small number of crewmen. "So few in the face of marauders surely waiting on the Bay of Biscay and off the coast of Africa?"

Amused, Lang offered, "This ain't no warship, Captain. We got only ten nine-pounders split between forward and aft. They're some protection from pirates and privateers. Our real strength, though humble it may be, comes from the sixty farriers sharin' these quarters. Each has got a musket and short sword. Never fear. They're fierce defenders of those horses. They love 'em like children. Besides, stealing a pack of hungry horses ain't a walk in the park."

Farther forward, under the forecastle, was the caboose, a black iron monster of a stove containing the only fire on the wooden ship. Rymer was introduced to the cook, a most vital crew member. His two assistants were obvious invalids; once ordinary seamen, the grizzled sailors appeared encumbered by twisted limbs and advanced age. Yet, they could fetch and carry from the deepest, most onerous recesses of the dank hold, where provisions were stowed in barrels, boxes, and bags. As containers were emptied, their wood became kindling for the stove's coal fire. Above, on the forecastle, live chickens, three goats, and a cow were confined.

Rymer and his guides descended yet another ladder, this one longer than the last. Mr. Cherry drew himself up to his full unimpressive height and remarked, "The horse decks provide more than eight feet of clearance between deck and overhead. You see, Captain, *this* being luxury. On the *Washburn* the horses enjoy commodious accommodations." Cherry reached high for the adjective. Gesturing ahead along the walkway, he said, "There's fifty individual stalls on either side. Many other ships you'll inspect today will gang as many as four in one large stall, and the animals will have to lean against each other." To excuse the arrangement on the other carriers, Cherry added quickly, "Although it might be confinin' to us, the horses seem to like the company."

At midships he stopped and placed his hand on the rough wood rack protruding from the bulkhead. "These feedin' stations will be stuffed with hay and the covered bin underneath filled with grain each mornin'. When we load 'em, the horses will be slung up from the litter, over the side, and lowered one at a time to the level of the stalls," he swung his hand in an arch. "Temporary planks'll bridge the gap over the hold. The rear gate to each stall'll be opened. The horse, standin' planks, will be released from the sling and led into the stall. The head'll face away from the hold and stick out here, on the bulkhead side of the ship where the groom can feed 'em. Then planks are moved to the next stall. Like clockwork, eh? By tomorrow, all the provisions will be stowed and we'll board the horses after dark, when it's cool."

The tour was beginning to take its toll; this second sweltering trek left Rymer's head buzzing. He felt faint. The inspection party picked its way past bails of hay and sacks of grain piled along the passage between stalls and bulkhead. The captain's eyes watered at the noxious stench rising lazily from the depths of the hold. The brackish slime was a hellish mixture of putrefied meat, rotten potatoes, rancid fruit, and horse manure and urine clung to ever-sodden corners where the oak ribs met the keel. In ordinary ships, closed decks confined the odor. The seeping saltwater dampened the ballast and provisions that lay on the keel and crept slowly toward the hull's low point at the base of the mainmast. Every day, the second watch exercised the bilge pump, a system of small buckets attached to a continuous line that dumped the waste out onto the main deck, where it ran through a sluice pipe into the sea. Yet, Mr. Cherry and Mr. Lang appeared not to notice the pervasive reek.

The fleet commissioner handed Captain Rymer over to the ship's veterinarian, who was unpacking in the cockpit. There, below the second horse deck and far forward, Harold Rainsby and his two assistants were stowing their medical instruments and supplies: coils of thick rope, twisted leather harnesses, tan canvas nosebags, shiny metal tubes, and curlicues of rubber hose pipes. The musty aroma emanating from scattered piles betrayed the equipment's age. Cherry's concern was evident in his parting comment. "You'll be sure to clean and air out, won't you, Mr. Rainsby?"

"Righty ho, Mr. Cherry. Don't give it a second thought. It's all good and proper, you can be sure." While freeing tangled leather lines drawn from a seabag, Rainsby gave a wave of his free hand. He had attended Sir Ashley Cooper's Veterinarian College, established at Greenwich in 1796. The Naval Board certified the graduates as warrant officers and deployed them throughout the transport fleet. The policy intended to stop the farriers' cruel and ineffective treatments, which centered on bloodletting and drenching the horses with everything from turpentine to gallons of fermenting compotes.

Rainsby was accountable to Cherry for the animals' health and welfare. He took a break from the stagnant humid atmosphere and leaned back, his spine crackling like dry kindling. "You know, Captain, this is the worst part of the voyage. The stink goes away once we're under way."

His large strong hand gripped Rymer by the bicep and pulled him out into the open shaft of the hold, where they could see the blue sky through the mast and yards. He pointed up and forward with the carpenter's hook he had been using.

"We'll run with the hatch covers off and those doors at the bowsprit wide open. Weather permitting, we'll blow the ship's entire innards with fresh air day and night."

Having discarded his dark blue frock coat before laboring below, the brawny middle-aged man in rolled-up shirtsleeves could easily have been mistaken for a common deckhand—except for his scuffed leather shoes and pale skin. His straight thinning hair, soaked with sweat, exposed large portions of pink scalp.

"I nearly forgot. Captain, do ya know about air sails? During a blow we deploy small sails rigged to direct the flow of fresh air down canvas tubes into the hold."

Rymer had never heard of such an odd, wondrous contraption, but it wasn't enough to divert his attention from his concern that the hatches wouldn't be battened down at sea. He asked, "What must be done, Mr. Rainsby, in a storm to prevent water spilling down the open hatches?"

"Not to worry, sir. Procedure calls for hatches to be closed in a storm. Selected planks from the galley to the quarterdeck will be removed to keep the air flowing. It's terribly important to keep the horses ventilated or they'll tuck up with miasma—a fierce thing to watch. My father, a farrier, told me, 'Once they sicken, you got to separate 'em from them that ain't.' That's why on each horse deck there are free holding stalls reserved for those that are sufferin'. Keep 'em apart no matter what the complaint, and the pestilence won't spread. Once, when I was a lad, shippin' with my father on a big carrier, out of four hundred beasts ninety-six came down with the staggers from poor ventilation. The doldrums off South America trapped us, you see. Not a breath of breathable air stirred for days. The horses dried up with ringworm. We almost lost them all in the end."

"Terrible!" the captain commiserated.

"That ain't all, young man! Sorry, sir, begging your pardon, but I get so heated up when thinking about that voyage off Cadiz. The fleet lost 259 out of 720 from pneumonia due to poor ventilation. The coughin' swept through the ship like Halley's Comet, it did, till you couldn't hear yourself think."

"Seafaring's hard on horses," Rymer agreed. "I can see that. What about water and feed. What bother can we expect?"

Rainsby was pleased that he was stirring the young gentleman's enthusiasm. "Mind you, a horse can go two days without water, if necessary, but not an hour longer. And when I say water, that's good clean water. Mr. Cherry must make sure that none of those casks are made of leaky pine. If air gets in, then the water goes bad, and if that happens, then we'll be in for it. We'll be stopping at Cadiz for salt licks and the Canary Islands for fresh water before takin' the plunge to Bermuda. I can tell you, sir, the issue of the water worries me most." From his lofty height of six feet two the veterinarian bent down into Rymer's face to relay a confidence. "Without water a horse's victuals don't wash out, and we'll have terrible trouble. The grooms will be up to their armpits cleaning them out. Or else there'll be twisted bowels or stagnatin' lungs."

"Mr. Rainsby, when you add all those concerns together with the long passage to Canada, it seems hopeless. What are our chances?"

"Now, sir, that depends. If I were a bettin' man, then I'd wager we'll make it in good form—that is, if the weather holds true and the sea runs clear."

Delancey Seaborne

Strictly speaking, transporting Wellington, his personal staff, and the household was the responsibility of the expedition's quartermaster department under Delancey. To Delancey's great joy, First Sea Lord St. Vincent intervened. He offered his newest ship of the line, the HMS *Caledonia*, the largest ship in the Royal Navy at 201 feet long, displacing 2,600 tons, and armed with 120 guns. Nothing on the high seas could match her. It wasn't her armament that made her attractive to Wellington, but her size. The duke had sailed a great deal, as had most soldiers, to India, Portugal, and the Mediterranean coast. He had crossed under both the Horn of Africa and the dreaded sea below South America. For all that, he was a notoriously reluctant sailor. He had weathered some of the worst storms recorded and had suffered intensely from mal de mer until an officer who had served in China told him that fishermen there chewed gingerroot. The duke was familiar with the flavor from his time in India, where he enjoyed the local cuisine. His batman always made sure that a box or two was packed with the mess kit.

In the third week of July, Delancey was on hand at Greenwich to ensure a safe embarkation and to receive last-minute instructions before parting from Wellington's traveling headquarters. The great ship had been decked out in flags on the stationary rigging. The ten massive forty-two-pound carronades, each weighing more than two thousand pounds, had been removed from either side of the quarterdeck to allow the staff considerable space to take exercise during the long voyage. There was no need to worry about the loss of firepower, since the remaining 110 long guns were at the ready on the three decks below the one for passengers.

Delancey was relieved to watch the masts disappear on the ebbing tide downriver into the fog. No speedster, the great ship would wallow its way across the Atlantic slightly faster than the slowest merchantman. The hold of the *Caledonia* was large enough to store not only a fine selection of victuals for the field marshal's table but also his mess party's needs for the duration of the fall campaign season.

During negotiations with the Royal Navy for escort vessels, Delancey requested a favor that the liaison officer of the Halifax northern fleet, responsible for protection of the convoys of troop carriers, granted with a wave of the hand. He had asked for a fast frigate to carry him and his staff to Canada so that they could proceed as quickly as possible to meet the arrival of the troops and provisions bound for Montreal. Delancey and the quartermaster staff would enjoy less space per person but a much-swifter crossing, and in all likelihood, they would arrive ahead of Wellington. A sailing voyage in 1814 across the central Atlantic in the heart of hurricane season was a gamble at best, and a warship was a better choice than a merchant vessel. But speed was of utmost importance.

Delancey's batman left only those personal items required for the voyage in the cabin the first lieutenant shared with the vessel's captain and then went below to oversee a party of sailors busy hauling the colonel's trunks, bits, and boxes. The smell of the sea and the damp wood that surrounded Delancey in the tiny chamber was pungent. It was a wet day; his dark wool cape hung on a peg and dripped rhythmically onto the plank deck.

The colonel dozed as the ship bobbed about the anchor hawser and strained at the hemp while timbers creaked somewhere within his afternoon dream. He could relax since Wellington was now at sea, just a day ahead of him. All was done that could be done. The rain had exhausted itself by the time twilight began etching the sky in orange-purple strokes. The wind of the capstan, pulling the anchor from the mud, woke him. The tramp of sailors' bare feet on the damp deck above was his signal to go topside and watch the main course sail fill with the warm breeze that would take the frigate from the harbor east into the widening estuary. Movement was slow at first, and Delancey studied the mast's progression against the side of the harbor fortress to assure himself that the ship was indeed moving and to measure its glacial progress.

Within thirty minutes, he saw the outline of Spithead in the dusk just before the *Endymion* turned southeast under the protection of the round brick fort in the center of the channel. Within ten miles another popped up like a cork in the center of the Solent. Bristling with cannon from its crenellated battlements, the fort secured the seaway from marauding privateers. The *Endymion* slid silently beneath their proud protruding gun barrels; no salutes were fired. The ear-splitting bursts of red flames and white smoke were reserved for the triumphant return. The narrow channel between the coast and the Isle of Wight was thick with troop carriers—all part of the lantern-lit flotilla bound for Canada. Wight, a large island densely populated with sun lovers and yachtsmen, was heralded as the English Riviera. To the Royal Navy it was an essential barrier that protected the entrance to Portsmouth's naval harbor.

Delancey wasn't alone as he watched dusk settle against the shore off Cowes. His staff, pressed shoulder to shoulder, gripped the wet rail of the quarterdeck's port side. The last of the amber lanterns faded astern, as the vessels passed the Needles, where the wind picked up from the east, slowing their progress and driving them toward the jagged shoreline that loomed astern. They were far short of the open water at the entrance to the Irish Sea. A strong easterly gale, though not as maddening as the southerly winds that prevent all movement toward the Bay of Biscay, was nonetheless treacherous.

Captain Hall pushed the crew aloft to shorten the sails and then swung around to the north in an attempt to venture into the English Channel and clear Dorset's beckoning hazards. There, on the ragged rocks, many ships had been wrecked and many men had drowned. In the age of sail the straight lines on the navigation chart, while helpful, were seldom achievable. If drawn accurately, the path of the ship would resemble a drunken sailor's gait. It took an experienced captain and crew to tack out, crossing the wind time and again, and avoid the lure of Davy Jones's locker in a forcing gale.

Lighthouse beams shot out a warning but could do little for a ship under the influence of the wild wind. With only sails, which provided not only headway but also steering, for propulsion, the entire convoy's mettle would be tested within sight of their homeland. Each crew member would compete alone in a contest against the elements. Quite suddenly, currents combined with the gale, which was blowing at forty miles per hour. The force of the wind could turn the bow toward land and toss it onto the rocks like a toy. Once ensnared in Nature's grip, there would be no reprieves, no quarter given. If the storm snatched control away from the crew by turning the bow to run with the storm, the ship would be driven inexorably toward the foaming shoals and rocky shore.

Delancey was propelled away from his comfortable perch among his staff by the rail. The men rushed below. The heading switched every few minutes, as the wind blew uninterrupted down the length of the ship. Cool wet spray, leaping over the plunging bow, coated Delancey's face. Gripping a storm line that had just been rigged for the crew's safety, he made his way to the frigate's skipper, who was braced behind the helmsman. The wind vibrated the standing rigging and set off a multitude of strident singing above the rush of air that drove Delancey backward, his cloak flapping wildly.

Above the storm's din Captain Hall was shouting orders, which officers and boatswain mates echoed. The brass trumpet, held flush against his mouth, propelled his deep, resonant voice as he called out, "Royals secured, top gallants down, gallants riffed up, courses clued up and braced around to port."

The ship's master bellowed, "All hands on deck!"

Delancey was caught up in the rush of sailors as they doubled up on each assignment. They seized the running rigging from belaying pins, where they were wrapped tightly. Chest to back in gangs, they struggled to turn the yards around against the wind's relentless pressure. They fought billowing canvas aloft by snagging handfuls of material in accordion pleats and tying them into long bundles, which reduced the area of the sail. The howling wind objected to this affront to its power. High up the two-hundred-foot mast, the crew members each used one hand for the ship and one for their balance, as they packed the small sail against the wooden spar and secured it in place. The mizzen topgallant shredded into rags, nearly causing the top men to tumble to the deck below.

Concerned that the ship was being driven backward despite the crew's exertion, Delancey looked to Captain Hall for reassurance. The man, though soaking wet, was calm. "Look at them, sir. I've trained them for the past two years. See how they climb like monkeys, haul like horses, and respond to commands like mercury through your fingers. My God, it's gratifying." He pointed aloft as the royal yard came down on a sizzling line through the spinning wheels hidden with the wooden blocks. Everyone and everything was in motion—except for Delancey, who stood amidships, his feet braced wide apart on the rolling, pitching slippery deck. He was proud to witness what men could do when they were well led.

"Sir, I've done this many a time," Hall mused, "but it still stirs my soul when I feel The Needles' wet gale in my face. Don't get me wrong. It's a challenge, and there are those out there in the darkness that'll flounder. Bright and early tomorrow, the smugglers and scavengers of Devon and Cornwall will leap with joy at the sight of a ship's broken masts, collapsed gunnels, and drowned sailors. This storm will sink leaky, rotten hulks, which should've been permanently moored years ago. Their greedy owners shamelessly scattered overinsured ships along this graveyard coast, taking the last measure of value for themselves."

Hall gripped the sodden soldier by the shoulder and grinned into his dripping face. He couldn't wait for one more gulp of fame and glory, now that he had had his first taste of the brew.

CHAPTER 7

Diversions and Death

"All warfare is based on deception. Therefore, when you are capable, feign incapable; when active, inactive. When you are near, make it appear that you are far away; when far, that you are near. Offer the enemy a bait to lure him; feign disorder and strike him."

—Sun Tzu, *The Art of War*

From front page of the *London Times*, August 5, 1814:

Strike now. Chastise the savages, for such they are. Make them pay. Our demands may be couched in a single word: submission!

From page two of the *Albany Evening Journal*, August 5, 1814:

What Are We to Do

This past year we have reported on the heinous harassment of British military misadventures against peaceful American villages whose only crime was to nestle on our undefended shore. Feeding on plunder, the lobster backs have become emboldened. This escalation threatens our very existence and demands a renewed call to arms. We must repel John Bull from our sacred shores and make him pay for his affronts with his blood.

On August 1, British harassment turned into seizure. Vice Admiral Sir Alexander Cochrane set loose his hired turncoat Captain Richard Coote on the trusting folks of New London, Connecticut. Flying false colors, he brought the *Comet* into port on the evening tide. On board, hidden belowdecks, skulked a company of Royal Marines bent on destruction. Once disembarked, they rampaged through the town, just as they did in our fathers' time. They turned their drunken wanton attention to the waterfront and torched twenty-seven moored craft, the source of livelihood directly or indirectly for scores of New London's inhabitants, before leaving the traumatized citizens in their beds.

It is widely reported that the scoundrel Coote was paid two thousand pounds rather than thirty pieces of silver. It seems the vile traitor is more skilled at negotiating his fee than Iscariot, but beyond that caveat there is scant difference between them. Are we to bow before such infamy? Where is our rallying cry?

But treason is not all we have suffered. The Royal Navy, not two days later, at Buzzards Bay in Wareham, Massachusetts, put armed sailors ashore, in the dead of night, to burn, rape, and pillage. To their surprise, our militia confronted the blood-thirsty scoundrels and trapped them like the rats they are. To save their craven skins, they took American hostages and used them as shields while fleeing. Are we to bow before such infamy? Where is our rallying cry?

The list goes on. At Fort Phoenix in New Bedford, Massachusetts, our artillery got the best of the Royal Navy frigate HMS *Nimrod* when it attacked the USS *Fairhaven*, which lay helplessly at anchor. Are we to bow before such infamy? Where is our rallying cry?

Some communities are already lost. That merciless Cochrane has even seized the defenseless Island of Nantucket. He issued an ultimatum to the undefended population to surrender and swear allegiance to the mad King George. Devoid of the protection of federal forces, they had no alternative except death and therefore signed away their precious freedom—won for them at great cost by their forefathers. We have lost contact, but not faith, with our brothers on that unfortunate island. Are we to bow before such infamy? Where is our rallying cry?

What is behind this sudden escalation by the redcoats? Their onerous intention is to reverse their ill-starred fortunes of 1776. Are we to bow before such infamy? Where is our rallying cry? If the British think they can return this gallant upstart country to the fettered status of colonies, our foes across the pond have once again made a serious miscalculation. It is our duty to disabuse them of their vaunted delusion.

To arms! Defend your honor, your family, your land, and your nation. To arms!

Sounding Brass

Within a week of Coote's attack on New London the president called a cabinet meeting in the corner room of the Executive Mansion. Madison didn't mince words. "Mr. Armstrong," he said, "Commodore Joshua Barney's harbinger is in the hall awaiting instructions. What are you going to tell him?"

The sailor brought word that in the Chesapeake the Royal Navy fleet under Adm. Sir George Cockburn had disturbingly doubled in size. Barney's feeble fleet of gunboats had been sniping at the British ships for the past year but could manage little else. The alarming communiqué also warned that his paltry flotilla was boxed in and that, in the commodore's view, Cockburn intended to land a large force on the Patuxent Peninsula. Barney's force was the last American navy element opposing, however ineffectively, the Royal Navy's rapacious designs. Along with the warnings came a recommendation: beach the fleet and rely on infantry. Sunk, captured, or blockaded on the eastern seaboard since the spring of 1813, the once triumphant navy of 1812 had been reduced to reporting on John Bull rather than resisting him.

Seated at his tiny table, one of a dozen in the large room, Secretary of War Armstrong answered confidently, "Sir, it's my belief that Cockburn's heading for Baltimore, *not* Washington. After all, what does this little backwater swamp offer other than we poor servants of the people?" He smiled at the absurdity of Great Britain spending assets to capture such a plebeian lot. "The Capitol and other central government buildings aren't even finished. There's not a single military installation of importance in the city. The government, as embodied by us, can simply walk away at our leisure, leaving them nothing more to conquer than the deserted streets and oppressive heat. The only army they'll find in this sodden place is an army of mosquitoes. They're not equipped to conquer and occupy territory. All the British can do is more of what they've done, which I admit is most disruptive and distressing to those living within twenty miles of the coast. But, after all, it's only twenty miles."

An exasperated James Monroe cut in: "Must I remind you, sir, those twenty miles include two inlets capable of supporting ships teeming with redcoats."

But Monroe's apt query failed to deter Armstrong. "Washington's not the target. Of that I'm certain. We'd better serve the crisis by acknowledging Baltimore as the prize drawing their avaricious interest. A dozen privateers, which have seriously challenged the Royal Navy's reputation, are bottled up there at anchor. Yes, vengeance's their game, not grand strategy. Baltimore's wealth will draw them north. Their predatory captains are interested in only one thing—prize money. We are, without doubt, safe. Baltimore, of course, must be reinforced. To that end I've dispatched an additional two hundred regulars to Fort McHenry. They'll guarantee that not so much as one thieving British vessel of any size will penetrate the inner harbor. I've directed the governors of Maryland, Virginia, and Delaware to summon the militia. At federal expense, no less! The commissary general of ordnance has thrown open the arsenals and armories, which will supply the troops marching to the shores of the Chesapeake. There, our brave soldiers will repel Cockburn's raiders. Raiders, mind you, *not* invaders."

Monroe pressed his objection. "Isn't it prudent to bolster Washington's defenses? Surely our back door is also 'thrown open' to military mischief. The port of Alexandria supplying the city is recklessly vulnerable. The Potomac's navigable to Fort Washington, a mile from the capital."

Armstrong replied quickly, brusquely, dismissively, "Brigadier General William Winder, the new commander of the tenth military district, appointed *personally* by the president, has assured me that he's made all necessary preparations." (What he neglected to note was that Winder wasn't *his* personal choice for commandant of the district. He had proposed Moses Potter, of the artillery, known for his distinguished war record. Armstrong knew that the appointment was politically motivated; it was expedient to please Levin Winder, Maryland's governor and William's uncle, especially since it was Maryland's militia that would defend the Chesapeake.) "The commander at Fort Warburton, across from

Mount Vernon, has fresh instructions and will soon be augmented by several hundred Maryland militiamen. The Virginia militia is currently mustering at Mount Vernon as I speak to secure the northern Potomac. While other cabinet members may panic"—he eyed Monroe derisively—"I assure you it's all sounding brass. Our government, homes, and families are safe."

Some in the room took the secretary of war's statements at face value. He was the most trusted military man in the capital. He had seen war both during the American Revolution and in Europe, where modern tactics had evolved before his eyes. Neither the misfortune of the American army in Canada nor the moribund morass into which the navy had sunk had tarred his reputation. The Revolutionary War was very much alive among the cabinet members, most of whom had served under arms. They believed that another war on American soil favored Americans and that John Bull would not risk it again.

Armstrong echoed their view. "England lacks the luxury of maintaining a standing army here against the will of the people. Their attempt this time will end as it did last time—with the lobster backs singing 'The World Turned Upside Down' as they march back onto their ships. Currently, the majority of the British army is four thousand miles away—except, of course, the troops in Canada, but they are decisively engaged on the northern border and having quite a time of it! Our militia can take the field in great numbers if necessary. Presently, the regular army is small, but it's growing as a result of new appropriations."

Again, Armstrong failed to mention the obvious: the militia was unarmed, untrained, unreliable, poorly supplied, and badly officered—in short, no longer viable. As for the regulars, it was true: Congress had approved the army's expansion, but between the approval and the enactment lay months, if not years, before the numbers on the page matched the numbers in reality.

The president demanded an answer to his original question: "What will you tell Commodore Barney?"

"Sir, I'll instruct him to dismount his cannons onto wagons, burn his boats, and march his four hundred men to Baltimore to aid in the defense of that city's outer limits."

All those present could hear Monroe's teeth-clenched sigh.

Dissension at the Dinner Table

That evening, the Monroes dined with the Madisons at the Executive Mansion. The sun had set, yet the humidity remained oppressive. The dwelling, replete with open windows and fourteen-foot ceilings, allowed a light leisurely breeze to circulate. At the small intimate dining table, draped in white linen, Dolley expressed doubt despite her husband's assurance that Winder was the man for the job.

"James," she said to her husband, as the black attendant offered a cheese plate to the president's guests, "I must confess that I'm not as certain as you are concerning General Winder's competence. He's a bit of dolt. Some say a bungler. Until just two years ago, he was a lawyer in Baltimore and not a very able one, I'm told. Worse, his only military experience is as a prisoner of war. His unimpressive record of underachievement hardly inspires confidence."

Monroe's wife nodded in agreement. After all, she was the source of Dolley's damning assessment. Bitty Kortright Monroe, of the Baltimore establishment, had little good to say about William Winder or his uncle. Addressing the president and her husband, she asked, "Are we to be left in the hands of a party hack who looks and acts more like an inept public prosecutor than a soldier?"

It was true: Winder was bald, bespectacled, and bewildered. It was unusual for the regal Bitty to voice such strong opposition. The wife of a diplomat and present secretary of state, she rarely criticized openly; however, the couples were old friends. At this private supper she didn't hesitate to voice her growing concern for the welfare of the capital and, most important, her two daughters.

Shaking his head, the president replied emphatically, "No, no! I appointed him on the party's recommendations. Before he could draw his sword, he was betrayed and captured. Through no fault of his own Winder was denied a chance to redeem himself on the battlefield. I'll not have his character besmirched for circumstances beyond his control."

James Monroe supported the two ladies. "Sir, I believe he's a rummy *well* in over his head. This summer he's done next to nothing to prepare for field operations. There isn't a staff to organize a defense because he hasn't established a headquarters or built a staff! All he does is ride daily alone throughout the district 'assessing the terrain.' His only military companion is Armstrong's outdated book, *Hints to Young Generals by an Old Soldier*. Winder doesn't have the excuse of youthful folly or aged infirmity for his neglect of the most basic duties of a commander."

The president, a literary man, offhandedly asked, "Is the book any good? Is it amusing? I must confess I have never delved into military science."

"It's nothing to hang your hat on. But neither is Winder. If he's our savior, then we are indeed ruined."

Winder's Nondefense Defense

Madison's wife and his guests were correct. Even though Winder had been in command since June, he hadn't started to assemble a plan for defending Washington until early August. By stark contrast to Winder's lethargy was his opponent's energy: British admiral Cockburn had spent the summer raiding Chesapeake Bay communities from Havre de Grace, Maryland, to Hampton, Virginia, across two hundred miles of interior coastline. Winder didn't budge. What were a few nuisance raids when measured against his larger pressing concerns? It never occurred to him that Cockburn might be using these forays to learn the intimate details of the tributaries for a much more devastating attack on the capital. Meanwhile, the American lion, Commodore Barney, had opposed the English fleet with a handful of outgunned boats crewed by gallant sailors.

Winder's palace guard, 380 regular infantry, 125 light dragoons, 120 marines, and a military band remained under his direct control. When he finally pulled together his staff, it was composed (unsurprisingly) of party cronies. The militia in the Washington region was composed of bands of friends who trained on weekends as a reason to be away from their wives. Their drill sessions were short, the subsequent parties prolonged. Uniforms were scarce, as were blankets, tents, shovels, axes, field kitchens, and transport. There was no system to resupply troops with flints, which were good for only forty shots. Even if there *were* supplies, no one had contracted for cartage to move the army. The men were told to bring personal items to maintain themselves and their buddies in the field. The regulars weren't much better prepared; some had enlisted to drink and loot. The thought of their country's survival was the furthest thing from their minds.

Like Congress, the lazy and reckless Winder bet on the strength of the state militias to join him on the battlefield and supply the numbers needed for a decisive victory. The brigadier general's inaugural order came on August 4, when he activated 4,000 militiamen to defend the tenth military district. He was unaware that of the 3,000 that Congress had summoned during the previous month, only 250 had answered the call.

Cochrane's Diversion

Vice Admiral Sir Alexander Cochrane briefed his principal commanders at Government House in Bermuda on August 8, 1814. He had relocated his headquarters from Halifax to be closer to the action and to intercept Wellington, whose arrival he expected within the fortnight. Cochrane had been faithful to his Admiralty orders that spring and summer. Trade, so vital to the New England merchants, had been throttled. Royal Marine raiding parties had burned out numerous coastal communities. The American navy was shut down. He and his officers had become rich from the prize money paid for captured American ships and cargoes. The vice admiral, aware of Wellington's September invasion scenario, began the meeting by announcing, "Gentleman, the time's come to end this Yankee Doodle Dandy."

Present on the open veranda of the bleached-white edifice and cooled by Atlantic trade winds, were Admiral Cockburn, Commodore James Gordon, and Captain Peter Parker. Enjoying a break from months at sea, also present were their subordinate captains, who echoed the vice admiral's sentiment. There were thirty in all, the finest serving naval officers of their time, each representing a vessel instrumental to the coming onslaught. Other Royal Navy ships posted to blockade American ports had been left on station. Hats off and swords stowed, every officer donned his best navy blue tailcoat, marked with gold braid and decorated with medals and stars. They all knew each other from youthful days spent at Dartmouth, from the rolling decks of yearlong voyages, and from moments of terror and courage shared in His Majesty's service. They were dedicated to their king— and their careers. Aware of their own inimitable place in the island empire's ancient history, these proud strutting knights of the sea saw the coming campaign as one more opportunity for fame and fortune.

Among the sailors that day was Major General Robert Ross, the expedition's appointed land commander. Newly promoted, he had commanded a combat brigade for

Wellington at San Sebastian, Spain, during that war's closing campaign. General Ross had embarked at Saint-Malo, Brittany, on June 2 with four battalions: the veteran 4th Foot Royal Lancaster, two battalions of the 44th East Essex Regiment, and the 85th (Bucks Volunteers) Light Infantry. All had been resting in the wine cellars of France since Napoleon's capitulation in April. Arriving in Bermuda on July 25, Ross added a battalion of the 21st Royal Scots Fusiliers from Genoa and a company of field artillery, which had embarked at Gibraltar. The welcome addition brought his complement to nearly four thousand fighting men.

Addressing the assembled officers, the boisterous Cochrane took pleasure in proposing the plan that, in the end, would profit them all and ruin the fledgling American government. A man who valued the finer things of life, he made sure the assemblage was well fed. A buffet table, beneath a green-and-white-striped awning, boasted a fine display of seafood as well as joints of pork and beef that had been roasted on a spit over a glowing charcoal pit on the beach below. Wine—liberated from a Frenchman bound to sell it to the Brahmins of Boston—flowed freely. Bermuda, while humid, lay peacefully on the northern edge of hurricane alley, where fortunately the fierce wind hammering the Caribbean had tapered off to a tropic breeze.

The host, grayed haired and overweight, offered a toast: "To the Duke of Wellington, author of our adventure. To finish the American War in our favor, the field marshal will lead an invasion down Lake Champlain designed to cut the rebels in half at their belt line, the Hudson River. Our role is diversionary. Some of you have raided coastal communities; others have disrupted the shipping off New England and the Chesapeake to our immense benefit. To distract the enemy's government and military away from the northern frontier, we're going to bring hellfire on Washington, Baltimore, Mobile, and New Orleans. I know that Washington offers little of value, but our endeavor will siphon off their interest and resources, thereby leaving the real targets poorly defended and ripe for plunder." Cochrane raised his glass of Bordeaux wine once again and turned to General Ross, conspicuous in his gold-braided red coat, a willing captive in a sea of dark blue uniforms. Ross, in turn, raised his glass in tribute to the Royal Navy.

At forty-eight, Ross was several years older than Wellington. He was the son of Major David Ross of Rostrevor, County Down; his mother was the half-sister of the Earl of Charlesmont, his patron for many years who provided for his education at Trinity College in Dublin. Ross, a brilliant combat leader, rose from ensign to regimental commander of the 20th Foot in fourteen years. A drillmaster and strict disciplinarian, he talked tough but cared for his men as if they were kin and willingly shared their hardships. Always leading from the front, Ross was popular among his troops. His three wounds, two of which had been serious, attested to his courage. He caught Wellington's attention at the Battle of Vitoria in 1812. From dozens of able commanders the duke chose him to promote to major general.

As Cochrane described the mission to Ross and the naval officers, they could see his blood rise. He was a man of passion bent on settling this war, which tied down half of his fleet with a boring wasteful blockade.

"General Ross, your troops, augmented by some of our tars, will conduct a brief, intensely destructive land campaign to raid Washington, burn it out, and confiscate any contraband capable of being carried. In short, destroy both the Americans' political and military establishment. You mustn't, though, take or hold anything that might threaten your withdrawal. Refrain from becoming decisively engaged and avoid capture. Ross, above all, do not hand the enemy a victory."

On August 16 the ships bearing the British soldiers slipped into Chesapeake Bay through the narrow opening between the tip of the Delmarva Peninsula and the long sandy shore of Norfolk, Virginia. A small provincial artillery battery at Hampton Roads Island fired short of its target as the enemy transports turned north and headed up the bay to join the major portion of Cockburn's fleet, which had been awaiting them.

Ross wasn't passionate but calculating. He had no ax to grind with Americans and couldn't relay the venom that filled Cochrane's parting words: "Come down on their heads like God's wrath!" Instead, the army general wrote instructions to his unit commanders that were short but strong: "Destroy, disrupt, distract, disorient, disorganize, and decoy American military and government at all levels. Above all, do not get trapped."

Cockburn on the Move

In the age of sail, broad interpretation of orders was condoned and independent action encouraged. Extraordinary deeds discovered and claimed for the crown vast territories and conquered exotic distant kingdoms without an umbilical cord back home. In that same spirit of adventure, Cockburn viewed his present orders. On the morning of August 18, Ross landed four thousand soldiers and sailors from Cockburn's fleet, anchored on the Patuxent River, near the fishing community of Benedict and just twenty-five miles—as the crow flies—from Washington, D.C. But his crow, if not airborne, would have to follow rutted dusty farm roads through several towns before reaching the capital's outskirts.

Ross anticipated stiff resistance, unless the other diversionary elements successfully distracted the American defenses. Although seen through the steamy morning river mist, they marched surprisingly unopposed. Unit commanders sought out local avaricious farmers for horses and carts. Although the British always paid in gold coin, they were unable to find draft animals, so British sailors spelled each other while hauling borrowed wagons loaded with powder and ball. The veteran infantry's inactivity during the long sea voyage had sapped its strength, turning once sinewy legs to rubber. Progress was slow and the element of surprise decidedly lost. Ross's column sent up clouds of dust visible for miles over the rolling green fields. With no cavalry to screen his approach, he feared ambush. Several platoons of infantry, mounted on saddle horses purchased from locals along the way, reported a cordial reception as they moved carefully northward. The next day, Ross paused just north of Nottingham to order his ducks.

Cockburn, who shared the trek, noted all harbor installations, shipping, and storehouses destined to be destroyed on the return. The field artillery, picked up at Gibraltar, was left on board the fleet in favor of a troop of Royal Rocketeers. Their lightweight "A" frames and unguided rockets were more mobile but less effective than cannons. Ross expected the missiles to panic the American militia.

Cockburn was well aware that the road to Washington would attract far too much attention and blunt the effectiveness of his foray. One of his subordinate commanders, Captain Parker, had suffered the loss of numerous British merchant ships under his protection to mercenary American privateers. Now on board the frigate *Menelaus,* Parker ventured an additional sixty miles north with a flotilla of a dozen empty transports in an effort to confound the American defenders. The movement, designed to resemble an attack, was merely a feint at Baltimore. By chance it reinforced Secretary of War Armstrong's myopic prediction and tied down Governor Levin Winder's Maryland militia. Parker didn't engage but rather laid off, outside the range of Fort McHenry's cannons.

Simultaneously, Royal Navy captain James Gordon entered the southern Potomac River, where it met the Chesapeake, and made a great show of moving ever northward, burning settlements as he slowly closed in on Fort Warburton. His impressive fleet of two frigates, three bomb vessels, and Congreve rocket ships raked the shore with gunfire, which terrorized the civilians nearby. Several smaller craft filled with troops harassed the riverbank and challenged the militia to fight. But the militia refrained. Local folks abandoned their homes as the tall masts and billowing sails moved upriver past the plantations and farms that hugged the muddy Potomac. The fishing boats, fleeing ahead of the British, spread the alarm as far as Alexandria.

Monroe Plays at Intelligence Officer

William Winder, wearing his usual blinders, was unaware of the two enemy diversions and therefore was unaffected by them. Reports of redcoats on the Marlboro Road drew him to Washington's outskirts. James Monroe commandeered a contingent of regular dragoons from the force husbanded by Winder and went looking for trouble. South of the Upper Marlboro, they encountered the first, though hardly the last, American refugees fleeing from Ross.

Monroe stopped a young man astride a dray horse harnessed to a wagon full of household goods and a family of four. The wife and small children took on the dazed look the secretary of state had come to know as minister to France during the Reign of Terror. Monroe, natty in civilian clothes, at first confused the stranger when he beckoned him.

"My good fellow! Where have you seen the redcoats?"

"At my place east of Nottingham, sir," he said, turning and pointing as if it were still in sight. "It's teeming with 'em by now. There's a swarm of redcoats on both sides of the road. They're buying all the horses and hiring carts."

"How many are there? Any cavalry? Any cannons?"

"Didn't stick around to write a book about it, mister. They aren't mounted. Didn't see no cannons." He looked to the sky and stroked his clean-shaven chin while his horse shook its head impatiently. "Saw some barefoot sailors pullin' a wagon full of straw."

From the sparse account, Monroe, an amateur soldier, deduced all good tidings. He tested his theory on the dragoon captain, who sat astride the horse next to him. The officer, quite a contrast, was clad in a short indigo blue jacket crossed with eight rows of straight silver braid that ended in curlicues.

Monroe, buoyed by the knowledge that he was heading in the right direction, said, "That's the first account we've heard free of hysteria and rumor. The absence of cavalry is most encouraging. The straw was protecting powder barrels, I'd say. And they're moving slowly, not by choice, I reckon. Heading our way certainly, but toward Baltimore or Washington? It's sixty miles to Baltimore, so why pick a route so far south? There are better roads farther north if that's the bastards' intention." Suddenly, an inspiration seized him. "Captain, they're coming *our* way! When they get to Bladensburg Junction, we'll know for sure."

The captain thought the secretary unduly pleased with himself.

Monroe smiled in triumph. "Who ever would invade without cavalry and artillery? This isn't invasion! It's a raid!" Monroe, statesman turned intelligence officer, sent a trooper back to inform the army what he had discovered and that he intended to press on and question more travelers. While accounts differed slightly, nothing changed except the numbers. He encountered a magistrate from Nottingham fleeing on a cart stuffed with records, who estimated the British advance guard at six thousand. Without confirming the intelligence, Monroe sent another dispatch of looming woe that panicked the capital city.

Late on August 20, a messenger carried yet another dispatch from Monroe bound for Winder, who was busy dithering at the bridge that crossed the swampy eastern branch of the Potomac, just west of Bladensburg. The long, low timber structure was the gateway to the capital city. Monroe's assessment was forwarded to Armstrong and Madison.

Armstrong, standing fast, told the president, "They'll turn north to Baltimore as soon as they reach the turnpike. I'm certain."

Madison countered, "If that bridge isn't destroyed, we'll be having redcoats as dinner guests." The president no longer believed him and pointed to the map on his desk. Recognizing Washington, D.C., for the prize it was, he began organizing the district militia to defend the mansion and Capitol. Armstrong's certainty of Baltimore as the enemy objective was being undermined. Now concerned that he might've miscalculated, he sent his only military engineer, Decius Wadsworth, commissary general of ordnance, to Bladensburg to form a blocking position. By the time Wadsworth arrived, Winder, confused, had inexplicably left the bridge. The village at the crossroads for Baltimore or Washington would soon become the focal point of the American defense without Winder, who moved south—alone.

On the east side of Bladensburg the hills folded together into open fields. Finding a point where the view was unrestricted, Wadsworth directed that defensive dirt revetments be dug. A scattering of troops arrived to form a crescent-shaped line on the low ridge. The Potomac was only fordable south of Bladensburg; there, the bridge waited.

Several thousand American militiamen were gathering in small groups on dusty roads southeast of the Potomac. They began to meander toward Upper Marlboro as the

British marched unmolested in the same direction. Ross's men weren't cheered, neither were they stymied. Local folks recognized the contrast between citizen-soldiers and professionals but were surprised to see Admiral Cockburn walking alongside common sailors. They knew his name and sinister reputation from newspaper accounts, and his presence was widely reported to both Baltimore and Washington. The only thing operating at full capacity was the rumor mill.

Disaster Looms for Washington

Early on August 21, an advance infantry platoon of redcoats, with muskets slung across their bodies and mounted on barebacked horses, blew through Blandensburg and out the other side. By late in the day the first true elements of the British column were nearing Upper Marlboro. By the next morning, the sanded cobblestone streets would be teeming with their British brothers by the thousands. Marching in order of fours, to the sound of ominous drums, they appeared invincible.

Winder vacillated with the arrival of every rumor. Camped at the Woodyard a few miles southwest of Upper Marlboro, he sat surrounded by regular troops and waited for good news that he was unwilling to create through his initiative and action. His palace guard consisted of 750 regular infantry and cavalry, some marines, and five guns. In the last twenty-four hours he dispersed an army of nine thousand men along roads connecting Baltimore, Annapolis, Washington, and Fort Warbuton. He had single-handedly constructed a battle line extending over a hundred miles. The majority of cannons were in Baltimore. Government clerks had commandeered the army's transport—with which he had been expecting to cross the bridge at Bladensburg—to move files and furniture west across the Potomac and north to the Harpers Ferry arsenal. By the night of August 21, the American field army was sleeping on the ground and eating whatever it could forage.

General Stansbury, a noted loudmouth and commander of the 20th Maryland Infantry Brigade, gave an unsolicited interview to the *Niles' Weekly Register*, a Baltimore newspaper. The resulting article read, in part,

> According to our own Brigadier General Tobias Stansbury, "The 20th will be the point of the spear that pierces the heart in the British beast." This proud day the citizens of Baltimore cheered the marching column of Maryland militiamen as they left the city to the sound of military music. Hearts stirred at the sight of a thousand of our finest sons, citizen-soldiers from the 5th Maryland. Colonel Joseph Sterrett posted himself in front of the gun carriages and, gleaming sword in hand, led the militamen, as they marched to the accolades of their fellow citizens. No finer troops have been seen in our streets since the days of our fathers.

They didn't march far. Five miles south of the city, they halted to set up camp and remained in place to protect Baltimore.

At the other end of the overextended battle line, Winder's reinforcements had arrived at Fort Warburton with new orders for Captain Dyson, the fort's commander. He was ordered to blow up the fort if seriously attacked by a large British force. There was no sense to the order, but it served to illustrate the hopelessness that Winder embraced so wholeheartedly, almost willfully.

Monroe appeared at the Woodyard on the night of August 21. Even though he had seen the British column from a considerable distance without a telescope, which led to his highly inflated reports of enemy strength, he did manage to convince Winder to send Sterrett's regiment to Bladensburg.

By the morning of August 22, Monroe had also managed to convince Winder that Bladensburg would indeed be the battleground and led the general and two thousand American soldiers on foot south toward Upper Marlboro. There should've been a compelling reason for taking the long route, but there was none. They had nearly covered the five miles when, to their shock, they stumbled across the British army's advance guard. At the sight of the distant redcoats, Winder lost heart and ordered a retreat that turned into a rout. Monroe dispatched another message to Madison, declaring that the British troops' intended target was indeed the capital. His earlier figure of six thousand enemy troops advancing north was now up to seven thousand—overestimated by three thousand soldiers. The report spread panic through the capital city, sending crowds of citizens mounted on all categories of horse-drawn vehicles west to Virginia.

The British Commanders' Conference

Ross continued to consolidate his force at Upper Marlboro, and wondered what the Americans were doing. Little did he realize that he would be unopposed until the following day, when he reached Bladensburg. Such a possibility was beyond the ability of his bellicose brain to comprehend. Protected in the center of the British formation was a fifty-man detachment of Royal Sappers and Miners (RS&M). These men were specialists trained and equipped to blow up military fortifications. Unmistakable at first sight, they wore tight black leather caps with protective plates that extended down the back to cover their necks. A single row of white metal buttons closed their short red jackets. Dark blue stand-up collars and cuffs gave them the appearance of soldiers. Their white pants were hidden under blue coveralls and they carried shovels and picks instead of muskets and bayonets. If Monroe had been the intelligence officer he claimed to be, he would've identified the unit and concluded that the British not only intended to occupy the capital, they were also determined to level the city.

Besides the sixty forty-pound rockets of the Mounted Rocket Corps, the navy dragged one six-pounder and two three-pounder field pieces. The mounted scouts reported that Bladensburg, nine miles north, was the enemy camp and strong point. While his troops consolidated at Upper Marlboro on August 23, Ross conferred with Cockburn over lunch. They had been invited to billet in a fine house overlooking the village green. Their somewhat reluctant hostess, Madam Charlotte Banks, had offered them accommodations in order to protect her house from looting British soldiers. Madam Banks's guests assured her that her gracious home and furnishings would be safe. She hadn't believed the posted notices that Ross had printed, offering immunity from plundering as long as the household didn't directly oppose the occupation, but she was surprised and pleased that the officers offered to pay during their stay for the rooms and meals.

On the shady patio the two officers enjoyed a cold lunch of gammon, fruit salad, and cheese prepared by the family cook. Cockburn, not trusting the water in the hot climate, had brought his own wine. Ross traced his plan on a map laid at Cockburn's feet. "Sir George, we're halfway to Washington and haven't seen, but briefly, the enemy in the field. My scouts report that they're gathering here." He pointed with the tip of his straight sword at the dot on the map—Bladensburg. "We haven't been able to determine their strength, but we'll surely find out firsthand and last minute against the ridge there, just before the bridge to Washington. There's scarcely any opposition shivering inside their untried militiamen, and their regulars haven't yet put in an appearance."

Cockburn advised, "These colonials are clever crooks. My father warned that they're not gentlemen and fight from cover like mountebanks. Be careful. They could have an unpleasant trick or two up their sleeves."

Ross accepted the caution but added, "We've little choice. We must fight the enemy where we find them. I've no cavalry and only a few artillery pieces. In essence we're a reconnaissance in force. If we find them too strong or too wily, then we can always withdraw down our same route to the safety of the fleet. Porter and Gordon must've made an impact: spreading the enemy out and preventing their massing anywhere but that bridge. Once we scatter them at Bladensburg, we'll be safe long enough to torch Washington. It'll be quite a bit more costly for the Americans than that 'tea party' they're forever trumpeting."

Cockburn, though a naval officer, had considerable experience with small land forays. "I agree. Let's have at them! We'll see if their red-white-and-blue, hit-and-run aboriginal tactics can stand up to His Majesty's most invincible soldiers."

"You know, I believe we can see the capital from Bladensburg. The map shows it as a mere six miles west. Gad, I'll bet it's hot and humid there!"

The evening of August 23, General Ross listed the troops available for the next morning's attack. It was an old habit from the Peninsular War, when he had been a subordinate commander reporting to higher headquarters. The list read,

> Four regiments, Infantry
> Battalion, Royal Marines
> Company, Black Colonial Marines
> Light rocket, Royal Artillery
> Naval rocket, Royal Marine

Naval gunners, 90
Navy sailors, 275
RS&M, 50

_____

Total 4,300

The total wasn't as large as he would have preferred, but he thought it would suffice. After all, he wouldn't be facing George Washington or Napoleon Bonaparte in battle.

The Blind Leading the Helpless

The bog on the Washington side of the bridge wandered for miles and was one of the finest mosquito-breeding spots in Maryland. Bladensburg, on a low ridge above the river crossing, blocked the sight of the British approach. Traditionally, the cluster of buildings was the last rest stop before entering the district's confines. Comprised of sundry services for travelers, the village provided rented rooms, eateries, livery stables, and a post office. Just to the east the American military elements began to coalesce to the left and right of the Wadsworth in a hasty redoubt that blocked the road from Upper Marlboro. On arriving on the evening of August 22, Stansbury's command absorbed the small elements coming in from all directions until his hodgepodge force grew to more than 4,100 men. With little control exercised by the Baltimore general, the troops ebbed and flowed all day until nothing was certain. The road network that converged at Bladensburg soon became knotted with desperate elements moving in disparate directions.

On the afternoon of August 22, the bewildered American commander grasped at every crazed rider who jabbered that he had seen the enemy column. Unfortunately, no coherent picture emerged from the ranting reports. All Winder could ascertain was that the British were in a column headed north toward Bladensburg and would intersect with a considerable number of his troops—perhaps that very day.

The next day Winder and his followers remained in bivouac six miles south of Bladensburg at Long Old Fields. Winder and Monroe were conferring in the open that morning when President Madison emerged from the tree-covered road on horseback. Armstrong and the entire cabinet had accompanied the president. Unprotected by minimal military escort, the entourage included grooms and civil aides, who followed the closely leading remounts like a pack of itinerant polo players.

Winder, always the sycophant, pardoned himself from the discussions, greeted the president, and bowed to the others in turn. The diminutive Monroe stood up in his stirrups to gain the lay of the land and disposition of the troops. "May I assume, General, that the British are down that road?"

"Yes, sir, indeed. Somewhere to the south—we encountered them yesterday but lacked sufficient strength to engage them in any meaningful way." Winder's voice quavered, as he pointed in the general direction of Upper Marlboro. "I've been waiting here till I better know their real intentions. Let me describe our defenses and pinpoint the deportment of the British."

The gentlemen dismounted and stuffed themselves into the white field tent, where the operations map lay on a rickety portable table. With a red crayon Winder drew circles and arrows that marched from the edge of the bay, to the east toward the Potomac's nearest branch, and stopped short by a half a dozen miles. "Sir, there are seven thousand enemy soldiers and sailors coming this way. We saw them here yesterday. Well, we think we did. So I withdrew to consolidate here, but then I began to doubt the redcoats' intentions. Several sightings have been provided as a result of Mr. Monroe's daring probes." He nodded at Monroe across the table in recognition of his assistance. "However, there've been others that suggest Baltimore is indeed the target. It's all very fluid and confounding and makes me believe that perhaps Major General Ross—that is, our opponent and my nemesis, sir—may have split his column of seven thousand. Or there are even more lobster backs than we've surmised. They may be moving along a multiple axis of advance, which would account for the confused picture we have today."

At this point Armstrong, attempting to redeem his egregious judgment by demonstrating his knowledge of international military matters, interrupted the briefing to ask, "Is that Robert Ross from the Peninsular War? He's a formidable member of Wellington's family at arms, to be sure. We're up against the professionals, just as I predicted."

Madison didn't find Armstrong's foresight particularly exceptional or helpful. Internally, the unsolicited news slid like a cannonball to the pit of his stomach. He looked at the secretary of war from the corner of his eye and shook his head. Groping for good news, he asked, "General Winder, how many men can we count on and where are they?"

"With us here and in the surrounding area, I'd say roughly 2,000 to 2,300 regulars, navy, and marines culled from the capital district."

The president witnessed Winder interrupt his own briefing to order Major Peter to lead a battalion of 800 regulars south for several miles until he located the main British force—without taking too great a risk. Even odder, the general dispatched a message for Stansbury ordering him to abandon his position on Lowndes Hill and move his entire formation south toward Upper Marlboro. These curious instructions perplexed Madison, but before he had a moment to consider their full implications, Winder further confused the chaotic situation by demanding the district militia of 1,700 to stand fast. The president, whom Winder was trying to impress with his ludicrous efforts and this inane display of self-negating decisiveness, could see that fragmenting one's command so near the enemy would only quicken the headlong rush to defeat. Even Armstrong, also taken aback, urged Winder to withdraw the entire army to Washington and there build a revetment around the Capitol and Executive Mansion.

"Excuse me, gentlemen. I must attend to the troops. I have a battle to fight!" With those parting words Winder rode off, leaving Madison, Monroe, and Armstrong to stare at a map filled with cryptic red arrows and meaningless red circles that translated into one chilling word: doom.

———

An officer reported to Stansbury that the British, only five miles away, were coming straight at his troops, only a mile or two east of Bladensburg. Stansbury ignored Winder's order and returned his entire command to Lowndes Hill to assume defensive positions.

By the dinner hour, Sterrett's 5th Maryland trudged in from its forced march. The general added his weary soldiers to the end of the line, where they stood and waited in vain for the British, who weren't coming.

When darkness fell, the men sat down where they had been standing for hours, and a thousand flickering campfires, fueled by clapboards ripped off the commercial buildings, sprang up. The cooking fires graciously marked the American position for the British scouts secreted in the line of trees a mile to the east. White chicken feathers, plucked from birds the troops had slaughtered on the spot, clearly delineated a path for Stansbury, who stumbled down the cluttered line to Sterrett's bivouac. Stansbury was noticeably nervous and no longer able to hide his lack of combat experience. Few whom he encountered along the insect-infested path were true veterans, but knowing he wasn't alone in his inexperience didn't reassure him. He despaired over the pathetic preparations he did make and the reasonable ones he didn't. Stansbury needed to commiserate with a fellow sufferer of the same rank. In private, both could be candid about their trepidation. The company of a close friend was his only available solace that terrifying night before the battle. Soon, their government, family, and fellow citizens expected them to vanquish thousands of Wellington's *invincibles*, proud warriors from the finest army in the world. Both were certain inexperience would mean they would either die or be disgraced that day—probably by noon—exposed as parade soldiers unfit even to command a company of tin toy soldiers. But despite Stansbury's search, Winder was nowhere to be found.

Monroe arrived around midnight and repeated the rumor that Winder was either captured or dead. He had vanished somewhere on the road when Ross attacked Major Peter's column on August 23. After midnight a messenger handed Stansbury a dispatch from the resurrected Winder, who had taken his wing of the army, led by Peter, back to Washington. Stansbury, feeling forsaken to face the entire British force on his own, vacated Bladensburg, marched across the bridge, and headed for Washington. When Winder heard of the move, he countermanded Stansbury's action and ordered him back to Bladensburg. In explanation, he relayed the latest information derived from interrogating a captured enemy patrol: "The British intend to attack the capital city from Bladensburg."

At 10:00 AM on August 24, Winder ordered his command, which had settled comfortably in Washington, to Bladensburg, where Stansbury was expected to defend the Lowndes Hill line. But Stansbury didn't trust that Winder would reinforce him prior to Ross's arrival and decided to remain on the west bank of the Potomac's east branch. Trailing behind his army, Winder, clueless as ever, slumped in his saddle. The president and cabinet followed, and the people who had stayed behind to protect their homes cheered them on.

Stansbury could've returned to the strong defensive position along the ridge on the east side of Bladensburg but feared that, if pressed, he wouldn't be able to move his command across the narrow Potomac bridge and would become trapped with his back against the river. On the Washington side of the river the land didn't support a feasible defense; there was no natural high ground with open fields of fire. Wadsworth had thrown up an artillery redoubt at the intersection of the Georgetown and Washington pikes. Although it was too large for Stansbury's small field pieces, it could be somewhat modified. An orchard dominated the center of the marshy land. To Stansbury's immense relief, Colonel William Beall arrived in a cloud of dust from Annapolis with his brigade of exhausted marchers, who had been on the road for twenty hours. Without a respite, they were directed to form a reserve in the rear.

While Stansbury was overwhelmed by the approaching British, who streamed over Lowndes Hill and found it empty, Monroe decided that the troop disposition was all wrong. As secretary of state, he took command and moved the formations while Stansbury's back was turned. Before the 20th Maryland field commander could react to Monroe's meddling, Winder appeared. He agreed with Monroe and, to show his power, also moved the artillery and rifle regiments. General Walter Smith arrived, promptly argued with Stansbury concerning who was the most senior general, and then took up a position across the Washington Pike with Barney's naval guns. In the end, American units of all sizes were converging willy-nilly and elbowing for a place in the front.

The British quickly cleared the observation posts from the village and broke into open order to cross the bridge. The 85th Shropshire Light Regiment was delayed momentarily by American artillery but soon dispersed into clouds of skirmishers, thereby nullifying the solid shot usually so devastating to packed formations. The light companies of the other regiments consolidated and then rushed across the bridge without incident. The poorly placed American gun positions allowed the enemy to find dead spots where they could move unopposed. Suddenly, the six-gun battery of the artillery was in jeopardy and left the field, losing one gun in the process. The river proved fordable north of the intact bridge, which the Americans didn't even try to disable. The 44th East Essex Regiment, wearing red coats with yellow cuffs and collars, attacked where the American resistance was weakest and began to roll up the left flank.

The Royal Rocket Battery fired its unguided forty-pound rockets, which burst into fireballs and showered fragments of hot metal casing onto the frightened soldiers. The unequipped and untrained American regiment, part of Stansbury's brigade, was most susceptible to the rockets. As Ross had hoped, the screaming cylinders, trailing prodigious amounts of white smoke, terrorized the Americans, who did not know such a weapon existed. While the rockets didn't cause gross casualties, many soldiers sought refuge in the capital. In their haste to flee, they left their muskets behind.

General Winder determined that the British Light Infantry was overextended and ordered the 5th Maryland to counterattack. He misread the situation, and soon the Americans were caught in a deadly cross fire from the east and the north. The American battalions stood at close order in the center of the field to engage the British, but the enemy fought as open skirmishers from two sides. In a reversal of the Battle of Concord, Massachusetts, in 1775, the Americans paid with their lives. Winder rode forward to rally the faltering troops. Confused in the face of enemy fire, he merely interfered instead of inspired. He shouted for Stansbury to withdraw but, as usual, moments later recanted. The 5th Maryland broke and fled, chased by redcoats.

Barney's naval gunner made an impression with shot and shell and stopped three charges by the British Light Infantry. Killing and wounding the enemy officers, who led from the front, the concentrated firepower of Commodore Barney and Major Peter drove the first wave of redcoats back across the marsh to the north. The 1,700 men of Walter Smith's district brigade were spread out across the Georgetown Pike in among the guns on the north flank. To the British they looked green, lacking uniforms and discipline. They became the object of a deliberate attack from a large British contingent of line infantry, supported by hellish rocket fire. Smith believed he could hold the ground, but to his appalled surprise Winder ordered him to withdraw to the center.

Barney was just as vulnerable, but he never received the message, if one to pull back was ever issued. Soon exposed, his command took volleys of fire from the north and east. The commodore, badly wounded, was taken prisoner. His last order was a robust, "Run for it, men!" Smith's ordered withdrawal and Barney's capture brought Winder close to panic. Twice, he ordered Smith to halt and face the enemy, only to countermand the orders within minutes. The entire American complement rose as one and moved off down the Washington Pike. Redcoats streamed across the bridge at Bladensburg. Enemy formations mingled with wounded and straggling Yankees. Winder sent word by horseback to the elements still in contact to break away and reform five miles down the road at the capital. The stream of moving men, some in blue uniforms, some not, turned into a torrent. If the British had been blessed with cavalry, they would've decimated Winder's army before its remnants had traveled two miles.

As it was, the enemy was also walking, and so it became a footrace by the evening of August 24. The militiamen broke ranks, scattering in the direction of their homes and leaving what little military equipment they possessed littering the path. Here with his army disintegrating, Winder truly succumbed to total panic.

Madison, Armstrong, and the rest of the cabinet witnessed the debacle less than a mile from the battle line. Scared men, many without weapons, ran past their president without even saying, "Hurrah!" The road to Washington overflowed, as the regular army, still in formation, plodded toward the capital. Armstrong urged the president to join the blue-coated column for protection, but Monroe suggested that the president disperse the cabinet members and direct them to convene at Kemp Hall on Market Street in Frederick, Maryland, fifty miles north of Washington. Madison consented, then turned his horse and rode for the west bank of the Potomac and then north toward Harpers Ferry. The government, the Executive Mansion, and Dolley were left to their own devices.

Ross claimed sixty-four of his men killed and three times that number severely wounded. The American losses were fewer—twenty-six killed and fifty-seven wounded—because many ran rather than fought. The battle had developed so rapidly that there were only brief periods of rifle action. No units had clashed in hand-to-hand fighting; no bayonet needed cleaning. It was less a stand than a rout. Most of the soldiers, sailors, and militiamen involved at Bladensburg never fired their weapons.

The Burning of Washington

The British occupied Washington and torched the Capitol, Executive Mansion, and other federal buildings along Pennsylvania Avenue. Some said later that Yankee Doodle looters were as responsible as John Bull. As they trudged north along the Potomac, Monroe and Winder paused to watch the glow in the sky to the south. They spent the night surrounded by a thousand regular soldiers turned refugees. Both men had more or less deserted; they made not the slightest effort to oppose the British or eject them from the capital city. Their grand strategy was rather simple: wait for the enemy to leave.

That night and the next day, Ross and Cockburn supervised the destruction of the Navy Yard and Washington Arsenal (today Fort McNair) at the fork in the Potomac River a mile south of the capital. An inquisitive element discovered a dry well at the arsenal and threw a blazing torch down to see what the Americans had dumped there before abandoning the garrison. To their surprise and regret, it had been filled with gunpowder, which exploded, killing twelve and wounding thirty. It was the most horrific engagement of the battle, but only one side suffered casualties.

Monroe rode to Alexandria and took charge of what military men and equipment there was to block the southern approach. He had received reports regarding the progress of Captain Gordon's fleet. Captain Dyson, commander of Fort Warburton, sent word that he would soon be attacked by water and land. As the enemy drew closer, Dyson expanded his orders, which stated he was to destroy the guns and fort if attacked by an overwhelming force. Prematurely, before a shot was even fired, he acted on them, spiked the guns, and ignited the powder magazine before abandoning his command.

By the last week of August, Madison requested that Armstrong resign as secretary of war. The ever-able (in his modest view) James Monroe accepted the temporary duty, while remaining secretary of state.

Cockburn, withdrawing all his elements, left on the tide for Jamaica Station to replenish and plan his return. Before September 1—the date set for Wellington's invasion of the United States—Cochrane had accomplished his mission; his destructive incursion had diverted political and, more important, military attention away from the Canadian border. Better yet, the frantic reports of redcoats marauding through the capital's streets bred hysteria and defeatism throughout the country. America was now primed for the taking.

Jackson the Peace Maker

While the British were sailing the Chesapeake, Madison had appointed General Jackson to conclude a peace with the Creek Nation that would put an end to the Indians' recalcitrant behavior and push the boundaries of the United States farther south and west. Jackson called for a convention of the chiefs for August, but Indian Commissioner Benjamin Hawkins told him that the Indians were not coming. In a rage Jackson threatened,

"Destruction will attend a failure to comply with those orders, Hawkins! If they don't come in and submit, a sudden and well-directed stroke may be made that will at once reduce them to unconditional submission."

The Indian chiefs finally gathered in mid-August at a camp in southern Alabama Territory. Jackson had been appointed in place of General Charles Pinckney, who had concluded a treaty with the other tribes that essentially allowed them to remain on their land, and the chiefs expected from him a similar offer. Jackson had other instructions and came down on their heads with outrageous demands backed by threats of further violence. Jackson was aware that the Creeks were still accepting arms from the British and offers of assistance from the Spanish governor of Florida. He repaid the treachery. Large tracts of land—far more than had ever been given up—were forfeited. When the chief protested, Sharp Knife, as Jackson was known to the Indians, declared, "The truth is, the great body of the Creek chiefs and warriors did not respect the power of the United States. They thought we were an insignificant Nation, that we would be overpowered by the British. You are fat with eating British beef." The Indians signed away their land in total defeat.

When Jackson returned from the negotiation in late August, a letter was waiting from his old friend George Grigg, a Washington colleague. It read, in part, "The British have burned Washington. They left as quickly as they arrived. Last evening a fiery glow filled the sky. The Houses of Congress are gone, as is the arsenal, dockyard, treasury, war office, presidents' house, ropewalk, and Potomac bridges. A smoldering remnant, the capital city now smokes on the bank of the debris-filled river."

Jackson was distraught. "Those bloody British!"

Lloyd's of London

In late August, a clerk at the marine insurance house mounted the dais behind the long mahogany table at the far end of the Members Hall. His presence passed unnoticed by several hundred well-dressed gentlemen in tall hats who milled about or spoke in small groups. Thick gray tobacco smoke obscured the room's business end, which rose off the main floor in a series of escalating platforms covered with refectory tables—an altar to commerce. On succeeding levels, clerks worked, white quill pens swishing on polished tabletops heaped with sheaths of paper bound with colored tape. Investment firms were separated by rows of eight-foot-high wood-paneled partitions along each side of the ornate vaulted chamber. On one side of the stanchions, bookcases bulged with parchments, papers, and engraved documents while silent clerks on high stools labored at their fold-down desks. The ceiling resembled a great ship's upturned hull with ribs exposed. Founded at Lloyd's coffeehouse in the mid-1600s, the exchange had grown until it required this massive hall.

Lloyd's of London was all about gambling: shipowners bet money that their vessels and cargoes would perish while the Lloyd's partners wagered they wouldn't. Each time a vessel arrived safely, Lloyd's retained the stake money. Only when damage occurred were the owners rewarded for their up-front money and paid off. It was a strange and highly speculative business, but actuarial statistics made it obscenely profitable. Unfortunately, it also attracted a few shady characters and companies prone not to honor their agreements. They were soon identified and separated. Despite this, Lloyd's success was built on trust, deep pockets, and a sterling track record.

The clerk stood alone between massive, deeply carved posts. The supports were from the unfortunate vessel HMS *Queen Charlotte*, which while carrying gold to pay Russia for her participation in the Napoleonic Wars, was lost to fire at sea. Recovered in 1800, the hundred-pound brass bell, corroded a deep green from immersion in the sea, had since been rung to attract the murmuring crowd's attention. One strike foretold bad news; two strikes, good news. That day the investors paused and waited, suspended like marionettes on strings, for the second ring that did not come.

"The consortium announces," the clerk said in a voice as clear as a bell, "that the sea has claimed the following vessels lost to the hurricane south of Bermuda this past month." Silence swept through the room. These men represented family fortunes that had been committed to the recovery of full value. Lloyd's of London allowed only those investors with a record of sound financial dealing to trade under its venerable name. On a particularly hazardous venture, several firms would join together, thereby allowing the entire voyage to be covered while lessening the risk to the individual broker. The loss of the *Queen Charlotte* had decimated the holdings of several partnerships.

A Caribbean storm had trapped several convoy cells of Naval Board merchantmen. All had Royal Navy escorts. The Parliament was willing to pay high premiums to insure warships against loss at sea by act of God. Recently, a Lloyd's consortium had paid a claim of a million pounds. A number of vessels bound for the Americas that summer had been reported overdue, which allowed underwriters to ask specialist brokers to reinsure their liability based on the possibility that the ship in question was a total loss. If the report turned out to be false, then the added premium was considered to be worth the gamble, but if it were true, then the additional cash was welcome at *any* price.

The clerk began alphabetically: "The *Ambrose*, victuals and uniforms, out of Liverpool, Naval Board contract, fifteen days overdue at Jamaica Station; the *Claudette,* general cargo. . . ." The final announcement was, "The *Washburn*, out of Chatham, horse carrier, Naval Board contract, presumed sunk."

An underwriter, desperate for additional details, elbowed through the ruined mourners to the disposition desk on the first level.

The clerk, displaying no perceptible emotion, retrieved a small, black, oilskin-covered book from a pouch marked with the broad arrow. Considering such a possession to be bad luck, the clerk was glad to be rid of it and dropped it onto the table as if it were a package of dead fish left too long in the sun. "Sir, two weeks ago, a navy cutter on her way home plucked it from the pocket of a dead man tied to a floating ship's hatch off Little Abaco Island."

The broker knew Abaco lay at the northeastern fringe of the Bahamas. The clerk had offered the waterproof hardbound volume, the kind used by campaigning soldiers, as evidence for the claim that was sure to follow. The broker's heart sank as he picked up proof that the *Washburn* was resting comfortably on the bottom of the sea; almost certainly there were no survivors. Nothing was asked or volunteered about the dead man. What did the details of a man's life matter to a broker? After all, the investors had insured the ship and her cargo, not the lives of individual crew members.

The broker, head down and cursing the bad start to a long day, accepted the book without question and returned to his cubicle. There, he hunted until he found the contract. He was relieved to realize it would be a limited claim: the *Washburn* was small and old, while her cargo of horses was of negligible value when compared to the *Queen Charlotte*'s cargo of gold. The broker and his partners could withstand the loss. Putting the diary aside, he went on with the day's business.

The broker's clerk, Jonas Weaver, a bachelor who occupied a room in a house between Lloyd's and Saint Paul's Cathedral, slipped the book into his case along with a partially nibbled chunk of cheese from lunch. At seven that evening, work finished, and Jonas walked to his local public house, the Londoner, for supper and a mug of ale, as was his habit. There, over two tankards of ale and a pork pie, he read from the diary he had taken from work. The script was broad, precise, and learned.

> Basil Ronald Lawless Rymer
> Captain, Royal Staff Corps
> Special Staff, Duke of Wellington

> The *Washburn*, John Rudge, Master, horse carrier out of Chatham Royal Dockyard, under Naval Board contract, bound for Chambly, Canada, July 1814

It began, as did so many of the personal accounts Jonas had read, at the beginning, at the bon voyage part of the voyage, so Jonas flipped ahead, letting the pages' curled edges scuttle through his bony fingertips and stopping only when the word "snapped" caught his eye. He wiped his lips with a napkin and scrambled back a few pages to locate where the episode started.

> —a black storm clouding far off to our front sent me to read the barometer in the captain's cabin. The master waved me in. I joined him, as he recorded the change in position of the pale-blue metal needle. A glance at the entry from the previous watch confirmed what we suspected—the pressure was plummeting.
>
> I told the master of the ominous clouds dead ahead that splayed out before the setting sun. On deck we watched the edge of the sky turn from silver to gold. Rudge told me to turn around, for another culprit was brewing off our stern. Gaining on us, the deep ebony mass was rapidly blotting the sky like an ink-spreading splotch. Rudge told me that we'd run before the storm and assured me that "it's not all bad news." We could make up the days we lost replenishing our supplies.

First Mate, Mister Lang, called for all hands. The crew was sent aloft to furl the fore and main topsails to prevent damage. The courses were clued up, fore and main, to prevent the masts from cracking under the strain. Even though both watches were aloft, the crew was few in number and the mizzenmast had to wait. By the time the sailors, exhausted by the urgent pace, climbed up to take down the mizzen topgallant, the pursuing wind had doubled in intensity. The crew fought to roll and secure the mizzen topsail. Under the pressure of the screeching wind the masts began creaking, as the bow was driven down and spray crashed over the foredeck. Mister Lang told me to go below in case one of the masts snapped off. The only staysails deployed were the spanker aft and the jib forward on the bow left to aid in steering.

Taking in the excitement, though, I remained next to the master at the wheel. Soaked to the marrow by the tons of cold water splashing and rushing about, I commandeered a lifeline that Rudge had ordered to be strung. The master, now at the top of his game, cautioned that steering was critical. "If we get crosswise, we're a goner!" He added, "Don't worry. I've ridden out many a storm and while it might take us out of our way, the burden belongs to Mr. Cherry and Doc Rainsby coping with the horses."

I'd nearly forgotten about the horses amid the exhilarating perils of the storm, which had grown so deafening that I could scarcely hear the master issuing commands to close all the airways, for fear of shipping in more water than the pumps could handle. He could see that the men cranking the water up from the bilge were beginning to flag.

Hand over hand, along the sodden lifeline, I crept to the hatchway. The pitching and rolling flung my feet off the exposed slippery deck that dropped out from under my scrambling boots. I feared letting go of the rope. An able seaman came to my aid and gathered me into his arms and took me below. He must've seen the panic in my eyes, for I believed I was about to be tossed overboard.

It took more than a moment to regain my composure, as the man who'd likely saved my life ascended the ladder into the teeth of the storm. Normally, I would've searched for dry clothes, but there was no point to that exercise. Below, the grooms were at their stations securing lines, to be used as handholds, along the passageway to facilitate ease of movement. The ship was becoming unstable, as it plunged and rose up in ever-deeper throes of angry green water.

I found Doc with three grooms administering to a mare, who had smashed her mouth on the stall's edge. I saw blood and broken teeth and the wild eyes of the animal, distressed beyond belief. Doc waved his hand at me to stay back, as his assistant poked the muzzle of his large caliber pistol against the white blaze on her forehead. He fired a ball into her brain to cease her suffering.

With the frenzy over for the moment, Rainsby left his underlings to cope with the dead beast and approached me. He said, "It's all that can be done. There's nothing else to do. Even in the best conditions the animal would be unable to eat and waste away."

Tonight, I lie in my swinging bed, rather than in the company of my fellow travelers, since it's impossible to move about this popping cork in the midst of this damnable storm, which has stubbornly worsened. The master believes that we're being driven by a storm toward another that's just ahead to the east of the Bahamas. Might we be sandwiched in between? A gut-wrenching thought!

August 11, 1814

The ship has traded in its usual groaning for eerie popping sounds as if her treenails are snapping off and loosening strakes pinned into the hull's ribs. Our rudder has already been carried away. We're towing a sea anchor not only to slow our progress, but also to keep our head with the wind. When I was up on deck at first light, the sea and the air were the same impenetrable white color. I couldn't discern the horizon. Cherry told me the animals are going mad from the incessant movement; several had to be shot to stop their frenzy. The closing of the ventilation system and the heat generated from the horses' hyperactivity have rendered it impossible to linger below for more than a few minutes at a time. Cherry, the master horseman, is beside himself and tells me that he's never seen a storm this vehement and violent. He fears for the horses' sanity—if not for the ship's safety.

I haven't seen the master since last evening. I'm told he's at the wheel, but the deck is so viciously kinetic that I dare not go topside.

I hear a bell tolling, the ship's bell. Has the clapper broken free? No, it keeps ringing in a rapid urgent rhythm wrought by a man's hand, I'm sure.

Is it a fire? I must go. God willing, I'll write again tomorrow. I've put my things in order and fear neither Nature nor man. I only hope He casts his benevolent gaze upon us in this time of dire need.

That was all that was written. Weaver closed the volume and tried to imagine the man's last moments, if he had continued to cry out for God's mercy or merely cursed His divine indifference. But a lifetime of clerking at Lloyd's had blunted that faculty. After all, there were only so many ways one could drown. Sunk was sunk, dead was dead, and in the end, a claim was a claim.

Jonas stabbed another chunk of pork pie, which he promptly put into his mouth. Within seconds, as was his habit, he was counting the number of times he chewed. He did not connect the importance of the lost horses to the formations that would have to walk nor the wagons that would fail to bring food and ammunition to embattled soldiers. How many other ships were never heard of again?

CHAPTER 8

Invasion!

"I have told the ministers repeatedly that a naval superiority on the lakes is a sine qua non of success in the war on the frontier of Canada."
—Arthur Wellesley, Duke of Wellington

Meanwhile on the northern front, the American navy protecting Lake Champlain had spent the winter and spring of 1814 building up strength to counter the Royal Navy juggernaut.

In March 1814 Commander Macdonough, having recovered from Commodore Pring's naval attack at Otter Creek the previous year, was ordered north once more. His meager naval force was supporting yet another American army invasion intended to advance forty miles to Montreal.

This time, Major General Wilkinson was the would-be conqueror of British Canada. He fostered a new adventure, leaving the South to Jackson, who had received a permanent commission in the army's regular ranks as a major general. The impetuous General Wilkinson was inspired by Jefferson's most recent witless boast to the Marquis de Lafayette, who had gained his renown during the American Revolution and was on a visit to the United States in the fall of 1813. The press widely quoted the former president's pledges to annex Canada. Confident in Wilkinson's ability, Jefferson had vowed to the Frenchman, "Before spring we will sup together in Quebec."

Yet once again, a few miles inside the Canadian border, the grand American attack had fizzled out and Wilkinson was relieved of command. The bedraggled American troops returned to Plattsburgh and Burlington to refit and to train under new leadership. Commodore Macdonough returned to boat building at Otter Creek.

At the start of the summer, while the Royal Navy was engaged in transporting thousands of soldiers to Canada, Secretary Jones's attention was turned from the blockade that kept the American navy bottled up and out of action. He became alarmed by the rapid pace of Royal Navy construction on the Canadian end of Lake Champlain and the stream of British soldiers landing in Quebec. Macdonogh received a letter from Washington:

July 4, 1814

Master Commandant, Lake Champlain
Commodore Thomas Macdonough, USN
Vergennes, Vermont

It's come to my attention that the complexion of the Royal Navy in Canada has altered rather dramatically. The Royal Navy has assimilated the Canadian Provincial Marine and has embarked on a program to construct a frigate, along with auxiliary support, strong enough to sweep Lake Champlain of an American naval presence. Such ambitions cannot be tolerated. I'm therefore sending you two hundred more joiners and shipwrights from Boston and New York, along with cord and iron to enlarge our own fleet. Do all you can to extend the limits of your yard's maximum capability. All efforts are being made to detail sufficient crewmen to your service.

Take to the lake at your earliest opportunity. Prevent Royal Navy adventures supporting British land forces. And keep me regularly informed of progress and any relevant events.

Signed,
William R. Jones
Secretary of the Navy

The secretary's message didn't surprise the young officer. For weeks Judge Sailly had been passing on hair-raising reports of a tall-masted frigate under construction at Ile-aux-Noix's boatyard. The Royal Navy's lake trials of the HMS *Linnet*, a new sloop of war, were conducted openly. U.S. customs agents observed the events, as they bobbed about for a better view on the watery border above Rouses Point, New York. American boat construction was progressing swiftly, but the promised sailors hadn't materialized. Jones didn't understand why men refused to serve on the lake. The prolonged British naval blockade had confined the American navy within its ports all along the eastern seaboard. Jones assumed that crews could be shifted north to Lake Champlain, but Macdonough feared that two factors would inhibit volunteers: the rumors of lake fever, which scared some, and the prohibition on prize money. If Macdonough were to man his new vessels, he would have to raise the crews himself.

By August 1 the commodore could not wait any longer for crewmen who might never answer the summons. The enemy's commitment to a building program and Captain Pring's recall, owing in part to his unsuccessful expedition the previous fall, meant that the lake was free of a Canadian maritime presence—for the time being.

Macdonough anchored the sloop *President* in Burlington's open bay. At a floating dock, a Vermont militia colonel, dressed in a green coat with red collar, lapels, and turnbacks, met his gig. Taking his guest by open carriage through the prosperous town, the colonel pointed out the repairs that had been made since Murray's raid the previous year. The tour was an unwelcome reminder of the American navy's inability to defend the city. Macdonough would've liked to assure the gentleman that such destruction would never happen again on his watch, but he couldn't and so remained mute. Newly promoted Brigadier General Macomb was found supervising gun crews as they limbered up the cannons. Others were packing tents into wagons in obvious preparations for an impending departure.

Always the cheery diplomat, Macomb greeted the naval officer with bravado. His handshake and broad smile were most genuine and welcome. "Thomas! How goes our brilliant navy?"

Macdonough thought the general had gained some weight over the winter; his face was round and ruddy, while his blue eyes sparkled with the prospect of adventure. He wore an embroidered, single, five-pointed silver star within a laurel wreath on either side of his dark blue stand-up collar. Macdonough had seen Macomb from afar that March through his telescope from his ship. He had watched the general trudge along with his men on the lake's western shore to and from Canada with the rest of Wilkinson's force. Hatless in the sunshine, his exposed head had revealed numerous strands of silver hiding ineptly within the thick dark curls that flopped onto Macomb's forehead and over his ears.

"Congratulations on your promotion to general," Macdonough said. "Well deserved it is! Especially after that trek north with Wilkinson."

"I noticed you were dragooned into the melee as well. I saw your ships clinging to the shoreline and about to have their bellies ripped out on the rocks. For what, I ask you?" Then he answered his own question. "For nothing! One can learn a great deal more from failure than victory, though. We ought to chalk it up to experience, wouldn't you agree?"

"Yes, sir," he agreed, "but I'd prefer a little success from time to time."

"So would I, Commodore, so would I. As you can see, we're about to embark on an endeavor in search of just such an elusive prey."

"Going on maneuvers?"

Macomb smiled. "Why no, not at all. Major General George Izard, our new commander, has ordered the northeastern army to consolidate at Plattsburgh. There, he's been directed to conduct a school for soldiers—all six thousand regulars! I feel most positive about this man. He's no Wilkinson—though as of late too many are." The general urged his visitor to walk with him out of the way of the bustling gunners. "You know, Thomas, I foresee a need for naval protection during this lake crossing. I know the Royal Navy's been quiet lately, but if those vile smugglers—or should I say vile *spies*—tip the British off, we could be ambushed on the water and utterly ruined."

Macdonough was pleased to assist and temporarily set his own needs aside. It was the best way for Macomb to learn about the commodore's shortage of qualified crewmen. "General, I heard about Wilkinson's court-martial and had thought you would take his place. I can only hope this Izard has some loins to gird!"

Macomb repeated his assessment. "He's no Wilkinson, thank God! Nearly three quarters of our men are new. It's high time we ran 'em through a vigorous training program, if we expect 'em to meet the redcoats and not turn tail."

This was the first Macdonough had heard of an imminent border crossing by the British army rather than the navy.

Macomb put his arm around the naval officer's shoulder and slowed their walk. He drew the commodore in tight and lowered his voice. "I hope to join the rest of the army at Plattsburgh by the tenth. Can you protect the crossing on such short notice?"

"Yes, sir. We'll stay north. You may not even see us, but you can count on the *President* and a dozen gunboats. I'd have the new *Saratoga* and even *Ticonderoga* as well—if only I had the crews. This past winter and spring we've spent an enormous amount of time and money building a credible naval fleet. We've been able to replace the *Eagle* and *Growler* with two new, bigger, more formidable vessels. The *Ticonderoga* has twenty guns, the *Saratoga* mounts twenty-six. We have enough material to build one more brig before the summer sailing season concludes."

The general cocked his head and pursed his lips, "Great news, Thomas. Just in time, too. While you're out sailing, we'll be digging in." Macomb's plan for Plattsburgh's defense, indeed for the entire North Country, involved an overwhelming need for naval support. Macomb knew the British would test those vessels to the breaking point, but he would save that tidbit for later.

"General, the news may sound good and may prove meaningful to victory, but, as is, I can't set out till I have fully trained crews. Alas, sir, there aren't enough sailors willing to serve on Lake Champlain. All I have from the navy are empty promises. If I don't start training crewmen soon, these vessels will be like thistles before the wind. British guns will blow them away. Sir, I once again require some of your soldiers, preferably those with experience on the water, but I'll take anyone."

The general could easily see the importance to his own plans of displaying power on the lake and therefore took little convincing. "How many, Commodore?"

Macdonough knew he had to be realistic, paring down the number to the absolute minimum. If Macomb and Izard were digging in, then they must be expecting an attack of considerable size and strength. They would only take on the enemy from a defensive position if their numbers were too small to engage the redcoats in the open field. While Macdonough calculated, Macomb provided a glimpse of his own dire need for trained troops.

"Commodore, it's no secret that the British will be crossing the border. Since June, I've been receiving reports that a considerable number of Wellington's heroes have been marching in Montreal's streets. Canadian newspapers are filled with speculation. The arriving British officer corps is toasted at summer balls and a veritable forest of masts has sprouted in the harbors of Quebec and Montreal. Governor Prevost has promised the people that the regular army will now bear the burden of the war. Izard believes that the new redcoat formations will take the offensive, and if they do, then Plattsburgh will be the first chance—let's not hope the last—to stop them."

Macdonough couldn't believe what he was hearing. He had never considered the possibility of a land invasion of America. British raids to protect those smugglers vital to support the army in Canada could be expected, but an *invasion*?

"Why Plattsburgh and not Burlington? There is nothing of value in northern New York."

"General Izard would agree with you. He reckons the British will most likely attack at Niagara. England's eyeing the west, he says. He's certain that northern Ohio, the Indiana Territory, and a little chop off the Illinois are bringing them in such force. Marshal Moreau continued to advise him until he left for Quebec and had convinced him that Napoleon's fall has renewed the crown's interest toward its former colonies. Izard tells me that he has a strategic outlook, one that I'm not sufficiently educated to appreciate totally. You see, I've had only provincial schooling at West Point. He also believes they intend to secure the southern shore of the Great Lakes to protect an expansion west to the Pacific. On the other hand, in my humble way, I've concluded that Prevost intends to resurrect Burgoyne's plan and strike south for New York City. If our northeastern army congregates on the western side of the lake, we can support either avenue. If Generals Brown and Scott call on us to reinforce Niagara or Ohio, we can respond from Plattsburgh. A march to Sackets Harbor and ships to Niagara can be accomplished in time to save the day. But, if they come due south, we'll meet them at Plattsburgh, where we'll be dug in and where you can protect our right flank from Cumberland Bay."

"Sir, if you travel west to Niagara, then no one other than the militia will be here to secure the shoreline." Macdonough, like so many other commanders, didn't trust the militia. He knew them to be wasters, drunks, and looters.

"No, no, my friend. I'll remain behind, huddled at Plattsburgh's dirt forts, spending the summer digging trenches along Saranac River's southeast bank. There, I'll be in the company of the sick, lame, and lazy—all those unable to make the trek."

The urgency of the situation was exceedingly clear. "I'll require an additional 250 men now, sir. If I can finish one more brig before September, then I will need another hundred."

"Commodore, I don't consider lending you troops as a loss. My right flank will lie on the bay's shoreline wide open to the enemy's naval cannon fire. By adding to your crews, I'm merely protecting myself. Cooperation by land and lake will be the only way we can hope to resist. You realize far more than most that no one's coming to save us. There isn't a federal formation between Plattsburgh and Baltimore, a span of more than five hundred miles south. We're on our own. We'll have to complement and suffice for each other."

Macdonough was relieved by the promise of help, yet plunged into deep doubt. "What if the British come our way? Will six thousand raw troops stop such an onslaught?"

Tipping his hat in farewell, Macomb promised, "It's a question I look forward to answering. I'll find your sailors in the ranks and send them over. You can be sure that once the hard digging starts, the volunteers will favor a free ride on a warship. Sail on, Commodore," Macomb said, to which Macdonough replied, "Dig on, General, dig on."

Delancey Brought Up to Date

On August 13, 1814, eleven days before the successful attack on Washington, Colonel Delancey stood on the heaving deck of the frigate HMS *Endymion* fifty miles east of Halifax. He and his quartermaster staff had embarked on July 16 and bypassed Bermuda in an effort to surge ahead of Wellington, confined on the plodding, pitching ship of the line. It had been hair-raising to career at eleven knots ahead of a storm front that chased them southeast.

Coming up on the port side, a Royal Navy message cutter from Halifax Station ran up and hailed the *Endymion*. Captain Hall pulled back his pace by bracing around the yards on the mainmast, thereby causing the ship to slow down and take on the packet shunted across via a high line.

The captain invited Delancey to share in the folded papers, tied with thin red tape. Some had surely come from Commissary General Robinson in Montreal. The oilskin-covered dispatch box was turned on its side, spilling out a couple dozen tri-folded documents, each wrapped in tape and sealed with either the Admiralty or the commissary stamp. The captain and Delancey stood by as the secretary sifted through the pile and sorted the documents into a stack for each. There was nothing of importance from Robinson except to confirm that all movements were on track and that the army was assembling in great numbers at Fort Chambly in Canada.

"Well, it's all good news. I was rather worried that some disaster had occurred while I've been cloistered at sea."

"Don't worry, sir," Hall snickered. "What could possibly go wrong?"

Hall passed a naval dispatch across the trestle table that had been moved by the steward against the window to capture the light. The document was a status report of the convoys destined for Chambly. An introductory paragraph relayed the weather reports for the past thirty days and the status of the trade winds, as culled from ships' logs in various ports across the Caribbean and Bermuda. It also included relevant items extracted from the blockade fleet along the eastern seaboard. Hall wrinkled his forehead, deep red from days spent in the wind and sun. Head down, he leafed through ship statistics, then his eyes rose upward and fixed on Delancey, who was running his finger down the columns of merchant craft bundled within numbered convoys. Hall, used to reading the lists of ship names, had gone quickly to the point of interest.

"William, look at page three. Convoy 7-20-CT." He was referring to the horse carriers, so vital to the coming campaign, from Chatham. The captain was unaware that Delancey had ordered Captain Rymer to that special duty against his desires.

"The *Washburn!*" the colonel cried. "Lost at sea—all hands. My God!"

Seek Forgiveness Rather Than Permission

Commodore Macdonough handed his second in command, Lieutenant Stephen Cassin, a dispatch from Secretary Jones that had arrived by the morning courier boat from Albany.

Office of the Secretary of the Navy   1 August 1814

Enclosed please find a copy of the joint regulation of the War and Navy departments for the government of their respective commanders, when action is considered. Take careful note of the following:

No officer of the army of the United States shall, on any pretence, command any ships or vessels of the United States nor shall officers of the navy of the United States, on any pretence, command any troops of the army of the United States.

William R. Jones
Secretary of the Navy

Curt and pointed, Jones's letter didn't address the pressing issue: the absence of navy crewmen. Macdonough was being asked to disregard his solution of using soldiers to perform as sailors.

"Stephen, unfortunately, I told the secretary that Macomb wasn't just supplying soldiers as crew, but that he'd agreed to leave his officers in charge since I have none."

"Sir, we can't afford to accept this communiqué. It's a court-martial offense if we do! I don't recall *ever* receiving this message. It must've been lost in transit."

It was a common, convenient excuse. Macdonough did not like Cassin's proposed solution, but no other was available. He was committed to his course of action.

"What does the secretary expect me to do without crews in the face of the enemy? I thought he would approve my initiative. After all, his Fourth of July order stipulated that I not tolerate any British incursion and take to the lake at my earliest opportunity." The commodore's frustration overflowed. "How can I do what he demands if I don't have the crews?"

Accompanying the dispatch was Lieutenant Robert Henley, the nominated commander of the new brig that Brown Brothers had knocked together in less than thirty days. Although Henley had been appointed in Washington, final approval remained the commodore's prerogative. A year younger than Macdonough, Henley was well connected in the capital. He had been denied prior commands as a result of his history of personality conflicts with senior officers and crews. A neat, aloof man of twenty-nine, he treated everyone below him with disdain and his equals in rank with intrigue and malice. His most recent failure had confined him to a desk at the Navy Department, but his family, well connected within the federal government, was influential enough to force his selection for command on the inland lake. Within the Navy Department few recognized the Lake Champlain's importance and instead concentrated on the sea-going navy, which hadn't actually gone anywhere in the preceding year. Since the American navy was very small, nearly all the officers were known to one another either personally or by reputation. Among junior officers, often crammed into tiny wardrooms at sea, tall tales and gossip dominated the conversation. So it was that Macdonough was less than pleased to shake Henley's hand.

"May I present my orders to take command of the brig *Surprise*?"

Macdonough's first words were cautious. "Henley, where is the brig *Surprise*?"

Henley, who hadn't bothered to change into suitable attire on this first meeting with the commodore, said, "It's your new twenty-gunner, the one just finished. When I accepted the command from the secretary, I took the first commanding officer's privilege and informed him that I shall call her the *Surprise*."

"You did, did you?"

During the brief exchange Henley didn't apologize for presuming far too much nor did he acknowledge Macdonough's position as master commandant of Lake Champlain or his title of commodore.

"Yes, indeed. Macdonough, it's a splendid name, since the enemy doesn't know she exists. Clever, isn't it? In fact, I admit that some in Washington didn't expect I'd find her finished. You're to be commended for the accomplishment, Macdonough."

Well aware of his superior's Irish temper, Cassin retreated into the background. The commodore, seething inside at Henley's sheer arrogance, kept his head, since a superior officer couldn't call out a junior. It was a terrible beginning. The last thing Macdonough needed was an unctuous political appointee relaying distorted tales of his own daring and other folly to Washington. Fortunately, Henley hadn't been present when the message from Jones was discussed. To remind the new officer of their respective positions, Macdonough dispensed with surnames; instead, he addressed the new arrival by his rank.

"Lieutenant, as commodore of this flotilla, I've christened her *Eagle*. And though *Surprise* may be a splendid name, I believe *Eagle* to be far more appropriate." As the officer in charge, Macdonough didn't wish to explain the reason for his choice, though it ought to have been obvious. Barely restraining himself, the commodore paused until he regained some semblance of composure and then announced to both officers, "Prepare for a three-day trip to Plattsburgh. There, I'll attempt to find a crew for the *Eagle*. Cassin, while there you will survey the bay." He nodded to Henley. "And you, Lieutenant, are dismissed."

Izard Has Second Thoughts about the Invasion

The commander of the northeastern wing of the American army, Major General Izard, had at first agreed with Secretary Armstrong's assessment. The British army would reinforce Prevost's men at Niagara and proceed to push Brown back toward the west and north to reach the Mississippi River. As of late, however, doubts fluttered like moths in his mind. Izard owed his promotion and, more important, his position to the secretary of war.

The general, a sycophant, had served in France as an aide to Armstrong ten years earlier. He had also edited the secretary's book on warfare. When Wilkinson was relieved, Izard, a newly appointed brigadier, had lobbied for promotion once again. Now in the position he desired, he began to question his fitness for command. He was finding decision making much more difficult than mere mindless agreement.

American customs agents' reports regarding British intentions countered those in the Montreal newspapers. Canadian accounts reviewed the composition of military columns marching west along the St. Lawrence. The agents spoke of troops consolidating at Fort Chambly at the confluence of the Richelieu and St. Lawrence rivers south of Montreal. In a rare moment of defiant courage Izard voiced an opinion that went against the War Department's view of the situation. The general pleaded for relief from his orders to go west in aid of Generals Brown and Scott. He could see that Wellington's intention was to strike due south down Lake Champlain, the shortest and simplest route to victory. Armstrong, ignoring the general's unsolicited notions, ordered him out of Plattsburgh on August 6. (The secretary had based his order on the estimate of his personal spy, a Plattsburgh lawyer living in Montreal.) Izard, unaware of the spy, continued to send daily appeals to Armstrong as further confirmations arrived that pointed to Plattsburgh as the redcoats' main target.

He confided to Macomb, "It matters not if they're wrong and I'm right. I'll be blamed for the mistake and drummed out of the army. I've been so careful for so many years to maintain myself within the War Department's good graces, but I'll be the scapegoat. Of that, you can be sure. Oh, it's dreadful, isn't it?"

What Macomb found dreadful wasn't Izard's career hazards, but rather his own realization that with three-quarters of his command gone, he would be alone with nothing but invalids blocking the path of Wellington's juggernaut. While most of the army prepared to move west, the remainder dug deeper, stockpiling ammunition and supplies on the peninsula formed by the Saranac River. In mid-August Macomb called on Major General Benjamin Mooers, the New York militia commander, at Mooers's home overlooking the future British lines. The regular army had dug a line across the center of his garden that reached down to where the river met the bay.

Mooers welcomed Macomb into the parlor of his large, two-story red-brick home. Unfortunately, the hammering on two blockhouses being built within fifty yards strained communications.

"I'd offer you some refreshments on this hot day, but I'm afraid I'm alone in the house. My wife's fled to Albany to be with her family during the crisis. It's not that she is afraid, mind you. She simply can't stand the constant din and disruption your soldiers are creating in anticipation of this perceived British advance."

Macomb wasn't surprised that the militia commander didn't support the view that the British were coming. That summer the militia had declined the offer to train side by side with the regulars; instead, they said they had to work their farms and prepare for the winter. From the outset Mooers's attitude made Macomb's visit contentious and his appeal for assistance most tenuous. It was a dangerous position for Mooers to take—even if there was no immediate threat from the North. Training at no cost with the regular army was rarely offered, and his judgment in this matter was now being questioned in Albany.

"General, there are those in Washington who would agree with you that this labor's all for nothing. But may I take you into my confidence?" He waited for Mooers to agree, but the latter was icily silent. Macomb took a breath and proceeded. "General Izard's leaving soon for Sackets Harbor. I'll be left here with those soldiers and heavy cannon unable to make the arduous journey. In the event that the 'rarity' becomes a reality and the British do attack south, if only in a feint, we must be prepared to defend Plattsburgh. To be a credible ruse, the British will send at a minimum several thousand marauders to garner headlines. But, sir, the people will suffer nonetheless. I am confident that's not what you want your constituents to endure."

"What do you propose?"

He handed Mooers an intelligence summary listing the units at Chambly. "Whatever the ultimate strategy, some of those redcoats are coming our way, which is why I'm continuing to dig in your garden. The regulars left behind won't be able to defend the town on their own. And Governor Martin Chittenden of Vermont has refused to send his militia to defend New York. Sir, I need your militiamen to stand with us."

Mooers bristled at the mention of the Vermonters' abandonment. There had been enough bad feelings between New York and Vermont since the British attack the previous year. "By God, sir, if that's the state of things, then it's my duty to notify Governor Daniel Tompkins that I should be released immediately to federal service along with the five northern counties." The militia commander saw it as a chance to play a role; besides, his wife was gone. He could have a hell of a good time on the federal payroll. He did not believe for a minute that there would be any serious fighting. That afternoon he dispatched a rider to Albany and took it on himself to call out the 2,500 men listed on the muster rolls at the armory located in the basement of St. John's Academy, in the center of town.

Army and Navy Come Together at Plattsburgh

Macdonough took all the seaworthy craft with him on his trip north to shake up the complacent crews and to test the ships. In the lead was Lieutenant Charles Budd, captain of the *Preble*, a very small but swift staysail-rigged sloop sporting seven, long nine-pounders and a crew of forty-three. Little more than a cutter, she was named in honor of Macdonough's old superior in the Mediterranean, where they had fought the Barbary pirates. Next came the *Saratoga*, the commodore's flagship, a three-masted, ship-rigged sloop of war with eight, long twenty-four-pound cannons; a dozen twenty-four-pound carronades; and six forty-two-pound carronades. Undermanned with a complement of 250, she was the fleet's biggest and best. Close behind was Cassin's *Ticonderoga*, a two-masted brig armed with four long eighteens and eight twelve-pound cannons and crewed by 115 former soldiers. Originally meant as a steam-powered vessel, the *Ticonderoga* had a hull design that made her a slow sailer. Well behind the other vessels, as a southerly breeze picked up, were a dozen seventy-foot rowed gunboats. The small latine sails did little to increase the boats' speed, and they required crews of sixty to row their oars for the forty-mile trip north to Cumberland Bay.

Right hand gripping the standing rigging for support, Macdonough stood on top of the port rail. Without an elevated bridge on the sailing ship, he couldn't see forward or aft from the helm of the single-decked sloop. Prior to leaving, the commodore had ordered the gun crews to fire at various rocks and outcroppings. On the fleet's return he planned to coordinate the firing and improve gun drills throughout the flotilla. As they passed the uninhabited Valcour Island, four miles south of Cumberland Bay, each vessel, including the single-gunned galleys, opened up on the trees and rocks in a heartening display of naval gunfire, Macdonough's calling card. His ships turned west into the quiet bay and dropped anchor two hundred yards offshore. The loud echoing reports of the guns brought out the entire town. Fearful of a Royal Navy visit, people came running to the beach to see what was happening.

Once the flotilla was afloat, Macdonough was calm when speaking to Henley. Leaning on the rail, the arrogant, ambitious lieutenant beheld Plattsburgh for the first time. The commodore quoted the statistics: "The bay's six miles across and sixty feet deep, generally, except for sandbars that stretch off each end of Crab Island at the bay's opening. The *Saratoga* draws eighteen feet and can approach no closer than where we are now. The winds in the bay are unpredictable, varying widely from those on the lake. The sailing season will close down the bay by November 1 and not open again till late March." He waved his hand loosely to indicate that the dates were uncertain and depended on the severity of the winter. "Have you ever sailed on a lake like this, Henley?"

"No, Commodore," he said, reluctantly accepting his subordinate position. After the jaunt north he realized that maneuvering on such a narrow body of water with an unidentified, most probably unqualified crew in an untested brig and in the face of the Royal Navy might exceed his own vaunted ability.

While the flotilla gathered and settled in safely, Macdonough and Henley examined the chart for a strategy that would protect the army's right flank and not jeopardize the fleet's well-being. "I must lend you Nelson's *Naval Wars*. In it, he recounts how the Royal Navy attacked twice in a situation similar to ours. At Copenhagen and again at Alexandria they bore down on moored fleets."

Henley interrupted. "Are you planning to moor in line like sitting ducks?" He couldn't believe he had heard correctly. Such a tactic was simply suicide—nothing more.

"I know what you're thinking, Henley, but you must consider the enemy's strength. If the frigate's as big as they say she is—that is, a third larger and more powerful than the *Saratoga*—and she's joined by three or four other ships comparable to ours, we haven't a chance on open water. The gunboats will never be able to keep up, which will leave the four of us besieged by the frigate's cannons. Reports indicate that the frigate's equipped with the latest Congreve short twenty-fours as well as a complement of carronades. Those cannons will outdistance us by hundreds of yards. She'll hover out of range and break our masts before moving in and raking us further. Our carronades, the bulk of the *Saratoga*'s firepower, extend only five hundred yards. A mere popgun's range, that'll have absolutely no effect on our foes. If their commodore's skilled—and most Royal Navy senior officers are not only skilled but also wise—he'll lie out of range and blow us out of the water. Our only defense will be to run."

"Run, Commodore? Run where on such a long narrow lake?"

"Exactly," he said. "Where indeed? Remember our mission isn't to defeat the Royal Navy but to defend our army's flank. That's the second good reason to fight from a static position."

"Static or mobile," Henley said, "it doesn't look promising."

"We must wring every opportunity from our plight," Macdonough said. "We have no other choice."

———

"General Macomb, I'd like you to meet a man with a new warship, but no one to sail her. Lieutenant Robert Henley is a captain without a crew."

Macdonough caught Macomb in a jovial mood; he had just received Mooers's pledge of a couple thousand infantry. "A pleasure to meet you, Lieutenant. Henley . . . don't I recognize that name from the hot summers I spent in the capital?"

"The pleasure is mine, sir. You could well have mixed with my people in that mosquito bog. I can tell you, sir, I'm glad to be out here on the open lake—in my element." Henley was particularly charming and deft where small talk was involved.

"Thomas, you warned me that you might raid my ranks one more time, but I must admit you have little hope of finding any lake seamen here. You have captured them all, I assure you."

"I know, but I've no choice. I need at least a hundred, and I'm willing to take anyone who can pull a rope or light a fuse."

"Well, gentlemen, I suggest you fan out across the peninsula and take anyone— that is, not exceeding a hundred anyones—who are willing to risk a watery grave."

The next morning, Macdonough and Henley breakfasted with Macomb in the open field behind Fort Scott, an earthwork for artillery guns named for Macomb's former commander, Winfield Scott.

"Sir, I've solved a portion of my problem. Your regimental band and several of their wives have stowed aboard my fleet this morning, along with a few invalids better off on the lake than on the land. But I must confess I'm still short sixty-five men. Your brigade sergeant major has suggested you give me the prisoners in the stockade. They'll be truly confined on board, especially since most can't swim. I promise they'll be too tired to cause mischief."

Macomb laughed heartily, slapped his knee and then Macdonough's back. "Well, I never! Women on a fighting ship! What a lark! And that sergeant major of mine, he's a wily enterprising old devil. Don't you see, my friend? He's talked you into taking the stockade off his hands! You better check your molars. He may've extracted them while you were making your appeal!"

Delancey Sets Foot on North America

On the shore of the Canadian bay stood Fort Chambly, a tiny rough-stone fort with square crenellated towers on each of its four corners. The short walk from the water's edge to the drawbridge on August 24 was the first time Delancey and his staff had felt the good earth under them for five weeks. Inside the commandant's office Commissary General William Robinson greeted the men. Since June, there on the broad plain beside the Richelieu River, he had been fitting together the pieces to make war possible.

Outside, on the two-mile-long concave shoreline, a circus of milling men, wagons, limbers, troops, and their families sent clouds of dust billowing into the sunny northern sky. The number of young children trailing along behind their mothers, each carrying a burden appropriate for their size, surprised the colonel. While children dumped armloads of firewood close by for the cook and laundry fires, the regiments' wives, relieved to be free of the cramped ships, were setting up tents. The fort's thick walls provided a refuge from the constant noise and acrid smoke.

Delancey craved the quiet of the ocean, the refreshing scent of the sea. "I'd forgotten the foul aroma of an army camp," he confided in Robinson.

"On the contrary, my dear Colonel, I like it. It smells like success."

Delancey felt an immediate affinity for this provider of tons of boxes and barrels filled with the necessities of life. "I've been pouring over your reports provided by the Halifax courier, General, with great interest. It appears that the lack of draft animals is our Achilles' heel. We've lost at sea a large portion of the horse carriers. What can I expect for transport?"

From the throng of people and provisions comingled on the fort's grounds, Delancey reckoned that moving it all at a snail's pace could doom the expedition.

"It's true, Sir William. Just over half of the livestock perished in the hurricane, but the mounts of the King's German Legion survived, as did those of the 19th Light Dragoons. I'm afraid it'll leave you with two squadrons of cavalry. If the force is to remain balanced, all the horses available in Canada will have to accompany the wagoneers and artillery transporters. Each foot regiment must be limited to five saddle horses. The officers will have to share mounts. There'll be a good deal of walking, I'm afraid—and a good deal of complaint."

Delancey agreed it would be only the first storm he would weather. The officers within the regiments were already disgruntled over being shunted to Canada. After the final battle of France, they had been expecting to go home to glory. Instead, they found themselves in yet another wilderness, one muggier and more maddening than any on continental Europe. The quartermaster general turned and whispered to his assistant, Major Colley Grant, "It's not all bad news. Wellington hates cavalry—or to be more exact—cavalrymen.

The major, an experienced intelligence officer and accomplished spy who had studied under Wellington, agreed with both assessments. "I understand that the King's German Legion is being favored, since they're Hanoverian and well disciplined."

Grant had replaced the deceased Captain Basil Rymer as Delancey's right-hand man and confidant. Thin from years of army deprivation, he knew no other life. He specialized in roaming freely and alone behind enemy lines and using a grain-fed stallion to outrun pursuers. The duke depended on Grant's observations, which were always reliable and detailed, and often praised the major as his "second pair of eyes." The two could be seen poring over maps after supper, with Grant pointing and Wellington questioning. Grant was one of only a few whom the duke trusted. He knew his place; he wasn't the son of a titled house and so maintained a respectful distance from the man he greatly admired. He expected to die anonymously one day in Wellington's service. Surprisingly, this belief was common among the enlisted and officers alike. They were content that history should know them only as the Duke of Boots' soldiers.

"General," Delancey said, "I'm most concerned to know if the *Mars* made it through. The ship carries the duke's personal belongings and the general staff's kits. His horses and foxhounds are on it as well." The quartermaster general failed to mention that his own pair of bay horses was among the staff's mounts. The colonel suspected that, considering Wellington's well-known criticism of the Naval Board, the *Mars* must've made special arrangements to ensure a safe passage.

"I knew you'd ask, Sir William. I've been tracking her personally since she left Deptford a day or two ahead of His Grace. She's been here and gone. You'll find everything in order in the center of the quadrangle." He motioned out the window to a pile of boxes and barrels peeking out from under canvas. Two red-coated soldiers stood guard. "I'm pleased to report that the animals are at a farm nearby awaiting your inspection, Colonel."

———

On August 29, Delancey received word at Fort Chambly that Wellington and Governor General Prevost would be arriving. The men crossed the dust bowl to the cheers of the assembled regiments and waving children. The clattering of the carriage across the wooden drawbridge announced their arrival at the camp. The horses slowed to a walk as they squeezed through the oval-topped gate into the courtyard.

Wellington alighted first. "Well, Sir William, congratulations! Most of us are here in one piece. The bloody navy nearly rocked me to an early death, but I prevailed. I hope never to see the *Caledonia* again. How are we getting on?"

"Your Grace, may I present Commissary General William Robinson? He has a great deal of good tidings to bring you."

The duke took Robinson by the arm and walked him toward the center of the quadrangle, where Wellington's property had been uncovered for inspection. Looking back over his shoulder, Wellington remarked to Delancey, "Shake hands with Prevost. He's got some good news for you as well."

The colonel saluted the lieutenant general instead. "Sir, I admire the defense you've waged these past two years. I've read your battle reports and foreign office memorandums with great interest. I fear Horse Guards doesn't fully understand the harsh climate you and your gallant men have endured."

Prevost tipped his hat in recognition. "So you're the boy quartermaster I've heard so much about. You've an awesome task ahead of you, my young friend, one, as you so aptly put it, 'in a harsh climate.' More than anyone else, I know what you're up against. Let me assist you at every juncture."

Delancey accepted with a slight bow the compliment and the offer. "You have good news, sir?"

"As I told His Grace, the diversionary plan has triumphed. Washington's ablaze, the Chesapeake's our lake, the Gulf Coast's threatened, and Madison's government is in shambles, cowering somewhere north of the capital. I can also report that, to our great advantage, my modest diversion is about to be accepted by the enemy." The men moved inside, where Prevost read a message from Izard to the American War Department. An American smuggler on Lake Champlain had intercepted it. The dispatch was a plea from the American commander that his orders be changed and that he be permitted to remain at Plattsburgh.

Prevost directed his aide to give Delancey the red leather-covered box with the governor's seal in gold fixed to the top. "Enclosed is a troop list, locations of our stock-piled provisions, and a delineation of all my troops allocated to your campaign. I'm transferring them to you. You'll find that they're not only experienced, but also well trained, disciplined, and willing. The French and Swiss are quite unique, but, of course, you're familiar with both from your Iberian experience."

"I gratefully accept the bounty in the spirit it is presented." Delancey was taken with the governor's military bearing, which wasn't typical of a man fulfilling both military and political roles.

Prevost directed the colonel's attention to the map on the wall. "I've moved my formations to St. John, ten miles south of Chambly, to provide room for you to muster your regiments and to prepare the artillery train for movement. The invasion is only days away. Isn't that right, Your Grace?"

Wellington merely smiled, examining the map of the border between Canada and the United States. Prevost and Delancey, meanwhile, slipped away to a small anteroom for some refreshment, where Prevost expanded on his news from America.

"I had the very good fortune to meet French general Jean Victor Moreau, who came up from the south to board one of your returning transports. He's on his way to join the Russians against Napoleon. Moreau's been tutoring the American officer corps since his exile in 1804. You must remember him from those postrevolutionary campaigns, victor at Hohenlinden and along the Rhine, don't you know."

Delancey was aware of the famous Moreau, one of the early commanders who led a victorious ragtag army of conscripts against formidable Austrian and Prussian regular formations. His bright light was snuffed out by the political intrigues of his wife while he was away in the field.

"He tells me that with Izard out of the way the only man who could cause you trouble is the militia general Andrew Jackson."

Delancey shrugged, "Who's he? Never heard of him."

"Moreau says he's a wildcat, more than just the fuss and feathers we've seen in so many of the backwoodsmen. Not only has he put an end to the Creek uprising that we have been backing along the Gulf Coast, but he also has a way with the men that stirs them up. They say he's worth a couple of brigades on the battlefield."

Delancey was interested from a purely academic point of view, knowing that he had no intention of stringing out his service in North America any longer than the present campaign. He pursued a line of questioning in case Wellington became curious over a newspaper article or war report from Horse Guards. "What feats of legerdemain has this Jackson performed?" he asked, hoping to hear a good story to tell the duke.

Prevost, anxious to impress went on with the tale. "According to Moreau, who was in the area at the time, Jackson was marooned in the wilderness of the Alabama Territory, blocking an Indian force from the villages in Tennessee when the militia came close to starving. The governor couldn't keep the supplies moving and the winter had descended into a killer cold snap. Past their enlistments, the men were yearning for home and hearth. One brigade packed up and began to move off north. Jackson knew that if one left it would start a torrent and the command would dissolve in the flow. The artillery was called out and stationed across the road. Alone, mounted in front of the guns, Jackson tried talking, telling them that a supply train was only a few miles away, which was a lie. He'd been promised relief but had no assurance that it was really coming. While the officers' resolve to leave began to wane, the men shouted for the general to get out of the way or they would fire on him. It was a full-scale mutiny. Jackson shouted for the gunners to light their matches. The mutineers began to murmur but stood fast. Jackson pulled a short musket from its leather sheath and laid it across the saddle. He cocked the hammer and turned his horse sideways, leveling the barrel toward the errant brigade. 'I will shoot the first man who steps beyond your colors,' he said. There was silence."

"Well," Delancey entreated, "what did they do?" He doubted Jackson had perished in the stampede.

Prevost finished the story. "Why they backed off and waited for the supplies, which didn't arrive for another week." Prevost paused. "They tell me Jackson knew his gun wasn't loaded. You can thank your stars, my dear Delancey, that you aren't up against Old Hickory."

Dreadful News from Ghent

Secretary of State James Monroe called on the president, who was residing with Roger Brooke Taney, at his Frederick, Maryland, home. After the Battle of Bladensburg, Monroe had traveled to the port of Philadelphia in the last week of August to establish a temporary State Department liaison office. There, he received a communiqué from Albert Gallatin that outlined Great Britain's demands.

Taney's spacious, washed-brick three-story home, dating from 1750, faced a small green square where the militia had mustered after the Boston Tea Party. Dolley had joined the president within two days of losing her home on Pennsylvania Avenue to the redcoats. She sat in on the discussions while waiting for tea to be served.

"Mister President," Monroe began, "Gallatin sent a copy of the treaty terms offered by the British delegates. Obviously, they were expecting a victory at Bladensburg, since the demands are most strident. At the Saint Petersburg talks last year, they were far more conciliatory." He handed the long tri-folded parchment across a still-bare tea table in the comfortable lounge. The document read,

> To settle the present conflict His Majesty's government offers the president of the United States of America the following terms: At the time of signing, both sides will permanently maintain those territories they physically occupy; the United States of America will establish an independent Indian state on its soil; and the Royal Navy will be allowed free travel upon the length of the Mississippi River. In return, His Majesty will reaffirm his recognition of the United States of America's sovereignty in all matters of international dealings and of its right to freedom of commerce on the high seas.
>
> Earl Bathurst
> Colonial Secretary

Shaking the document at Monroe, as if the secretary were its author, Madison stood up, removed his metal-framed spectacles, and shouted, "Absolutely outrageous! This amounts to redrawing the boundaries established by the Treaty of Paris in 1783."

"Gallatin's accompanying note declares quite openly," Monroe said, pausing to pull it from its leather case on the table and to raise his silver-framed spectacles, which dangled on a thin black ribbon around his neck, "that Great Britain wants war to cripple us and to aggrandize the crown at our expense. We offered to revert to the prewar status quo and requested the end of impressment for all time, payment for damages inflicted on the United States during the war, and, further, that in the future neither the United States nor England would induce the Indians to become combatants. Clearly, our reasonable position has made no impression on the British delegation. They perceive that weakness motivates our rational attitude. The delegates feel that they hold the whip and the reins, not to mention controlling the spurs!"

With a gasping release of breath, Madison sat down next to Dolley on the divan and put his head in his hands.

"My God, so it's true," he said softly, his voice tinged with awe that such a remote prospect had become an impending reality. "There's no chance cooler heads in London will prevail as some assured me." He had been hoping that the intrigues, coastal disturbances, and raid on Washington were just ploys to make him give up the war and settle. "It's an invasion. They're coming in for the kill."

Wellington's War Council

On the simmering morning of August 30, all the major military commanders were summoned to Fort Chambly's open quadrangle and seated on long benches. The men, their gold and silver braids glinting in the early hazy sunlight, wore a variety of colors: red for the infantry, dark blue for the artillery, buckskin for the chasseurs, and green for the light rifles. Most had been in Canada for the past two months. The 1st Battalion, 8th Regiment of Foot, as well as a contingent of sailors, had marched from New Brunswick, 250 miles east, to release their transport animals for the next phase. All senior officers agreed that morale was low; the sooner the campaign began, the sooner it would end. (Wellington shared their anticipation but kept private his conviction that they would all be needed the following year to fight the Russians and Prussians in Europe.)

Not a man to share much of anything, Wellington began with the briefest outline of the coming invasion. "Gentlemen, we'll be three large brigades with a fourth left in reserve at St. John."

Delancey, standing beside the duke and ready to answer any questions about the details, pointed to the map hanging for the occasion on the quadrangle's inner wall.

His voice clear and clipped, Wellington continued: "Major General Frederick Robinson will lead with his brigade of 3,400 men. I'd like to introduce his deputy, who accompanied me on the voyage. Brigadier General Benedict Arnold Jr., son of the great American patriot and loyal British subject, will be with the vanguard of the 3rd Foot and will cross the frontier first."

A murmur of approval trickled through the assembly. "It looks as if His Grace plans on treading heavily on the American rattlesnake," Major General Sir Henry Torrens, Somerset's deputy chief of staff, was heard to say. "Don't Tread on Me" had been the American rallying cry of the rebellion.

The duke allowed for the distraction to inject some needed venom into the proceedings. "Manley Power will lead the 2nd and Thomas Brisbane the 3rd brigades. You are all students of military history. I am, of course, referring to the old American road to war. We'll follow that road once more. I expect to meet the American army at Plattsburgh, where they have dug a defense. The Royal Navy will seek out and destroy their American counterparts. We'll capture its transports, sail to the southern end of Lake Champlain, and there, demand terms. General Sherbrooke is in the territory of Maine as I speak, moving south toward New Hampshire."

Delancey pointed to the map once again, and Wellington continued: "The Royal Navy's operating from Nantucket Island, where the citizens have pledged an oath to King George. As you may have heard, the American capital, like the American government, is a smoldering ruin. We will force a peace that favors His Majesty and flaunts the grandiose posturing of that presidential troll, James Madison."

Wellington sat down to face the assemblage and to listen as his quartermaster general and commissary general continued the briefing. Interested only in assessing the mood of the officers' corps, a crucial component of victory, he didn't interrupt.

Macomb Makes the Most of a Bad Predicament

General Izard was unaware that the War Department had been torched and that the president had dismissed the secretary of war following the attack on Washington. His numerous appeals requesting relief from the movement orders didn't find an audience, and on the evening of August 29, the first element of the northeastern American army boarded boats destined for Whitehall, nearly a hundred miles away at the southern tip of Lake Champlain. By noon, the artillery, ammunition, and provisions had been dragged to waiting rafts and before nightfall on the following day, all 4,500 men—those fit enough to journey to Schenectady, through the Mohawk Valley, and onward across Lake Ontario—had left.

Brigadier General Macomb gathered the sick and lame at Fort Moreau, an earthen redoubt, in the center of the American defensive position.

"I'll tell you what I know," he said. "The British army's expected to invade at Niagara." The mood lifted visibly at the announcement that the danger had passed. "We mustn't let our guard down, though. There's every chance the British bastards will attack us to mislead us about their true intentions. We'll keep digging, improving our positions, and making room for the New York militia, which ought to swell our ranks by a couple thousand. Our navy will be on the bay to support our efforts and defend us from a lake attack. Follow your officers' directions and all will be well."

However, Macomb soon learned that Mooers's volunteers fell *far* short of the call. Only a disappointing seven hundred men milled around in civilian attire at St. John's Academy, the muster point in Plattsburgh. In the basement, the armory sheltered sufficient muskets, balls, and powder to arm 2,500 soldiers. A welcome contribution was a troop of New York State dragoons, reported to be north of Plattsburgh and moving toward the border.

Macomb chuckled to his aide, "The British will mistake their red coats and sausage-roll leather helmets for their own troops and will allow them freedom of movement in Canada. Those horsemen are my eyes and ears, Lieutenant, my eyes and ears."

Prevost Brings News

That night General Prevost returned late from Montreal and was warmly received by Wellington in his fortress quarters. Delancey had sent out the order for the first brigade to move to the border, south of Lacolle Mill, a spot that had witnessed three abortive attacks by the Americans within the last two years. The second brigade was sent close behind, followed by Brisbane's combined force of British, Canadian, and French militia.

Prevost, quite pleased with himself, took a few minutes to settle in and put his audience at ease. "Your Grace, my diversion has spirited away Izard and three-quarters of his command down the lake and off to a pointless rendezvous with no one. A fledgling brigadier and 1,500 invalids defend Plattsburgh tonight. The way to New York is clear."

Wellington, equally pleased by the enterprising Prevost, offered refreshment: a ruby red Madeira. "I selected this vintage myself on a trip to the island," he said. "May I toast your initiative, Prevost, and the certain success you've wrought?"

Delancey, joining the toast, asked, "Then it's on for tomorrow, Your Grace?"

"Yes, Sir William, it is indeed—first thing. May God help them—just not too much."

Cutting Down the American Flag

The rising sun streaked across the lake north of the tiny Rouses Point customs station. Masquerading as British cavalry officers returning from an early morning hunt, Lieutenants Matthew Standish and Roswell Wait saw an illuminated cloud of dust climbing through the mist.

Standish drew a brass telescope from the stiff leather case on his belt. Dismounting behind Wait, he steadied the extended barrel, drawn out in sections, on his comrade's shoulder.

From the cover of the trees lining the Canadian road a British officer on a dark horse emerged. A color guard and ranks of redcoats followed him.

"Ros, there they are—coming straight for us."

Wait heard the first throb of drums, deep and distant. The lieutenants mounted their horses quickly, expecting an imminent encounter with enemy scouts, but none came forward. The column grew longer by the minute—four abreast, crossed white belts at shoulder arms, burnished bayonets fixed and ready for action.

"These fellows sure don't need a cavalry screen or cloud of skirmishers," Standish observed.

Wait, beholding the first of Wellington's invincibles, said nothing.

Mounting up, they spun their horses around and spurred them toward the frontier, a quarter mile south. Standish joined his troops at their bivouac south of Rouses Point and sent a pair of dispatch riders to Macomb. Just before 11:00 AM, supervising the mounting of cannons at Fort Brown, a three-sided earthen redoubt high on a bluff at the edge of the Saranac River, Macomb received the message and read it with deep concern. He wasn't surprised but found the information far too sketchy to be useful. A regular cavalry scout would've waited longer and provided the column's size, speed, and composition.

"This report," he said, handing it to Major John Wool, a former student of his at West Point and a fellow comrade at Queenston, "is of use to newspapers but useless to the art and business of war."

"General, we're served by amateurs. Consider us lucky that the lieutenant didn't bring his entire force to deliver the message. Perhaps he'll stick with the British and be of some value, after all."

"Even if this crossing's only a feint, at best Plattsburgh will be destroyed and at worst we'll be taken prisoner. Defending we have a four-to-one advantage over our taking the offense. The river's our best ally and the navy our next. Yet, if we don't get some assistance from Sam Strong and his Vermont militia, I doubt we can hold out against a brigade of British regulars. Send swift word south to Macdonough to hurry. He should be here by now!"

Major General Mooers rode up on his lathered black mare. Long, frazzled white hair, matching his frenzied mood, stuck out from under a black flat white-plumed hat. He pulled the wild-eyed mount up short before the dirt berms, where Macomb and Wool were standing, but he remained mounted. "My God! Macomb, you were right! Have ya heard? The redcoats are at Rouses Point and headed straight for us!" Steadying his horse and leaning over to hear, he whispered, "What are your orders?"

"Where's your formation, General?" Macomb inquired calmly, hoping his tranquil demeanor would imbue the militia commander with the same attitude.

"We're still forming—more than a little short, I'm afraid—but these are my best boys. They're drawing weapons at St. John's Academy Armory. Should I bring 'em over here?" He didn't pause for an answer. "Some town folk are leaving by the Catherine Street Bridge, others are afraid to abandon their property, and still others are forming a committee to welcome the enemy! The weasels!"

"How long before the militia's ready to take to the field?"

"Well," Mooers replied, shaking his head, "I don't know. They're trickling in from the farms, but as the British come on down the road, they'll overtake many of my citizen-soldiers."

"I think you should stay at the armory on the other side of the river until we better perceive what the redcoats' intentions might be." To Macomb it was becoming all too clear. Why would Wellington require a feint? It would take at least a week before the War Department knew the enemy had crossed the border. Who would they trick with a false show? Additionally, Macomb was beginning to doubt the militia's reliability. It may well be a good idea to leave them outside his defensive line for the present—or at least until they revealed their true mettle.

For the next four days Standish and Wait tracked alongside the British column's eastern edge and sent dispatches every few hours to Macomb, each one more informative than the last. None was more appalling than the first message, which recounted a feast for British officers paid for in gold coin and served by the citizens of Rouses Point.

Redcoats Plunge South

Smugglers' Road, which ran beside the lake, seemed ideal for the army's use, but its condition had deteriorated to marsh and mud. The British were forced west for six miles before turning south once more for Plattsburgh. Misled by the smugglers, who had described the road as sturdy, the British soon realized that the route south was barely a farm track through the wilderness. The column, ten miles in length, found the rutted narrow path too fragile for heavy wagons. Siege artillery, ammunition, and provisions, dragged by high-priced slow-plodding oxen, lagged behind the main body. Progress slowed while Wellington's impatience quickened. The next twenty miles proved long and torturous.

Riding behind the second brigade and in front of two nine-pound field gun batteries, Wellington fussed at Delancey. (The other four batteries were divided between Power's and Brisbane's commands.) At the end of the column and in front of the commissary supply and repair train of a hundred wagons, the families trudged along in the siege artillery's dust. Late, and therefore last, was the rocket brigade of 210 men on horseback. Since the natives appeared friendly, there was no rear guard other than the rocketeers. The folks of the northeastern United States, living so close to the border, took the invasion rather causally. Intermarriage and cross-border business had been going on long before there was a United States.

On the afternoon of September 4, Delancey rode up beside the duke to report that his staff tents were set up next to a farmhouse. Wellington preferred his tent and camp bed, when suitable housing for a gentleman of his rank wasn't available. He was a Spartan in the field; his mess wasn't grand and neither were his furnishings, but particular attention was paid to the wine.

"Sorry about the pace, sir. The road's nothing but an old Indian trail tangled between farms. Long as we pay in gold coins, the natives are cooperating. They charge high prices to haul off broken-down wagons and offer replacements only out of the goodness of *our* pocketbook. The commissary general's been forced to commandeer the horses of the 19th Dragoons, compelling them to march on foot."

Wellington smiled but didn't turn his head to acknowledge the deprivation they were enduring. "God, I wish I could've done that to Uxbridge in Spain." (Lord Uxbridge, his cavalry commander in Spain, had run off with his brother's wife.) The joke lightened the mood.

Delancey continued his report. "Remember Captain Ardal Quincannon, commander of the Staff Dragoons, our scouts at Salamanca?"

"Of course. I'm old, Colonel, no doubt, but not ancient."

"He's turned up with a full troop topping a hundred. It seems his ship went into port to refit, and he managed to expropriate saddle horses at Nantucket Island. I've assigned them to Colley as scouts, if you don't mind."

Quincannon's dragoons were experienced hunters, who had been vital to Wellington's maneuvers in the past. A special troop of selected cavalry from Ireland, they were grandly clad in bright red jackets, blue cuffs, and collars piped in white. Black shako headgear with white plumes covered their heads, while dark blue coveralls with double red stripes running down to their black riding boots concealed their white leather pants. Chunky, round, white metal buttons were sewn on every three inches between the stripes to protect their legs from scrapes. On either end of their saddles, "SD" was embroidered in white. Couriers, scouts, and guides, they were the duke's favorites.

Wellington knew the ubiquitous Quincannon but never admitted the captain was Irish. The duke never considered himself to be Irish, though he was born in Ireland, but rather a guardian of the Irish. "Just because a man's born in a stable, it doesn't make him a horse," he would say to anyone who broached the subject. He often complained about the Irish troops' indiscipline and drunkenness, yet he valued their troublesome service.

Through the fourth day of the march there was still no contact with the American army. At first light on September 5, Delancey pressed Quincannon to locate an alternate route to Plattsburgh because the column was bogging down from its own weight on the solitary road. Six miles north of town the captain probed a side road to the east that soon turned south and skirted the western edge of Cumberland Bay. The quartermaster general diverted the third brigade and the remainder of the column's military portion down that road.

"Sir, I can report that we'll take Plattsburgh from the lake side as well as from the land. Quincannon's dragoons, however, haven't made contact with the enemy today, even though they're less than six miles from the city."

"Perhaps the Americans are sleeping, Delancey," Wellington suggested wryly. "Do you think we should wake them?" The duke had been reading Prevost's field action reports of the past two years; nothing in them suggested a penchant for a vigorous defense to match the Americans' vociferous patriotism.

"Perhaps they've abandoned the town, as they did last year, and moved down the lake behind Izard?"

"No matter. We'll fight them where we find them. Have you heard from Yeo? When will his fleet be ready?"

Delancey was reluctant to say. "Commodore Yeo has relieved Captain Fisher, the man who constructed the new frigate, and replaced him with"—he looked at a communiqué that he pulled from his coat pocket—"Captain James Downie."

Wellington, miffed by an answer that had nothing to do with his query, asked, "Who the deuce is he?"

"When I asked Prevost about Yeo's change so late in the game, he said, 'Yeo's prone to rash inexplicable actions beyond the reach of mortal man's comprehension.'"

"Sounds like the bloody navy. They're a jealous bunch. He mustn't have liked the cut of Fisher's jib." The duke had become warily used to the gulf that yawned between the two services. "Delancey, send a message to Prevost about the timing of naval support. He's supposed to be in charge. Let him sort it out."

Just in Time

The American ships, pushed by a strong following wind, plowed the narrow passage past Valcour and entered Cumberland Bay from the south. Before his ships could anchor, Macdonough left his flagship *Saratoga* and beached his gig at Fort Scott. There, an officer lent him a horse for the climb uphill to Macomb's headquarters behind the center of the American defensive line. It was a warm and sunny autumn day. A stiff breeze rustled through the few trees that hadn't been cut down for revetments. The maples that dominated the town beyond were already turning rust red and burnished gold. The general was conversing with a dragoon, who stood by his sweaty horse. The horseman mounted and spun off before Macdonough had reined in his own borrowed animal.

"Ah, Thomas! Just in time. I saw you enter the bay. You're most welcome, I assure you." Taking the commodore by the arm, as was the general's wont, he led him into his white canvas tent and to the map that lay spread out on the field table. Briefly, Macomb outlined his defensive plan. "As you can see, I've integrated the New York militia into the regular units. Perhaps that'll steady them up, eh?"

Macdonough saw working parties containing blue-coated regulars and a substantial number of other men in irregular hats and leggings. They were handling large guns and stacking black cannonballs at Fort Moreau. The three earthen forts—Brown, Moreau, and Scott—were arranged in a crescent, all within easy reach of the other.

"Sir, the flotilla—that is, the *Saratoga*, the *Ticonderoga,* the new brigs *Eagle* and *Preble*, and a dozen gun galleys—are maneuvering into a line from above the Saranac River to below Fort Scott." Macdonough, turning from the map, pushed the tent flap wider. "My starboard guns will protect you from a lake attack while my port side guns will engage the British army positions north of the river. Do you approve?"

The general, who admitted that his knowledge of naval warfare was limited, asked, "Do you intend to anchor?"

"That I do, sir. The galleys will maneuver and attempt to board enemy vessels while the four major ships will remain static, directing accurate gunfire at major targets. I'm afraid my crew's poor sailing skills limit us to a static, though hopefully effective, defense. I can't hope to sail and fight at the same time. My men aren't ready."

"Commodore," Macomb said, "it's a wise man who realizes his limitations and maximizes his strengths."

First Man Killed

On September 5 the armies clashed at Culver's Hill six miles north of Plattsburgh. Scaling a low rise, topped by a small stone farmhouse, the battalion commander of the East Kent Buffs Regiment, silhouetted himself long enough for Private Sam Perry, a militia scout, to kill him with a rifle shot to the chest. Angered at the loss of their commander, the lead element of Robinson's brigade charged over the hill and down the far side toward Wool's men, who were spread out on either side of the dirt road. Not stopping to drop their packs or deploy into line formation, the nearly out-of-control redcoats presented their rifles in groups of four and fired unrestricted volleys, as they ran down the road.

The fierce onslaught surprised Wool, who ordered an immediate withdrawal. Limbered up in haste, the two cannons, though loaded, withheld their fire. Wool's men yanked the artillery pieces around and pulled them down the road a long mile before stopping at the next low ridge. There, Wool regrouped and presented another obstacle. The British once again took up a column of fours and proceeded as if nothing had happened. Wool rushed to a stone wall at Sampson's Corners. The gunners fired the twin field guns once, which belched canister; then limbered up; and scurried off before being overrun.

———

A mile north of Plattsburgh, where Dead Creek emptied into the bay, Lieutenant Colonel Daniel Appling established yet another blocking position. At nearly the same hour on September 6, Brisbane's column emerged from the forest road and saw Appling's line. At the British column's head was de Meuron's Swiss infantry, dressed in red coats with light blue facings outlined in white metal buttons and topped with black shakos. An element of the American rifle regiment, hidden from view by the soldiers' green jackets, engaged the skirmishers at long range. Surprised at the accuracy of the enemy riflemen, the Swiss ducked for cover among the low, thick scrub brush that covered the ground down to the shore. The remainder of the British and Canadian units rushed forward and spread out along the shoreline of the bay. The riflemen were pushed back by the volume of musket fire that snapped above their heads and kicked up the sand in front of the creek bridge. The creek was not deep and soon redcoats were wading across, forcing Appling to withdraw in stages into Plattsburgh's outer limits.

Macdonough, on board the *Saratoga*, saw the infantry's plight and slipped anchor, allowing his ship to drift into range. He knew that Appling's scant force of a hundred Americans couldn't hope to hold the bridge area. Yet, the *Saratoga* could distract the enemy with cannon fire. Her first shots from two of her four long-range naval cannons caused Brisbane to reconsider capturing the little bridge.

After an hour of stalemate the British brigade commander brought up his field guns and arrayed them along the shore. In the interim Macdonough had launched a half-dozen rowed galleys, each mounting a single cannon in the bow. A donnybrook began close to shore. Billows of white artillery smoke obscured Macdonough's view. He soon realized, as the south wind cleared a passage, that the boats weren't nimble enough to take on the field guns and called for their withdrawal. Without cannon fire from the boats, Appling and his men were on their own.

———

Although the redcoats forced Major Wool from every farmhouse and stone wall within six miles of Plattsburgh, he never gave Robinson a moment's respite. Mile by mile Wool retreated, stopping where he could to fire a volley and discharge the two cannons before limbering up and moving once more. In town a footrace developed between the seventy-seven men of Appling's rifle regiment and de Meuron's Swiss soldiers. Wool withdrew to the center of Plattsburgh, heading for the approach to the Bridge Street Bridge. Waiting for Appling, he fought off skirmishers from Robinson's brigade. The redcoats swarmed between houses and flushed out the American infantry. Macomb's cannons were static in the earthworks on the south side of the swift Saranac; houses, barns, sheds, churches, stores, and mills blocked the artillery's line of sight. The gunners were unable to distinguish friend from foe.

Macomb watched the action from the top of the blockhouse next to Mooers's home on the bank of the surging river. He sent a message to Wool by runner: "Give up the town. Bring Appling and all across the bridge."

Exhausted, Wool hurriedly threaded his troops back through town, past the houses and barns, to the stone bridge over the Saranac River. Appling's men made it to the north bank and put down a devastating line of musket and rifle fire, allowing Wool's men to begin crossing the bridge. The horses pulling the two cannons clattered a hellish rhythm as they careened across into the American lines. Together, Wool and Appling, under scathing volleys of enemy musket fire, mingled the remnants of their units and pulled up the planks as they crossed. They piled the heavy timbers into a makeshift wall, thus sealing off the only bridge for a mile. Wool's cannons were yanked into position on the American side of the wall and commenced firing. Between the American fusillade and the turbulent river, British hopes of a swift victory withered away.

A Siege Begins

Unopposed red-coated regiments arrived hourly throughout the night of September 6. Plattsburgh, a town of a thousand inhabitants, would swell to more than ten thousand men by morning. Half of the townsfolk had fled south to stay with more safely situated relatives and friends. Farm fields surrounding the clusters of houses and churches bloomed with regimental tents, each staked out in a precise rectangle. The British did not fear an American counterattack. The road, not the Americans, had taken a toll—mixing baggage and confusing provisions. While men could move more than two miles an hour, the wagons of artillery, ammunition, and victuals stalled, broke down, and lost momentum.

Wellington expected a visit from his quartermaster and commissary generals when he arrived at the substantial red-brick, multistory Georgian house that he'd commandeered to serve as both his living quarters and headquarters. It sat on the village's northern edge, just out of range of the Fort Brown battery a mile and a half away.

Delancey was the first to arrive and settled into a chair next to the duke, who was sitting at his large campaign desk, which had been set up in the spacious front lounge. Delancey laid out a sketch map, which he just finished, on a large piece of parchment. "Sir, we are here." He put his finger on the dot next to "HQ" in black ink, which lay at the intersection of the two main streets that led into the center of town a mile east at the edge of the Saranac River. "There are no significant elevations. We are on a high point here; the ground, which is open farmland and homes, slopes gently down to the lake. The main road is in front of this house and is built up with farms and brick houses along its length to one of the two bridges that cross the river." He traced the path and Wellington noticed the large number of structures dotted along the roadway. "The first and main bridge is of stone, fifty yards long, defended by artillery, and extends Bridge Street into the enemy lines. The enemy also defends the second bridge of timber a mile south on Catherine Street. Three miles southwest is the only ford across the river and is the site of an abandoned military cantonment. Elsewhere the river cannot be forded owing to its swift current. The Americans have abandoned the village of Plattsburgh and withdrawn into a strong defensive position on the peninsula bounded by the Cumberland Bay on the east and the river on the north and west. Within their lines are three earthen artillery positions marked here, here, and here." Delancey touched each symbol with tip of his pencil. "I have drawn an arch to show the range of their guns, which you can see fall short of this headquarters. The American navy is anchored in the bay, and I have dispatched a copy of this map highlighting the enemy ships and artillery positions to Commodore Downie. I know, sir, that you will shortly be reconnoitering the ground for yourself. I must warn you that there are some snipers about and a good number of citizens have remained in their homes to protect their belongings."

Wellington, concerned that the local population be protected, remarked, "Have you posted the assurances that they will be safe from intervention?"

"Yes, sir, they appear to be very cooperative."

"Sir William, how long before I can expect the artillery to be operational?"

Before Delancey could answer, the commissary general, late, entered the room and was directed to a chair opposite Wellington.

The duke didn't scold him for the column's tardiness. The field marshal, a practical man, had just ridden the same route and witnessed the challenges that could be expected to plague the endeavor throughout the campaign. The two experienced staff officers knew there was no need to provide excuses, only their professional estimate.

Delancey spoke first. "By the evening of September 9, all the guns will close on Plattsburgh."

Wellington nodded, "And the navy? Where is His Majesty's renowned navy?"

Robinson took that question. "Sir, while at Rouses Point the day before yesterday, I saw a magnificent sight. The new frigate, sails full, was test firing her guns. The entire fleet, gathered off the point, was waiting for the wind to allow them to sail south."

"So it's the wind and not the navy that's delaying our plan?"

"I believe it is, sir."

Robinson was only partially correct. Captain James Downie had been unable to crew the *Confiance* with sailors and, instead, embarked with three hundred soldiers from the 39th Foot to man the guns. Downie posted a Royal Marine at each cannon and carronade to assist with the training. He had spent the last three days shaking down the ship and heating up the guns. Downie, battle hardened at age thirty-three, was not happy to be thrown into battle under such constrictive conditions. But Yeo had snatched him from command of a frigate off Halifax in order to relieve Captain Fisher, who had become too friendly with Governor Prevost. And now the problem was his and his alone.

————

Brisbane's brigade occupied Plattsburgh and sniped at the Americans each day and night while waiting for the artillery to arrive. Beginning on September 8 and continuing through September 9, the American artillery, safe behind the dirt forts, sent red-hot cannonballs hurling and crashing into town. To deny the redcoats any cover, homes and businesses along the river's north side were burned to the ground.

Sailly called on Macomb when the judge's office was destroyed by a sizzling, particularly effective shot. "My God, General! You were sent here to protect us from the

British. Unlike you and your rabble of irregular regulars, they've behaved like gentlemen, paying in gold for every inconvenience, while your men, like vandals in the night, have burned me out and left my family with nothing. *Nothing!* Your guns have laid waste to my practice. What do you intend next? To impress us to dig our own graves?"

The judge was just the head of the line; many more homeowners and businessmen were waiting to vent and accuse Macomb of gross negligence and willful perfidy. They threatened to ruin the general's career by informing the government of his outrageous behavior. But Macomb had a war to fight, and he pressed Judge Sailly into service to deal with the locals' discontent.

On the evening of September 9, the general was holding his own but wondering what Wellington had in mind. Two-thirds of the British—clearly visible by their campfires on the high ground on the town's northern edge—were idle.

Captain George McGlassin asked for a moment of the general's time. He seemed preoccupied as he set down a folding camp chair beside the tiny field table.

His manner's strange, Macomb thought.

"McGlassin, are you still suffering from lake fever?"

Having been bedridden for the past week, the captain was indeed running a considerable temperature. The big, red-faced Irishman was trying to minimize his wretched condition. The general observed beads of sweat collecting like dew on the bald dome of his head.

But McGlassin waved it off. "I'm fine now. Just a bit tuckered is all. I'm told the redcoats are diggin' in a battery of rockets across the river from Fort Brown. We can't accept that, sir. Those are the devil's machines and will panic the militia. They're already restive after Culver's Hill."

"I agree, but I can't get a good-size force across that river, not even from the Catherine Street Bridge. There's at least a British regiment sitting between the bridge and the battery. If I take the offense, they'll blast me on open ground."

The captain insisted. "A large force can't do it, sir. You're correct. But a small raiding party could stir 'em up and destroy the launchers and maybe the whole stock of rockets. After midnight I propose to take a raidin' party of fifty men across the river. They won't be expectin' us. We'll catch 'em with their pants down and wallop them good."

"I must say, McGlassin, no one but you would devise such a hair-brained risky scheme." Macomb liked the big fellow; he had depended on him for the past two years to handle the tough jobs and see them through. Sitting and waiting for the enemy to attack didn't fit either man's style. Still, Macomb didn't think McGlassin had the strength. "Are you well enough to take on this mission? You'll have to swim the river. There's no other way. Remember you've got to get there *and* back."

"The cold water will do me good. Wash away the last of my fever, sir." For the past week the captain had looked longingly from his tent cot at the cool rushing water and had wished he could let it run over his feverish body.

"Take fifty fools, George, and good luck to you. If nothing else, it'll put a spark back into our weary soldiers."

That moonless night, the raiding party moved to the river's edge. McGlassin tied a rope around his middle and left a coil on the bank. His lieutenant secured the other end of the hemp to a stout tree. The small party huddled together in the brush at the edge of the shallows.

"Take the flints out of your rifles. I don't want one to go off and give us up for crow bait," he cautioned in a harsh whisper. "On the other side we'll split in two. I'll take the left, and the lieutenant will take the right. I'll give a shout to start it off. Then, bayonets fixed, up over the revetment. Rout them out, break the launchers, and set fire to anything that'll burn. Independent action—give no quarter—take no prisoners."

Skilled in Indian hit-and-run tactics, his raiders were well trained for this night of revenge. As McGlassin slipped silently into the stream, the freezing water soaked his clothing and reduced the fever ravaging his body.

"Sling your rifles. When I get across and tie off, I'll give three pulls. Then follow me. And take care of each other."

That night the water near the opposite bank reflected the blazing fires lighting the work site as British soldiers finished the battery. An additional hundred men had been attached to the rocket brigade to boost its strength so that the construction could be completed by morning. A solid dirt bank, twelve feet high, had been thrown up to protect the rockets on three sides. Gun ports were unnecessary because the wooden launch rails leaned against the embankment, inclining the unguided missile toward the Americans.

When construction was finished, a salvo of twenty screeching rockets, spewing trails of white smoke, would streak across the sky. The internal fuse, cut for time of flight, would ignite the charge, which would detonate the canisters filled with metal fragments. The shrieking would cease when the charge exploded in a red-yellow fireball. A shower of hot metal would scatter in all directions, killing and maiming. But if McGlassin could knock the battery out with this preemptive raid, the American soldiers would be spared, for a short while at least, from the deadly projectiles.

Once across the raging currents, the big man lay spent on the opposite bank and struggled to maintain consciousness. Spitting up water that had gushed into his gaping mouth as he attempted to breathe in midstream, he was afraid his spluttering gasps would alert the British sentries. But the noise of the rapids and the racket of the workers concealed his presence. Tying his end of the rope to a tree, he gave the hemp three hard yanks. In his fevered brain only one thought prevailed: "Those rockets must be silenced."

The other members of the party came across, hand over hand, resisting the river's downstream pull. McGlassin held his finger to his mouth, urging them to be quiet as they left the water and joined him only yards from the British observation post. Holding their muskets at port arms, the parties separated and snuck through the underbrush that the British had neglected to cut down. Once in position, the captain waited until he was sure the other half of his raiders were in place on the opposite side.

He triggered the attack when, jumping up on top of the berms, he shouted in his booming voice, "Attack from the left! Attack from the right!"

Screaming and whooping like Indians, the raiders leaped over the top and skidded down the loose dirt. The British, armed with only shovels, were jarred from their boring tasks by the raucous onslaught. The rocketeers became disoriented. The wavering light from the campfires did little to identify the attackers. Slashing at upturned shovels, slicing at shadowy figures with his sword, the captain crossed the battery on the run. Unarmed, most of the enemy raced to the battery's open side and the safety of the darkness beyond.

The battery commander, attempting to defend his ground, took command of a group of men who had been charging in good order. Sword drawn, he led them into the fray. A bayonet sliced through the back of his sleeve; he whirled to parry the attack. Only then did he realize he had assumed command of the right side of the American raiding party. He too fled, running through the briars and brambles at the water's edge and shredding his dashing uniform in the process.

Within ten minutes the ground was clear, several dozen shadowy bodies lay crumpled, silent or moaning, barely visible near the glowing fires. McGlassin's lieutenant positioned a dozen men with loaded rifles to ward off a counterattack, and the captain directed the rest of his rangers to destroy everything of value.

Time was short. Surely, the gunners would be back.

The disruption would not stop the battle or win a victory for the tiny embattled American army. It was a demonstration that soldiers were willing to risk their lives in the face of overwhelming odds. The next morning both sides of the river would be buzzing with the heroic account. It would give heart to the Americans, who needed something to grab onto that terrifying day to come, and would show the British counterpart that they were about to pay for their aggression.

Wellington Goes It Alone

On the morning of September 10, Delancey reported the raid and the resulting delay, but Wellington was unconcerned by the news. It was the tardy Royal Navy that made him anxious.

"Sir, I have another disturbing report to relay. It came in early this morning from Colley. The Vermont militia commander, Major General Strong, has hijacked a considerable flotilla of lake craft. Colley believes that Strong has defied Governor Chittendon's prohibition and plans to come to Macomb's aid. The report reads, 'Strong is capable of fielding more than two thousand troops at a landing site near the mouth of the Salmon River, five miles south of the Saranac.'"

Wellington went to the map on the table.

"Colley—what would I do without him? While an additional two thousand militia won't change the outcome of the battle, they could cause me casualties." The duke, no squanderer of lives, always aimed to preserve his force. Wellington pointed a brass divider at a line on the map. "That road will bring them up behind the Catherine Street Bridge or to Pike's cantonment at the ford."

The field marshal knew he enjoyed an overwhelming presence at Plattsburgh and saw no need to suffer unnecessary casualties on behalf of the recusant navy. So far from England, he would find replacements difficult to obtain. Besides, he never chose to fight when he could maneuver. Why wait for Commodore Downie and the fitful lake winds, only to allow Macomb the reinforcements that he couldn't expect for himself? It was true that the Vermont militia was of little ultimate use, but strange things happened in the fog of war. Since, as was his custom, he hadn't revealed the details of his battle plan to anyone, it was quite easy to alter it on the spot.

Straightening up from the table, Wellington asked, "Has the siege artillery closed?"

Not wanting to linger over the previous night's debacle at the rocket battery, Delancey replied quickly, "Yes, sir. They took up a position adjacent to the rocket battery this morning. The combination ought to provide sufficient men to defend both against further disruption."

Wellington bent over the map once more.

At that moment 1,500 Americans defended against the duke's 15,000 invincibles. Delancey waited for instructions, which came speedily enough. "Delancey, before noon, order Brisbane to put everything he has against the Saranac River. Pin the Americans down with artillery; drive their fleet out of the harbor with the siege guns. Send Power, followed by Robinson, two miles inland up the Saranac River to Pike's cantonment. Ford the river in strength. Leave Power to deal with Strong here," he said, pointing to the road to Salmon River. "And send Robinson against Macomb's rear." He made a broad sweep of his hand, fingers flat like as an arrowhead. "You'll find me near the Sailly house at noon." Wellington paused. "That is, if you need me."

CHAPTER 9

Wellington Plunges South

"The eyes of America are on us. We must defend to the last extremity. Fortune always follows the brave."

—GEN. ALEXANDER MACOMB

Commodore Macdonough's flagship sat at anchor. The range of the British heavy mortar battery had compelled him to slide his fleet farther out into the bay, thereby limiting his targets. He watched helplessly as rolling clouds of white smoke obscured the battlefield. Every cannon and thousands of rifles spat out red and orange flames. A baffling wind cloaked enemy targets and friendly units, merging both until they were indiscernible. The handful of long-range naval cannons capable of reaching enemy lines depended on the system of floating buoys that marked the target line to the Sailly house and adjacent British units. The sudden arrival of Yankee cannonballs at the mansion knocked Wellington off his perch and forced him to move farther inland.

Decisively engaged in the fight of his life, Macomb lost communications with Macdonough. When the commodore made out small boats loaded with redcoats rowing toward the American side of the Saranac, he sent a half-dozen gun galleys. Their skipping cannonballs cracked against the flimsy craft, showering the water with wreckage and dismembered limbs, which floated on the turbulent surface for a few seconds before sinking in lazy spirals to the river's bottom. Laden with pouches of lead musket balls, the redcoats tried to swim for the nearest shore, but American sharpshooters in trees along the bank picked them off.

A recent target in front of the Sailly house, Wellington sent a six-gun field battery forward to the riverbank. Their long-range nine-pounders engaged the gun galleys and drove them out of range once more.

Macdonough received word that Major General Strong was calling for transport. The *President,* though still under repair, was soon under way to bring the Vermont militia to New York. Delancey reported the unopposed crossing at Pike's cantonment and the rapid deployment of both Power's and Robinson's brigades. Withholding no reserve, Wellington chose to smash Macomb's army as quickly as possible. He left Macdonough's fleet to the Royal Navy, hoping the American ships wouldn't slip away in the interim.

Macomb knew instantly from the ferocity of Brisbane's assault—nearly five thousand muskets supported by six batteries of guns—that the end was near. The restored rocket battery's first salvo struck the blockhouse next to Mooers's home, killing the soldiers inside and setting it ablaze. The flames could be seen along the entire front of the American lines, and the sight decimated the entrenched soldiers' morale. Macomb, watching from the attic window of Mooers's house, saw the British form for an attack. He rushed out into the melee. While bullets snapped around him, he ran the hundred yards down Bridge Street to the river.

Finding Wool with Martin Aikin's Volunteers adjacent to the stone bridge in the center of Plattsburgh that had been fortified with the planking, Macomb asked, "Where are Wellington's other two brigades? Do you think they'll force a crossing here?"

"Don't know, General," Wool replied amid the screeching, deafening sounds of battle. "I've got my hands full. But I reckon the bastards will sneak up from behind. I'd watch my rear—if you take my meaning." An enemy cannonball impacted against a tree; an explosion of fall foliage scattered above their heads. Wool hollered to the cannoneers, "Change to canister, and give those bastards so eager to cross a watery grave!"

"These redcoats are all yours, John. I'll find my own."

Macomb dodged his way uphill to Fort Moreau, where his horse was sheltered. Behind the guns and beyond the range of the British fire, he took the road that paralleled the river in the direction of the Catherine Street Bridge a half mile southwest. He rode bent over in the saddle to avoid the stray bullets that sizzled through the trees. Shattered branches fell on him. As he approached, leading elements of Robinson's brigade came into view. Macomb watched the Cameronian Scottish Rifles, kilts flying, run to engage a detachment of the American 15th Infantry, which came out to meet their charge. The Americans attempted to form a line, but the Scots overwhelmed them. The only other Saranac River bridge, made of timber, which Macomb intended to burn in an emergency, was suddenly caught in a vice with redcoats on both sides of the river applying pressure. At close order, marching to the drumbeat of 120 measured paces a minute, the 27th Inniskillings broke through to the bridge, which was now irrevocably lost. Brisbane's right flank poured across the river.

The American defenders fragmented into smaller groups and, attempting to reach the safety of Fort Brown, ran up the road in Macomb's direction. The general stopped the near rout, gathered the remnants of bridge defenders into a semblance of a formation, and led them to join the garrison fighting at Fort Brown.

"Our perimeter's being squeezed into a nutshell," Macomb told his aide, Lieutenant Lewis G. DeRussy, the engineer who had designed the forts. The lieutenant now ardently wished he had barricaded the rear of the forts as well.

———

Leading the envelopment, Robinson barked from his saddle over the roar of the attack, "Adjutant, send the 76th to the right flank. Let's see if Wellington's West Riding Regiment can break these Yankees. It'll be a fitting battle honor for His Grace, a present from my brigade."

The battalion of six hundred rampaging redcoats split off from the main column at quick time and headed straight toward the rear of Fort Moreau a quarter mile away.

Macomb swung his black stallion around and galloped like a young scout to warn his main battery to turn the guns around. Less than a hundred yards away, the general drew his sword to show his business was urgent and shouted, "Look to your rear! Look to your rear!"

The crews, stunned by the sight of redcoats and the rhythmic sound of pounding battle drums, swung the guns around. The thousand-pound cannons resisted, preferring to remain in their recoil ruts. Macomb rode on to Fort Scott and took personal command of the infantry reserve, composed of men from several regiments who possessed enough mobility to trot along behind Macomb as he drew them up the embankment to take the 76th Foot in its flank. The American charge forced the regiment back at a trot to the safety of its brigade, which soon massed once again. And once again, Robinson charged, thrusting a bristling wedge of bayonets at Fort Moreau's bewildered cannoneers, as they lit their last charge. Within minutes Robinson closed the gap in the red line of British wrought by Macomb's reserve.

It was hopeless. Robinson alone had far more power than Macomb's entire command. The American general, overwhelmed and defeated, turned to DeRussy. "It's too much. It's plain murder to continue." He rode forward alone, hat in hand, sword in its scabbard, and delivered his force into the enemy's hands to prevent the slaughter that would've followed any further vain attempts at resistance.

The news of the victory spread north to Canada at the speed of a dispatch rider. It was dark when the sixty miles lay behind the string of exhausted post horses. The following morning Prevost's daughter Ann opened the Montreal morning paper to read to her mother over coffee and toast. The headline blared the news in the boldest of print: **Plattsburgh Falls!**

"Father will be pleased," the girl said. Then she mused, "I wonder what they'll make of it at Ghent?"

Macdonough Decides to Fight Another Day

Macdonough feared the silence after the battle more than the battle itself. The white veil lifted slowly to reveal unarmed exhausted men in blue uniforms sitting out in the open.

"Ship's Master," the commodore beckoned, "the battle's lost. There's no time to lose—up anchor, make a signal, take to the lake! Helmsman, Valcour Passage, if you please. All hands make sail."

It was three o'clock, and fortunately, there was still no sign of the Royal Navy. The wind that had brought Macdonough north and frustrated Downie was dying away. It would soon be replaced by a northerly gale, which the *Confiance* would ride south, leading the most powerful fleet ever seen on the lake.

The American crews, fearing the Royal Artillery would reposition their siege mortars to the water's edge, labored to turn their ships away from the shore. The square-rigged combatants hoisted every inch of sail they could raise. The oarsmen, praying for a following wind, rowed as never before to increase the distance between themselves and the enemy guns. Macdonough kept his eyes on Cumberland Head at the bay's northern tip. If the wind changed from the north, it would surely bring the Royal Navy with it. The *Confiance* was so large he knew her masts would be visible above the tall pines on the point.

The master of a customs cutter hailed Macdonough. As the sides of the two vessels bumped together, a rolled weighted message was pitched at the *Saratoga*'s boatswain mate, who took it to the captain. Macdonough learned that his service vessel, the damaged *President*, was engaged, along with everything that could float, in transferring the Vermont militia across the lake to the Salmon River. The commodore scribbled a reply to Strong:

Plattsburgh taken by British land force at 3 PM. Royal Navy fleet expected at any moment. Suggest you remain in Vermont.
—Macdonough

With the army lost, the young American commodore assumed command of federal forces in the Northeast. He called for his captains—Henley, Cassin, and Budd—to join him, as the fleet slipped slowly south between Valcour Island and the New York shore. There, they anchored.

Cassin, face still blackened from the fountain of sparks that had fizzled up from a touchhole igniter, arrived first. Henley was full of "sage" advice as soon as his heels hit the wet deck. Budd, the most junior among them, was quiet yet nervous and anxiously watched for signs of the enemy.

"We've lost the west side of the lake, but we still have Vermont to support the fleet. The British army can't move farther south without having lake superiority. We now stand alone against the full brunt of the Royal Navy and His Majesty's army—particularly its artillery. If we prevail, the invasion will have to winter here, and our army will have the time needed to regroup. If we don't defeat the *Confiance* and her sisters, Wellington will reach as far south as navigation and the mercurial winds permit." Macdonough paused to articulate their plausible options, but Henley preempted him.

"Commodore, if Valcour was good for Arnold in '76, then it should be good enough for us now. It's nearly the same story anyhow, except Arnold faced a larger fleet and still took them to task here in these narrow waters. We can form a crescent and pick them off. Only one of Downie's ships can pass this way at a time."

Macdonough was familiar with the past and rather tired of it. "Things have changed, Henley. There's a huge victorious army three miles up that shoreline, and they're heading south to engage Strong and those Vermonters who may've crossed over. They'll be on that bank within the hour." He pointed to New York, two hundred yards off the starboard side. "Wellington's artillery can line up, wheel to wheel, and blow us from the water before the Royal Navy even arrives. We cannot stay here."

Henley, wishing he had thought first before spouting an impromptu useless history lesson, dropped his head.

The commodore didn't wait for anyone else to interject. "If we confront the enemy on the open water at the lake's widest point, then we can maneuver. Perhaps the *Confiance* is not as nimble, and we can rake her across the bow. However, our crews, though well-meaning and courageous soldiers, don't have the skills we'll demand. So we'll have to tear a corner from Benedict Arnold's page," he said, nodding to Henley. "We'll sail down the lake to our base at Otter Creek, where we can get support. There, the lake's somewhat narrow, and there, we can compel the Royal Navy to fight on a reduced front, cutting the number of guns directed at us at one time. There, too, we can fight from anchor to improve our aim while they will have to maneuver."

Cassin spoke up. "Sir, I agree, that's our only chance. But doesn't it change the ordnance? The *Confiance* has dozens of long-range cannons, and we have only a handful. Our carronades won't reach beyond five hundred yards."

Macdonough tipped his hat. "It'll be a bloody day. May God grace us with His benevolent gaze. Sometimes he favors the Davids over the Goliaths—or so I've been told. To your ships, gentlemen."

Battle of Lake Champlain

Earlier Wellington had reported the American fleet anchored in Cumberland Bay, where the Royal Navy could defeat the enemy's navy in detail, but Commodore Downie was unable to shake down the *Confiance* quickly enough. Worse, the prevailing southern wind prevented him from sailing. Late on the evening of September 10, the wind changed, allowing the British fleet to careen south in search of its quarry.

The single light sails on the eleven rowed gunboats provided some propulsion but not enough. Seventy men pulling on oars couldn't keep up with the square-riggers. Intended to protect the larger vessels from boarding parties, the gunboats receded from sight. Downie, new to the lake, was reluctant to leave them behind. As darkness lifted at 6:00 AM on September 11, leaving a mist hovering above the placid water on the wet dreary morning, his flotilla gathered off the head of Cumberland Bay.

A small picket boat with a party of British army officers set out to meet the flagship. Delancey rendered a salute and accepted honors on boarding the *Confiance*. A gun salute, under the circumstances, wasn't appropriate. The colonel wore a short, unadorned red tailcoat with a dark blue collar. By contrast, Downie's long-tail dress coat, heavy with wide gold piping on navy blue, reeked of navy formality. Every edge and seam was wrapped in braid. His low half-cocked hat was also encrusted every few inches with gold lace.

"Commodore, the duke begs your indulgence, but he's unable to come out while the army's consolidating its position. I'm happy to report that the American army has been vanquished with minimum casualties on both sides. The prisoners will be evacuated via land, which will leave all the craft you can capture free to move our army south."

"Sir William, please pass on my congratulations to His Grace on a signal victory. What's the disposition of the American fleet?"

"They slipped anchor before we could reposition our siege guns and sailed south through Valcour. I believe they're intact." Delancey handed Downie a list of the American vessels along with pertinent observations. "Your orders are to confront the Americans where you find them and destroy them."

"Sir, the *Confiance* alone is capable of sinking the entire flotilla!"

Satisfied that he could now answer all the duke's inquiries, Delancey quickly departed to allow the bellicose Downie to get under way.

————

At four that afternoon, sailing to a thirty-knot following wind, Downie thought he caught a glimpse of the *Saratoga*'s 150-foot mainmast against a gray sky. The lookout, perched 200 feet above *Confiance*'s deck, cried out, "Sail ho!"

Earlier, knowing he could take her later, Downie ignored an alert regarding the possible nearby presence of the *President*. The lone transport, limping and listing to port, wasn't worthy of the name "quarry." Wellington could use her later to help move the army. The American fighting fleet was Downie's intended prize. Standing atop the starboard rail and looking through his glass, he counted three, perhaps four, square-riggers emerging into view. *They must be moored in a line*, he thought. *Their sails are furled. What luck.*

The *Confiance*, launched just two weeks earlier, was as unfamiliar with the lake as was her captain, who had to this point relied on the experience of Pring, his second in command, but he was now leading the flotilla in the *Linnet*. Constructed mostly of pine procured from American smugglers, *Confiance* was as green as her soldier crew. But it didn't matter. She was simply a floating gun platform armed with the latest cannons that Woolwich produced. At a mile her twenty-four-pound solid-shot could drill a crisp charred hole in one side of the *Saratoga* and a gaping rupture, with wooden planks like broken petals, out the other.

"Well, Simons," Downie said, directing his comments to the shipwright, William Simons, "once again we British will be spilling blood—Yankee blood—into this ancient waterway. But mark me, sir. This'll be the last time, for we shall never forfeit our control of it again." Downie pulled an ornate pocket watch, a gift from his adoring sister, from an inside pocket and glanced at the date. "The 11th of September will be a date that'll live forever in the history of this land and the hearts of our countrymen."

Simons was more concerned with the new ship's performance than making grandiose historical claims. During training the shipwright had noticed that rough planks caused the giant cannons to jump in recoil. Pulling them back into position took a dozen fit men. Downie felt the implacable weight of history on his shoulders, and he signaled, "Form a line—attack!"

The four ships tacked to port and opened their gun ports.

Downie ordered his first lieutenant, "Mister Robertson, run out the guns."

The midshipmen, leading each gun section, echoed the officer's order. The Dorsetshire soldiers followed their Royal Marine gunners to the main deck and hauled the 2,500-pound cannons into position. Eighteen mammoth guns per side, along with one in the bow and a pair of thirty-two-pound carronades aft, stuck their black snouts out past the gunwales. Each had been preloaded with bar shot—two iron balls, like barbells, welded together between a foot-long iron bar, a lethal configuration.

"Shoot for the rigging, Lieutenant, and bring it down on their heads. We're about killing crewmen—not sinking prize ships."

The *Confiance*—courses clewed up, royals down—sailed slowly north. "There are only a few American cannons within range of us, sir, but be careful, Robertson, the wind's pushing us toward the damn Yankees. As the lake narrows, we can count on just two rotations before being squeezed down to five hundred yards and forced to anchor adjacent to Macdonough's battle line. We must turn them to kindling by then or we'll pay too high a price."

Commanding the *Linnet*, Pring led the pack, followed closely by the *Confiance*, the *Chub*, and the *Finch*, each trailing a hundred yards behind the other. The low throw weight of their long guns diminished their usefulness, but Downie wasn't concerned. The *Confiance* alone could more than compensate for the difference. With starboard sides exposed, the Royal Navy fired as first little *Preble*, then *Ticonderoga*, then *Saratoga*, and finally *Eagle* appeared over the front gun sites. The rippled salvo from twenty-eight cannons shattered the seldom-disturbed silence of the northern lake. Strung together by ropes, the British gunboats huddled behind the Royal Navy battle line and waited to deploy on order and board the shattered American ships.

For the slightest of instants, the cannonballs hung in the smoke-filled air. Then they descended like a giant's wrath.

———

Before the Royal Navy arrived, Macdonough had called out all available small craft from Otter Creek. To leeward of the four anchored American ships, he tethered dozens of small boats and filled the craft with gun crews from the short-range carronades and light cannons; the substantial hulls of *Saratoga* and her trio of sister ships protected the men. There, in safety, the crewmen wouldn't be called forward until their weapons were within range of Downie's closing fleet. The American ships would have to absorb the first two enemy passes. During that critical time the *Saratoga* would rely on her six twenty-four-pounders, the only guns to match the *Confiance*. Only the six large cannons on the *Saratoga* were crewed.

The commodore believed that the ever-narrowing lake and strong northern wind would drive Downie's ships within range, and then it would be a different story. The

Yankee "smashers"—carronades with heavy shot propelled at low velocities—would crash by sheer force through the enemy hulls, causing mass casualties and splintering obliteration. *All will be well,* Macdonough thought, *if we can just hold out that long.*

Isolated on his flagship, the commodore heard the guns' belching baritone reports just before the cannonballs arrived. Some shot skipped short, its speed sapped by the waves, and splashed the *Saratoga*'s hull harmlessly with sheets of lake water. Others sizzled through the rigging, snapping lines, overshooting the men in the small boats, and ultimately sinking harmlessly to the bottom of Champlain. Macdonough knelt behind a massive iron twenty-four-pound gun, waiting for a clear shot at the *Confiance*.

"God, she's a brute," he said when he first beheld her. He cautioned his gun captains over the din of the shelling, "Concentrate on the big ship. Take your time. We may not get a another chance."

Further conversation was cut off when a handful of British cannonballs, tossed like marbles, struck the masts and rigging above the Americans' heads and showered them with splinters, twists of hemp, and blankets of shredded canvas. An enemy bar shot hit a mast, cracking it with an ear-piercing snap. The sound was buried beneath outgoing blasts from *Saratoga*'s cannons. But Macdonough kept his cool, holding back his cannon fire for the perfect moment.

———

Although the *Confiance* possessed a shot furnace to heat her cannonballs so that they would set the enemy's vessels on fire on impact, Downie refrained from using it. Like the rapid beat of a snare drum, another ripple of gunfire erupted all along his line while he calculated the looming prospect of substantial prize money—perhaps enough to win him Prevost's daughter Ann, who had caught his eye as she had Pring's. Burned-out hulks held no value, but a great country estate could be purchased from this catch.

Downie shouted, "For your purses's sake, keep your aim high! All repairs to captured ships will be subtracted from your share." The *Confiance* had reached the end of her first pass, and her crew left their guns to maneuver the ship back to the west. The brisk wind from the north contained an unexpected and uncomfortable chill. The *Linnet* swung wide and as it did, the *Confiance* was forced to use only her staysails fore and aft to complete the turn. It was a precarious moment. Too many minutes passed as the soldiers-turned-seamen labored with unfamiliar lines.

———

Macdonough's fifteen years of experience at the gun as a midshipman and lieutenant bore fruit. He ordered that two cannonballs be loaded into the breech. It was risky, but what action wasn't that day? Just before the *Confiance*'s bow crossed to the west, he yanked the lanyard on the flintlock igniter, sending sparks into the thin column of powder that lit the main charge in the breach behind the doubled shot. The gun roared as if it might crack wide open from the internal outrage. But instead, it spat out its deadly contents.

The fly time allowed the *Confiance* to swing her bowsprit safely west but exposed nearly the entire length of her open top deck to the twin destroyers as they descended with no intention of dispensing honors. The first cannonball split the foremast at the height of a man while the second passed over the open hold, nicked the mainmast, and shattered the ship's doubled wooden wheel, killing instantly, horrifically, the helmsman, master, and lieutenant. Still caught in reverie about the treasure the American fleet would earn him, Downie was untouched. No stranger to carnage, he ordered, almost perfunctorily, "Boatswain, clear the deck, man the tiller on the orlop deck, set a relay for commands, and get the casualties below to the cockpit."

The *Confiance* had veered closer to the American lines than planned but still remained out of range of the enemy's cursed carronades.

Far more dangerous now at two thousand yards, the *Confiance*'s guns became murderously accurate. It would be her last track before Macdonough could call forward his carronade gunners to even the fight.

The rough decks caused a delay as the British crew repositioned the ponderous Royal Navy cannon. Heaving, sweating men levered the stout metal pry bars to force the gun muzzles outside the ports, where the blast wouldn't singe the ship's gunwales. Downie, his back to the mainmast, was below on the gun deck. On his knees he could see the *Confiance*'s guns begin to bear on the *Saratoga*. "Level your tubes, gunners. Shoot for the top of the rails. Sweep the deck free before they can harm us. Fire as you bear!"

The barked orders were echoed eighteen times. Sailors, confined in the darkness of the gun deck, watched through square gun ports for their target to come into view.

————

Macdonough's glass told the story of his magnificent shot. "We hurt her, boys. We hurt her bad. Look at her lose way."

The gun crew scarcely heard his words as they wet swabbed the hot barrels' bore and poked leaky flannel bags of powder down them. A strong black-faced man in a torn and faded red shirt heaved a cannonball to the lip of the recoiled cannon, and a buddy rammed it home.

The commodore stepped behind the gun, drawn forward on small, fat wooden wheels, and knelt on one knee. His left hand gripped the last of the protruding rings in front of the round base plate. He rested his cheek on the warm metal and sited with his right eye. The aft quarter of the *Confiance* was sliding by. He didn't have much time. He rolled slightly to one side to avoid the recoil and, as warning to his crew, shouted, "Fire!"

Simultaneously, and astonishingly, a tremendous clang resounded as a British cannonball ricocheted off the muzzle of Macdonough's gun. The impact snapped the metal trunnion straps holding the barrel to its carriage. The massive seven-foot black-iron barrel, weighing two thousand pounds, rose like a mighty vengeful whale from the deep, stood on end, and crashed down on the stunned commodore, fastening him onto the deck and flattening him. A spinning chunk of iron, chipped from the American cannon's muzzle, whistled through the air in a high arc and, with an anticlimactic splash, sank into the water.

Macdonough was dead. His face still held a wide-eyed stunned expression.

The hopes of the American navy declined rapidly. Lieutenant Cassin, unaware that he was now commanding the entire effort, called forward the carronade crews, but it was too late.

The Royal Navy cannonade littered the deck with chunks of masts, sharp splinters, shredded swatches of canvas, coils of standing and running rigging. Returning gunners who found certain carronades operational were restricted to discharging only one preloaded shot. Downie unleashed a swarm of British gunboats, which slid in under the trajectory of the firmly mounted carronades. Unable to depress the barrels, the Americans were as helpless as their ships. The Yankee gunboats, believing there was no chance to resist, turned and fled farther south toward Fort Ticonderoga's protective stone walls to fight—perhaps—again.

Fighting the north wind every step of the way, Downie departed the scene that night via a captured cutter. By morning, frustrated, he abandoned the boat at the Salmon River for a borrowed horse. Fitzroy Somerset, surprised to see the commodore alone and expecting the worst, greeted Downie and quickly ushered him into Wellington's mess, where Brigadier General Macomb was both guest and prisoner. Delancey rose, offered his chair, and ordered a plate to be brought for the weary commodore.

The duke quipped, "Commodore, the dust on your uniform tells me that you're no longer counting the waves. Allow me to introduce General Alexander Macomb. You two haven't met, have you?"

Downie hadn't met Macomb or even spoken directly to Wellington before that morning. Ignoring Macomb, who rose, the commodore blurted out his news. "Your Grace, I could've sent a messenger, but I wanted to deliver my report in person: We've wrested complete control of Champlain. Your land force can begin to move unhindered farther south down the length of the lake."

Macomb wasn't surprised, for both he and Macdonough had been outnumbered, outgunned, unsupported, and abandoned by Madison's administration in the face of a vast foe. The diversionary attacks at Washington and Baltimore had deprived Macomb of any hope of assistance.

A Cry to Arms

From the *Albany Evening Journal*, September 13, 1814:
Here is the talley of our misfortune, read it and weep for those who suffer.
August 24—Washington, District of Columbia
September 2—Nantucket Island
September 4—Penobscot, Maine
September 11—Plattsburgh & Lake Champlain

Word has reached us that the large British land-and-sea force that attacked Washington has entered Baltimore's outer harbor and is preparing to seize the city within days. We have not lost, but we *are* losing.

New Yorkers—leave your fields, bid good-bye to your families, and bring your rifles, for we are besieged. The king's intentions are clear. This struggle to free ourselves from foreign rule, which we believed we had won a generation ago, has just begun. It may take the season, it may take a year, it may take a lifetime, it may take our children's lifetime and that of their children. But God Almighty has ordained that we, firmly ensconced here in the New World, must live free to govern ourselves—or not live at all. We did it before, and with God's help and assistance, we will do it again.

It is our pledge, it is our right, it is our duty, it is our heritage, it is our future. In God We Trust!

To arms, to arms!

A few inglorious days later in Philadelphia, banker, printer, publisher, and Irish freedom fighter Mathew Carey read similar pieces and snorted. He didn't share the authors' confident certitude. Sentimentality and false pride weren't going to rescue this frail fledgling experiment in creating an enduring country ruled "by the people for the people." True, the Americans had bested the British in Baltimore, but that wasn't a triumph of arms, only and merely a respite, a temporary reprieve. Carey's bitter experiences in Ireland had caused him to fear Great Britain's inexorable economic system, which enslaved the people and cleared the land for the privileged. He recognized the Baltimore "victory" for what it was.

"The Yankees never faced the full brunt of the king's forces," he told his wife over morning coffee. "Like Washington, this attack was just a raid, my dear, timed to divert attention from Wellington's drive in the North. There's no doubt that the British will consolidate their gains on the Atlantic Coast and Lake Champlain and then threaten our very survival if we don't surrender."

There was only one solution. Carey hated the thought of taking money from the avaricious London bankers under any conditions. He despised them and thought they were in league with the devil. He tried to reject the thought but knew that if British money were not infused into the veins of this war, the first "republic" would collapse. The time had come to take the money to build the army and navy or die. No alternative existed.

Which Way to Turn?

The day after Baltimore's successful defense, Madison established his government in a set of commercial storage buildings off Pennsylvania Avenue that had been emptied prior to the British arrival.

A week after the victory at Baltimore, Monroe, now heading both the State and War departments, sent Albert Gallatin a summary of the military situation and British gains in the North as of September 15. He urged the delegation to stall or adjourn and further cautioned, "Under no circumstances are you to sign *any* agreement or letter of understanding. The winter's our only hope, and we shall use it to our utmost advantage. There is no intention on the part of this administration to quit the war as long as the British occupy our land and blockade our coast. While events of the past month have been most alarming, we have not yet begun to fight!" Invoking John Paul Jones was perhaps theatrical but also appropriate. Still, brave quotes were one thing; money—a great deal of it—was the only means to survival. "Our friends abroad have been most encouraging," Monroe wrote, referencing the secret financial assistance promised by London's independent banks. "Their support will allow us to reestablish our military and right the present imbalance."

In a cabinet meeting on September 16, Monroe laid out the military situation for the few members in attendance. Cabinet colleagues regarded the routing of the British at Baltimore as a great victory, but the loss of Lake Champlain had made little impression. It was *so* far away and no cabinet members had ever been there.

"Plattsburgh was nothing—a mere demonstration," the ever-witty Secretary of the Treasury Campbell quipped, dismissing it with a wave of his hand. The politicians who filled the room were pert regardless of the burning of Washington, which to many from the North was a blessing. Later they could move it back to where it belonged: New York or Boston.

"The British will withdraw as soon as we withdraw from Niagara," another added. "The sooner we withdraw, the sooner this trouble will be over and we can return to trading with England, as we did before. The war's all a terrible misunderstanding. Surely, that much is evident, Mister President."

Most members nodded in murmuring agreement.

Monroe couldn't believe his colleagues' flippancy. "This war is neither a good-natured horse race nor a frivolous ball. War isn't a matter of whim. It's war, gentlemen! Declared by Congress! It must be fought *here* and *now*, or we'll lose forever and the British will take whatever they choose—our lands, our citizens, our honor, and our lives!" Monroe, wound tightly by his own rhetoric, was growing hot under his high starched collar. "Sir," he said, turning to the president, "we are engaged in the preservation of our unique nation, the most singular and sterling in existence, one that many of us rebelled to create and that *some* of us are still willing to die for!" He turned to Campbell and asked harshly, "How do you think the British will treat us? I'll tell you—with taxation, oppression, and subjugation." The murmuring ceased.

"I propose that the regular army be increased from your authorization of twenty thousand to fifty thousand men and that the state militias be federalized in the present emergency—*today*." (The regulars had never exceeded fifteen thousand.)

"Fifty thousand!" said Campbell, a former senator from Tennessee. He grew decidedly less mocking as he reminded those present that the Treasury was virtually empty and that the call out on the bonds had yielded only 20 percent of their value.

Since Campbell hadn't been informed of the clandestine arrangement with the bankers of London, Monroe said, "I believe that Wellington's presence a hundred miles inside our border will energize considerable monetary encouragement for our cause."

Such a vague statement was difficult to debate, and the passion for argument had diminished markedly. All Campbell could say was, "Sir, the country's coffers are open and waiting. For all our sakes, I hope your confidence is well placed."

Madison would've then turned to seventy-one-year-old Jefferson, but he had hurried away to his beloved Monticello and was unreachable. The former president's misplaced faith in Napoleon's unending success, the American navy's confinement, the burning of Washington, the losses of Lake Champlain and the territory of Maine, the relentless blockade, and crucially the decimation of trade—all fell to Jefferson's egregious miscalculations and advice. Madison turned to Monroe and placed the burden on his shoulders. The president pleaded with him to extricate the nascent nation from the nefarious mess that threatened its existence and to do so before the British arrested and hanged them all.

Monroe's solution was to reincarnate the Continental Army of his youth. Once again, the ranks would fill with hordes of single-minded free men to preserve and defend the idea of free people under their own rule. Before fielding an army, however, there was the question of funds. The lack of money had nearly undone the American Revolution and now during this Second War for Independence the Treasury's echoing emptiness could easily undo the nation.

The secretary left the capital secretly that night for Philadelphia.

A Treacherous Passage

"It'll take more than brotherly love to save our way of life," Mathew Carey told the secretary when they shook hands in front of the Bank of Philadelphia. It was sunny, but a chilly breeze was blowing from the north. Was it a hint of winter or Wellington's cold breath? Hope dwelt in the men's eyes on that late September day. They stood only blocks from where it had all begun nearly forty years ago at Independence Hall.

The pair settled in Carey's dark, wood-paneled chamber deep inside the bank. "Mister Secretary," the Irishman said, "having this British aristocrat camping on our soil makes me uncomfortable. We must do something about it, don't you agree?"

Monroe nodded, pleased by Carey's refreshing defiance after the cabinet meeting. He brought his host up to date on the military situation, which held few surprises for the Irishman. England threatened the new nation on three sides—Wellington in the north and the Royal Navy on the east and Gulf coasts.

Monroe grew expansive and (he hoped) persuasive. "Sir, there's no possibility that a foreign army or crowned head will sway the balance, as France did once before. America's conspicuously alone. We have all the elements to defend ourselves excepting one—money. Delegate Gallatin, Sir Josiah Wedgwood, the financial institutions in London, and, most important, you are our only hope to defeat the British. I understand that foreign banks strongly desire to protect their substantial investments in the United States and, to do so, are willing to provide the means for our resistance and ultimate victory. We intend to build a credible army that will bog Wellington down and bleed him. We'll make it prohibitively expensive to sustain his huge hungry army and navy at a distance of three thousand miles across the Atlantic. If the British become weary and Europe becomes unstable once again, as it has always done, Britain will relent. Although funding for the creation of a meaningful force may come through a circuitous route, avoiding the price we shall all pay otherwise will be well worth the effort."

"Mister Secretary, permit me to say," the banker paused and leaned forward in his brown leather chair, which creaked noisily, "you personally have assumed an enormous burden and a daunting task, the success of which will inscribe your name in stone next to that of Washington. I thank you on behalf of our ungrateful country and our unknowing children. I'll assist you every step of the way. You've a friend in me, sir, and the Irish take the notion of friendship to heart."

Carey's pledge relieved somewhat the tremendous tension Monroe had been feeling. He was on uncharted waters, true, but he was no longer a sole voyager. He now had a fellow passenger, who was also a keen navigator of treacherous waters. Experience warned him to be wary though. What else did this man want for ensuring safe passage?

Carey, always the banker, asked, "Mister Secretary, how much do you need, how will you spend it, and, most important, how do you intend to pay it back?"

A New Army by Spring?

Back in Washington in borrowed rooms, Monroe relieved Brigadier General Winder of his command, not only for the loss of the nation's capital but also for supporting his equally inept uncle, Maryland's governor, Levin Winder. Meanwhile, the president notified the governor of the federalization of Maryland's victorious and beloved militia.

Monroe took stock of the regular army. There were fourteen thousand fit for duty. Major General Andrew Jackson had assumed command of the 7th Military District and its three thousand men to defend Mobile, Alabama, and New Orleans, Louisiana, from the Spanish and British. Major Generals Jacob Brown and Winfield Scott together held the combined bulk of the fighting army's committed force. Their 3,500 troops at Niagara were about to be joined by Major General George Izard's command of 4,500 soldiers, still in seemingly perpetual transit, somewhere along the Mohawk Trail. In the west, with only 1,000 fit regulars, Major General William Harrison was relying primarily on militia from three states. Macomb and his 1,500 men were prisoners of the British. That left approximately 2,000 regulars for duty at Baltimore.

Monroe's first act as secretary of war was to change the mission of the army in the north from offense to defense. The second was to order the ever-marching Izard to countermarch to Saratoga. The third established a training and logistics cantonment at West Point and a cannon factory across the Hudson at Cold Spring Forge. All this was accomplished with the stroke of a pen.

His pressing challenge was to find that "man on the white horse" who would lead the army against Wellington and fight him, if not to a decisive victory, then to a standstill. Harrison—at first glance the most successful field commander thus far—wouldn't abandon his beloved frontier while it was imperiled. Brown, a good fighter though a bit of a scoundrel, was plagued with accusations of lining his pockets with British embargo gold and would therefore hardly be able to inspire the sacrifice and effort required. Scott, young and brash, was a good field man but not a great thinker. Izard was an unknown variable, well educated but without credentials to support his selection. And a long list of politically connected failures were not considered: Henry Dearborn, James Wilkinson, Wade Hampton, and others either too old or alcoholic.

The one man left standing was the experienced, obnoxious, tough, heroic, ruthless, outspoken, headstrong, cantankerous, outrageous, and slightly infirm—a bullet still dwelled in his body from a duel—Andrew "Old Hickory" Jackson. If summoned to Washington, would he come? If he came, would he take on the thankless task or would he curse the secretary and storm back to the bayou? And if he accepted the appointment, could he beat Wellington?

A Wild Goose Pens a Letter

Mathew Carey would've liked to have boarded a ship for Dublin to meet Harold Scoff and the cabal's other principal members from the Bank of Ireland and the Hamilton Bank of New York. As a rule, such meetings were cordial affairs held in a modern metropolis, where a man could enjoy the diversions of a great city. When they were among themselves, international financiers commonly laid politics and borders aside. In their "real" world, which neither appeared in newsprint nor was discussed on the floors of government assemblages, deals could be struck for the benefit of all.

However, Carey's freedom-fighting activities in Ireland made him a persona non grata anywhere the Union Jack flew. As a result, his deals required couriers and code ciphers and encountered needless delays. Under the circumstances and in the interest of expediency, for it was nearly November, Carey personally composed a letter to Scoff.

[Note to clerk: Show to no other officer of the bank. Encode without signature—C]

October 25, 1814

My dear Mr. Corcoran,
My client gratefully accepts your offer of assistance with the expedition, which is undertaken with high risk. Enclosed is a list of the sums required prior to commitment of the venture and an interest payment schedule. My bank will be honored to accept the allocation through channels previously arranged during consultation.
    Regard this letter as a binding fiduciary obligation on the part of my institution.

    Sincerely, in the greatest of faith,
    Monk

Carey signed the letter "Monk" in reference to the turncoat of the English Civil War. Benedict Arnold Sr. had also used the alias; Carey hoped it would mislead any inquiries.

Besides Carey's obvious enterprises was a hidden one: he was the shadowy leader of a secret society, the Wild Geese, made up of ex-patriots exiled from Ireland who devoted their lives to the expulsion of Great Britain from their homeland. Thousands of Irishmen, declared outlaws for acts of sedition at home, had resettled in foreign lands, vowing to return to the emerald island one day to free their nation. They could be found scattered in Napoleon's armies and navies, but they maintained close ties to the mother country through local anonymous chapters while they waited for the day when they could return home and lead their countrymen in rebellion. The chapter leaders, members of the Committee of Correspondence, used encrypted communiqués sent by couriers to maintain cohesion in the long-term struggle. America unknowingly harbored hundreds, perhaps thousands, of Wild Geese.

Carey referred to his brothers in the chapters simply as Irish-American Club members and rarely used *wild geese* in conversation or correspondence. One day Carey intended to return to Ireland as the leader of an avenging army of Wild Geese. He was a loyal American, but his heart had never left Ireland. While the money lent by London's banking community would provide for the creation of a new regular American army to rescue his adopted country from Wellington's army, it would also train an exiled Irish army that would eventually rid Ireland of English rule. It was a dangerous game, but one he thought well worth playing.

When Carey left Ireland under the protection of honorable men inside and outside the British establishment governing Ireland in 1804, he wasn't alone. While many dissidents were imprisoned and publicly hanged for treason, others slipped away and during the intervening years continued to do so. While abroad, the Wild Geese received financial support from the organizations in Ireland that expected them to return when the time came to cast out the British. These exiles learned trades useful to the coming war of liberation. Some turned to government administration, others to financial institutions, but most became soldiers. Napoleon welcomed them, as did the Austrian, Prussian, and Russian armies. And when the Napoleonic Wars neared their close, many immigrated to America, where they joined the effort against their common enemy. They learned the necessary languages and fought as if the lands were their own, but in the back of their minds their escapades abroad were mere interludes until they could return home.

Monroe's suspicions that money men harbored hidden agendas were well grounded. But if he had known that an Irish legion would first defend the United States and then carry that hard-won freedom and all it promised to Ireland, would he have objected? Carey thought not.

The letter was the first of many acts Carey would perform to assist in the fielding of an expanded regular army. He began a campaign in the *Pennsylvania Herald*, his newspaper, urging men to join the army to resist Wellington's occupation of northern New York. He hinted that the bounty of $164 and 120 acres of western land was about to be increased. He enlisted newspaper owners throughout the country to rally the citizens and wrote editorials reminding people of Burgoyne's old battle plan and of Wellington's nefarious intentions to split the country. The secretary of war and the president applauded his efforts.

While he waited for the money to filter in from the Scoffs, who were accumulating millions from their partners, he wrote to the president of the Bank of Ireland, an old friend, to remind him of the Wild Geese's commitment and to encourage the banker to speed the process along. Carey traveled to New York City with two goals in mind. The first was to call on his banking friends at the Hamilton Bank. Although its founder, Alexander Hamilton, had been killed in a duel with Vice President Aaron Burr in 1804, the institution and economic practices Hamilton had inaugurated survived his untimely death. An agreement to mask the origin of the transfer was quickly concluded. The funds supplied through the Bank of Ireland would be split equally between the Hamilton Bank and the Bank of Philadelphia. In previous years both the Bank of Philadelphia and the Hamilton Bank had abstained from purchasing government war bonds. To the government's great relief, Carey, as promised, influenced both institutions to gobble up every Treasury offering the moment it was released. The origin of the money would be so convoluted that no one could trace its source. Flush with cash as never before, the administration placed orders for military provisions at record levels.

The other purpose of his visit was surprisingly more delicate, as it concerned people rather than institutions. Carey was the houseguest of his old friend, Thomas Addis Emmet, New York's Irish-American attorney general and brother of Robert Emmet, who had been hanged by the British in 1803 for sedition. Thomas, a young-looking fifty-year-old, short and broad, was the leader of the Wild Geese in New York and was driven to vindicate the murder of his brother and others who died at the hands of their overlords. His wealth and power placed him at the van of the movement.

That rainy night the two men traveled the wet streets of the largest city in the country to the Bowery, where only the brave ventured after dark. Dressed in clothes as dark as the night, with large collars pulled up to conceal their faces, the attorney general and Carey stepped from the carriage; the former led the latter to an alley and from there to the back door of McGee's Pub and meeting house for the Wild Geese. Seated on a stool by the double doors to the cellar, a surly man in a soaked tweed coat stood up and yanked the doors open. He tugged the front of his cloth cap as the expected guests passed quietly down the broken stone steps.

Passing moldy beer kegs strewn about the dirt floor, Carey could barely see the crack of light that issued from under a scarred door at the far end of the passage. Suddenly, out of the darkness, a second shabby man stepped in front of Emmet and said, "This way, Your Honor." He rapped a prearranged rhythm on the wood and the door cracked open. A bright blue eye appeared, lit by a stubby guttering candle. The eye looked Emmet up and down. "Welcome, Your Honor."

The subterranean chamber was much larger than Carey expected. To his right was a makeshift bar, made of planks resting on tall barrels. He could smell beer in ceramic pitchers, even though the air was thick with tobacco smoke. Dozens of men seated along the walls rose, tankards in hand, as the party was led down the length of the room to a broad table. On either end were brass candlesticks, each with four arms, that imbued the room with a monastic look. A Kerry green flag with a white harp emblazoned in its center was draped loosely across the back wall.

Standing on the far side was a man whom Carey knew well—Liam Sampson, president of the United Irish of America. A big, broad-shouldered specimen, Sampson stuck his massive hand across the table and gripped Carey's hand. He held it and pulled the visitor toward him until the banker was leaning across the tabletop. He put his other hand around Carey's neck and kissed him quickly on the cheek.

"By God! I knew it'd be you who'd fire the cause. I hear from the counselor you've come to give the Wild Geese back their wings. Bless you, my fine man." He released the guest from the chokehold just in time to save Carey from blacking out from lack of oxygen. "Come round and take the place of honor, while our Father Brian evokes the heavens on our glorious cause."

Carey followed Emmet around the corner of the rude table, soaked and stained with beer, and stood silently while the priest gave a brief invocation.

Emmet spoke to the congregation first. "I'll not tell you this man's name, but I assure you that he's suffered more for the cause than any man here tonight. He's an important brother, honored wherever you find him but not to be identified publicly as one of us until the day we march triumphantly into Dublin. Through him we'll banish the king and all his men from our oppressed, precious island."

Carey took the introduction in stride. "Sons of Eire, I've come here tonight to tell you that at last we've been given the means to do God's work. The dreaded British are once again about to subjugate the Irishman, this time here in this glorious refuge and blessed land. They are less than two hundred miles north of us! The blood and sacrifice of the American army and navy have slowed down their invasion. The British have been forced to winter over on our soil but plan to take this town, this *very* street, next spring. You can stop them, as your fathers and grandfathers did in '76. I—an Irishman in exile—have hold of the means. Do you have the will?"

Fired by Carey's words, every man leapt to his feet and cried out, "Erin go bragh!"

Carey sat down. It was up to Sampson and Emmet to give the assembly organizers their marching orders. Carey felt young again; a fire had been rekindled deep inside him. He would swap places with Sampson if he could, but that wasn't his role—unfortunately.

Before he left the city two days later, the recruiting stations were overwhelmed by long queues of shabby men, mostly Irish, led there by the Wild Geese.

Carey's closed coach, mired in traffic, slowly wound its way out of the city. He sank back in the black leather bench seat. A small metal box, filled with hot coals, warmed his feet. A horsehair blanket, lined in red felt, covered his lap and hung down to the floor. Suddenly, the door to his carriage jerked open and a red Irish face poked in. "I hope your honor's of a fightin' persuasion. We need officers too, ye must be knowin'."

A handbill fluttered onto his knees, before the door slammed shut. It read,

YOU VOYAGED ACROSS the ATLANTIC to be FREE.
WILL YOU LET the BLOODY BRITISH OPPRESS YOU HERE?
RESCUE YOUR ADOPTED COUNTRY!
SAVE YOUR FAMILY FROM THE LOBSTER BACKS!
MAKE YOUR MOTHER SMILE &
YOUR FOREFATHERS PROUD!
Sign up at the CANAL STREET IRISH CLUB
for the NEW YORK IRISH BRIGADE!

FREE BEER & VITTLES!
ENLIST & COLLECT $264 & 120 ACRES OF LAND

Carey noted an extra hundred dollars added to the recruiting bonus, offered only at the Canal Street Club. It had been Carey's idea, and he intended to duplicate it in Philadelphia to draw Irishmen to the colors. If it produced twenty thousand recruits from the teeming cities, the $200,000 would be well spent.

Old Hickory Leaves the South

Preparing to attack Florida and involved in a planning session at his temporary headquarters in Mobile, Major General Andrew Jackson was surprised to receive a War Department envoy. He was well aware that Washington was against his excursion into Spanish territory. The government realized the foray would only provoke Spain's ally, Britain, to greater mischief. But still the previous secretary of war, Armstrong, had given Jackson his begrudging consent.

When the interruption occurred on the evening of the planning session, Major Davy Crockett had just given the floor to the militia's Captain Sam Houston, who was reporting on the fitness of their patchwork force of regulars, militia, and Indians. Recognizing the visitor at the door, Brigadier General John Coffee, Jackson's cavalry commander, halted the proceeding. "Cass! Welcome!"

Brigadier General Lewis Cass had been appointed a colonel of militia in Ohio from the earliest days of the war. A small-town politician, he had done well and was promoted to brigadier under Benjamin Harrison despite his party affiliation. While Cass recovered from wounds suffered at the Battle of the Thames, Monroe seconded him to the War Department staff. During the Creek War, he had been both Hull's and later Harrison's liaison officer in Jackson's headquarters. Unknown to those in the map room, he had accepted the task of coaxing Jackson into leaving his beloved South and committing to command the new army against Wellington.

"What in tarnation," Jackson roared, "blows an old politician out of the heavenly Ohio Valley and into this alligator swamp?" His tone was warm, which was unusual when he greeted a staff officer sent from the War Department. "My grapevine said a fancy fellow was beatin' up the dust, but he was described as a walleyed misfit in a borrowed general's uniform! I figured it was a War Department toady determined to stop my operation."

"Andy"—Cass knew better than to call Jackson "General," a title he never allowed a friend to use—"the president sent me on this miserable trip. I never would've stuck it out for anyone other than you."

Jackson recognized trouble when he saw it; Cass looked like a black cloud about to rain on him. He seemed gaunt and a great deal older than his thirty-two years. Jackson had heard that he had been wounded at the Battle of the Thames just over a year ago. It was only natural that the general had been interested in the fight that had ended Chief Tecumseh's tempestuous career. He looked carefully at his old friend and fellow warrior. "How are you, Cass?" he asked softly.

"In the pink, Andy, except for these here saddle sores." He rubbed his backside.

Pleased, Jackson shifted his tone. "I hear tell you left Harrison because the big fightin' was over. That why you're here? To join in the killin'?"

"I was thinking of joining you on this little soiree, but the president asked me to join a bigger show. While Baltimore's survived intact, northern New York and Lake Champlain haven't. Wellington's occupied it all, along with the eastern wing of Maine. He hasn't returned to Canada. The British, fifteen thousand of them, are wintering north of Albany. Wellington's back in Montreal, prepping thousands more for a spring campaign—most likely pointed at New York City—to cut the country in half. That red-coated duke's gonna take the whole country, Andy, unless someone can stop him. And the president thinks that someone is you."

Cass paused, his narrowing eyes fixed on Jackson. Both knew what was being offered—what opportunities, what obstacles.

"Well now, you came *all* the way down here to lure me from my home, my kin?"

Cass cut him off. "We're all kin now that Wellington's boots are under our table, Andy." He knew that Jackson harbored a pathological hatred for all things English. The scar on his forehead from the British officer's sword may have healed—but only on the outside.

Jackson was silent, a rare state. All the eyes in the room watched him. He turned away from Cass.

"Well, Coffee," he said, "someone better promote you to major general because Cass, my new chief of staff, and I are leaving for Albany." Jackson moved close to Coffee. Putting his hands on the cavalryman's shoulders (Old Hickory tended to touch a man when he had something important to convey), he said, "It's time to get off your horse, stop havin' fun, and go to work like the rest of us. John, my old friend, I'm about to ruin your very promising career. You're now the commanding general of the 7th Military District!"

That evening Jackson supped alone with Cass. It wasn't fair to Coffee to remain visible after relinquishing command. It would only confuse loyalties and encourage commanders to second-guess their new general and his orders.

"Cass, I'll retire to my home if you don't accept the chief's billet."

"Not me, Andy. I'm too junior, and my hip gives me trouble."

Jackson shook his head. "Any man who rode from Washington to Mobile must be capable. I couldn't be more insistent. Remember: you'll be the one to inform the president that you not only failed to twist my arm to accept the foolish job but also influenced his finest general to quit the field and return home to his lovin' family."

Cass needed no further incentive to accept. "It'd be an honor to serve you in *any* capacity—even as a fellow prisoner in an English hulk."

"Well, chief, we're officially an army of two. Where are we goin' to find the other thirty thousand soldiers good enough to best Wellington?"

Just then, Crockett and Houston slipped into Jackson's tent.

"Why you only need two more, not thirty thousand, Andy, and here we are."

Houston added, "God sent, I do believe."

Crockett and Houston had disengaged from Coffee's 7th Military District and attached themselves to Jackson's new command. The pranksters, approximating an attentive pose, stood at the side of the small rickety supper table.

"My God, but you two are *terrible*-looking officers. What'd'ya think I should do with these sorry examples?" Jackson asked Cass.

"Well, sir, you can't leave 'em here. They'll scare the troops. It's best if we take them along and save Coffee from hangin' 'em for impersonating officers."

Meanwhile, Major General Izard's 4,500 exhausted soldiers ended their odyssey at the old battlefield of Saratoga, twenty miles north of Albany on the bank of the Hudson River. The troops who had marched from Plattsburgh during the last days of August now fearlessly blocked Wellington's path south. They'd have fought the devil himself if it could've freed Macomb's imprisoned soldiers, who'd been taken to Quebec.

It took three weeks of steady saddle-weary riding for Jackson, Cass, Crockett, and Houston to trek more than eight hundred miles on poor roads to reach Washington. Each night they poured over the British order of battle and the battle map of Plattsburgh Lieutenant DeRussy had drawn and that had survived the capture of Macomb's command.

In a rented house near the burned-out shell of the Executive Mansion, the president received Jackson and his chief of staff. Secretary Monroe stayed in the background and let the two men become acquainted once again. Madison had known Jackson as a member of Congress and had, at the time, found him argumentative, brash, extremely opinionated, and a pain in the backside.

But times had changed. In Madison's opinion, Andrew Jackson was the only man who had a hope in hell of containing the British. The bald president was nearly a foot shorter than the impressive, white-haired military hero. Contrasting figures, they stood facing each other before the restored painting of Washington that Dolley had saved. The large portrait, housed in a new gilt frame, overwhelmed the small dwelling's parlor, where a pleasant ceremony was conducted in the presence of the executive staff: Jackson's swearing in as the commander of the Army of the United States. Departing from the tradition of military districts, Monroe justified the title change based on the acute national crisis that demanded men from many places. When the spectators cleared out of the parlor, Madison adjourned to the adjacent dining room, where Jackson took the floor before a massive hanging map portraying the eastern seaboard north to Quebec and south to Norfolk.

The newly appointed commander wore a plain blue tailcoat with dark cording across the chest and a single row of gold buttons down the center. Large, gaudy gold epaulets, with a pair of embroidered silver stars in the center, were buckled to his broad shoulders. (In the field the expensive shoulder boards had remained in their black leather case.) His tight, light brown buckskin pants' legs were tucked into high black riding boots. His eagle hilt sword was left with his hat on the narrow hall table just inside the ornate glass front doors.

Jackson's assessment of the enemy began with a short review of Wellington's order of battle, past history, performance, and intentions. Then he switched to the subject that most interested Madison and Monroe: defeating the duke.

"I intend to build a force of 25,000 newly minted soldiers to be trained in conjunction with 45,000 federalized militia from Massachusetts, Connecticut, New York, New Jersey, Vermont, and New Hampshire. My headquarters and training base will be at West Point. There, through the winter and into early spring, I'll forge an army that'll fight him north of Albany. We won't require any fallback position. I won't forfeit any more American soil to the bloody British. We'll make our stand and prevail. It's up to you, sir, and your government to support me. For if you quibble, procrastinate, backslide, shilly-shally, or change your mind in the heat of the moment, then all will be lost. These are grave times, sir. Am I expressing myself clearly enough, Mister President?"

Madison wasn't used to such a forward challenge, but under the circumstances perhaps it was warranted. He excused the verbal affront—*To be expected from a true military man*, he thought—and nodded in agreement, not wanting to risk a statement that could be challenged later.

While Jackson, with all his brash no-nonsense attitude, could intimidate the federal government, he held no sway over the states and, therefore, left the bureaucrats to line up the ducks. The general departed the capital with Cass, Crockett, and Houston for West Point, a civil engineering military school founded in 1802, and a gun metal foundry that had turned out cannon barrels since 1767. A hundred miles north on the Hudson, the new arsenal at Watervliet, which had begun building gun carriages the year before, would be expanded to serve as the headquarters' provisioning center, dispensing victuals, uniforms, equipment, powder, and shot.

Political Dissension over Military Matters

The state governors, highly independent and almost pathologically reluctant to participate in federal endeavors, saw the British occupation differently from Madison and Monroe. They considered armed conflict only one answer and, in fact, felt that in the face of an occupying and blockading enemy, deploying federal troops was not necessarily the most prudent course of action. Federal troops hadn't yet earned a battle reputation that inspired the states to hand over their militias. Still, an infusion of federal money held the promise of better business and individual enrichment.

Thus, a great deal of debate would be necessary before the governors released their "private" armies. The war, highly unpopular, and federal embargoes, even more unpopular, had caused immense hardship in the industrial north. When the federal government called for the militias to defend the seacoast early in the war, Massachusetts and Connecticut refused outright. Quoting from the Constitution, they declared, "Only in the instance of the maintenance of the laws of the Union, the suppression of insurrection, or to repel invasion would the states have to relinquish control of their militias."

Since 1804 Great Britian had encouraged New England merchants to trade with England and defy the restrictions Jefferson and, later, Madison imposed. As an act of conciliation, the Royal Navy allowed New England merchant ships alone to pass through the blockade. This act of friendship, which was in the economic interest of both England and New England, formed a bond between the otherwise enemies and distanced the five northern states from their own federal government. As war loomed, many influential New Englanders objected to *Mister Madison's war*, fearing an end to the prosperity that lay with England. They rejected the federal government's interference, favoring a negotiated conclusion to hostilities. Now the unthinkable had occurred: invasion. The British descent on the United States empowered the president to federalize the state militias. In a turnabout that fall of 1814, reeling from attacks on its territory of Maine and the nearby island of Nantucket, Massachusetts governor Caleb Strong asked Madison for federal troops. There were none to spare. Strong was told to fend for himself. Angry, Strong declared that he was willing to give up expansion westward in favor of maintaining trade with England and immediately ending the war at the treaty table. (England had made it known that it wanted free military access to the entire length of the Mississippi River.) The Republican-leaning press featured cartoons of King George enticing New Englanders to leave the Union and return home to the monarch's open arms. Undaunted, by such slurs, New England politicians convened a secret convention at Hartford, Connecticut, concerned primarily with limiting the federal government's power.

Nathan Dane, a mill owner from Lowell who sold cloth to the British army, was the convention's prime mover. A veteran of the Revolutionary War, sparked by and steeped in principles of liberty and individual rights, he nevertheless viewed this conflict from a purely monetary perspective. He favored a separate peace for the New England states. He was a recalcitrant, small, wizened man, who at age sixty-two relied on a cane to navigate the aisle and steps to reach the podium of the Hartford State House. His gray eyes matched his hair, which flopped over his forehead. He expressed the views and true feelings of the New England merchants and manufacturers suffering over the loss of British and European orders. Taking the floor on the first day, he spoke in a high-pitched but clear voice: "Great Britain curtailed the Orders of Council two years ago and since Napoleon's defeat this past spring the Royal Navy has ceased impressment of American seamen. These were the prime objections to the conduct of Great Britain. What are we fighting for? I ask you gentlemen. Mister Madison is nothing more than a military despot bent on conquering Canada, for what?"

The convention delegates signed seven resolutions concerned with states' rights and the retention of state militias by the governors. Some firebrands called the proposals ultimatums and said they would seek assistance from the king if they were not adopted. The facts were that the militias needed federal assistance. Massachusetts had seventy thousand militiamen who were unable to take to the field because the state didn't have the resources to feed or equip them. Most of the other New England states had similar shortcomings in numbers, arms, and provisions.

The participants, not the most closed-mouth citizens, leaked news of the "secret" convention to Monroe. They told him that the convention members could be considered a voting bloc but that those present planned to defer any further discussions after the seven resolutions were signed until contracts for war goods were permitted. Monroe informed the president, "Sir, I must support the New England states' economic interests in light of congressional spending. I believe that a special consideration should be sought on their behalf. After all, the war burden on the North will shortly increase as the spring campaign commences. Troops—that is, militia—will come voluntarily from New England to round out Jackson's army. But most important, sir, with the wolf not just at our door but across our threshold, this is no time to start squabbling."

To maintain a viable war effort, Madison consented to the loathsome blackmail and issued an executive order favoring manufacturers in the New England states.

Prevost Toasts Smugglers Turned Merchants

When Prevost released command of the army in Canada, he turned his vast talents to the political game, so often of equal importance to the fate of even the most formidable military ventures. When he arrived in the spring of 1812, his predecessor provided a report from an English spy sent to assess the feelings about the effects of Jefferson's embargo. John Henry continued his service for Prevost, poked around the coffeehouses of Hartford, and ascertained talk that trickled into the street. The first session of the "secret" convention had convened to discuss federal actions. Henry's report of the delegates' ramblings read,

> There seems but one opinion, namely, that they [embargo restrictions] are unnecessary, oppressive, and unconstitutional.
>
> It must also be observed that their execution is so invidious as to attract toward the government officers the enmity of the people, which is, of course, transferred to the government itself. So, in the case of Massachusetts, it will likely take any bold step possible toward resisting the execution of these laws. The British cause may calculate upon the hearty cooperation of the people of Vermont.

In an interview with Prevost, Henry surmised that the return of English rule had a better than 50 percent chance, which military action could easily sway in favor of King George. Prevost saw it as his duty to exacerbate the situation and encourage New Englanders to defect to the crown. The smuggling industry on Lake Champlain ended, bowing to an open market, now that Wellington had temporarily relocated the northern U.S.

border south of his army's winter quarters at Whitehall. Commissary General William Robinson and members of his staff were invited to a meeting with former smugglers, many of whom were local and state officeholders. The crown paid all the expenses. Some were farmers, and others were transporters, suppliers, and manufacturers from Vermont, New Hampshire, and northern New York.

At Ramezay House, Prevost's residence in Montreal, the governor-general addressed them over a seven-course repast prepared by his French chef. In most genial tones he began, "My dear guests, let us drink to the support of our gallant troops, who will winter deep inside America and perhaps remain for some time." He paused to chuckle at the prospect of a new border. "I propose a continued cooperation between the commissary board and our new American friends, who have been so generous in the past. I also believe fervently that such cooperation could be very profitable in the future, when our army achieves the final victory. As we all recognize, the winter is unpredictable, and we are all concerned for the men in the field who suffer severe hardship—stoically." He was rambling, as was his custom. "Their discomfort could be somewhat mitigated, if we all do our best to preserve humanity while governments haggle. Raise your glasses, gentlemen. A toast to ardent cooperation for the sake of His Majesty's soldiers—and the inhabitants of His Majesty's former colonies, so reduced, oppressed, and impoverished under the supposedly liberty-loving government of the United States."

Glasses clinked and the free champagne flowed.

Coffee's Success and Preparations for Battle

After the Battle of New Orleans on January 8, the American postal system, which had offices in eight hundred locations from Georgia to Maine, was overwhelmed. Paying two cents for a reporter's story sent on January 10, the owner of the *Albany Evening Standard* published its contents in the January 25, 1815, edition:

John Coffee, New American Hero

The hither-to-unknown Major General John Coffee of the cavalry, with a force of 9,000, comprised of regular army, Tennessee militia, and Jean Laffite's pirates, stopped the invasion by British regular forces of redcoats and rocket artillery on January 8. Coffee, a veteran commander under Andrew Jackson during the Creek War, maximized the marshy terrain and fortified former canal ditches into an impenetrable defense. The British, unsure of themselves amid the bayou's mud, bugs, and vermin, struggled to approach the city and lost many of their 7,000 weary troops along the way to fever and exhaustion. They threw themselves against an impregnable wall defended by *Americans* of all ages who had vowed that the English would never take New Orleans. British commander Sir Edward Pakenham, Wellington's brother-in-law, was wounded during the fighting, and the Royal Navy fleet withdrew in disgrace to Jamaica.

God willing, we as a nation shall prevail over these inimical interlopers, as our Southern brothers did with such ferocity of purpose and élan. Citizens of the *United*

States, you ignore such a glorious example as that established in the annals of history by the defenders of New Orleans at our peril.

Lieutenant Colonel Davy Crockett, delighted with news of the New Orleans victory, greeted the general as he entered the breakfast room in their new headquarters to join Chief of Staff Cass and Major Houston. "Andy, looky here! Old Coffee and the boys have set a high standard for us to follow, while we're living mighty high on the hog up here in Yankee country. We cut loose from the swamps, but those gators are lookin' our way to see if we'll do as well."

Crockett, respectable in his new dark blue uniform, had tamed his look but not his manner. He was still a frontiersman and wished he hadn't missed the lickin' that Coffee had given the lobster backs.

Jackson, though pleased, was less rhapsodic over the victory. He didn't equate the two British armies. "I wish we had Coffee's odds, Davy. He was near two to one for, and we're double that number against, as we sit here eatin' breakfast and about to freeze to death."

Houston still had a bit of the lost boy in him. He was quiet. He had abandoned his family farm before his teen years and joined a band of Cherokee Indians. Adopted by the chief as his son and named Raven, Houston grew up as a member of the tribe. When he reached twenty, he left the Indians and scouted for Jackson's Tennessee militia. At the Battle of Horseshoe Bend he transitioned back to the white man's world. General Cass utilized the newly promoted major's stealthy craftsmanship by appointing Houston chief of intelligence. Jackson approved, and Houston agreed to lead a band of Indians and white trappers to scout behind British lines. Within days they were to leave for their first reconnaissance around Wellington's camp south of Ticonderoga near Whitehall, on Lake Champlain's southern tip. The mission entrusted to Houston in writing was simple, predictable, and nearly impossible to fulfill: "Discover the enemy's strengths and weaknesses. Detail his formations, observe his supply lines, and uncover Wellington's intentions." The last part weighed heavily on Houston's usually ebullient spirit.

————

The West Point military school had been shut down while its cadre formed the nucleus of the training command. The departments of records, billeting, school of the soldier, marksmanship, gunnery, officer training, and supply and clothing were established in a cluster of gray stone buildings.

As the recruits arrived and as the freezing winter closed in, they outgrew the available shelter and were housed in flapping tents. Trudging reluctantly, they were introduced to formation drill on the huge flat parade ground perched on the cliff's edge above the Hudson River. Over Governor Winder's bombastic objections, additional troops were taken from the two thousand regulars now idle at Baltimore. After reviewing the drubbing the

British had suffered in September, Jackson assessed the chance of another raid on Baltimore as slim. He told Monroe, "If Cockburn returns, it'll be behind me at New York City." The secretary agreed with this view.

The regular regiments from Baltimore were broken up as they arrived. To their surprise and pleasure, the soldiers were promoted up the grades on the spot to fill the vacuum of officer leadership that the twenty new regiments, numbered from the 20th to the 40th, needed so urgently.

Jackson told Monroe, "I don't have a hankering for the past. This is the *new* army of the United States. It begins here and now. These are *my* men; they've no other ties to the past. We must make history, not study it."

Cass was keenly aware of U.S. demographics. While Canada's population was roughly 700,000, America boasted 7.5 million. There was a fairly even distribution of northern Europeans across the country, with perhaps more from the British Isles than from other European nations. The expanse of ocean, availability of ships, and cost of transit had limited migration. As the chief of staff walked about, observing the progress—slow but progress all the same—he noted a highly unusual infusion of Irish lads from New York and Philadelphia. He knew the difficulties of recruiting off the farms and small towns, where the men tended to join the militia for varied reasons, not least the ability to return to sow and harvest crops vital to their families' and communities' survival.

Jackson, immersed with the artillery, made it a point to dine each evening with the principal members of his staff. During and after the suppers, served in the officers' dining hall adjacent to the chapel, he would quiz the men regarding progress and suggest alternatives. Cass sounded off one wind-blown evening about the origin of most of the new recruits. Others chimed in with similar observations, though no one before had articulated the matter.

"Andy, I'm not adverse to Irishmen or Scots or Germans or French or anyone willing to help us give Wellington a whippin' he'll never forget. I know many of the recruits are Irish and find it curious," Cass said.

Jackson perceived the political ramifications of his chief of staff's remark. "Irish, you say? Now ain't that most interestin'."

Crockett had seen that face before and knew some deep thinking was occurring before their eyes. "I'm a thinkin' the same thing you are, Andy. The Irish despise the British as much as you do. Makes them fight like all Billy, don't it?"

"Too true, Davy. Let's take advantage of that hatred that keeps them all together and put it to use. Why not form four brigades, two from New York City and two from Philadelphia? Make up the first four brigades of three each all-Irish regiments. Now then, . . . " Jackson gazed at the timbered ceiling of the hall and counting the rafters like ranks of men. "Any Irish left over should be scattered in single grenadier companies to add punch to the formations."

"Yes, sir. Four Irish brigades, each with a bright green flag led by bagpipers and drums. That oughta make Old Nosy [Wellington] take a dose of his own medicine."

"Well done, chief!" Jackson said, boxing Cass's ears playfully. "Irishmen loyal to the king and Irishmen disloyal to the king—that ought to put the wind up. I do believe it is time to pass the port, gentlemen."

Jackson slept soundly for the first night since taking on "this fool's command," as he called the U.S. Army.

The one-man Office of Army Heraldry employed bands of ladies in church societies to embroider new colors: regimental flags bearing the arms of the nation sitting atop a scroll containing the regimental number on blue backgrounds. Departing from tradition, the Irish colors were sewn on a field of bright Kerry green. The Catholic ladies of Cortlandt Manor, laboring by night before blazing hearths, ornamented each corner of those flags with small gold harps. Not to be outdone, other ladies' sewing circles took license to sew on shamrocks, harps, or Celtic crosses just inside the fringed corners.

———

Jackson had little experience with large amounts of artillery, but he knew the value of massed cannon at critical junctures. Each morning, he was rowed across the Hudson by the patrol that maintained the chain barrier at the narrow switchback below the parade ground. At Cold Spring Forge two vital operations needed Jackson's personal touch.

The first was the manufacture of six- and nine-pound cannons at the Cold Spring Foundry. Jackson had directed that six- and nine-pound barrels, the same size as those the British used, be made. If the guns were identical to those of the Royal Artillery, then British ammunition could be used in them. Since before the American Revolution, the foundry had been making gun metal from the rich iron ore deposits nearby. At the coldest time of year it was extremely difficult to make cannon barrels because gun-metal smelting required a higher temperature than ordinary iron smelting, a temperature nearly impossible to sustain long enough to pour a tube. A special double shed, with straw wedged between the walls for insulation, was constructed. Red-hot sparks from the process rocketed out in all directions and set the building's inner confines on fire. Men with buckets of water stood by, ready to douse the walls and themselves within the superheated confines.

Artillery drill, a series of steps and movements characterized by teamwork and brute strength, challenged neophyte gunners. Here Old Hickory was in his element. Moving a thousand-pound field piece into firing position was a hardscrabble affair. Stripped of his officer's coat, Jackson took a turn behind the single wooden gun trail. He helped pry the cannon a foot or two to the left until the muzzle's front blade sight rested dead center on the target half a mile away. Jackson's steaming breath condensed on the back plate as he put his cheek on the rim and elevated the tube with the screw mechanism underneath.

The student crew smiled and nudged each other.

"I'll bet you a day's pay, Michael," said one member, "that this old fellow couldn't hit the broad side of a barn."

Michael, who had labored along with the general to position the gun, assumed Jackson hadn't grown so much gray hair sitting in an officers' tent. "You're on, but I'll take my winnings in beer."

The men didn't know that Jackson's prime amusement in past winter camps had been shooting grazing deer with a six-pounder: the ball reached the animal before the sound of the gun; the result was called dinner. Jackson lit the fuse from the side and jumped clear of the great recoiling wheels. The nine-pound cannonball, though not visible, hissed as it passed down range and splintered the old target wagon.

When the last bit of shattered weathered planks settled along with the dust, Jackson turned to the private who had bet against him. "Now remember that, soldier. Never bet against your general or a sure thing, or in my case—both!" Jackson donned his dark blue undress jacket and strolled off.

Madison's Angst

In Washington, Christmas was a time for prayer but not rejoicing. The joy came in January, when the outcome of the Battle of New Orleans reached the capital city. Madison and Dolley dined at the Monroes' spacious Georgetown home, which hadn't been damaged by the attack four months earlier. After dinner the ladies reviewed the plans for reconstructing the Executive Mansion and skimmed over the decorations. Many small items of furniture had been spirited away before the British could destroy them. Dolley had a list of all the drapes and rugs in storage.

Alone in the library, the president and secretary sat in soft leather chairs and lit their cigars while balancing thin-stemmed glasses of port before a flickering, crackling fire. Appearing smaller than ever in the large chair, the president asked, "Why doesn't Wellington attack, even if it *is* winter?" He threw his free hand up. "We are undefended. The great duke must know that. If Ross could take the capital with a handful, then surely Wellington could take New York with his army! Is he toying with us? Taunting us? I know he's driving me to distraction!"

Monroe, who had spent the last three months reading every text that remained in the burned-out national library about modern warfare, replied, "Wellington's at the very end of his supply line. If the British stay in one place with all those troops, then a supply system can deliver the mountain of provisions. The system's strength comes from repetition. But if he moves his force farther south at this point, then the system will break down, leaving him precariously vulnerable. The winter's been rather mild, comparably speaking, and Lake Champlain's remained clear of ice. But it wouldn't take much to snip that thin thread he's hanging by—especially if he moves away from the water."

The president sipped his port and cleared his throat of its winter rasp. "I suppose fifteen thousand men do consume a great deal, eating three meals a day. But James, there's nothing at Whitehall other than a harbor. If he pushed Izard aside, then he could take Albany and spend the winter inside a city capable of supporting him without a need for a long, tenuous link to Canada, couldn't he?"

Monroe thought a moment. "If Wellington took on Izard's dug-in force at Saratoga, away from his support base, he could repeat Burgoyne's folly at Bennington and lose a considerable number of troops. Wellington fought the French in Spain, where he was always outnumbered. He's not a waster of men so far from home. He'll not risk a fight unless there's a clear, manageable outcome. I read about his early campaigns. While he takes risks, they are minuscule. He'd much rather preserve his force until he can predict the result, to a degree most gamblers would dream of, before committing to battle. It's a good way for him to prosecute the war—for us, that is!"

What the duke's history didn't tell Monroe was that Wellington had other agendas to address. He wanted a swift political solution and was counting on his victories at Plattsburgh and Lake Champlain, combined with the devastating attacks on Washington, Baltimore, and New Orleans, to compel a treaty before spring. He wished to return with his army intact to fight the central European countries coalescing against England in the power vacuum created by Napoleon's defeat.

While this strategy would have consoled Madison, something else was afoot. Wellington was communicating with Halifax Station. He asked Cochrane to send Admiral Cockburn to Jamaica to load the New Orleans army on board in order to reinforce Sherbrooke, who planned to come south and support Wellington's left flank. Thus he could spread the American army perilously thin from New York through Massachusetts.

When Wellington confided his plan to his quartermaster general, Delancey said, "It'll be like shooting fish in a barrel, Your Grace."

The duke smiled and replied, "Sir William, may I offer a note of caution? Refrain from getting *into* the barrel before you shoot."

CHAPTER 10

The Blaze in the Barn

"Battle should be offered only when there is no other turn of fortune to be hoped for, as from its very nature the fate of battle is always uncertain."
—NAPOLEON BONAPARTE

The diversionary attack on Washington by Ross and Cockburn focused the Americans' attention on the Chesapeake Bay and the threat of losing Baltimore. Macomb's and Macdonough's weak, abandoned forces succumbed to the land and lake attacks of the British. There were no American troop formations between Wellington, wintering at Whitehall in New York, and the nation's capital. The American navy was out of action, and the remaining army formations were committed to defending the Gulf Coast and Niagara.

Wellington expected the Lake Champlain victory and subsequent occupation under the Union Jack a hundred miles south of the border would prompt the American president to sue for peace, thereby allowing the duke an early return to England. Still, he had to plan for a long, unpleasant American winter in the event Madison committed to the war for the long haul.

The duke directed Delancey, "Sir William, put out a web to gather every crumb concerning Jackson's slightest activity. I must know his strengths and weaknesses before spring."

Major Colley Grant, chief of the British spies, deployed his scouts and began to collect information about the events occurring in Saratoga, thirty miles south of Whitehall. There, the British expected the Americans to entrench once again and wait out the winter. The duke, though, had no intention of roosting in a tiny provincial village and, with gratitude, accepted Lady Prevost's invitation to winter at Ramezay House in the heart of Montreal. To everyone's surprise, the arctic winds and brutal cold had yet to come by the first day of 1815. Wellington traveled north on an empty transport ship that had been commandeered from the Americans. Boats crammed with red-coated regiments, bound for Whitehall, flooded the Richelieu.

The duke remarked to his aide, Captain Ronald Ulysses Burgh, kin to Wellington and dazzling in his white-plumed cap and bright red coat, dripping with gold braids, "They're really more of a demonstration of our intention to crush Jackson should Madison be foolhardy enough to continue this farce. But I don't believe, Burgh, we'll have to employ these lads in the field come spring."

Wellington's dull gray cape, which nearly touched the deck, was a stark contrast to his aide's ornate uniform. "I'm making a big show in hopes that Washington's politicians will hear of our growing numbers. My bit of theater may make Madison come to his senses and settle this damn thing. I hope he's quick about it, before the St. Lawrence freezes."

The King's German Legion

At St. Jean the duke debarked. Fresh troops from Ireland, who had been lounging around cook fires, lined up to board the transport for its return voyage to Whitehall. A sharp stab of cold wind, a harbinger of worsening conditions, spun off the river.

Happy to be on horseback once again, Wellington decided to ride alone the ten miles north to Fort Chambly.

Burgh, staying behind with the baggage, reminded the duke, "Sir, the King's German Legion is waiting to escort you to camp."

Wellington was particularly fond of this disciplined corps. The splendid Hanoverian troops were tied to George III through his great-grandfather, George I, Elector of Hanover. When the Stuart line ran out in 1714, the dukes of Brunswick-Lüneburg proffered the Protestant great-grandson of James I as a viable candidate to assume the English throne. As a result, the white horse of Hanover was added to the English king's arms. In 1803 Napoleon overran Hanover. Loyal Germans, escaping to England, formed the legion under George III to fight the French. All branches of the army were represented in their ranks. Fighting alongside the British in Spain, the legion proved to be indispensable in battle. To preserve the force at the war's end, the duke had arranged for the corps' nucleus to be transferred to Canada as a part of his army. Traversing the Baltic, North Sea, English Channel, and mid-Atlantic delayed its arrival considerably. In fact, the King's German Legion was the last to transit the St. Lawrence that winter. And Wellington was glad to have it.

From the Journal of St.-Jean-sur-Richelieu:

January 2, 1815

On the hard-packed road at the edge of the village, Major General John Sontag, commander of the King's German Legion, waited patiently with a platoon of jostling dragoons astride black horses. The great Duke of Wellington appeared delighted when greeting his old comrade-in-arms before taking his place at the head of the mounted escort. A detachment of twenty horsemen astride magnificent ebony horses wheeled into place in a column of two wide. The weather was mild, and they rolled their gray cloaks onto the backs of their dark blue, yellow-trimmed saddle blankets. The crowd flowed from the dock through town to the meeting place. They cheered and banged pans in the traditional welcome. The duke smiled, waving to the throng lining the road on either side. At the command, blades, flashing in the sunlight, were drawn to present arms. The white gauntlets held massive, straight sword hilts against the left hip. Short carbines, hanging limply on the right side of their white cross belts, were not fired in salute for fear of alarming the animals in the nearby market. As they marched smartly off, their bouncing blades reflected the midmorning sun's rays. The distinctive brass German Legion helmets, with flowing black horsetails streaming behind, gave the riders an air of speed. Dark blue, stand-up collars piped in yellow contrasted with their short red coats. A wide plastron of blue plunged down the front of their jackets to their white sword belts, the edges spun in yellow worsted. Rarely have we seen such splendor in our midst. But it is only fitting, given the arrival of such a man and warrior as Wellington.

Wellington was delighted by the honor and its smooth execution. "My dear Sontag, I'm happy to see your dragoons haven't changed uniforms to the European style. Sometimes that makes it difficult to tell friend from foe, and we'll surely want to make such distinctions when next we take the field. You can't imagine my pleasure at having your boys with us in this wilderness. This isn't cavalry country, mind you, but on Saratoga's plateau you'll be most useful. Has anyone advised you that only the 19th Light Dragoons and a few staff guides will make up your mounted element?"

"Your Grace, it's of no matter to me. The King's German Legion requires no augmentation." Sontag spoke with a German accent. "Ve are self-contained and quite able to fight alone. But that's not necessary. Along with the 1st Dragoons, I have three line infantry regiments—the 3rd, 12th, und 14th—as vell as one *Scharfschuetzen* [light infantry] battalion of four companies who vill fight like your red Indians. You vill soon inspect a battalion of my foot artillery—vith eighteen nine-pounders und three howitzers. I've also responded to your call for engineers. I brought you a company of sappers und another of pontooneers. You see. I don't forget." Sontag's twinkling eyes brightened the duke's spirit. "Are you aware, Your Grace, that my family members vere with Burgoyne in '77?" As a rule, Sontag addressed his commander as "Vellington," but he hadn't seen the duke since the latter's elevation.

"I must admit, John, I'm not conversant with Burgoyne's complement [of soldiers], but it wouldn't surprise me at all. Your ancestors are as much a part of this army as are mine."

Wellington rarely used a colleague's Christian name, but the ebullience barely contained behind Sontag's weathered red face made it impossible to call him general. During the unhurried ride to Chambly the two comrades revived their shared memories of past battles and lost friends.

In front of the stone chapel, on the plain behind the fort, the King's German Legion, happy to be off the swaying transports, waited in ranks. Unlike the British army, the German soldiers accompanied their precious horses on the ships. The bond between German troopers and their beasts resulted in the flaunting of Naval Transport Board regulations. But no one objected.

Wellington and Prevost Discuss Circumstances and Strategy

While snooping around the edges of Saratoga, Grant sent weekly intelligence summaries about Jackson's preparation and intentions to Wellington in Montreal. At Ramezay House the duke was enjoying the governor's hospitality. The three-story, gray stone chateau provided comfortable refuge from the cold winds careening off Hudson Bay. The large staff, which scuttled about on woolen slippers, polishing the parka floors as they went about their rounds, tended the fireplaces day and night. The heavy drapes, closed by the early afternoon, helped keep at bay the deep cold settling over the capital. Each morning, seated across from each other at a large ornate table in the library, the duke and governor shared information and ideas. A slew of maps, one thrown over the over, covered the table's large surface as other scattered papers overflowed onto the floor. It was impossible to discern which belonged to whom, but it didn't matter since they were becoming gradually, undeniably, a team. Both educated in France, they often lapsed into French.

The two men shared a penchant for learning as much as possible about their adversary's intentions. More important, Prevost's ties to certain garrulous members of Vermont's and New Hampshire's political structures were strengthening daily. The governor provided Wellington with valuable tidbits about the internal wrangling in the United States between the states and the federal government. General Sherbrooke, wintering in Maine, was also advised of New England's growing discontent and instability. By mid-January, the three leaders were sharing military intelligence as well as the latest political intrigues. When combined, their disparate views and disconnected information created a comprehensive picture of New England's strengths and weaknesses.

Wellington found his derisive perception of Americans was perhaps prematurely formed and certainly misplaced. "Sir George, I must confess that my comprehension of American culture is paltry at best. You must've learned their peculiarities. What drives them to take such risks to such rash ends? Why would they ever declare war on England? We're the Americans' best friend. They were once a valued part of the realm, and after they rebelled, we took them back without prejudice into the fold. If the truth be known, the Americans' logistical support through the port of Lisbon was vital to me during the Peninsular War. I'm doubtful I could've hung on against the French without their merchant shipping. I owe them a debt."

"Remember, Your Grace, the New England merchants supported you, *not* their federal masters."

"Sir George, I can see there's a dichotomy between the states and Washington. Are these people even capable of governing themselves?" Frustrated at the thought of wintering over, Wellington admitted, "Ah, I'd like to be rid of this campaign and return home before Europe flares up."

"Your Grace, the Americans complain that England doesn't respect their sovereignty, but they trample on Canada's. What's good for them is good for them. They have no interest in being a good neighbor. I can explain the American cause of this war with a simple old joke: The Yankee says, 'I'm not greedy. All I want is all land that adjoins mine.'"

Wellington cut the thin red tape that bound a rolled copy of the *Albany Evening Journal*, sent courtesy of Grant. "You know, Sir George, during my last campaign I often found the Paris newspapers so valuable that I became a subscriber." Wellington chuckled at his own joke and then added, "I understand Napoleon was a regular reader of the *London Times*. Of course, some planted lies are placed there to mislead, but in general, early in a campaign, that is, a great deal can be winkled out from between lines of newsprint."

Wellington began to read an article prominently situated on the paper's front page:

Jackson's Promise and Plea

Major General Andrew Jackson, hero of the Creek War, has established his headquarters at West Point. There he is building an army that he promises will "eclipse the invaders."

Governor Daniel Tompkins has announced the establishment of a partnership between the state's manufacturers and the War Department to supply the nascent United States Army with everything it requires—from gunpowder to gaiters—to oust the lobster backs from American soil and into the Atlantic, where such crustaceans most reasonably deserve to dwell.

The two leaders have met at Watervliet Arsenal, where bids are being processed. In a recent interview, while touring the waterfront in Albany with the governor, Jackson issued a plea for volunteers to join the regular army. Besides a land grant of 120 acres, men who enlist for two years' service will receive a bonus of $164.

"Sir George, who's this Jackson fellow? I don't recall reading about him till now."

"His men call him 'Old Hickory.' He's mightily single-minded and tough. Doesn't give an inch. Jackson's a noted Indian fighter, a hero of the Creek War, though the Americans employ a very broad definition of 'hero.' He turned against his Indian allies quickly enough. Dispossessed them without a qualm. Of course, they're savages, but one's word is one's honor. He's no gentleman, I should think. My friends in New Hampshire tell me he's a frontiersman and firebrand who disregards states' rights. In truth, he's a brawler and habitual duelist. Recently, he's been harassing the Spanish in Florida. Jackson prides himself on preferring the direct approach. I'm told he's reading everything he can get his hands on about you at the military school library. I'll have my staff put together a dossier on Jackson that'll include the Creek Campaign."

"An interesting fellow," Wellington mused. "We'll have to keep a keen eye on him."

Old Hickory on the Ground

One trait both Wellington and Jackson held in common was a gift for recognizing and maximizing terrain. Pausing at Watervliet Arsenal before the final leg of his journey to Saratoga, the American commander reviewed the provisioning for the coming battle. Governor Tompkins had assured Jackson that he would assemble an armada of boats to transport the army from West Point, eighty-nine miles south of Albany, to Saratoga, thirty-five miles north of the arsenal. The river was navigable above the narrowing Hudson by bateaux and sloops. While Jackson's army fought the river current north, Wellington's army, only thirty-six miles above Saratoga at Whitehall, would be slowed by several fatiguing portages. The circumstances thereby negated whatever advantage the situation of one afforded to the other.

Leaving the governor to wrestle with how he would keep his promise, Jackson stood on the prow of a sailing sloop headed north. A westerly wind pushed his sloop abeam up the river. He went ashore at Gates's Landing, which was named for Horatio Gates, the commander who had beaten the British there in 1777. A watch officer who ran the picket boat patrol lent the general his horse and provided a guide to General Izard's headquarters. A well-trodden dirt road wound its way up the backside of the two-hundred-foot palisade to a plateau. There, behind Bemis Heights, which masked the headquarters from the north, Izard occupied the same set of stone farm buildings abandoned by Gates a generation earlier.

Major General George Izard, desperately thin from campaigning, was waiting at the hitching rail in a worn, unadorned blue field coat. His fruitless march, begun at the end of August in Plattsburgh, had continued nearly nonstop. The unremitting rigors of the previous month had clearly diminished the general. He was no stranger to Jackson, who nonetheless was shocked by his fellow officer's appearance. Jackson, who had served with Izard briefly at the start of the Creek War, found him nearly unrecognizable. The long trek and deprivations suffered by his command had gone not only unheralded but also ignobly unnoticed.

"General," he said, "I was alerted you would be coming. Our positions are ready for your inspection. I'll tell you up front: we're in a pitiful state. Morale's low. But we're the only thing this winter between Wellington and New York City. That causes me no end of anxiety, General."

"You must call me Andy, George. There's to be no ceremony between us. How are you, my old friend?" His tone was warm, filled with deep concern for a fellow soldier who had done what he was told to do by those who should've known better. Izard sparked up a little as he and the former Indian fighter spent a few minutes recalling a far different war.

Jackson reached out to touch Izard's shoulder. There was little flesh clinging to the bone. "How have the victuals been since your people left Plattsburgh?" he asked.

"Well, you know what they say. You're not hungry till you can wipe your face with the slack from your belly."

Jackson was appalled. "Your people have done us all a great service, George. I'll see you right."

"Compared to my men, Andy, I'm in rude health. You'll see soon enough," the weary commander said, motioning toward their waiting mounts. "My men are determined to avenge the comrades they lost at Plattsburgh. Yes, they're in sorry shape, but the sight of a redcoat will bring them back from the brink."

Izard led Jackson to a field table covered in a yellowed map and offered him a cigar. "Andy, before we take a gander at our position, let me show you the map Granny Gates used—nothing changed. Gates and Arnold fought an offensive battle." Izard traced a line with the tip of his yet unlit cigar. "They took on the enemy strung out in a line extending from Coulter's farm, Freeman's farm across the valley to the great ravine and redoubt, which anchored on the Hudson River."

"Ya know, George, the duke's complement is more than twice the number Burgoyne had in '77. In those days, though, the shoe was on the other foot. Burgoyne thinned his force out at the unexpected and costly battle at Bennington. His trains, strung out back to Canada, had cut his field strength even more, and he was forced to defend. He counted on marryin' up with Clinton from New York City and another column that had come down the Mohawk Valley that was defeated near Utica. Clinton left him high and dry. As great a victory it was here that day, only the ground is the same today."

"I know, Andy. We needn't concern ourselves with taking the offense with raw troops that form the bulk of the army." Izard traced his finger along the lower edge of the old map. "Bemis Heights and the ridge that runs to the east and rises to the point, high above the river, will serve us well. The Neilson farm dominates the landscape, giving us a clear view over the middle ravine all the way to Freeman's farm and middle ravine."

"George, could you see the enemy advancing on Bemis Ridge?"

"Andy, our artillery could have a field day once they clear the woods in advance of the ravine. It's a good thousand yards of open ground. You'll see, the point, above the river and high up to the right, is the key, though. I would double the guns up there and put a good reliable force next to them for protection. If we cover this long ridge with troops, no matter how green they may be, we can stop the redcoats dead."

They rode, side by side, up the gradual slope to Neilson's farm, perched at the top of the conical hill, which rose to the highest elevation for miles. Along the way, ragged soldiers emerged from double-thick tents to stand at modified attention and render a sad salute.

Jackson muttered, "Thank you, thank you for your devoted service."

It wasn't his usual response to a salute, but the soldiers' pitiful condition told a stark story he had seen before, during his own retreat from New Orleans many years earlier, when he too had been abandoned by his government.

The soldiers' plight nearly overshadowed the ride's purpose. Jackson wanted to see the old battlefield he had read so much about. He remembered Benedict Arnold's disobedience in front of Granny Gates and his heroic actions that had rendered him an invalid. Walking his horse down the precipitous north side of the heights, Jackson began to appreciate how the hill dominated the surrounding landscape. They walked faster now, due east, along a dirt track that paralleled the American line for nearly a mile of open country. All the while, Jackson had been eyeing the point's artillery position near the river.

"I see you've an appreciation for the guns, George."

Ahead was the eastern anchor of the American line. Atop a continuing rise of a hundred feet sat a dozen cannons—all that Izard could muster. To the north, facing the potential enemy was a sharp hundred-foot drop-off. To the east, an unassailable cliff provided a field of fire that commanded the only road south as well as the aquiline Hudson River.

"From there my guns can dominate the entire right flank," Izard said, pointing his gloved hand. "In fact, there, over two miles north, is the great German redoubt where Arnold was wounded. I'm sure that's where Wellington will rest his eastern flank."

Once behind the point's guns, Jackson was surprised to realize that the position was more than two hundred feet above Gates's Landing on the Hudson. The promontory was crucial terrain; it allowed access from the west up the only road he had just walked.

"By God, George!" Jackson exclaimed. "To the east you can put a stopper in the road and the river.

All that Izard and his troops had been through twisted inside him, as he gazed at the empty landscape that would soon turn red—first with British uniforms and then enemy blood.

"None shall pass," he agreed.

"Granny Gates may not have been much of a fighter, but he was a hell of a military engineer." Jackson's voice dropped; he was about to admit something that galled the old Indian fighter. The words came out slowly yet firmly: "We can't take the offensive, George. They'll not put a bullet in me at the great redoubt, but by *God*, we'll put plenty in them on Bemis Heights. We'll sit tight"—he slapped the frail officer's shoulder, nearly knocking him from his saddle—"and let them come at us. Our children will read about this third engagement at Saratoga and swear to the Heavens how wonderful we were."

Jackson was doing his utmost to conceal beneath a veneer of threadbare humor the acute apprehension he felt. He had to display incurable optimism in the hope it would be contagious. When the day came to confront the finest army in the world, Jackson's men had to believe that victory was not only possible but also probable. If he could, he would call on the indomitable spirit Washington had summoned in others at Valley Forge.

Before dark, Jackson descended alone to the landing for his return trip south. Major Houston, who had been north observing the British, waited to report.

"I'll not ask how you knew I was here, Sam," Jackson greeted him. "A good intelligence officer knows where to find not only the enemy but also his leader. What can you tell me about the redcoats?"

"The fifteen thousand troops Wellington had at Plattsburgh were just a beginning. The figure's nearly doubled. His intentions are clear: he's preparing for further offensive action in the spring." Houston paused to let the grim prognosis sink in and then repeated a rumor overheard at a tavern in Whitehall. "One of his brigade commanders boasts that he'll reside in his father's house at Courtlandt Manor. That's five miles from West Point, sir."

In the dim light they shoved off, propelled by a stiff frosty breeze from the north. Houston's information—which included detailed estimates of troop strength, myriad descriptions of mountains of supplies, and vivid accounts of roads clogged with plodding refugees—weighed on Jackson. He dismissed his old friend with his thanks.

"You best get something to eat, Sam, and, if possible, a peaceful night's rest."

Alone on deck Jackson brooded, muttering to his absent wife as he sometimes did when possessed by inner duress. "Ah, Rachel, what have I gotten into? I'm just an Indian fighter—plain and simple. Fighting redcoats won't be the same as fighting savages."

The coal fires hung in the damp riverside air at Watervliet Arsenal's line of forges. The wavering light silhouetted the blacksmiths, hard at work on the gun carriages.

"But fight them we must," he said, as the lights of Albany slid by. "Fight them we must."

His Majesty's Benevolent Care

Houston, skilled at the subtle art of espionage as he was, was still not aware of Major General Sir John Sherbrooke's four thousand British troops comfortably ensconced that February in Bangor, Maine, and wintering on the backs of the local community.

Oddly Sherbrooke was not there with them. He was attending a conference called by Vice Admiral Sir Alexander Cochrane at Bermuda. There, Admiral George Cockburn and a still-recovering Major General Sir Edward Pakenham along with the staff were preparing an early spring offensive to support the duke.

Cochrane greeted his guest on the veranda of his whitewashed headquarters above the bright blue bay currently filled with men-of-war.

"Gentlemen, what better place to conduct a winter conference, eh? I'm sure that the great duke would love to be here, but unfortunately he's ice-bound in the Canadian wilderness. A toast then. We wish him well and look forward to our meeting here at the victorious end of this campaign to restore the American colonies to His Majesty's benevolent care."

"Here, here!" they cried, before draining goblets brimming with the finest Madeira.

"Now to the plan. The duke's expecting General Sherbrooke to arrive at Saratoga by the last week of April. Accompanying him will be the bulk of the New Orleans force, which my flag intelligence officer tells me has been posted to Gibraltar—that is, according to New York City's newspapers."

A roar of laughter filled the room.

"I believe we have a surprise in store for the fabled Andy Jackson that'll send him rushing back down south to early retirement." A note of glee touched his raspy voice; he cleared it away with another sip of Madeira before resuming. "Pakenham's army is in

Jamaica, refitting as I speak." He raised his replenished glass. "After voyaging peacefully up the coast this spring, he'll join Sherbrooke at Portsmouth and drive *hard* on the Yankee's right flank. They will put an end, no doubt, to Yankee Doodle Dandy."

The wounded Pakenham rose unsteadily to his feet. "I'll do just that, Sir Alex, if you'll transport my horse and me to New England without killing him or me on one of your dreadful ships."

A genial laugh slipped free from the army officers and a more guarded one from the navy. The army never ceased to criticize the navy for the unpredictable weather and hazards of transport.

Cochrane sat down, grumbling to himself. Pakenham's lighthearted yet poignant comment irked the admiral. For all the collegial good cheer, the general's remark held a stinger: many transports had indeed floundered and perished that hurricane season.

Federalizing the American Militia

Jackson's hands were full. He had taken on the task of building an army bereft of the able assistance from the government. That February, twenty thousand regulars were certified as fit to fight and sent, a regiment at a time, up the Hudson River to Watervliet while state militias straggled into West Point for training.

The winter favored Jackson. Farm folk were eager to avoid cabin fever, nagging wives, sick children, and a perilous shortage of alcohol. But even so, obstacles and opposition existed.

Jackson asked Houston to prepare an assessment of the northern militias for the general's eyes alone. It read,

> The New York militia displayed a strong hankering to repel the invader from the state's soil. However it is led by political appointees of little military experience even this late in the war.
>
> Unlike your experience with the Tennessee militia, the New England militias, like their political backers, tend to be mostly unreliable when supporting federal orders. The attack on Washington and the British marauding all along the eastern seaboard turned attention away from the northern threat. Connecticut's small contingent, only 1,500, under General Cushing, who has a poor reputation, is not interested in federal service and might be expected at West Point by spring.
>
> The New Jersey governor was concerned, with good reason, that the British might land somewhere along their long shoreline while the bulk of his fighters were helping the northern neighbor. As a result, authorities are withholding their militia.
>
> Massachusetts is splitting its force between eastern and western counties but can be expected to fight in good order.
>
> Vermont was divided along other lines. Its inhabitants had reluctantly joined the federation in 1793, after remaining independent for nearly a decade after the

Treaty of Paris. However, the commander of Vermont's militia, Major General Sam Strong, is at odds with Governor Martin Chittenden, who ordered the troops not to train with the regular army beyond the state's borders. He insisted that they remain at Bennington to block the British from crossing the lake. Strong disobeyed and joined Jackson. A great deal of pressure has been brought by the political organization in the state, and if it weren't for the support of the militiamen, Strong would be replaced. He may be replaced before the spring along with those officers who back him.

New Hampshire's citizen-soldiers, perhaps the best of the bunch and certainly the most skilled, are of one mind: the troops accepted federalization, but many of their officers, politically connected to the state house, were carping over having to leave their homes unprotected from Sherbrooke's covetous gaze.

In my estimation the militia, though large in number, is poorly officered with men who are more concerned with reputation and future prospects. Therefore, their units should be buttressed with regular units close by.

Nonetheless, by the end of February, Davy Crockett was able to provide figures to the visiting secretary of war who had come to West Point to find answers for his colleagues in Congress. Jackson welcomed the visit as a chance to show off his system to induct, train, procure, equip, provision, and transport the army. It was the first attempt to establish a professional field force capable of defending a nation that had just begun to emerge. Monroe kept asking the same question: "Where is the money being spent?"

Crockett tried to stay on track, concentrating on the work accomplished rather than the funds. "Sir, the militia's integrated into the army and trainin' under Andy's command here on the plains. I've some gross numbers that tell the story. We bleed off some deserters every day, of course."

Monroe read the document quietly, taking it with the grain of salt that Crockett suggested.

Militia Infantry Complement to Date
Fit for Duty
February 22, 1815

New York	14,000
New Jersey	9,000
New Hampshire	3,800
Massachusetts	10,000
Vermont	2,500
Connecticut	1,500
New York dragoons	250
Total Militia:	41,050

"As you can see, Mister Secretary," Crockett clarified, "these round figures equal a tad over 41,000. Add that to Andy's seven brigades of regular infantry and supporting artillery, estimated at, say, 20,000. Our brigade numbers are somewhat smaller in number—between 2,500 and 3,000—than the British equivalent. Andy believes"—Davy looked in Jackson's direction for support—"with inexperienced troops and officers, bigger brigades would be difficult to handle. By spring, we'll take the field at Saratoga against"—Crockett stroked his chin—"say, roughly 30,000 redcoats."

The secretary looked startled and aghast.

"Those figures are based on Sam Houston's watching the goings-on at Whitehall." Crockett paused, waiting for Jackson or Monroe to interject, but neither obliged. The two men, sitting side by side at the broad polished table, looked at each other with the same feeling gnawing at their insides.

Monroe spoke first. "Have you got enough, Andy, to take on Wellington?"

There was real apprehension in Monroe's voice. The secretary's mind raced to find a corner of the republic with untapped reinforcements but couldn't think of any.

"I do, if they fight like wildcats," Jackson sighed. "But those are just numbers, sir. There's more to battle than numbers. Didn't General Washington teach you that, Mister Secretary? I took a good look at the position Izard's assumed on the old battleground. It's damn fine. That ground's our best ally. I can defend at Saratoga, but I cannot attack. My green troops can't fight in the open or seize the high ground that Wellington's sure to defend. I must wait for him, gentlemen. I'm not comfortable waitin' for the likes of John Bull, but that's what needs doin' and that's what I'll do. You won't find Izard's 4,500 lost souls in my count, sir. If Wellington were to attack today, Izard's troops could be taken by a handful of cooks, farriers, sappers, and regimental wives armed with sticks and stones.

"Those neglected boys and their abandoned commander have given all they've got to give. They are merely sittin' on land that at present is uncontested. I figure it won't be long. Then we're goin' to pay."

"Are you telling me, General, that those boys are a spent force before they've even fired a shot?"

Jackson looked down his hawk nose at Monroe. "Those 'boys,' as you call them, were wasted through government bunglin', sir! To relieve the corps I'm sending the bulk of my cavalry as well as some artillery. They're capable of manning the guns on Bemis Heights and the point. There are two infantry brigades heading up the Hudson to fill the gap at Saratoga. Izard will withdraw his men to Watervliet to recover and refit. We've lost our only veteran brigade through wanton neglect, Mister Secretary."

Monroe took the criticism well. After all, it hadn't happened on his watch.

Good News for Wellington

Along with the report on the proceedings at Bermuda and greetings from his wounded brother-in-law was a document included from the colonial secretary in London.

In Wellington's absence on January 20, Great Britain, France, and Austria signed a treaty in Vienna pledging mutual support in peace and war. An attached note read,

Arthur,

You are responsible for this fortuitous outcome, which will surely preserve our national position in Europe—no matter what takes place. It is not a secret and has raised eyebrows in Russia and Prussia. War in central Europe has been avoided. Be assured that you have my full support to finish the American affair to our deserved advantage.

Bathurst

Wellington should have been elated that the earl's initiative had prevented the European powers from forming a coalition excluding Great Britain and, in all likelihood, the resumption of war. Instead, the duke received the news as official notice that, for the foreseeable future, he would be marooned in this blasted unwelcoming North American wilderness. He grew melancholic as the first blizzard howled like tormented souls around Chateau Ramezay and snow piled up to the windowsills.

Just a couple months later, on March 20, at St. Jean, Wellington boarded a cutter for Whitehall. He was looking forward to a day or two spent taking in the sun on the quarterdeck—a welcome relief after the cloistered confines and rigid routines of Ramezay House. His pack of foxhounds sniffed about the cargo, amusing the crew.

But events were about to overtake the duke. A hundred miles south, Sam Houston came in close contact with British scouting parties. British agents, recording the river traffic, nosed around the Hudson's banks. Both sides employed the same local Indians, rendering spying far simpler and efficient. Houston had furnished them with an article, cut from one of the latest New York City newspapers, fully expecting it to stir the pot.

Colley Grant's face grew as red as his coat at Houston's special delivery. It wasn't the kind of information that could wait for the regular weekly summary. Grant, abandoning the slow rowboat, resorted to riding a horse for the frantic thirty-mile trek to Whitehall. He reined in at the stone barn headquarters and interrupted Delancey's lunch.

"Colley, what's the panic? Are the Yankees coming?" the colonel joked.

"Not the Yankees, Colonel." He thrust the article across the table right under Delancey's nose. "Read this."

It only took a moment.

"My God!" he declared. "Get a fast boat fitted out and crewed. I'll be at the dock soon as possible."

Delancey jotted down a quick note of explanation to his deputy, who was busy enlarging the camp to accommodate two new brigades, while his servant packed his kit. Within the hour the two men were watching an increasingly petulant, turbulent sky from the deck of a bobbing craft and privately urging the wind to send them north to Wellington with all greater alacrity.

"Do you think he knows?" Grant asked.

"He *must*, that is, if he's still in Montreal. But I believe he intended to leave St. Jean this morning—weather permitting. I'm hoping to meet him en route."

Delancey and Wellington were on a collision course. At dusk, Grant saw the dim lanterns on Wellington's approaching craft. Delancey lit the baskets of fagots hung out on the yards in a signal to stop. The two wooden hulls bumped hard together, and Delancey and Colley jumped across to Wellington's cutter. Wellington, hailed on deck minutes before, was waiting.

Delancey spoke first, breathless. "Your Grace, he's done it! He's escaped! Napoleon has been welcomed ashore in the south of France and is heading for Paris. Europe's in a panic."

American Reaction

The news of Napoleon's return brought Jefferson out of self-imposed retirement and back to making mischief in the capital. Invited to a cabinet meeting, he proclaimed, "England will turn its back on us once again. When your house is on fire, you forget about the blaze in the barn."

Monroe agreed. "Napoleon will demand Great Britain's attention. There is no doubt. But, gentlemen, this momentous event's nearly four thousand miles away and a month old. By now, Europe could've turned over once again. The situation's highly volatile and frankly, at this late stage in our war, of little value to us. Napoleon could've been arrested, shot, or indeed proclaimed emperor once again. It does not matter in the short run. In the next thirty days, while the Ghent talkers hold their breath, Wellington will be compelled to attack. He can't just sit and wait for the next packet boat to bring instructions. The duke needs no further clarification, I assure you. Wellington is committed—regardless of what happens in Europe."

If Andrew Jackson had been in Washington, instead of Saratoga, he would've endorsed the secretary's view of events. Jackson told Crockett, who knew next to nothing of European affairs, "It's certain the duke will see Napoleon's return as a spur to finish the American war with the utmost haste. He may strike us quickly, catch us on the hop, and not wait for perfect conditions. The duke's known for surprise attacks, Davy. He knows that Napoleon's return may impede the flow support from England. While those in Washington are buoyed by this development, it may wreck my timetable. By God, now's the time to step up production, kick supplies out of Watervleit, and get the gol-darn artillery limbered up. The more noise and activity to confound the enemy, the better for us.

"Sam, throw up a smoke screen. March the troops to the great redoubt and send countermarches back. Do *whatever* you can to flummox the British snoops into thinking we're strong and eager for battle." Excited now, Jackson continued, "Davy, increase activity all along the front. In the rear build more cooking fires with plenty of wet wood. Send the cavalry to drag bags of hay to stir up dust plumes." Jackson turned to Houston again. "Sam, cease scouting the enemy and concentrate on sending false signals north.

Get the newspapers printin' stories about the rapid increase of both regular and militia strength. In short, boys, while we prepare, mislead the redcoats into thinkin' we're no easy target, by God."

Prevost Plays a Card

As the first week of April ended, Prevost arrived at Whitehall. He didn't come north by boat but rather from the east on horseback. Sherbrooke had lent him a troop of British dragoons to cut across New Hampshire and Vermont, both to provide safety and to frighten the locals.

"Your Grace, I've many intriguing political developments to report. The rumors are true. The Ogre's once again on the throne. But the Congress of Vienna has declared him an outlaw. Europe's mobilizing, and England's sending an army under Lord Uxbridge to Belgium."

The duke's deep disappointment was conspicuous to all those present. "Once again, Sir George, I've missed my chance at Napoleon. What is it about my star? Now my critics will place me on the second shelf. Worse, Napoleon's return has transformed our expedition into a *very* expensive sideshow." Wellington felt abruptly alone, isolated, ignored, while England's focus shifted once again to Europe. Despondent, he asked, "Is the goal of this campaign worth the lives of those who will surely perish in the next few days?"

Prevost said nothing. There was nothing to say. After a couple minutes, he sought to change the mood. "I've brought not only daunting dispatches but also more delightful ones. More regiments, thawed out of the St. Lawrence, have joined Sherbrooke's men and are moving south. His seven thousand fresh troops are traveling—unopposed, mind you—down the Connecticut River."

"How's that possible?" Wellington asked, skeptical.

"The militias from Vermont and New Hamphire have joined Jackson at Saratoga, and according to reports from the Royal Navy's blockade, they've left the Portsmouth Harbor in New Hampshire undefended. Cockburn's fleet, with Pakenham's seven thousand veterans on board, is expected to land shortly and link up with Sherbrooke. Your brother-in-law's command will be a welcome addition to our cause. I expect, Your Grace, they'll be here by the first week of May."

Delancey was recording the interview, making notes as fast as his quill could dip into the inkwell and scrawl across the paper. "Your Grace, I presume I can plan to move forward on May 1. Will that suit you?"

Wellington's eyes sparkled, for the first time in months, at the prospect of finishing this business. "Sir William, if all goes well, I could be home by early July. There should be enough war left in France for me by then, I should think."

"Long as we tend to the war here first, Arthur," Prevost said, tracing Pakenham's path on the giant map that hung on the makeshift headquarters' wall. "Marching west, they'll pass through Concord and Keene, swing north above Bennington, and cross the Hudson at Schuylerville."

The duke calculated the marching time required in his head; it wouldn't take long. "That'll suit us very well. We will engage the Yankees at Saratoga and set right what Burgoyne set awry." Wellington's thoughts raced ahead to a new battle on that old battlefield—one that would be his for sure. "Taking into consideration Prevost's news, what can I expect to field at Saratoga, Sir William?"

Delancey scribbled a quick addition to his standing figures and, anticipating further questions, read from the order of battle he had just pinned to the side of the map board. "I forecast," he said, "that by the first of the month, here at Whitehall, we'll have Robinson's brigade of 3,400 men, Power's brigade of 3,300, and Brisbane's brigade of 4,500. We replenished Brisbane with the reserve from St. Jean and moved all his Canadian troops to Brigadier de Salaberry's Brigade, which now totals 4,300 men. We'll also have Sontag's German Legion with 4,000 troops, Sherbrooke's command with 7,000, and the Royal Artillery and transport with 1,000 men combined. We'll have forty cannon and howitzers, plus a brigade of Royal Rocketeers, with another 250. Pakenham should join us en route with an additional 7,000 troops. I've estimated the artillery with Sherbrooke and Pakenham to equal about 500. I believe that the final total under arms at Saratoga will be nearly 35,000 soldiers."

Somerset remarked, "I believe it's a figure not too far from that at Salamanca—your greatest triumph, Wellington, if I may indulge in making such an assertion."

The duke, recognizing the similarity, retorted, "And do you suppose that Jackson's the equal of the defeated Marshal Marmont?"

Ignoring the remark, Somerset tried to evade the duke's barbed tone by shifting the focus. "Wasn't Pakenham there that day as well? It appears British history is about to repeat itself, but this time at the Yankees' expense."

Delancey could not resist joining in. "Didn't some Frenchman say that Your Grace defeated forty thousand with forty thousand in forty minutes?"

Prevost welcomed the positive portends and was not to be outdone. "My New England contacts claim that Jackson has sixty thousand. But, of course, two-thirds are untested militia, which ought to bring the odds down to a more palatable one to one, I believe."

Wellington listened to his comrades' encouraging banter and flattery with only half an ear. In his mind he was envisioning Jackson and what nasty surprises the self-taught dueling frontiersman was planning for him.

May 1815

As predicted, Delancey launched his military machine south like a red-tipped dagger. A cavalry squadron of staff dragoons led the army along the Wood Creek Road. Robinson's brigade and a battalion of Royal Field Artillery followed. Behind the 3rd Regiment of Foot was a combined band from all three regiments. They alternated between "The Girl I Left behind Me" and "The World Turned Upside Down," the latter being played this time in gleeful anticipation of the American upheaval to come. As they entered each hamlet, the music was repeated, notifying the citizens along the way that their world was changing.

The soldiers marched down the dirt road through the village of Fort Ann, a common stop on the old road to war. The lead brigade bivouacked in the square at Hudson Falls while its officers billeted with families. The column undulated south like a red snake, clinging to the upper reaches of the twisting Hudson River, where the shallow water metamorphosed into whitewater rapids. A number of towns responded to the British arrival by evacuating homes and taking the road south, ahead of the column. By the second day, thousands of marching feet had beaten the road to fine dust. Gritty granules spilled over the tops of the soldiers' shoes and slipped inside their buttoned gaiters, much to the men's irritation. Most citizens remained, though, believing the posters that proclaimed, "No harm is intended by His Majesty's forces to those who showed civil obedience."

It wasn't until the third day of marching that the last of the Whitehall elements found space to take to the road. A solid mass of red deluged every town and village, broken only by the blue of the Royal Artillery and the gray of their limbers and rumbling supply wagons. The incessant pounding of hooves and the rattle of cartage drowned out the sounds of everyday life. Thumping regimental drums proclaimed doom for those who dared to stand and fight. Wellington's troops were unopposed but not unobserved—Houston and his scouts couldn't believe their eyes at the magnitude of soldiers in lockstep coming their way.

Houston reported to Jackson, "The redcoat patrols are sniffing about our flanks, countin' noses and markin' trails. I wouldn't be surprised to wake up to a raiding party or two 'round my tent."

"Sam," he said, "get Davy to put a screen out by Freeman's farm and set an outpost up on the old German redoubt above the river. I doubt Wellington will do anything drastic, but he may want to spook our young soldiers with a rocket demonstration. He's no Indian fighter, but according to what I've read, he's a quick learner."

As the battle drew near, Jackson could thank his stars for one thing: Saratoga was too far from Washington for the politicians to meddle under the guise of "helping" and "observing" and "inspecting." Comfortable at his headquarters behind Neilson's farm, he requested one final estimate from Houston as the last American units closed in on the heights.

"Sam, before you pull your boys back and we show our colors, what's it gonna take to tweak this thing in Wellington's favor?" Jackson was looking for their trump card.

"Andy, those field guns. . . . I never seen finer crews. I watched 'em drill in the evening before settin' up camp. They can fire twice as fast as ours and can hit a pine cone swingin' in the breeze at two thousand yards. I seen a batch of rocket troops, quite far back, so Old Nosy may be thinkin' of savin' 'em till later."

"Those fireworks could fill your carcass with thunder and lightning," Jackson said, trying hard to keep a sunny disposition in the face of the English juggernaut. He knew others were questioning Houston as to how Old Hickory was enduring the pressure. Optimism was Jackson's only parapet.

Crockett, the Indian fighter, had little experience with enemy cannon. Jackson, who never had more than a dozen guns to manage, had been tutored at West Point that past winter on the use of field artillery. While Davy watched, the general had the batteries placed where he specified as they came up behind Bemis Ridge. Taking a page from Gates's book, Jackson installed his six French-made twelve-pounders and the same number of old eight-pounders in earthen redoubts high up at the point. There, on the line's eastern end, the big guns would interdict the river and road if the British chose to outflank him. The Vermont and New Hampshire brigades, his most experienced militia units, were given the mission to protect the guns and stop a likely British approach.

"Davy, you needn't worry," Jackson said. "Those guns at the point will anchor our right flank." He penciled in the remainder of the six- and nine-pound batteries of field artillery on Crockett's map.

"Andy, spreading cannon batteries between the foot formations will keep the infantry steady." Crockett marked in the infantry along the heights' front slope, alternating regulars with militia.

"I hate to fragment cannon fire, Davy. I'd rather combine them into blocks. The cannons will still help skittish infantry maintain their courage."

The line extended over a mile, allowing units to stand in lines three deep, though staggered to meet the demands of uneven ground. A large reserve of six brigades, comprised of four regular and two militia, mustered behind the high ground, which protected them from direct cannon fire. On the morning of May 5, soldiers in blue watched the mist lift from the middle ravine to reveal red dots moving along the high ground to the north.

Houston, along with a body of Indians and scouts, filtered back through the American lines. A nervous sentry fired a warning shot at their approach. Soldiers rushed to their positions, and sporadic firing popped all along the line. Puffs of white smoke sprang up, generating hysteria among the green troops. But the young Irishmen from New York City, aligned in rows before Neilson's farm began to shout for English blood—a demand that would be answered soon enough.

Establishing a Presence

At the end of the march, Wellington took up residence in American general Philip Schuyler's old homestead next to the river. The following morning, assured that the Americans had withdrawn from the German redoubt, the duke joined the march as it trudged out of Schuylerville on its final leg. He followed in the dust of Robinson's lead brigade for two reasons. First, Wellington didn't trust the grudge-holding Robinson's reaction at the sight of the rebels who had imprisoned him as a lad. "The brigade commander's judgment might be clouded by past experience," he warned Delancey. The duke saw no need to rush at the enemy. Second, Wellington liked to be far forward to observe and judge the ground for himself. The terrain was new to him, making him nervous. He had the map Delancey provided lying open across the saddle. At a walk, the command party followed the column as it turned away from the river and onto the road leading up the giant ravine, carved by ancient torrents of water that had split the rock, to the old battlefield.

"Burgh, just look at that palisade. It must be a sheer three hundred feet high. Make a note to Delancey to establish a major battery up there, where the Germans built the great redoubt." He stopped his horse against Burgh's and tilted the map, so his aide could see the position.

They rode on behind the last squad of the Connaught Rangers. The dust from the road coated the rangers' yellow collars and wide white cross-belts, turning both to beige. Coming up on higher ground a quarter mile on, Wellington could just make out the buildings of Freeman's farm and checked them against the map. Using the farm as a reference point, he stopped his horse and pulled out a collapsible brass telescope from the round leather case buckled to the saddle. He looked with anticipation south, across the middle ravine and freshly cleared rolling hills, for a glimpse of Nielson's farm on Bemis Heights. The duke thought he could still smell the residue of gunpowder that had soaked into the ground after a generation of rain.

"Ah, there it is," he shouted to Delancey, who had come up onto the ridge, twenty yards away. The colonel trotted over along with Grant, who had been down in the middle ravine when the American line opened up with its musket fire.

"Were you the cause of that ruckus, Colley?"

"I might've been, Your Grace, but I believe it was their own scouts whom we drove back into their lines." Grant stood in his stirrups to see Wellington's map. "Are we going to fight the battle anew?" he asked Delancey. "Or just reenact the past?"

The question was a trifle brusque but valid and valued. Wellington stepped in to answer, since he had yet to discuss his plans with anyone, not even his quartermaster. "Colley, the ground's unforgiving and leaves us paltry choices. The weaponry has changed little in thirty-eight years, but I don't plan to make the mistakes of the past. We have Burgoyne to thank, for he tells me what *not* to do." Wellington tapped the map with the end of his telescope. "The Yankees are untested regulars and muddled militia led by a general who has never commanded more than ten thousand soldiers and rarely even that much. He dare not attack. And it's even doubtful that he could pursue. No, Colley, Jackson is wedded to that ridge. I'm not going to weary my solders by digging a defense. I intend to unleash an offensive as soon as we are in position and knock Jackson off his perch!"

———

Three days passed before the British army coiled out of range of the American cannons. Much of Wellington's army was in plain sight while others were concealed in the folds of the uneven ground. The aggressor had the advantage of focusing his wrath on a precise avenue of approach, and the defender had to spread his forces thinly and widely across all possibilities, further weakening Bemis Heights.

Wellington, conspicuous in a plain, dark blue frock coat among a sea of red uniforms, rode the length of Burgoyne's old lines. He had studied the battle from maps during the long voyage and had run through many scenarios, both as ally and as adversary.

Before dark, he rode again with Delancey and discussed his plan. Delancey had few questions; the ground had been fought for once before and little remained unclear.

Standing before a hanging map at the field headquarters, Freeman's farm, Delancey passed on the duke's intentions to the regiment and brigade commanders. Pakenham was still absent but expected momentarily. Brimming with confidence, Wellington felt that Pakenham's presence was unnecessary for the assault but would be crucial for the pursuit.

"There'll be three attack columns, each providing their own reserve," Delancey began. "On the far left General Sherbrooke will advance with his two brigades, Scots in the lead, and engage the point to divert their attention from the American center. This feint will minimize the supporting cannon fire from our main thrust at the point. The main attack, down the center, will consist of three brigades, with Robinson in the lead, followed by Power and Brisbane. General de Salaberry will form the army reserve to Sherbrooke's right. Be prepared to exploit the main attack. The interim objective is Bemis Heights, specifically Neilson's farm. The primary objective is the complete destruction of the American army. On the far right flank, the supporting attack of General Sontag's German Legion will probe the enemy flank for weaknesses and exploit them in concert with the attached cavalry corps. The guns will remain under the duke's direct control. All standing orders are in effect. I invite your questions, gentlemen."

Previous days had allowed uninterrupted reconnaissance by the British officer corps—much to the irritation of the Americans, who watched through telescopes. General Strong, on the point, was taken by their counterparts' casual approach, whose picnic atmosphere permeated the entire affair. Clusters of officers and aides, in brilliant uniforms stopped to eat and drink within range of the American cannon, daring the enemy to expose the positions of the artillery. It was an old trick.

Colonel Sir Augustus "Hugh" Fraser, regimental commander of the Royal Scots who was expected to lead Sherbrooke's attack, stood up. "I don't suppose you expect my boys to climb that bloody point and take those big guns, while the rest of you piddle around down here, do ya? Kilts can get very drafty in high places."

"Hugh, you're there just to distract, disrupt, and deceive the militia. Keep your own casualties to a minimum," Delancey said and then added, "The Lord willing, we'll all keep our casualties to a minimum."

Wellington Makes the First Move

On May 8 Wellington made the first move with his artillery. Three six-gun batteries slid down a path into a crease in the rolling terrain, which protected the artillery from direct observation and bombardment by the American cannons on the point. The British engineers had sneaked in to prepare these hidden cannon positions while Crockett was distracted.

Concerned with counterbattery fire from Bemis Heights, the duke relaxed astride his horse, telescope in hand. Under Delancey's control, the army moved with confidence. Clustered on high ground near Freeman's farm and awaiting instructions, many members of the command group stood by behind the duke. The staff, many clad in dress uniforms, commented loudly about the most inconsequential incident, distracting Wellington, who had only to turn around to restore order.

Along the battle line American solders listened nervously to the rattle of gun limbers and the jangle of horse brasses carried on the low morning breeze that wafted across the undulating field. The waiting soldiers remained silent, each committed to his thoughts of family, loved ones, the enemy, tomorrow's ration of salt pork—anything but Death's famished skeletal figure.

Soon the murmuring began. "When will they come at us, Sergeant?"

"Sooner than we'd like, but never soon enough," was the reply.

————

Alone on horseback, Jackson inspected the six reserve brigades lounging on the ground. They stood up within their formations as he approached. Hidden behind the heights, uncertain of what was happening, they appeared nervous. Houston rode beside Jackson and took mental notes for Crockett, who was sequestered with the general's assembled staff at Neilson's farm.

Jackson moved around the end of the ridge to the flank guard posted on the far west wing. The confusion rife in the ranks of the Massachusetts militia and the 5th U.S. regulars, clustered on flat ground with little protection, concerned him. While repositioning the elements to take advantage of a low cut in the ground, he remarked, "Sam, I don't like the look of these men."

"They're mighty scared, Andy. Wonderin' what's gonna burst out from behind them."

"Get back to the reserve," Jackson ordered, "and move two brigades forward, so these boys can see they're not alone."

Houston gathered together the New York Militia Dragoons, the American Dragoons, the 3rd Massachusetts, and 7th Regular Infantry and directed them forward to within sight of the troops at the end of the American line. Then he rejoined Jackson. Old Hickory was on the move once more, this time farther up the line, when the first crackling ripple of enemy cannon fire announced the start of another Battle of Saratoga.

Jackson took shelter with Colonel Michael Cleburne, a native of Cork and one of the Wild Geese under the green flag of the 1st U.S. Regulars. "Steady, boys." This was the best unit in the American army. They were very efficient and required little outside instruction.

Turning his attention to the action, Cleburne ordered, "Hold your fire." His instruction echoed via myriad voices across the three kneeling lines of blue-coated soldiers. "Wait till their red coats are within a hundred yards."

The British artillery's solid shot fell short, bouncing in crazy unpredictable arcs. Wherever they alighted, whatever they touched, they destroyed. American artillery batteries, on either side of the regiment, returned fire with poor results. Jackson was surprised by how quickly the Royal Artillery touched off a second and more accurate burst. This time some of the nine-pounders hit the ground just before the American line and then bounded high, clearing the formations and rolling harmlessly over the ridge.

"Sure now, General," the Irish colonel said. "They're just gettin' the range with that salvo." He turned to his men and shouted, "Get ready, boys! The next balls have got our names on them, to be sure!"

Jackson recalled Houston's earlier warning about the guns as the next volley of a dozen iron balls streaked through the formation, cutting down young soldiers three at a time. Many didn't even have time to scream. Jackson, in the thick of the artillery barrage, spurred his horse out in front of the line and waved his hat, as was his wont, to notify the entire front to withdraw over the lip of the heights to the secondary positions prepared behind. The prearranged signal was gratefully obeyed in the face of the bounding cannonballs. Each soldier was silhouetted at the top of the ridge before disappearing behind it.

The duke pointed out the maneuver to Delancey, "A reverse slope defense. My God! Where'd he learn that?"

"You have to blame your chroniclers for that, Your Grace," Delancey replied. "I did mention Jackson's access to the military school library during the winter, didn't I?"

Wellington, clearly amused, turned to his military secretary, "So I'm fighting myself, eh? By God, he's flummoxed me. I've no cavalry in the center to exploit the vacuum created by his pullback. Send the infantry forward, Delancey. I'm sure this fox will bring them back to fight on this side of the ridge. My artillery will have to hold fire when they mix at close quarter, though. *Damn* him."

Delancey sent a dragoon officer with a message to the chief of artillery that ordered him to hold his fire in the center and to reposition the guns at his pleasure. The gunner moved his howitzers forward with the infantry. The indirect looping trajectory of the five-and-a-half-inch stubby-barreled guns, unlike that of the direct cannons, could reach over the ridge to explode above the heads of Jackson's sheltered regiments.

"The raining shrapnel ought to disrupt them, at least," Delancey told Burgh, who replied, "And perhaps lop off a few of their best heads."

Delancey turned to a deputy. "Go forward and adjust the main infantry attack accordingly. Look to the right at the militia on the heights. They're restive and ill prepared. Turn their flaws into our assets, my boy."

Along the Front

The point's heavy guns were repositioned when it became plain that the British weren't interested in skirting around the Americans' far right flank along the river or over the adjacent road. Doubling the guns directed at Sherbrooke while supporting Bemis Heights, the Yankee gunners rained cannonballs down like hellish hail. The flamboyant Colonel Fraser pulled his kilted infantry back and took cover. However, the cannonballs were unable to deter Robinson's advance in the center. Like a madman, he rushed his regiments onward and his troops appeared to be intact.

On the left of the heights the New Jersey militia, which hadn't been engaged up to that point, began to shake when Brisbane's brigade rushed over to their side of the American line. At the command post behind their center, Crockett was dealing with a torrent of escapees, who had simply dropped their packs and weapons and tried to run away down the back of the ridge. Jumping into the saddle, Crockett grabbed one of the regimental flags and rode into the crowd. The number of deserters was growing alarmingly.

At his most profane, Crockett shouted obscenities and waved the colors. "Stop, you blasted bastards! Don't you skedaddle, by Christ! Get back in the line, you craven varmints! What kind of men are you? Imbeciles! Blockheads! You damn morons, get back to your regiments!"

Some fugitives turned around, bending to pick up their cast-aside muskets.

Crockett raised his voice higher, "Jackasses, cowards, you shame your mothers!" Running down one sprinting deserter, he reached for his collar and snatched him up. "Don't you dare flee on Andy Jackson!" Crockett, furious, spurred his horse back and forth across the ridge as he screamed abuse. "Varmints! You there, you son of a bitch!" he hollered above the constant roar of the surrounding artillery. Billows of white smoke from the opposing guns mingled in the still air as if from one source.

The redcoats deployed across the bottom of the heights and began to climb like goats after the fleeing Yankees. The Royal Artillery cannons paused to redeploy while the Americans continued to heat theirs with volleys of grapeshot that showered the advancing British regiments, staggering many as if their legs had been knocked from under them.

Unaware of the crisis at Neilson's farm, Jackson led the New York militia and regulars off the reverse slope, over the top, and down the heights. He stopped to reform them in three lines a hundred yards from the top. Their unit officers took over and began pouring musket fire into the redcoats at the foot of the incline.

On the American left flank, the Massachusetts militia, bolstered by the 5th U.S. Regulars (Irishmen from Philadelphia), prepared to withstand a cavalry probe by Sontag's famous dragoons.

The horsemen, in perfect parade order, pivoted into a long thin line fifty yards away. They unhooked their short carbines from their white shoulder slings and delivered one volley of musket balls from the saddle. The Americans, who had never set eyes on dragoons before, stood silently, awed by the spectacle. The two hundred aimed shots were fired at the same instant and slashed through the ranks.

It was the first incident of mass casualties for the Americans. The wounded writhed in pain, shouted for revenge, or begged for help. The dead lay there in shocking dismembered configurations. Thrown back by the withering fire, the enraged Massachusetts men had to recoil—but only for an instant. The horsemen casually clipped their spent short muskets back on and wheeled for the charge.

But it was the American infantry that charged the cavalry. Yelling and cursing, officers running in front, swords held high, the breach was closed by bloodshed. The sight of four thousand infuriated men, racing with still unfired muskets, bayonets fixed, caught the English dragoons unprepared. They had never witnessed such behavior before. Their commander ordered a hurried retreat under the protection of German artillery, which came to the rescue of the harassed dragoons.

The unsteady New Jersey militia began to crack. Brisbane, at the head of the trailing brigade, shifted farther to the right to dilute Wellington's main attack. The brigade commander believed that he saw an opportunity to rout the wavering New Jersey men. Perhaps he could even roll up the left flank onto Bemis Heights.

Jackson, behind Cleburne's Irish troops, rode back over the heights and called forward the 3rd and 4th Regulars, who responded quickly. They had been sitting and absorbing enemy howitzer fire. Anxious to leave their killing confines, where it was raining exploding bits of metal, they followed the general. Sam Strong's big twelve-pounders on the point were definitely impacting Robinson's and Power's brigades.

But Robinson would not let up. He was avenging his family and the wrongs to himself. When his colors fell at the cost of an officer's life, he seized the flag and drove up the ridge into the face of the American Irish. His lead battalion of Buffs melted under the threshing musket fire and stopped. The Inniskilling, next in line, took their place and followed the brigade commander.

Cleburne recalled an action in Spain when he served with the French chasseurs. The British officer in command of the 95th British Rifle Regiment had massed his riflemen in three rows and cut the Frenchmen to ribbons. Cleburne had practiced the formation and trained his men to conduct a rolling fire, rank after rank. While one loaded, another fired and a third took aim. Packed shoulder to shoulder, company tight against company, they followed the commands of their officers, standing at the side of the solid blocks of resolute troops. Cleburne gave the command, "Fag-an-Bealach." It was an ancient war cry from Ireland meaning "Clear the way." The captains beat time with their unsheathed swords. Jackson standing in the rear, holding his horse, watched the precise exercise wither away rank after rank of redcoats. The Irishmen spat out a rolling fire much like the artillery and burned out the heart of the main British attack.

Robinson, wounded now but not down, turned his back on the Americans and called for support. "For the king and our land—"

Exposed, he was shot through in a dozen places. His thirst for revenge may not have been slaked, but it had ended.

The Retreat

The redcoats' energy had been exhausted. They collected their wounded and escaped under a renewed barrage of Royal Artillery fire.

The day was still young, however, and Jackson feared another attack. The American soldiers collapsed where they stood. They called for powder and ball along with buckets of water to relieve the incredible thirst brought on by a massive expenditure of adrenaline.

An hour passed and then another. The battlefield was silent.

Once again on horseback, Jackson rode along the jagged front line. Men smiled when they saw how freely and easily he rode with his sword back in its scabbard. They shouted at him, "We sure done good, General! We beat 'em bad, General!" Jackson touched the brim of his hat in salute as he trotted along. He was as amazed as they were. They had just halted the best army in the world.

Not until he reached Crockett, still tangled in the New Jersey ranks, did he learn of the cost of the battle. "We beat 'em off, Andy, though casualties are terribly high. I put some wild cat into those New Jersey boys. They'll settle down now that they're veterans."

Crockett paused and breathed in the air, still acrid with gunpowder. And then he asked the one question for which Jackson had no answer: "What about tomorrow, Andy?"

CHAPTER 11

The Battle of Saratoga, Day Two

"The paths of glory lead but to the grave."
— Thomas Gray, "Elegy Written in a Country Churchyard"

Jackson, grateful for the steadfast Irish brigades, knew that the professional British soldiers, resting now beside thousands of campfires, had his measure. Jackson had no more tricks up his sleeve and tomorrow would be a hard slog. As he lay exhausted on his canvas cot, the thought of death crept into his troubled mind. It comforted him, and he prayed for forgiveness before falling asleep.

Wellington had the same concern as Jackson—what about tomorrow? He sat alone in his tent near Freeman's farm while Delancey pulled the army back together. The duke planned alone, never trusting in the judgment of others. When his quartermaster general appeared with the casualty figures, Wellington was more interested in his efforts to refit the troops.

Delancey presented a detailed list by regiment: "Sir, the main attack sustained 10 percent casualties, concentrated in the lead and follow-on brigades, while Sherbrooke reports a total loss of four hundred soldiers, a quarter of whom were killed."

Wellington took note. He had no choice but to recognize the invulnerability and strength of the guns on the point.

Delancey continued uninterrupted. "The King's German Legion is intact. Sontag reports that his command will turn their left flank tomorrow, drawing Jackson's reserve out from behind Bemis Heights. He asks that the main attack be assigned to him and that de Salaberry be deployed to support the right flank." He paused for comment or instructions, but Wellington remained mute.

Believing he may have overstepped his bounds by passing on Sontag's request, Delancey's attitude grew more formal. "Your Grace, Lord Fitzroy assesses morale to be high across the officer corps. I've evacuated the casualties to the great redoubt and will spend the night distributing ammunition and victuals. I perceive no significant limitation in our capability. And if I may risk an assessment, I suspect Jackson's shaken after this extraordinary day. Fitzroy doesn't believe he'll hold together. Nor do I."

"Any word of Pakenham?" Wellington inquired. His gaze remained firmly fixed on the document he had accepted from the quartermaster general.

"Only that he's expected," Delancey said and left quickly. There was much to do.

Alone again, Wellington ruminated on Jackson. During the battle the duke had observed the Yankee's behavior: he had left his staff to lead and rally the troops at critical moments. The American soldiers were most likely buoyed by their initially successful stand, but were their leaders shaken by their losses?

Wellington was concerned with the ground and the role the guns of the point would play the following day. They had dominated the battle thus far and would protect the center again on the morrow since they had survived their first engagement intact. How should he approach the enemy tomorrow? Maybe Sontag really did have the answer: go out on the open flank where terrain wasn't a factor. He could reinforce the King's German Legion and let the Germans roll up Jackson like a carpet, but that would give the victory to the Germans and the Canadians. And Wellington wanted to ensure an ample portion of glory was reserved for England as embodied in none other than the duke himself.

After dark, at the evening meal in the duke's mess, conversation rattled along the length of the long linen-covered table. All the general officers were present; the duke rose and offered a toast to the fallen. Like always, the meal was light and the fortified wine heavy.

Delancey, seated near the duke, offered, "Jackson showed a level of professionalism we didn't expect. His withdrawal behind the ridge, minimizing the covering cannon fire, was a rather unwelcome surprise. His ability to maintain cohesion within the ranks is also impressive, a tribute to his training program. Yet, his weakness is his militia. Those troops near Neilson's farm were skittish, and if I'd seen it sooner, we wouldn't be sitting here tonight, but instead we would be on our way to Albany."

"Don't trouble yourself," Wellington said. "Insight is too often a matter of hindsight."

Somerset addressed the duke: "I agree, Your Grace. We planned a set-piece attack and failed to exploit in time. Believing no enemy could stand against us, which is so often true, fails to prepare us for the unseemly exception."

He sat down and called for more port. The warm light from the brass candlesticks reflected the decanter's crystal facets in multicolored dots of light on the large tent's canvas as the decanter went from hand to hand on its depleting journey. As they drank, the generals dissected the day's decisions, efforts, and turns of fortune. Wellington sat, gravely quiet and quite still—except for the hand petting the head of his favorite foxhound, which lay beside his folding camp chair.

Outside, the sound of the soldiers' campground and the smell of bubbling hot pots drifted in through the open tent flap. A sudden commotion erupted. The sound of hooves pawing the ground turned everyone's head toward the open tent flap.

With a swirl of blue cape lined in orange, the visitor entered. His face appeared new to most but was familiar to Wellington. His brother-in-law, splattered with mud but recovered from the wounds inflicted at New Orleans, walked the length of the tent and embraced the duke.

"Gentlemen," Wellington said, his voice a bit more festive, "may I introduce the late Major General Sir Edward Pakenham, a valuable servant to His Majesty and an invaluable relative of mine. The infernal Yankees thought they slew him at New Orleans, but won't they be stunned to find him resurrected tomorrow at Saratoga?"

Another Visit, Another Camp

At nearly the same hour, Jackson received visitors of unknown origin.

"Andy, you're gonna have to come with me to headquarters," Sam Houston said, pulling at the general's arm.

Jackson had been sampling a meal of turkey buzzard gizzards baked in cornmeal pan bread. Reluctantly, he gave up his place at the campfire, where he was so often most comfortable. His soldiers stood as he did. "Stand easy, boys," Jackson said. "We're all just soldiers here in the dark."

After tripping over tent ropes and accidentally kicking over a wash pan, the general greeted a party of civilians well dusted from their long journey. Jackson knew that a delegation from Washington would come sooner or later. But he counted it a blessing that they had arrived after—instead of before—the battle. Still, he didn't want to make time for them. He wanted to devote tonight to a long walk through the camp and be seen by the troop—for he too was a soldier—before whatever tomorrow would bring. If Jackson was lucky, come sunrise, Wellington, with Napoleon nibbling on his mind, might cut and run back to Europe, leaving the field to the American army. Of course, he realized this was improbable, but regardless, the image offered him a modest measure of solace.

"Andy, I'll let these gentlemen introduce themselves. They're from the North, *not* the South," Crockett warned.

The self-appointed spokesman offered introductions: "General Jackson, may I present Their Excellencies? Governor John Taylor Gilman of New Hampshire and Governor Martin Chittenden of Vermont. The other members of our party are John Harper and Ephraim Somes of New Hampshire, Marcus Allen and Addicus Bell of Vermont, Major Derrick Rodgers, and your humble servant, sir, Randolph Pew of Maine."

Each in turn stepped forward and extended a hand to the general as Pew uttered their names.

"Well, it's an unexpected pleasure to welcome you all to my headquarters. Have ya been to the point yet? That's were your folks are perched." The general gestured to the east. "Your soldiers performed gallantly today in the face of a *very* determined enemy. Your states should be mighty proud of their offspring."

Governor Gilman spoke next: "No, sir, we haven't. We thought it proper to get your permission before roamin' around your camp. We know you're preparing for tomorrow's interlopers and don't wish us to intrude, but we have information that I believe is of value to your army."

The governor's offhand reference to *your* rather than *our* army disturbed Jackson. Were these birds here to lend a hand or to test the mood of the battle? What were they looking for—a chink in the armor to spread to the newspapers? Jackson was well aware of the objections to the war these particular politicians had voiced during the long winter while the army was being pieced together. *Don't let on*, he thought. *Keep an eye out.*

"Thankee, friends, for your consideration. What compels you to go so far out of your way?" Jackson asked, glancing at Crockett, who was equally bewildered, for a clue.

"General, we," Gilman said, pointing to his group, "met at Concord and came by way of Keene. We thought it'd help your gallant effort if we met with our militiamen and brought good wishes from their folk. But the movement of a massive column of redcoats delayed us for days. To the best of our knowledge, they came ashore from a British fleet hailing from Jamaica and anchored in Portsmouth Harbor. I, that is, *we*, believe that nearly eight thousand men, configured in a corps with horse-drawn artillery but little cavalry, landed. We trailed behind them—*behind* them, mind you, sir—crossing the Hudson near Schuylerville this afternoon, which means that this influx of redcoats must already be. . . . I'm afraid we haven't brought you good news. Still, knowing is better than guessing, though guessing can sometimes be more entertaining."

Jackson was grateful for the warning but displeased by the man's tone. "This is indeed unwanted though timely news. I thankee, gentlemen, and would very much like to dawdle with you, but as you can possibly appreciate, there's much to do. Please visit your constituents. Davy, give 'em passes and a guide to the point. Now pardon me, gentlemen, and good evenin'."

Jackson patted each on his shoulder in appreciation, as they filed out. His mind was simultaneously paralyzed and galvanized by the new variable embodied in the unexpected arrival of thousands of veteran British troops. He turned to Houston for his perspective, but Houston only shrugged.

Something bothered Jackson about the encounter with the New Englanders. In all his days in the field he had never experienced a visit from a politician, much less a whole delegation. "Sam, somethin's up with those fellows. Those Yankees from the North have always stood in opposition, closely tied to tradin' money—always votin' against support for the militia. Now they are right friendly, can't do enough for us. Tellin' tales about the British as if butter wouldn't melt in their mouths."

Houston replied, "I'll keep an eye on those varmints for you, Andy. Could be a tall story about those reinforcements. Maybe they want you to give it up tomorrow and settle over the table and save their boys' skins."

Worms in the Wood

The party of politicians was escorted along the dark trail east through the sprawling camp, dimly lit by cook fires fueled to last all night. The soldiers expected an early call to arms. Men in various stages of undress appeared out of the shadows, carrying bits of food, bottles, boxes, and open wooden crates. Some were clearly happy that the day was over. Fragments of campfire talk could be discerned as the party made its way through the camp: "By golly, we whooped them lobster backs!" and "We gave 'em one hell of a lickin'" and "Tomorrow they'll turn tail" and, most prevalent, "I hope they pull out by morning." There was no blood lust in the American ranks. Nervousness pervaded the smoky air as the visitors gained the road leading to the point and passed silent sentries, who probed the darkness with their rifles for the sound of enemy movement.

The party walked their horses for fear of stumbling in the pitch dark on the deeply rutted track. The guide stopped several times on the steep climb up to the guns on the point. The trek was made more treacherous on that moonless night. Out of breath and clearly fatigued, Governor Chittenen remarked, "I pity the poor British soldier who attempts this ascent under fire."

Curious, the American guide thought, *that he should pity the enemy?*

He took them to the tent on the redoubt's south side that housed Major General Sam Strong's headquarters. Strong was conferring with the New Hampshire brigade's commander in an effort, ultimately fruitless but always essential, to anticipate and prepare for the next day's uncertainties. The visitors, some of whom were kin, were greeted as friends. They had known one another for years, coming together in private business, political, and familial associations. Recently, however, Strong and Chittenden had had a falling out over whether the militia should support the federal government. Strong was unaware that at this late date, Chittenden intended to reconsider the topic.

Gilman, speaking first, relayed the same information he had passed on to Jackson. He let it sink in for a moment. Strong squirmed in his seat. He had seen enough redcoats that day to last him a lifetime; he wasn't looking for any more.

"General," the governor said, "it appears to us, and all sane men with open critical minds, that Wellington will use the new influx of troops against your American right flank. You think your position is solid on the point, but will it sustain an attack from four more determined brigades? I've been advised that Wellington nearly took you today with *far* less."

Surprised that Pakenham had survived New Orleans with a viable command, Strong shied away from Gilman. He looked at the floor and pictured a mass of red flowing up the front slope of the point. "I believe it'll be a hell of a show, Governor. Will you be staying on with us to see it?" he said. "How did Jackson take this news?"

Strong knew that the day had been a close run and that the center had nearly collapsed with the weight of Wellington's onslaught. His mood began to shift as doubts surfaced about American success the next day. Strong had never felt that his militia was a part of the federal army; rather, he felt his troops were considered mere stepchildren, second place to the regulars. At first he had agreed with the Vermont and New Hampshire militias' assignment to the right flank, but he was troubled that if the center didn't hold they would be left high and dry with no escape route. Jackson could withdraw and leave them perched on the point all alone. Strong bit his lip at the image.

Governor Chittenden lied in a voice slicker than ice. "We've just come from the headquarters. Jackson is deluded into believing that your position is unassailable. I could see from the maps hanging on his wall that he plans to abandon you and put most of his troops on the far flank, where he thinks the British will attack in force. Your men, sir, will be deserted when he pulls out to the south under Wellington's assault. The regular army will be preserved, if for nothing else, to fight another day somewhere else."

The militia generals looked warily at each other.

Chittenden delivered the final cut: "Your militiamen are the rear guard, only you haven't been told, as yet."

The words hit Strong like a cannonball. Even a casual observer had come to the general's own conclusion. Strong felt trapped, caged like a pet bird on the point.

Gilman spoke more resolutely. "Tomorrow Jackson will cast you aside, leaving your commands stuck up here surrounded by the British. Those who don't die in the assault will be condemned to rot in the dank hulls of British prison ships. You know you'll be compelled to surrender to save lives. Surrender's a terrible legacy for a family, don't you think? But we didn't just come here with declarations of doom, General. We offer hope. You can do something to save your men from such a horrific fate."

Strong and the other generals on the point felt torn by the news and trapped by their predicament. They recognized that Pakenham's brigades had intensified the danger. The balance, so precarious earlier that day, could certainly swing in the enemy's favor.

Strong became suspicious. He thought, *What's going on here? Why are these men here? They are after something. They have not shown their hand.* The general warily addressed Chittenden: "What do you suggest, Governor?"

"Let your men become the nucleus of a new army, one that's independent of the inept U.S. president, who has started a war he can't win. Madison's like a child setting home and hearth on fire to see the flames flicker. We've been traveling in the company of Major General Sir Edward Pakenham, who assures us that he'll welcome the addition of your brigades into his corps and will even offer you and your officers commissions in His Majesty's army. Such a profitable alliance has been common talk in New England since Jefferson began his mad vendetta against England."

Strong had never heard a Vermonter utter the words *His Majesty*. They had always said, "That crazy king" or "that mad tyrant." The mood toward England had certainly improved in Vermont. However, no one in the tent, Strong noted, objected to the term; were they of one mind?

"Many of your neighbors and a goodly number of your own soldiers would welcome a return to the mother country. The economic disaster visited on our frail economy since allying ourselves with that vicious, self-vexing federal government has been immense. They've failed us at *every* turn. Those Virginian 'gentlemen' have dominated the government since the country's beginning. They don't care a whiff about us 'citizens' up north. They see us as bill payers. Not equals. We—your political leaders and, may I say, the king's men—are offering you a rare opportunity to become a hero to your state and your family."

The implied flattery pleased Strong, and the proposal being articulated interested him. Exploring the matter, he asked, "How would I contact Pakenham at this late hour to discuss the method of transfer—if we were interested, that is?"

"Sam," the garrulous governor said, "may I introduce Major Derrick Rodgers of His Majesty's Royal Staff Corps? He'll be your liaison and has your signed commissions with him, along with the necessary signals and contacts to integrate the Vermont and New Hampshire militias into the British army."

Strong, undecided, parried for time. "Gentleman, you've presented a dilemma that's not mine alone. You've handed me a weighty problem, one that'll determine the fate of generations to come. I must confer with my officers and those of the New Hampshire militia. The lieutenant will find you accommodations for the night. In the morning I'll give you our decision."

Gilman objected to the arrangements for the night. "It isn't that late. Can't we re-trace our steps through the lines and—and witness the affair in the morning from behind the lines? We have played our part. It's now a military matter, don't you agree, Sam?"

Strong enjoyed watching the politician attempt to wiggle out of the dilemma. "Governor, which line would you hide behind since you don't know our decision as yet? It could be very dangerous for you behind the loser."

———

Strong issued an officers' call for later that night. Senior and junior commanders crowded into a large mess tent. Viewed from the outside, it appeared to be a normal gathering, perhaps a last-minute update. The men expected that their officers were confering in secret over the strategy of the coming battle.

General Strong, a man of confirmed opinion and known for rarely struggling with decisions, stood erect behind a field table. Flanked by his staff, he was nervous, unsure, and unusually undecided. As the tent filled to capacity, beads of sweat formed under his high stiff collar and trickled down his spine, and chills ran up his back, over his shoulders, and down his arms to the tips of his fingers. Candlelight cast shadows against the white canvas, enlarging the figures inside to a size large enough to decide the question. He couldn't make the choice alone. He knew that much.

Strong addressed the hushed assemblage and reviewed the circumstances in which they found themselves. He concluded, "The question you must answer is this: should the Vermont and New Hampshire militias continue to defend the United States of America or should we, for the good of our citizens"—his voice rose and cracked—"change allegiance?"

He took a seat, leaving the discussion open.

Intrigue before the Battle

With the arrival of Pakenham's command through the welcoming port of Portsmouth, New Hampshire, Prevost's efforts on behalf of the king were undeniable. While Wellington was fighting the military campaign, critical as it was, Prevost was waging a political campaign within the structure of the northern New England states that was proving to be just as consequential.

In an effort to enlighten the assembled mess and situate their current circumstances within a more meaningful context, Prevost chronicled his efforts thus far: "Lords Liverpool, Bathurst, and Carlisle gave their support to my policy of offering commissions to officers of the New England state militias if they'd bring their troops over to the British army. To further subvert our adversary's perceived ambitions, I included incentives and rewards for political leaders to encourage their assistance. As a fellow political figure of an adjoining state, I welcomed them back into His Majesty's family. But I advised them to band together and offer the king a new dominion." Prevost refrained, wisely, from suggesting that they become a province of Canada. "The prime minister has agreed to charter the territory of Maine and the states of New Hampshire and Vermont. The Prince Regent has established the 'Dominion of Columbia' with Portsmouth as the capital. He's also offered credentials marked 'Sir John Gilman, KB, Governor-General of Columbia' and 'Deputy Governor-General' to 'Sir Martin Chittenden, KB.'"

Delancey, intrigued, asked, "Why would Chittenden agree to being offered only second place?"

Prevost explained, "The deciding moment came when General Strong hijacked the Vermont militia against the governor's orders and took it to join the regular army, thereby leaving the state totally defenseless. Jackson's ties to the South and Madison's own peccadilloes further exacerbated the situation. I could never have accomplished anything without such 'treason.' I prefer to call it 'fidelity.'"

Wellington, dubious about Prevost's vaunted accomplishment, interjected, "*Treason?* A rather odd word to use in this case, don't you think, Sir William?" He turned his attention to his quartermaster general, whose plans such treachery would seriously affect. Speaking rapidly, as was his custom when splaying out options, Wellington summed up the situation. "One of three things will happen: first, the militia, which appears to vote on everything, including the color of its hose, may reject the offer and fight from a very strong position, which would hurt us tomorrow as it did today. Second, the militia could remain neutral, refusing to take orders from Jackson and leave the field, denying their commander their invaluable gun support. Or third, the militia could join Pakenham and turn its guns on the United States Army while we roll up Jackson's right flank. I suggest you write a plan and take into account all three scenarios in your considerations."

Delancey worked through the night, altering the next day's designated maneuvers to reflect two major changes: the arrival of Pakenham's seven thousand soldiers and the possible defection of the point's militia.

The Cards Are Reshuffled

Brigadier Benedict Arnold Jr., the new commander of the lead brigade, took advantage of the morning lull before the battle. He stood on the high ground to his brigade's right and observed Bemis Heights through his father's leather-bound telescope. He felt his father's presence, not garbed in a red uniform but rather in blue, on the same spot looking in the other direction. He'd grown up with family trials and tribulations that, in some lasting way, stemmed from the soil of Saratoga on which he now stood. Chroniclers often wrote that if his father's wound had been fatal all those years ago at the great redoubt, Arnold Senior would've been the first American elevated into the pantheon of immortal heroes. But his father's choices had rendered all that moot. Now his son was back to avenge his family in exile.

Early in the morning of May 9, Crockett found it necessary to consolidate units owing to the enemy's action. The 2nd New Jersey, the 2nd and 4th New York, as well as the 2nd U.S. Infantry flags were removed from the field. Overnight calculations tallied 6,000 wounded or killed. By the time the morning had broken free from its nocturnal fetters, deserters resulted in a nearly equal number destined to be removed from the roster. The moonless night made it possible for the militia and regulars simply to melt away. The one bright note was the arrival of two squadrons of the U.S. Army's Light Dragoons, whose uniforms were a contrast to those from New York State: the regulars wore short blue jackets piped and corded in white while the New York dragoons remained clad in red with yellow markings. Brigaded together on the far-left flank, they provided a possible countermeasure to the mounted troops of the King's German Legion.

———

The only visible change in the British center was the thinning of Robinson's brigade. The new commander, Benedict Arnold Jr., made a request of the duke: "Sir, though my brigade's reduced in circumstances, may I have the honor of leading the main attack?"

The duke, who counted on family zeal when including young Arnold in the expedition, saw an irony in the appointment. But he felt that the troops should have an opportunity to avenge Robinson's death. A closer look exposed 1,000 missing from the lead brigade's three regiments and consolidated company of light infantry skirmishers. Wellington wagered that the Americans wouldn't notice the thinning of the ranks with Power's brigade drawn up close behind and Brisbane's poised to exploit any weakness.

Wellington was gratified by Arnold's request. "Brigadier, I expect nothing less from the son of one of the most gallant fighters this land has ever produced."

Jackson Doubts

Jackson was preoccupied that morning with how best to deal with the addition of Pakenham's division. He had not expected to be confronted by another famous warrior. The newspaper reports from New Orleans must have exaggerated the carnage. Because of the freedom of action that Wellington garnered with the Americans wedded to Bemis Heights and the point, several choice gambits were possible.

"Davy, if I were Wellington, given an influx of fresh troops, I'd reinforce the Germans on my right flank, so they could sweep around the flank." Jackson stabbed a finger at the map pinned to the tent wall. "There, out of range of the point's guns and away from our strength in the center, would be Wellington's best bet."

The sagacious Crockett felt unsure. "If they do as you're a-sayin', Andy, those lobster backs will have to move a goodly portion of their artillery to yonder hill at Charfield's farm first, and I ain't seen nothin like that this morning."

Houston agreed. "Nothin' movin on their right this morning. They're sittin' tight as a cottonmouth under a rock, just waiting for the chance to strike."

The American commander could see he was outnumbered.

"Davy, you're learning about guns, ain't ya? But keep in mind, hidden batteries can fool ya." Jackson thought for a minute. "You're right, though. I must be losin' my touch. Sam, can you find Pakenham without getting yourself kill't? Wherever Pakenham goes, so goes the main attack."

"I've been a waitin' for a decent job," Houston said. "I'm terrible tired of being your dogsbody. Even if I couldn't, I'd skedaddle, 'cause I'm losin' my reputation as a fightin' man sitting here with sorry old Crockett."

Crockett took exception to the choice of the word "old" since they were nearly the same age.

Houston continued, "Andy, I'm certain they'll be a-comin' at us from the right, down below the point."

Jackson replied, "Sam, you're as rambunctious as ever. Get yourself up on the point and warn me if you see anythin' of Pakenham."

The morning stretched on, but the low ground remained cloaked in fog. Each side watched the other for the slightest glimpse of enemy movement. Jackson grew nervous, moving the reserve on his left flank forward, still concerned as he was that the King's German Legion might become the main thrust.

Wellington Moves to Observe

With Wellington in the lead, the entire British headquarters, obscured by morning mist mixed with campfire smoke, moved forward. The duke chose to monitor the battle from the high ground beside de Salaberry's Canadian brigade. There, he could watch the ravine on either side. A thick gray mist veiled the valleys between the low hills. Peering through his glass, he noticed the point's militia guns above him were primed and manned.

"Well, Delancey, the militia's up there and appears ready to fight."

"The question remains, Your Grace, on which side will they serve?"

Wellington placed his bet. "I wager they'll stay with Jackson. It's hard to change sides in the middle of a battle. I saw it happen only once before—in India. You may remember the fight at Seringapatam, Delancey. Like then, I predict this too will be a bloody day."

"Your Grace, it's risky to stay so near the action. You're a bit too close for my comfort."

Wellington believed he lived a charmed life. The many close calls he had survived throughout his active career only reinforced that belief.

"Nonsense, Sir William. Let's see if I'm correct. . . . The militia's had all night to decide. Let's take advantage of the fog. Give the order to advance. The test will be if the point fires at our lead brigade."

The Last Battle of Saratoga

The fog settled slowly, masking both the sight and sound of the plodding British columns. The lead element, commanded by Brigadier Benedict Arnold Jr., absorbed the dampness into its woolen uniforms, which hung limp on the soldiers' sodden forms, matching the wetness of the forest trail. Their famous bright red color was soaked to a dark maroon that ran into the crisp white of their cross belts, changing the white to a curious pink. The direction of the march became confused, reduced to a probe, with the skirmishers creeping forward at a nearly imperceptible crawl. This day would not be a rush to judgment but a heavy storm extended in both depth and breath.

It was not yet noon when Arnold broke out into the open just in front of the enemy and ordered, "At quick time, forward march." Turning in the saddle and drawing his father's sword, he increased the pace and shouted, "For the king and for my father!"

The brigade was eager to avenge the death of General Robinson and sprang into action. Grim-faced and narrow-eyed, the Irishmen of the Connaught Rangers took the lead. An amalgam of light companies, taken from within the brigade, fanned out at the base of Bemis Heights. The sharpshooters knelt to fire carefully aimed rifle shots at American officers. They swarmed in loose order, picking off leaders to panic the New York militia blocking the road over the heights.

Arnold brought his regiments abreast and delivered the first volley. Like a farmer's sharp scythe, the salvo cleared away the first line of defenders. Artillery from both sides split the air with a deafening barrage that drowned out the shrill cries of the wounded. The rocket corps, silent the previous day, sent thirty unguided forty-pound rockets screaming overhead to impact helter-skelter along the ridge. Trails of white smoke streaked low above the advance while the scream of the projectiles frightened not only the horses but also the troops. The duke remained unimpressed by the whizbangs but admitted they were "worth the gunpowder."

The American soldiers held their breath as the blue sky was striped with thin bands of white smoke. A second, third, and forth flock of terror followed shortly behind the first, momentarily blotting the sun with thicker smoke. The American line quivered. Jackson mounted and spurred his horse in between the New Jersey brigades. He attempted to repeat Crockett's rallying display from the day before. Spurring his mount, Jackson rode parallel to the lines in the space near the top of the heights, exposing himself to enemy cannonballs, daring the Royal Artillery to bring him down. He was well aware how hard it would be to hit a moving target along the crest. A dozen cannonballs screamed by harmlessly, impacting somewhere out of sight to the rear.

In the heat of battle, with the American army committed to a static defense, little could be accomplished from the command post. The rockets were having an effect, turning the 3rd New Jersey militia to jelly. Crockett left the command post and careened down the backside of Bemis Heights and led the 7th Brigade of regular infantry up behind Neilson's farm to block the deserters' path. The Philadelphia Irishmen, held in reserve for the occasion, responded quickly, eager to join the fight. Just to the left of the New York Irish regiments, their colors extended the line of green flags farther to the west along the ridge. Jackson joined Crockett, letting the Irishmen flow past and mingle with the militia that was taking the brunt of Arnold's ferocious attack. The Philadelphia regulars' formation stopped and formed a line of battalions abreast. Accompanied by the color guard, their commander moved to the front, drew his sword, and commanded, "Fix bayonets!" The Royal Artillery seized the opportunity to elevate its guns calibrated on the New Jersey front line "up two hundred." The brake in the cacophony lifted the heads of Arnold's men toward whatever great event was about to take place in the sky.

"Forward, 7th Brigade!" shouted the general as he stepped off at quick time with the green flag flapping beside the Stars and Stripes. The battered New Jersey militia parted as the Royal Artillery opened up anew, drilling holes in the regular infantry as they marched down the slope into the face of the shot and shell. The Irishmen wanted to prove they could stop the British advance.

Power's brigade shifted to the right, away from Arnold's right side, to receive the charge and laid down a devastating volley of musket fire. But the Philadelphia Irish, with the momentum behind them, had no choice and kept coming, buoyed by the rapid drum-beat of the musicians close behind. The sound, in tune with the speed of their bursting hearts, drove them forward as the ranks thinned. Power's veterans had met Napoleon's French the same way far from Saratoga and defeated them. The thin red line, two deep as Wellington had taught them, brought every weapon to bear as the Americans passed through the artillery barrage to be met by withering musket fire. Power was shot down, and his color guard fell on top of him. Another officer scooped up the grounded green flag and brought it back through the line of bayonets. They could go no farther.

The New York Irish regulars on the American right stood fast and gave the bullets back as fast as they received them. The 1st U.S. Regulars, Irishmen from New York City, under Cleburne moved out of line and poured enfilade fire on the duke's Connaught Rangers, who took offense and charged Cleburne's troops. It was a mistake and caused an opening in their flank that the newly massed American artillery, between the 1st and 2nd New York militia, rushed to exploit. Separated from the remainder of Arnold's regiments, the gap in the British lines grew wider.

Jackson, seeing the opening, rode pell-mell down the ridge, leading the 3rd and 4th New York militia into the rift. Fearing a loss of control at this crucial point and showing the intrepidity his family was no stranger to, astride his charger Arnold sped across the field—rounds snapping all around him—pulling the Inniskillings and Buffs back into the line and closing the gap.

Smoke from the volleys of Cleburne's massed muskets hung in the still air. Gaping mouths inhaled the acrid vapor, residue from a thousand muskets. It shortened the breath and filled the eyes with tears, obscuring friend from foe. The disorganized formations flourished bayonets and fought hand to hand. Hats were knocked to the ground as men wrestled, blood flowed, and comrades fell.

Curses filled the air as the clash between Irish Rangers and New York City Irish turned into a donnybrook of Old and New World kin fighting on behalf of outsiders. No quarter was given. Brisbane, who wanted to exploit the weakness of the New Jersey troops on the heights, was instead compelled to swing to the left, and not the right, to help plug the hole.

The British army now commenced a general advance on the left and right. The King's German Legion attacked the American far left, where two brigades of Philadelphia Irish supported the Massachusetts militia. The German drummers beat a deliberate pace at an odd menacing cadence, slower than the British standard.

Far more shocking, the accompanying brass band of dark-skinned Moors in multi-colored North African costumes blew a foreboding dirge that chilled the 5th and 6th U.S. Regulars, recruited from the Philadelphia Irish community. They called for their own bag-pipes and skirled the pipes at full volume to drown out the Germans.

Leading, General Sontag moved to the side along with the king's colors—blue with the initials GR for George Rex stitched in the center and a white horse of Hanover em-broidered in each corner—to allow the infantry to advance. The general held his dragoons back but uncovered a hidden battery of artillery. The heavy guns reached the American lines before the legion arrived and cut paths with bouncing cannonballs that slew half a dozen at a time.

Knowing that Jackson was unaware of the legion's penetration, Crockett left the New Jersey contingent, which was no longer endangered, and careened down the heights, where he managed to combine the fire of three American batteries to counter the German artillery. The Yankees commenced counterbattery fire. Boiling clouds of white smoke shrouded the melee and obscured the legion's attack from Wellington's telescope.

Sontag wasn't concerned with the rest of the battle. He was in a world of his own—beyond the control of Delancey. A professional soldier who bristled at the title "merce-nary" the press often placed on him, the German commander viewed George III as his own elector. His disciplined soldiers, though dressed in red like Englishmen, wore distinc-tive markings: shiny breastplates embellished with a lion and supported on a looped belt bearing the raised letters *King's German Legion*. The troops' formidable appearance and steady movement seemed to foretell victory.

Crockett could see that the battle was going to be a set piece in the open, on flat ground, without cover. He called the reserve forward. *It's simple, really,* he thought, *the first side to give an inch loses.*

The carnage began in earnest. Once discharged, muskets were not reloaded as the front ranks clashed, using their weapons to club or stab each other. Soldiers cursed in both languages. Entangled and crushed together by new Irish formations pressing forward from the rear, the soldiers belied the supposed "art" of warfare. Empty muskets meant the melee descended into a brawl. Crockett, mounted in between the Massachusetts militia and Irish regulars, cried, "Bang 'em, boys! Break their skulls!" A regular major, one of the Philadelphia Wild Geese that Carey provided, pressed against the side of Crockett's horse and cried, "Sure now, Davy, it's just like killin' Germans at Jena, only with better company. By glory, there is nothing like a good donnybrook to get the blood boiling and settle the troops down to good old head knocking. Don't concern yourself, Davy: my lads have been deprived long enough. They itchin' to send these hirelings to hell. You should know that the reserve is no place for an Irishman."

Expensive muskets became long clubs to bludgeon the way forward through the mixed mass of swearing wild-eyed soldiers. The fracas became a shoving contest as the ranks thinned out. Arms became lead and mouths dried like the inside of a work glove. Men flagged, staggered, and fell out. Some were tired, many bled, and others died.

Both Crockett and Sontag stopped their artillery and sent the cavalry into the fray to break the stalemate. The Americans rounded the eastern edge at full speed, only to receive a volley from the Germans, who had stopped in extended order. But the Americans' speed and open order negated the effect. The gap, a hundred yards broad, was finally closed. Too fast for the Germans to hook up their carbines and draw their heavy straight swords, the American dragoons struck like lightning, breaking the enemy formation and scattering the King's German Legion to the wind. The infantry battle wavered back and forth until Crockett pulled them back to a new line, this one tucked behind the western edge of Bemis Heights.

Wellington saw that the Americans' center was holding. He noticed his opponent feed in troops and maneuver the reserve with skill and even some aplomb.

"Delancey," the duke said, "I can take the point if the militia fights, but it'll cost me Sherbrooke's two brigades and perhaps Pakenham's. I can beat Jackson, but no more than that."

Wellington began to outline his options to Delancey. "We can take Albany. New York City's a plausible destination, and then what? Weakened, could we stay while the Americans mustered yet another army as I carried on with ever-diminishing resources? With no hope of reinforcements from Europe, while Napoleon and Uxbridge steal my thunder, I'd only get weaker."

Realizing that Wellington was talking to himself and that the questions were rhetorical, Delancey remained mute. His superior, however, did not.

"We can accept this as our final position and fortify a line to Portsmouth, our supply port and escape route. Then it's up to the politicians to settle this unpleasant matter. So what do you think? Will the militia fight, or won't they?"

Delancey kept silent. He wasn't sure if this question was rhetorical or not, and Delancey still had no answer to offer.

Jackson Decisively Engaged

After stabilizing the line, Jackson returned to Neilson's farm and looked for Houston, but he wasn't there. Neither was Crockett, who had left to confront the King's German

Legion. The general was alone with his nervous staff. The battle raged below, but little had changed. Casualties rose on both sides as the sun made its way across the sky.

Suddenly, Jackson noticed that the guns at the point weren't supporting the center of his line. In the midst of the fighting he had assumed they were compelled to be otherwise engaged. But he had been wrong.

Above the low-lying smoke, he could see the point clearly now. Lifting his telescope, the general was the first to see that the Vermont militia was marching down the road after abandoning the redoubt. Moments later, he recognized the New Hampshire flags close behind. What did it mean? Was Houston bringing them to attack Pakenham's flank, still invisible from the heights?

As Jackson gazed at the point, Houston arrived on his lathered horse. "Andy, I've a message from Strong."

To Commanding General   May 9, 1815
Army of the United States

Sir,

In light of the United States government's continued unfair & biased treatment toward us and the enlisting of our people against their wishes, the states of Vermont and New Hampshire and the territory of Maine have seceded from the Federation of the United States. His Majesty, King George III, has taken the above dominions under his gracious protection. The military formations under my command have been assigned to His Majesty's army under His Grace the Duke of Wellington for instructions.

      Samuel Lawrence Strong
      Major General
      Army of Great Britain

Jackson was stunned and flummoxed. "That *Benedict Arnold*, that gol-darn Strong! He's defected! Taken the entire force with him."

He turned to Houston for an explanation.

"Andy, I met that pesky delegation again—you know, Gilman and company. They're rats, turncoats. They lied their way in here last night, the seditious bastards. They turned Strong against us. I've learned the varmints traveled under the protection of the British! Those mountebanks held me, against my will, till the time was right to march into the arms of the British. They tell me that the British Mission in Washington, on behalf of the those varmints, intends to deliver a formal declaration of the secession to the president."

It was Jackson's turn to be silent.

CHAPTER 12

"This Isn't War"

"Insight is too often a matter of hindsight."

—DUKE OF WELLINGTON

S trong's troops, muskets slung upside down over their shoulders in resignation, marched down from the point. The discussion the evening before had gone long into the night. Opening the floor up to debate, Strong took himself out of the argument. At first there was indignation; then the crowd of officers began to swing to resignation. The pragmatic were heard along with the hysterical. Major John Banks was the first to change the mood toward defection.

"Our land and families are behind British lines. Do you think, even if Wellington is defeated, they intend to withdraw and return to England? They're here to draw a new border, and in all likelihood, when it's all said and done, many of our homes will be in the king's territory.

Captain Homer Wilks added thoughtfully, "Even if we win here tomorrow, our army can't pursue. We haven't the means. We'll fight this over again somewhere nearby. This isn't the end but the beginning. I don't want to spend the next few years away from my growing family, fightin' in some hopeless war.

The commander of the New Hampshire brigade, who saw the advantage to a commission as a general in the British army, noted, "Jackson is no friend of ours. He favors his regulars, we all know that. Stickin' us up here out of the way was an insult to our courage as fightin' men. When he pulls out—and that is what he is plannin' to do—we'll be prisoners of war, shipped off to England to rot in hulks or starve to death at Dartmoor."

The powerful specter raised more objections to remaining loyal to the United States. Being wounded or even dead was frightening, but it paled in comparison to rotting in the bottom of a stinking vessel moored in a forgotten bay. Becoming a prisoner of the British was too high a price to pay for these citizen-soldiers.

Another chimed in angrily, "What about our families? With us gone who will feed 'em? Who will take our place and watch them grow up?"

Colonel Hammond of Portsmouth, a member of the state legislature, was in favor of feathering his own political nest in the new dominion but used a different justification for defecting: "Jackson is another of those thieving Southerners who hate us New Englanders. We all know General Jackson has no love for the North. Madison pulled him out of the South to humiliate us. I see Jefferson's hand in all this. Once they beat the British, they plan on keepin' the regular army up here to make us kowtow to their Virginia ways, by golly." Hammond knew his fightin' words were bound to stir up more resentment.

Wilks rose again and forcefully said, "We merchants need England far more than we need Washington. It's English trade, generous trade, that has kept us afloat since the Revolution. They've treated us fair, by God, and we ought to be grateful they stuck with us after all those doin's in '77. I think they've our welfare at heart. England made us a generous offer. We all have kin in the British Isles, and I for one want to go over to their side. We've much more in common with the British than we have with those Southerners." He spat out the word. "It's good for business. That's all I'm sayin'." Heads bobbed in agreement, and a low murmur of approval began to spread.

Diminutive Captain Louis La Cateau, a trader in potash and lumber, added another dimension. "Smugglin', as you know, has been my livelihood. I would surely like to stop runnin' and hidin'. It takes a lot out of a man, I can tell you." There were many who smiled but identified with the little man.

Wilks had been the first to say it out loud: "Go over to their side." It was out in the open now, and it wouldn't go away. There was no more talk of supporting Jackson or the war. Strong listened to a mounting shift away from Jackson.

The unspoken fear in the room full of soldiers burst from the mouth of Mister Callaway, not a soldier but a sutler. "If you fight again tomorrow you all could be killed. Those extra troops, fresh veteran troops, are comin' our way, boys." He pointed to the northwest. "They ain't goin' to march all around to the other end of the line before they strike. They're coming straight at you all. They'll be charging this here ridge—you know it and so do I. I ain't lookin' forward to that." The officers looked at each other. They knew their men would agree with the sutler.

Isaac Branch, the commander of the Maine contingent, stood up as the spokesman for his men. "Canada's our near neighbor. I can testify that Canadians are happy and prosperous under the Union Jack. There isn't a lot of kerfuffle with the central government. They leave their folks alone to get on with livin'. Nobody's tellin' them who to sell their stuff to or askin' them to pay for expansion westward. They're left pretty much on their own to take care of home and hearth. We of the far north, if we were voting now, would go over to the British."

Hammond, the politician, saw the moment was critical and jumped up. "He's right. It's time to stop jawin'. We're all of the same mind. Let's vote."

Strong agreed, "It's gettin' late, and you've got to get back to your men." To appear fair and hoping there was still some support for continuing the fight, he pleaded, "Aren't there any arguments for staying with Jackson and fightin' to the end?" Clearly the force of his neighbors' feelings weakened Strong, and he reluctantly and quietly slid away from his previous support of Jackson. He reminded himself that this was the militia, not the regulars. Voting on major issues had always been this way.

Branch nailed the coffin lid down when he took the floor once more. "When Sherbrooke crossed the border, we asked for federal troops to come to our aid. Mister Madison told us to fend for ourselves. That's what they think of us northern boys; we're nothin' until they need us and then we're members in good standing. What'll they do for us if we win this battle—nothin', by Henry."

Hammond also had more to say. "I've only one more item to consider before we move for a vote. Tomorrow will be a slaughter. Many of our kin will weep for us and our cause as they hang the Union Jack out the window."

With that, Strong took the vote: "All in favor of staying with Jackson and fightin' on to victory say 'aye.'" The junior officers looked for a signal from the senior members, but they remained mute. Strong knew plenty were undecided, and even a goodly number preferred to honor the memory of their kin who had fought to found the republic of the people. But the heat of the arguments had melted their resolve. It wasn't ever a good idea to debate life over death. Life would always prevail in the long run. "Well," said Strong reluctantly, "there is no need to go any further. We're of one mind."

Pakenham's Men Rise from the Ashes of New Orleans

Sherbrooke's division, with Pakenham's units close behind, waited for Strong's turncoat army to sneak north up the road beside the Hudson River. It took an hour before the British could resume the attack along the ridge on the Americans' right flank. The Canadians, under de Salaberry, stayed put in reserve behind Wellington's command post. Sherbrooke immediately attacked the exposed flank of the combined brigade of the 7th New York and 1st Connecticut on the end of the American line. Colonel Cushing's Connecticut militia fell back when the Royal Artillery opened with a salvo, leaving the colonel alone with the color guard. The 1st U.S. Regulars couldn't disengage from Arnold. The 4th New York and 3rd U.S. Regulars in reserve turned to absorb the retreat of the line regiments, thereby reducing the line's cohesion.

The American guns, all four batteries, began to fire wildly northeast at anything red. Sherbrooke's fresh brigades deployed in good order to assault the confused Americans. Pakenham's men remained in column, marching with drums hammering, filling the air with strident music and the eyes of the American infantry with red uniforms. The defecting brigades from Vermont and New Hampshire faded away into the smoke along with Jackson's hope of victory. Wellington watched, unsmiling. "Sir William, this isn't war. It's just treachery. How can we be a part of this despicable slaughter? What's keeping Jackson? He must surrender now. He *must*."

A spate of unruly American cannonballs whistled through the trees and bounced about the British command group. Branches fell, dirt sprayed, turf tumbled. Horses were spooked, and chaos ensued. Wellington, who had been in the thick of things before, pulled his horse under control. By the time he did, he was alone except for Delancey, who lay crumpled on the ground.

Vaulting off his mount, the duke cried out, "William, can you hear me? Where are you struck? William!"

He straightened the body and gently rolled his friend onto his side. The red of the coat disguised the pooling blood. Wellington's hand was warm and wet. He called for his surgeon, who rushed forward, his medical bag flying behind.

The doctor knelt on the opposite side, one hand supporting Delancey's head while the other searched for a pulse on his neck. "He's alive, but his heart's fading."

Two medical assistants scurried up the knoll with a folded stretcher. Wellington helped lift the limp body onto the litter.

Somerset dismounted, awaiting instructions. The duke turned to him and ordered, "End this needless carnage. I, for one, have had enough. I only hope Jackson has! Finish it off, Fitzroy—the usual terms."

The military secretary pulled his portmanteau up on his saddle, took out a stubby pencil, and wrote instructions for his clerk.

Army of the United States
Major General Jackson,
Commanding Officer

The Duke of Wellington, Commander of His Majesty's army at Saratoga, New York, will accept your surrender and offer terms designed to preserve the lives of your soldiers. Cease hostile actions immediately, maintain your position, and lay down your arms. Display a white flag at your headquarters at Nielson's farm. Terms will be offered upon your compliance.

Signed,
Major General Sir Fitzroy Somerset, KB
Military Secretary

An aide took the paper to a clerk for transcription, waited, and then rode off at speed, displaying a flag of truce.

Wellington quit the field. He didn't enjoy war; he thought it fruitless, always the cause of another war. Alone in his tent, the duke mourned the loss of Delancey. Even after commanding during so many battles, he took the death of soldiers hard, and Delancey had been more like a son to him, an extension of himself. The two had been together since India in 1797, living under canvas and fighting the climate, dust, mud, disease, vermin, bugs, and politicians. They had suffered through long stormy voyages and rejoiced on distant victorious battlefields. They had beaten the French, fought with the Horse Guards, and wrangled with Parliament.

Sitting with his head in his hands, he recalled so many other comrades who had died sweating with fever or smashed and bleeding. They had all been proud and strong, both young and old, tightly confined in uniforms soaked with sweat or stiff with ice. They had campaigned over corpse-strewn fields for their king and country.

Will it ever end? he thought. He knew the answer, and it discouraged him.

Jackson Accepts the Inevitable

Near the end, Jackson's center was pressed on three sides into a perimeter at the pinnacle of the heights. While his left flank held, Crockett made an all-out commitment of his infantry reserve and cavalry to try to blunt the efficacy of the King's German Legion. The lost cannon support from the point and the defection of nearly six thousand soldiers were hefty blows.

Jackson fumed to Houston over the betrayal. "Cowards, Sam. They're just cowards. Those filthy buzzards! What's happened to the Yankee spirit I was told about as a boy? If only I could bust loose and pierce the enemy's heart with my fine boys from Tennessee. God, how I miss them!"

The American commander left his tent and mounted his waiting horse. Standing in his stirrups, where he could be seen, Old Hickory made one more attempt to drive a wedge into the implacable red tide. He was aware of the risk of exposing himself and dismissed a warning that he could be killed. "I'm too damn mad to be killed!" he cried. "Even God would curse those bastard traitors." A man of honor all his life, he couldn't comprehend the treason perpetrated on his army.

He spurred his horse into the midst of the 4th U.S. Regulars, his saber reflecting the harsh noonday sun. The Wild Geese clustered around him. He felt at home in their midst. He wished his Irish father, whom he had never known, were looking down on him there with those Irish boys he had trained to fight. He prayed, "Give me strength and give me victory." He felt the power he had known as a young man when he first met the British. "Now, boys, bring your anger to bear on these Englishmen, revenge hundreds of years of oppression." He felt the scar on his face. "Crush them where they stand." His blood was up. "Fag-an-Bealach—clear the way—we're coming through!"

A wall of blue met a wall of red; the sound could be heard miles away as men swung muskets by the barrel, crashing the heavy brass butts down on British skulls. Cannonballs bounced into the fray, indiscriminately killing and maiming friend and foe. Jackson cried out for vengeance. Bayonets, streaked red, plunged into chests and backs while the blood ran warm down the stock and over the warriors' hands. Teeth clenched and eyes burned while sweat soaked through the thick uniforms. Men driven to their knees supported their dying frames on broken muskets. Horses screamed, struck with bullets, as their officers crumpled over their necks and slid to the ground in a loose heap. The uneven ground was carpeted with bodies, making it impossible to stand and deliver a blow. Yet the British regiments pressed on like a red machine, crawling forward up Bemis Heights. The massed regimental drums never stopped beating out the death knell. The skirl of the bagpipes screeched above the melee, and men died where they stood.

It was inevitable, though. Jackson's horse became nervous, unable to move forward, blocked by a tangle of men swirling about. The blue was slowly yet surely moving to the rear. The regiments became squashed together, losing their cohesion and distinction. One of the few officers on horseback, Jackson could see through the smoke the approach of fresh red columns. He recognized the first as Sherbrooke's Scots and surmised that they led Pakenham's division.

The loss of the point's guns and the New England militias' betrayal had destroyed Old Hickory's plans to defeat the British. He had believed, from the beginning, it was possible. In his heart, which overflowed with love for this land and hatred of the British, whom he had first met in battle as a boy, he would never quit. But American life could be saved—even at this late hour.

Reluctantly he broke contact and pulled his horse from the fray. Carefully the wounded animal picked his way against the grain to the headquarters at Neilson's farm. A British staff envoy came forward under a white banner with Wellington's ultimatum. Jackson was quiet for some time, undecided, but when he accepted, he did so quickly. Another Battle of Saratoga was over.

A second order, which should've been penned by Delancey, was distributed to Wellington's brigades.

Execute the general advance and secure the primary objective, Bemis Heights.
Take prisoners to the rear and secure them in the temporary stockade provided in the middle ravine.

Delancey, so certain of victory, had prepared an internment camp for Jackson's army on the low ground on either side of the creek that ran through the middle ravine.

Jackson relinquished his sword and colors. His thoughts turned to his soldiers and the families who waited at home. His responsibility was clear. He couldn't save their dignity, but at least he could preserve their lives. He rode among them now.

"It's over men. Cease fire, ground your weapons, and follow me."

The general pulled back on the reins, raising the head of his bewildered horse. Slowly, the animal reversed and turned back toward Neilson's farm. The British allowed the blue infantry to break contact halfway up the rise while their officers repeated sundry orders: "Cease fire. Look to your colors. Regroup. Stand to." Within the hour, Somerset arrived with a small party of staff officers.

All along the heights' forward slope, strong men carried their weaker and wounded brothers to a medical point. The cannons, still hot, were silent, and the air was slowly clearing of the smoke that had dominated it. The ground was disturbed, rent open in places, and littered with the debris of war. Bodies lay entangled, friend and foe, comrade with comrade. Wounded horses struggled vainly to get to their feet. Men bled, mourned, or sat despondently staring with vacant eyes.

Within a mile in any direction the world was unchanged, unaware for the moment of the catastrophe.

To the Commanding General,
Army of the United States
Bemis Heights, New York
6th May 1815

Terms of Surrender
In view of the conflict fought by the forces under the command of Major General Andrew Jackson this day and the inability of the said force to defend itself any longer, the following terms are offered by the commander of His Majesty's forces:

All members of your command must surrender their arms to the forces of His Majesty, King George III. His Grace, the Duke of Wellington, will ensure the safety and good health of those who comply.

In turn, all regular members of the Army of the United States will be interned for the duration of the conflict. The members of the militia, with the exception of the commissioned officers, will be released to return home unimpeded. The said officers who pledge not to engage in further hostilities against His Majesty's forces will be paroled to their homes.

If these terms are acceptable so signify with your signature.

The following morning, on horseback before his defeated army, General Andrew Jackson led his color party to Wellington, who was waiting at Freeman's farm. There, years earlier, General Burgoyne had surrendered His Majesty's army.

Jackson rendered a salute that Major General Somerset returned. Drawing his dress sword from its copper scabbard, he inverted it and silently offered it to Lord Somerset, an officer of equal rank, who passed it to the duke. No words were exchanged. Jackson had been betrayed, not beaten, and Wellington didn't covet this victory, brought about by political intrigue, as he once envisioned he would. The American commander turned his horse and rode down the slope toward the British lines, where he believed he would be led into captivity.

The colors of the U.S. Army and the regiments were surrendered, cased, and deposited onto an artillery cart. The combined British bands played a dirge as the regiments passed. Individuals grounded their weapons carefully in stacks by the thousands. Soldiers no more, the plodding defeated men, eyes to the ground, assisted their wounded brethren down the dusty road, which was flanked by redcoats standing at attention, their glittering bayonets fixed. Numerous wagons, American and British, carted the wounded to the hospital in Schuylerville.

Not present for this debacle, not invited, were the Vermont and New Hampshire militias, whom Wellington directed to be deployed along the 43rd parallel, the northern border of Massachusetts. The duke, knowing that no army waited in opposition, sent Pakenham south to Cohoes, New York, which rested on the same parallel. Slowly over the next month, the British expanded the line west a few miles to Rotterdam, only twenty miles north of Albany, the capital of New York State.

With the ceremony over, Somerset hailed Jackson. The two men, side by side on horseback, drew close together. Before Jackson could speak, the British military secretary thrust a document tied in red ribbon across to him.

"His Grace would like you to grant him a favor, General. He requests that you take this to your president. He knows you to be man of honor and can trust you with this highly personal, confidential message for President Madison. Can I inform His Grace that you've accepted the mission? Of course, you're not compelled to do so, but it would give the field marshal great comfort to know that it's in safe hands."

Fearing a trick, Jackson inquired, "You want me, your prisoner, to leave for Washington as an envoy for the British commander? Are you offering to parole me as long as I never take up arms against Great Britain?"

Somerset replied, "There's no conditional offer of parole, my dear General. You're free to do as you like. You see the note contains the duke's apology for the treachery that transpired during the conflict. I'm sure you can see that it's a matter of honor for His Grace. So would you be so kind?"

Jackson said, "I should like Colonel Crockett and Major Houston to accompany me on the long journey, if that can be arranged, Your Lordship."

Somerset granted the request, and the three rode south.

General Jackson, the orphan boy who had broken all the rules from youth and fashioned a life for himself on the frontier, hoping to make the new land safe for immigrant families, had been taken from his element and thrust into prominence. Presidents counted on him, soldiers revered him, his country trusted him, and now at the most critical moment in his life he had failed. It was a dark ride south. Would he be vilified, blamed, court-martialed, and shot? He was sure he would be.

Confusion

Within two days, messengers from New York governor Tompkins's office transmitted the news of the American defeat and the loss of the army to Baltimore and Washington. Tompkins particularly highlighted northern New England's treachery.

In Massachusetts and Connecticut, the returning militia spread the tale quickly. The two state houses were thrown into chaos. A Boston newspaper headline read, "What Are Wellington's Intentions?"

The mood of the people south of the 43rd parallel was split. The vast majority, when faced with relinquishing all their ancestors had fought and died for, remained loyal to the United States. Those who spoke for unification with England found their homes and businesses vandalized and burned. As in the past, British sympathizers, old-fashioned Loyalists, escaped north across the border to seek citizenship in Columbia. The Albany statehouse reeled from the loss of thousands of square miles of land and scores of communities. Many New Yorkers were transformed overnight into the king's subjects without the benefit of choice. Wellington's dismissal of the militias confused politicians and citizens alike. It was interpreted as a humane gesture, but was it?

Madison's Remorse

In the evening, on the day after the second battle, the devastating news of the army's destruction and the northern militia's treason reached the president, who had counted on Jackson defeating the king's men.

Madison cried to Dolley, "What'll become of our country, of us, of our future? Oh, why did I insist on war?"

His wife, more frightened by the future than concerned about past errors, asked, "What will the British do, James? Will they march south to New York City and be satisfied, or will they continue to Washington to arrest the government and restore the colonies?"

Monroe rushed up the front steps of the partially restored White House, threw his hat on a workmen's table in the charred lobby, and burst through the French doors into the president's temporary private accommodations.

"Have you heard, sir? Could it be? First reports are often wrong, you know." The president's stricken face told the secretary all he needed to know. "Mister President, with the loss at Saratoga, there's no field army left to resist."

"Why has Wellington released the militias?" Madison asked.

"The duke has excused the militias, finding them unworthy opponents. He's unable to feed them, so why keep them? If he must fight again, why waste scarce resources guarding prisoners? He'll march our regulars back to Canada, out of his way, I suspect. I'm told that a line is being established north of Albany. Sir, everything's in disarray. No one knows what's next. The press reports panic-filled streets in every town."

Madison sighed heavily and then said, "Call the cabinet for tomorrow morning and prepare to move west into Virginia."

———

The following morning, the president and the cabinet came to order in the only room fit for a conference. No sooner had the meeting started than an usher interrupted. "Sir, the chief of mission from Great Britain is here to see you."

"Fine. Ask him to wait . . . somewhere. Find a suitable spot. Gentlemen, what am I to say? Does he expect us to surrender?"

"The moment demands a delicate approach," Monroe advised. "Just listen. Don't commit to anything. That's why we have a delegation at Ghent."

Madison felt like a schoolboy with the truant officer waiting at the door. He stood up, determined to deal with the consequences of his policy, and slipped out the door to a small anteroom containing salvaged furniture, a small round mahogany table, and two straight-back chairs. Monroe stood against the wall behind the president. There were no curtains on the windows or rugs on the newly sanded floor.

Surveying the room, the president was embarrassed for a moment about its decrepit state. Then he remembered that it had been the British who had burned the house. He put his jaw out. "Yes, what is it, Sir Charles?"

Charles Bagot, baronet, had held the British Mission together during the war years after the British ambassador had been recalled in July 1812. "Sir, I have instructions, which I was directed to open if Lord Wellington attained a certain degree of success. I think we'd all agree that he has achieved that degree."

Sir Charles waited, but there was no reply. Madison and Monroe looked at each other. Was he suggesting that the military action had subverted the Ghent talks?

"May I proceed, Mister President?"

Madison remained stiff, highly apprehensive.

"Sir, in view of Napoleon's return, which you can appreciate has drawn England's intense interest, it is in His Majesty's government's interest to offer reduced terms to settle this conflict between our two great countries. To expedite the matter, the same document has been offered to your delegation at Ghent. May I leave it with you in hopes that this conflict can be settled as swiftly as human endeavor will permit? Thank you, Mister President."

Monroe accepted the packet sealed with red wax. "Much obliged, Sir Charles. We are also most anxious to bring this affair to a peaceful end—with little change in our relations. Please inform your government of our stance."

Sir Charles stood, bowed slightly, smiled now that his uncomfortable business was completed, and left.

Back in the cabinet room, the bewildered president passed the parcel to Monroe, who examined the contents. On reading it, the secretary of state was livid. "My God, this is impossible! They propose that in view of the defeat of our army, the presence of Wellington at Saratoga, and the king's establishment of the Dominion of Columbia, that a new boundary commission be established to recognize and solidify the situation. They cite the 43rd parallel as the new border separating the king's possession from that of the United States. Quick! A map!"

There was none in the room.

Jefferson, once again a guest, piped up. "It's the spoils of war. They demand that which they've conquered. Nothing changes for that bunch of robbers."

In the face of the crisis those present simply ignored the former president. An aide returned, paging wildly through an oversized atlas, and plopped it onto the table. A double page extending from the Atlantic coast to Ohio caught everyone's attention. Monroe traced the faint line that began just below Portsmouth, New Hampshire, and extended through Saratoga across New York State.

"Why that's a frontier close to hundreds of miles long all the way to Buffalo," Monroe said. "In addition to the states and territory, we'll lose Lake Ontario and the length of the St. Lawrence as well as the Mohawk Valley."

Madison traced the line with his finger. "Well, they got what they wanted—a land route to Quebec and protection for the Canadian border. I see Prevost's hand in this."

"Impossible," Monroe said again.

Report to the President

"Failure, that's what it is—it goes by no other name," the once-proud Jackson mumbled, as he perched sadly on his horse. The animal and the rider both had their heads down as they plodded south of Albany on the turnpike that wound through small towns toward Washington. Astride on either side of Jackson, screening him from the folks who stood at the sides of the road or approached hoping to speak to the general, were Lieutenant Colonel Davy Crockett and Major Sam Houston in sweat-soaked woolen uniforms that hung on them like the grief they bore. The three riders were alone; their army was now a throng of prisoners of war.

"You can't go blamin' yourself, Andy. Those snakes in politicians' skin did you in. Why, they'd sell their own mother for a vote or a bribe," Crockett said. He believed the truth in his words, but he was also trying to reason Jackson out of the black mood that possessed him before he saw the president.

Houston chimed in. "That's right, by gum, Andy. What chance did ya have when a chunk of your army skedaddled, leavin' an open flank and a fresh bunch of redcoats lickin' their chops. We were betrayed, plain and simple. That's how it was, and that's how folks will see it."

The conversation didn't change Jackson's mood. Neither did the whole torturous trek across rustic roads over the span of dusty days in which they was little to do but ride and ruminate. *Remorse* was too academic a word, not nearly visceral enough to describe Jackson's state of mind over his army's destruction. He was not a loser, or at least he had never been one before.

South of Baltimore, a dragoon escort met the three riders. The party traversed around the city at night to avoid contact with the bewildered citizens and questioning reporters. The first official account had to be given to the president and not in fragments to the press.

With the reconstruction of the interior of the president's residence now in full swing—though it was expected to take two years—the commander's quarters at Fort Washington near the Navy Yard was converted for use by the president and cabinet.

James Monroe greeted the party. "General," he said, stretching out both hands as Jackson reached the top step of the front porch. "Gentlemen," he said, nodding in acknowledgment at Crockett and Houston, who, though lagging behind by a step, saluted in return.

Jackson curled the corners of his mouth up slightly, chagrined. He felt deeply that the pitiful state of affairs resulted from his own disgraceful conduct. He managed to utter, "I have lost it, James. I have lost the whole army—"

"Nonsense, Andy, you were betrayed. We know the story. The papers are full of the dishonesty, calumny, deceit, and pettifogging. Those turncoats disgraced their ancestors who died to rid this land of John Bull. By God, I wish I could get my hands on them! Come along, Andy. The president has something in mind he must talk to you about."

For now the mindless recriminations and finger-pointing were held in abeyance as Monroe escorted Jackson into the presence of the president and cabinet members.

Madison crossed the planks of the expansive parlor. "My dear General, what can I say? By God, you fought like a wildcat, you and your boys." He looked to Crockett and Houston, who were shocked and pleased by such kind recognition. "We've heard it all. Many reports from all corners have told us of your gallant stand, personal courage, and steadfast resolve to defeat those bastards. Stabbed in the back by your own officers—lied to by those mountebanks Gilman and Chittenden—my God, sir! The perfidy is too great. My senses balk at their pernicious audacity."

Madison grasped Jackson's thick, meaty hand with his own in a grip that conveyed how sincerely the president felt the sentiments he expressed.

"We'll have none of it! The British will pay. Our people are made of sterner stuff. I've promises from every corner to help us seek revenge for the injury and treachery visited upon you and yours. The nation will not surrender. Our army will take to the field again. And I beg you, sir, to be at its head as its commander once again."

Ghent, Belgium

By the end of June, one great event had occurred in Belgium and another was about to happen.

Napoleon defeated the Prussians at Wavre and within days confronted the combined army of Great Britain and the Netherlands south of Brussels at a small hamlet called Waterloo. Lord Uxbridge commanded the northern allied army, but without the Prussians' assistance, the allies were driven back to Brussels. At Ghent, Uxbridge held on until the Austrians and Russians crossed the Rhine and drew the emperor away to guard his back door.

The head of the U.S. delegation, John Quincy Adams, had received the same document of English terms and wrote for instructions. Within the month an American naval officer delivered the president's instructions, penned by the secretary of state.

> Mister Adams and fellow envoys,
> In view of the British forces blocking our ports and military elements occupying our northern regions, it is imperative that this matter be concluded. The proposed solution, which I believe has also been provided to you, is acceptable to this executive. I ask that it be agreed to without amendment. This will end negotiations and close the proceedings that you and your colleagues have so diligently conducted.

> Signed,
> James Madison
> President
> United States of America

By September 1815, the Senate had ratified the treaty, signing away all land claims north of the 43rd parallel. Maine, Vermont, New Hampshire, and the northern portion of New York State west to Buffalo were lost. Great Britain discarded its earlier demands for British maritime rights on the Mississippi and a separate Indian state, and agreed to recognize American sovereignty on the high seas. Naturally, the American embargo against Britain and the British naval blockade were abolished. Slavery was not addressed except that both nations expressed an interest in ending the trade. The king delivered on his promise and established Columbia as a dominion of Great Britain. Madison remained president during that uncertain year of 1815.

Home at Last

Wellington arrived home to the usual honors and the admiration of his patron, the Prince Regent. When asked what Parliament could do for His Grace in light of his North American triumph, he replied, "I should like to take command of the pursuit of Napoleon." The Horse Guards, chagrined over the performance of Wellington's brother-in-law, who was pinned down in northern Belgium, granted the appointment and fulfilled the great duke's ambition.

Before he reunited with his wife, Kitty, who had continued to irritate him during the North American Campaign by including snippets from the scandal newspapers and political rags from London, he sought to fulfill one last self-imposed mission. He traveled the hard roads north to Scotland to deliver a letter.

Wellington and Lady Magdalene Delancey had never met, though they had become familiar through a shared flow of letters. She received the duke with trepidation. He thought her a frail wisp of a girl, deeply sad, even lost. She knew of Delancey's death but not of the circumstances. Cloistered alone in her private sitting room, she struggled to be brave before the most famous living man in Great Britain.

The duke, seated beside her on a divan, took her small, gloved hand. "My dear, your William was taken at height of the battle. It is my fault. I should've been more careful. I found this letter to you that he would've finished if God had not intervened."

He gave her the two loose pages, which she began to read.

My Darling Girl,

The torment I have suffered in the wilderness will climax tomorrow and my work will be finished. I'll be allowed at last to return to you. I have had enough of this blood sport and will leave the army for good to be with you in Scotland.

Today we fought our second battle since coming here to this primitive land, where I was born. It has no hold over me, and I thank God for leading my family to the British Isles, where I found you. I miss your soft ways, your tender touch, and your sympathetic gaze, which warms my heart. I look at your portrait, framed inside the cover of my portmanteau, each morning to start my day and by candlelight each night before prayers. My request is always the same: my dear God, I ask that you please give me your speed to bring me safely home to the side of my love, never to leave again. Tomorrow we'll end this business of war, and I will finish this letter, God willing.

When she looked up, she was alone in her grief. The duke had gone.

Strong's Depression

Following the British guides, Strong led the three militia brigades across the Hudson River and took up a position just north of the Massachusetts border. Within the week he learned of Wellington's departure for Montreal and then England and the establishment of a military district for the new Dominion of Columbia. He was not surprised to find that newly promoted Major General Benedict Arnold Jr. was made commander. Strong's three militia brigades were integrated into the force, which contained an equal number of British regulars.

Strong's first meeting with Arnold was cordial. Commanding only the Vermont brigade of the militia contingent, he was weary and content with fewer responsibilities. Still in his Vermont militia uniform, but with the piping of a British brigadier general sewn to the sleeve, he accepted the pay but felt he was torn by two opposing worlds. There was the threat of an American border attack, but the chances were slim in light of the recent capture of Jackson's army. Soon the militia was sent home on leave while the British shouldered the burden of watching for hostile activity along the Columbian frontier. At home near Burlington, his reception was mixed. Naturally, his family was overjoyed that he had survived the ordeal. His wife, Martha, clung to him as if he were a new groom, and his three daughters, all in their teens, heralded him as the savior of their world. But on the street some crossed over to avoid contact. Others readily approached the general and offered congratulations, thanked him for his service, and probed him with questions.

A neighbor and former smuggler, Lucas Reynolds, and others like him enthusiastically embraced Columbia as a splendid outcome. "Sam, how is it that you came up with the notion of formin' a new country?"

Strong tried to relegate his role in the process and told them, "I'm just a soldier, nothing more. Others must take the credit for the affair." His modesty belied his true attitude, for he was thinking more clearly in hindsight.

"Sam, what's the story? How are things going to go now that we're back to being a country of our own?" Though, many citizens had taken to Columbia, they hadn't yet grasped that they were the king's subjects.

Strong was afraid to bring up King George and the allegiance formed by the deal. He answered truthfully, "I don't rightly know. I'm a military man, not a politician. It's in their hands now over in Portsmouth. You'll have to ask Lord Chittenden. He's number two in this new government. I expect, though, that things will be a might more calm. There'll be some straightenin' out to do and agreements with the folks across Lake Champlain, but you can count on Canadians. I predict a long and pleasant association with Montreal. It could be a good thing."

He smiled, optimistic at the prospects, but inside he had lost something. Strong wasn't a free man any longer. Even though the king liked him and gave him a job and a commission, life wasn't as it had been before. The king had a string on him. He knew now how Benedict Arnold Sr. felt when he went over to the British. Strong continued his leave through the fall and into the winter; there was no need for him to return to the border. The Americans posed no immediate threat. The British put him on half-pay, and the cold months closed down the farm until spring. He was spending a great deal of time in the tavern, drinking much more than he had before.

———

"Evenin', Sam. Mind if we join you?" A tall man in an old army overcoat approached Strong in the tavern one evening. "Can I buy you a drink? Rum, isn't it? I remember from the old days after a good hard drillin' and turkey shootin'." Two more companions nodded their greetings and pushed in.

Strong knew the party well. They were officers in the local company of the militia. Happy to see old comrades, he slid over to the wall on the shelter bench. The three men— Courtney Hodges, Langford Beale, and Liam Emmons—were only a few years younger and long-term militia veterans.

Hodges, who made the first overture, sat across the table on the opposing bench. The other two looked around the room, checking to see who else might be in the tavern that blustery evening. "Sam, I'll never forget that night on the point when you got stampeded into agreeing we ought to give it up and save our own skins. It was a wretch for you, for me, and for the boys." He nodded to the other two, who had settled on the ends of the benches, making a foursome around the scarred table.

Sam was relieved to hear the words; these men knew he wasn't in favor of abandoning Jackson and seemed sympathetic over the outcome. "Boys, it was the worst night of my life. Those snakes from the state houses turned my stomach, and I wanted to shoot 'em on the spot. Lily-livered cowards, look what they've done to our lives. They made us into nothing more than the king's lackeys. God, I am ashamed. Jackson counted on us, and we turned tail and ran like whipped dogs."

"Well, Sam, that's what we wanted to talk to you about," Beale said, lowering his voice so Sam could hardly hear him. "We ain't alone, General. There's plenty others out there who don't want His Majesty poking his nose into their business."

Emmons, an attorney, said, "I've had my ear to the ground, Sam. There's a movement going on all over the state, but mostly over here in the east. We've been talking to an old friend in Plattsburgh, Judge Sailly. He says that the leaders in Washington aren't going to stand for loosing a chunk of the country and that Jackson has been appointed to raise another army. Monroe's gone to France, now that Napoleon's back on the throne and beat the British and Prussians in Belgium. Sailly—he's a Frenchman—says there's a good chance that the two countries will join up and make a run at Columbia before it gets a good start.

He thinks a hostile underground movement, like the one in Spain a couple years ago against the French, could pin down the British and disrupt the takeover." The three conspirators were risking their lives talking about sedition with a brigadier general in the British army, but they thought they knew Strong's true allegiance.

"General," Hodges reached across the narrow table and firmly grasped Strong's hand, "will you take command, or will you be another Benedict Arnold and waste your life lickin' their boots?"

Emmons, an Irish immigrant, suggested, "We should call ourselves the 'Wild Geese.'"

APPENDIX I

British Army at the Battle of Saratoga, 1815

The Duke of Wellington's Personal Staff, Canada, 1812

Major General Lord Fitzroy James Henry Somerset, chief of staff/military secretary
Captain Ronald Ulysses Burgh, later Lord Downes
Major General Galbraith Lowry Cole
Lieutenant Colonel Alexander Dickson, chief of artillery
Lieutenant Colonel Sir Hudson Lowe
Lord March, the young son of the Duke of Richmond, Wellington's great personal friend
Commissary General William Henry Robinson
Major General Sir William Stewart, adjutant general
Colonel Sir William Delancey, quartermaster general
Major Colquhoun "Colley" Grant, Delancey's trusted spy and intelligence officer

Commanders

Major General Sir John Sherbrooke
Major General Sir Edward Pakenham
Major General Frederick Robinson
Major General Manley Power
Major General Thomas Brisbane

Troop Units

ROYAL ARTILLERY
    6th, 9th, 10th, and 12th companies

CAVALRY
    1st Squadron of the 19th Light Dragoons
    1st Squadron (minus) of the Staff Dragoons
    1st Squadron of the King's German Legion

INFANTRY REGIMENTS

5th (Northumberland)

6th Warwickshire

8th Kings

9th East Norfolk

41st Regiment of Foot

49th (Hertfordshire)

100th (Prince Regent's County of Dublin)

1st (Royal Scots)

2nd (Queen's Royal) Regiment of Foot

3rd (East Kent) Regiment (The Buffs)

13th (1st Somersetshire)

70th (Glasgow Lowland)

27th Inniskillings

57th (West Middlesex)

58th (Rutlandshire)

62nd (Wiltshire)

76th West Riding

82nd Prince of Wales Volunteers

88th Connaught Rangers (the Devil's Own)

89th Regiment of Foot

90th Cameronian

98th (no affiliation)

99th (Prince of Wales's Tipperary)

102nd Regiment of Foot

103rd (no affiliation)

De Meuron Swiss Regiment

CANADIAN ELEMENTS

104th Glengarry Light Infantry

10th Veteran Battalian

6th Fencibles

Voltigeurs Regiment

Chasseur Regiment

APPENDIX 2

U.S. Army at the Battle of Saratoga, 1815

Major General Andrew Jackson's Staff
Brigadier General Lewis Cass, chief of staff
Lieutenant Colonel Davy Crockett, operations
Major Sam Houston, intelligence

Troops
ARTILLERY
> 6 batteries of nine-pounders
> 1 battery of twelve-pounders

CAVALRY
> 2nd U.S. Dragoons
> 1st Squadron, New York State Militia

INFANTRY
> New regular regiments numbered 20th through the 40th assigned to seven brigades:
> 1st Brigade
> 2nd Brigade
> 3rd Brigade
> 4th Brigade
> 5th Brigade
> 6th Brigade
> 7th Brigade

NEW YORK MILITIA
> 1st, 2nd, 3rd, 4th, and 5th brigades

MASSACHUSETTS MILITIA
> 1st, 2nd, and 3rd brigades

NEW JERSEY MILITIA
    1st, 2nd, and 3rd brigades
NEW HAMPSHIRE MILITIA
    1st, 2nd, and 3rd brigades
VERMONT MILITIA
    1st and 2nd brigades
CONNECTICUT MILITIA
    1st Regiment

AUTHOR'S END NOTE

Many happenings in this book have a true track, taken from history and events as they occurred. However, the one alteration, the Duke of Wellington's acceptance rather than rejection of command to take the expedition to Canada, has made this tale what it is. Prior to that fictional event, the paths followed by Europe and North America in this book were portrayed honestly. It is my contention that had Wellington commanded at Plattsburgh on September 11, 1814, events in North America and Europe would have been profoundly different.

To make the transition from truth to fiction, I interjected fictional letters, newspaper articles, and official documents to illustrate the possibilities in addition to quotes and accounts that I found in regimental museums, the newspaper branch of the British Museum, the Public Records Office at Kew, the Military History Institute at Carlisle, the National Archives in Washington, and the family papers of Sir Christopher and Lady Dolores Prevost that I saw in Portugal, Christmas 1996. I found it unnecessary to add more than a handful of fictional characters. The vast majority of characters are real people who feature in the history of the age.

I hope this book will compel the reader to search out the true record of this fascinating time in Western history and read the good histories written by those who have devoted themselves to telling the tale as it actually occurred.

BIBLIOGRAPHY

Brands, H. W. *Andrew Jackson: His Life and Times*. New York: Doubleday, 2005.

Carman, W. Y. *The Royal Artillery*. Reading, UK: Osprey Publishing, 1973.

Chandler, David. *Dictionary of the Napoleonic Wars*. London: Arms & Armor Press, 1979.

Congreve, William. *Details of the Rocket System*. Finsbury, UK: J. Whiting Publishing, 1814.

Elting, John. *Amateurs to Arms! A Military History of the War of 1812*. New York: Da Capo, 1991.

Everest, Allan. *The Military Career of Alexander Macomb*. Plattsburgh, NY: Clinton County Historical Society, 1989.

Fitz-Enz, David. *The Final Invasion: Plattsburgh, the War of 1812's Most Decisive Battle*. New York: Cooper Square Press, 2001.

———. *Old Ironsides: Eagle of the Sea—The Story of the USS* Constitution. Lanham, MD: Taylor Trade Publishing, 2004.

Flint, Eric. *The Rivers of War*. New York: Ballantine Books, 2005.

Griffith, Patrick. *French Artillery*. London: Almark Publishing, 1976.

Haythornthwaite, Philip J. *Nelson's Navy*. Reading, UK: Osprey Publishing, 1993.

———. *Wellington's Military Machine*. Tunbridge Wells, Kent, UK: Spellmount, 1989.

———. *Wellington's Special Troops*. Reading, UK: Osprey Publishing, 1988.

Hickey, Donald R. *The War of 1812: A Forgotten Conflict*. Urbana: University of Illinois Press, 1989.

Hofschroer, Peter. *The Hanoverian Army of the Napoleonic Wars*. Reading, UK: Osprey Publishing, 1989.

Katcher, Philip. *The American War, 1812–1814*. Reading, UK: Osprey Publishing, 1992.

Longford, Elizabeth. *Wellington: The Years of the Sword*. London: Harper & Row, 1969.

Macdonough, James. *Limits of Glory: A Novel of Waterloo*. Novato, CA: Presidio Press, 1991.

Miller, John C. *Alexander Hamilton: Portrait in Paradox*. New York: Harper, 1959.

Neillands, Robin. *Wellington and Napoleon: Clash of Arms.* London: John Murray, 1994.

Park, S. J. *The British Military: Its System and Organization.* Cambridge, UK: Rafm, 1983.

Pimlott, John. *British Light Cavalry.* London: Almark Publishing, 1977.

Remini, Robert V. *Andrew Jackson and His Indian Wars.* New York: Viking, 2001.

———. *The Battle of New Orleans: Andrew Jackson and America's First Victory.* New York: Viking, 2001.

Shepperd, G. Alan. *The Connaught Rangers: The "Devil's Own."* Reading, UK: Osprey Publishing, 1972.

Von Pivka, Otto. *The King's German Legion.* Reading, UK: Osprey Publishing, 1974.

ABOUT THE AUTHOR

Colonel David Fitz-Enz was a regular army officer for thirty years. While a platoon leader of Army Combat Photographers in Vietnam in the 173rd Airborne Infantry and later in the 1/10 Cavalry, 4th Infantry Division, Fitz-Enz was decorated with the Soldier's Medal for heroism, the army's highest award for life saving with extreme risk to his life; the Bronze Star for Valor with four oak leaf clusters; and the Air Medal for sustained aerial combat. He commanded the 1101st Signal Brigade, responsible for operation of the Moscow Hot Line. In Europe he served on board General Haig's airborne command post and later in 1984 was special assistant to the Supreme Allied Commander Europe. Colonel Fitz-Enz has appeared twice on C-Span Book TV from the National Archives and the Army War College. He is published in *Military Review* and *Military Illustrated Magazine*, and lectures at the National Army Museum, London. He wrote his memoir *Why a Soldier* for Random House. His book *The Final Invasion* won the Distinguished Writing Prize from the Army Historical Foundation, and he was granted the Military Order of Saint Louis from the Knights Templar for contributions to military literature. He has since written *Old Ironsides: Eagle of the Sea*, been named a Distinguished Scholar at Marquette University, and appears in *Who's Who in America*.

Married to Carol, his research assistant, they have three sons and live near Lake Placid, New York.

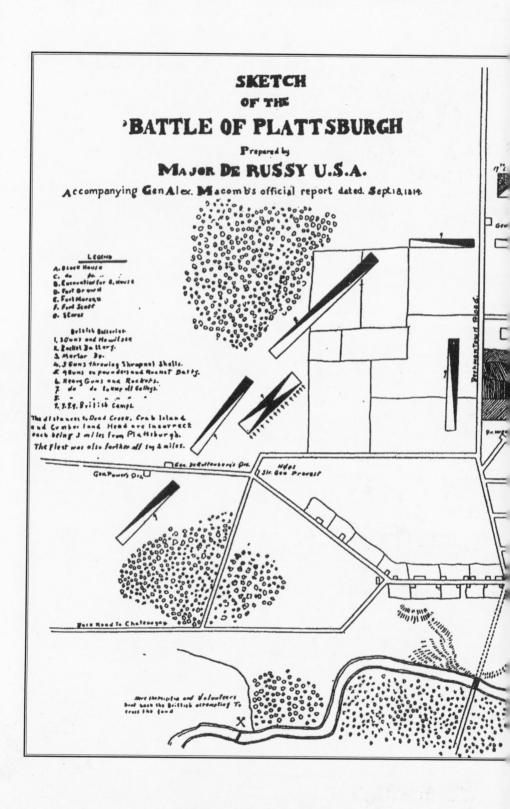

SKETCH
OF THE
BATTLE OF PLATTSBURGH
Prepared by
MAJOR DE RUSSY U.S.A.
Accompanying Gen Alex. Macomb's official report dated. Sept 18, 1814.

LEGEND

A. Block House
C. do do
B. Excavation for B. House
D. Fort Brown
E. Fort Moreau
F. Fort Scott
G. Stores

British Batteries
1. 3 Guns and Howitzer
2. Rocket Battery.
3. Mortar Bo.
4. 3 Guns throwing Shrapnel Shells.
E. 4 Guns 24 pounders and Rocket Batts.
6. Heavy Guns and Rockets.
7. do do to top of College.
8. " " "
9. 7. 8. 9. British Camps.

The distances to Dead Creek, Crab Island, and Cumberland Head are incorrect each being 3 miles from Plattsburgh.
The Fleet was also farther off say 3 miles.

Gen. Power's Ord.   Gen. DeRottenberg's Ord.
Hdqs Sir Geo Provost

Back Road To Chateaugay

Here the militia and volunteers beat back the British attempting To cross the ford

Beekman Town Road